The Jou
West In

Isabelle Lewis

ISBN 0-9741125-0-X

Printed in Canada

Printed on Recycled Paper

Published June 2003

Dedication

I dedicate this book with fond memories of my great grand mother, Catherine Letteen, and all those who have passed on in the family during my lifetime. I miss them dearly. I would like to include my mommy, grandmother Marie Letteen, with special gratitude for her unconditional love and support of me. Mommy, the positive impact you have made on my life cannot be compared to any other.

I also thank Gideon Lewis, my husband, who joined me in planting the seeds that bore the fruit, producing our two loving and caring daughters, Tahanique and Monique Lewis. The three of you are the rocks that prevent my falling when I stumble.

Remembering the song "That's what friends are for," I couldn't have asked our heavenly father for a better friend than Theresa (Jennifer) Kirby, who must be included in this dedication in a very heartfelt way.

Testimonials

The Journey of a West Indian Soul brought tears to my eyes and laughter to my soul at times.

Jerry Williams
Brooklyn, NY

Lewis pens a damning account of the very real, disturbingly banal, oppression of class, race, nationality and gender bias. She endows her bony heroine, Lola, with ceaseless adaptability and stamina that belie her years.

Minnie Cato
Caribbean Life Newspaper

Lewis did a remarkable story of one woman's courage and determination to overcome.

Nanette Campbell
New York., N.Y.

Acknowledgements

Iwould like to thank Him who is greater than me, in whom I believe, for His blessings, acknowledging that I would not have been able to complete this book without His daily presence in my life.

I would like to acknowledge my ancestors, both remembered and forgotten, for their sacrifice, guidance and love. It is on their shoulders that I leaned and sobbed as I wrote this book.

Next, I acknowledge those who have passed in my lifetime: my maternal great grandmother Catherine Letteen and grandmother Marie Letteen; my great uncles Joseph, Mantu, Jefford and Comince Letteen; my great tanties Cumsie Cane, Babe and Roberta Letteen, my cousins Emma and Nellie Cane, Clever Spencer, Hudson Cupid, Doris Dublin, Eugenia Toby, Hubert Letteen and friend Earlene Horne. They made an impact on my life for which I am forever grateful. I love and miss them dearly.

For the mothers of the village, including my own, who have toiled and endured many sufferings for the survival of their children and themselves—I honor all of you. Witnessing the hardship of your lives has inspired many like myself to seek a life which is different.

In the spirit of love and the affirmation of God blessings, I accept the enrichment of the love and support of my family— Gideon, Tashanique and Monique Lewis—and my siblings— Maugarite Brown, Maybelline McDowall, Roxeyanna Peters, Nicole Danzell, Garvey, Terry, Macabe, Muanna and Icena Pope.

Remebering the different stages of my life, I am eternally grateful to those who have motivated me academically—Theresa Cuffy,

Sisters Theresa and Eugene, my former mentors and educators and Oscar Allen (Brother A), who taught me the power of self-determination. I extend a special thank you to my best friend Theresa (Jennifer) Kirby for our many years of friendship and her endless support.

To the mothers, fathers, sisters and brothers, especially those living in third world countries who have had experiences similar to those described in this book—I have written this book with you in mind, praying that it might give you some hope for a better future.

Special thanks go to the following associates and friends: Rosemary Owens, Lorna (Grace) Robinson, Henrietta Hinds, Louise Jarvis, Paula Polite, Paula Thigpen, Hilda Massenberg, Mary Lou McBride, Josephine Anderson, Geraldine Sweeney, Jennifer Huggins, Ruby Thompson, Verold Prince, Jennifer Ryan-Bailey, Anita Ryan and the late Carolyn Scott. I gratefully thank my editors, Dr. and Mrs Dom Roberti, for their assistance.

The Village

Friends and other people have told me that I am different. Different? I often ask myself what they mean when they say that I am different. No one has ever clearly defined for me what they mean by saying I am different. Some have explained that I am what most of them would like to be: blunt, honest, outspoken, and right to the point, that I call it as I see it. Those comments are not a surprise to me. I knew and recognized very early in my life that there was within me a sense of justice, a driving ambition, and an intense sensitivity to shame beyond what is found in other people.

Other people cry when they are sad and laugh to acknowledge joy and happiness. Other people seem to enjoy themselves when they are among friends and free of burdens. I, on the other hand, seem not to know what happiness is. My "different" life has filled me with anger and turmoil, so much anger and turmoil that I am unable to appreciate the beauty of life. I am unable to smile when there is a need for me to smile, because I am always overwhelmed with a feeling of shame, and it hurts to smile. There are times when I am hurting deep within my soul and yet I am unable to cry. No

1

one knows of my past, and I fail to realize that my past and its secret have destroyed my soul ever since I was a child.

I was born Belitha Parker in December in a village on a tiny Caribbean island called St. Vincent, in the West Indies. The first known human inhabitants were Carib and Arawak Indians. Most landmarks, including the towns and parishes, have French names from the period of French domination of the island. The Spanish and British also ruled the country at different stages. The Europeans imported slaves from Africa to work on the plantations, but now, as on other Caribbean islands, slavery has been abolished. St. Vincent, with its scenic green pastures, luscious fruit trees, and vegetable plants, remains an island of paradise. Partly surrounded by the tranquil, clear, blue waters of the Caribbean Sea, it has mostly black sand beachfronts. Although the climate is tropical, the ceaseless trade winds result in tolerable temperatures the year round. Along with its natural beauty, St. Vincent is blessed with the pleasant disposition of its inhabitants, the majority of the black people being warm, friendly, and hospitable to strangers. Like most inhabitants of St. Vincent, I am a descendant of black slaves.

My mother told me that I was born on December 26th, even though my birth certificate indicates December 29th. According to my birth record, my father is unknown. Someone fathered me, but he was nameless. My birth record lists New Delphia as my place of birth. New Delphia is a small area located close to Amondid Village. Most islanders think that it is part of Amondid Village. Amondid Village had a population of approximately 200 to 300 villagers during the 1960s. Even though there are many different shades of black in my village, we are all alike black people.

I remember vividly how things were with the villagers and the village during my early childhood and beyond, when the people in my village, like those of any other village in St. Vincent, lived communally. We lived together in houses of one of the three types found throughout the many villages. The first type was constructed of sticks and clay, their roofs being covered with grass. The grass roofs had to be replaced after a year because they would rot. The grass also harbored dangerous pests like centipedes and scorpions. When it rained, these insects would often crawl out of their hiding places and crawl onto the bodies of the occupants of the houses, sometimes biting them, leaving welts. These houses had windows without glass, being boarded up with lumber. The floors were of compressed pounded dirt or were covered with wood. Referred to as thatch houses, they were owned and occupied by the poorest people in our village.

Houses of the second type had two or more rooms and were made of lumber. The windows might be glass or might be boarded up, and the roofs were covered with galvanized corrugated steel sheets. The floors were always covered with some sort of wood. These houses, referred to as board houses, were owned and occupied by the so-called middle class.

The third type of house, built from cement mixed with sand, had glass windows. Like the second type, these had roofs covered with galvanized sheets. These houses were referred to as wall houses. If there was such thing as the rich in our society, they owned and occupied these houses. At different times I have lived in each of these three types.

Although some of the wall houses had kitchens and bathrooms within the same dwelling, most did not. The thatch houses and the board houses, in those days, all had bathrooms and kitchens as separate structures. Even though some people had gas or oil stoves, they did most of their cooking on wood fires. At times the wood fire was so hot that it could singe the hair on your hands, as well as some flesh and skin, if you were not careful when cooking. I remember burning three of my fingers in a wood fire. I was roasting a breadfruit, one of our native foods, a starchy fruit with a green skin. I screamed at the top of my lungs from the heat and the pain. Then there was the smoke, so intense that your eyes would shed tears as if to provide water for cooking. Even people with gas or oil stoves often used wood fires for cooking, because firewood was so plentiful in the forest and fuel for the stoves cost money. It was also believed that food cooked on a wood fire tasted better. Since there were no conventional ovens, the villagers baked in empty cooking-oil containers.

These aluminum containers were approximately four feet high and three feet wide. The villagers cut the bottoms out of the containers and added baking racks made from recycled metal, similar to those of conventional ovens. The ovens were kept outdoors. A wood fire burned on the outer top of these ovens. To heat it for baking, a coal fire was made on the inside bottom. Bread would bake in approximately thirty minutes, cakes in an hour or more. Like foods cooked on a wood fire, bread and cakes baked in these ovens were among the tastiest I ever had.

It was one thing to endure the heat and burns when cooking and baking with a wood fire, but quite another to use latrines with no running water. The latrines, detached from most houses, smelled like decayed corpses. One was alert while sitting on the seat, which harbored big, ugly roaches with long whiskers that crawled on naked buttocks. Unexpectedly, you felt these creatures on your buttocks while you were in the middle of relieving yourself. Frightened, you jumped from the seat. The oil torch or flambeau used to light the latrine went out, and your surroundings became pitch dark. Unable to see, you groped your way towards the house and stepped onto the cold, terribly cold, back of a frog with your bare feet. Terrified, you screamed, "Help! Help!" Family members heard your screams and rushed to assist you. After they realized what your screaming was about, you became the laughing stock of the evening. Like other villagers, I experienced many of those incidents.

We fetched water for drinking in buckets from public pipes or from a spring—less than one percent of the villagers had indoor or outdoor plumbing. We bathed and washed our clothes in the river that flowed through the village. Women and girls carried basins or pails packed with soiled clothes down to the river to wash them. As men did not wash their own clothes, the mothers, wives, sisters and daughters bore the agony of washing the men's tough wrangler pants, stained with dirt and perspiration, leaving bruises on their bare hands. Some of the men came to the river to bathe, walking past the women without acknowledging their presence, let alone their hard labor.

Although a few villagers fetched water from the river to bathe at home, most took their baths at the river, in private areas surrounded by bushes. As children, I and my brothers and sisters usually took our baths in these private spots at the river, too. But sometimes we made dams to contain water four to five feet deep. Children would swim in these man-made pools every day until it rained, when the pools would burst and overflow. Then we resorted to taking our baths in privacy again, until we could make new pools. We made pools collectively and had fun doing it. The children enjoyed the activities at the river, but were forced to stop at times to allow the feces of some despicable human to flow down stream past them. Some villagers moved their bowels in the river even when they knew people downstream were washing and bathing. The river also provided us with crayfish. Children and adults both fished in the river, but the children had the most fun. As children, we pushed our hands under stones in the river to catch crayfish. Sometimes, instead of catching crayfish, we would find some other water creatures pinching and snapping at our fingers. River crabs and lobsters caught our fingers in their claws, leaving painful, bloody cuts. But we continued to fish the river, regardless of the danger.

Children also had fun in school. From ages five to seven, we attended a small one-room school in the village, after which we moved on to a school in another village nearby. We walked to school in small groups, climbing trees together along the way to get fresh fruit. Tangerine, orange, plum, avocado and mango are among the many fruit trees that grew in the yards or in the fields. Children would pick other villagers' fruit without their permission, some children picking and gathering the fruit while others stood as lookouts for the owners. When we heard the alert whistled, we ran through bushes to hide from the owners. If the owners caught the children, they whipped them or took them to their parents for an even worse whipping. But punishment did not deter children, including me, from picking other peoples' fruit.

Because most of the adults in my village had no more than an elementary education, cultivating the land was the main source of income. They grew vegetables for local consumption and for export. The banana crop was the most important cash crop, and the people of St. Vincent took pride in cultivating them. The bananas were exported to England weekly. Some parents took their children out of school one or two days each week to assist them in this enterprise. The children carried bananas on their heads for miles, from the banana fields to a station where the crop was graded for export. A bunch of bananas is approximately three feet long and weighs over thirty pounds. Children struggled, with their necks twisted, as they carried these heavy bunches of bananas, too heavy for some to carry. We carried them because our parents insisted.

Children also assisted with the cultivation and reaping of other crops, particularly yam and potato. They plowed the earth to plant the seeds or vines for the crops, and they weeded the acres of fields, too. Plowing the earth is hard work, but weeding the crops is even worse, especially for the yams. Men did not weed. The females, women and children alike, did this backbreaking work— work that left thorns in their fingers, sometimes too painful to remove. Although this type of work was tedious and punishing to children, many children abandoned their education and resorted to farming because they knew of no other way to make a living.

In those days, the villagers helped one another with farming and shared their produce with one another. They grew most of the crops that they ate, except for a few imported products like rice, Irish potatoes, and salted cod. Imported goods were a regular part of our diet, but they were replaced by local products when they became scarce. Crayfish caught in the river and fresh fish caught in the sea substituted for the imported salted codfish. Most villagers preferred fresh fish, not only because it tasted better but also because it was less expensive than the imports. Besides, local fishermen made a decent income from selling their fish. Fishermen would notify the villagers of their catch by sounding a shell. When they were plentiful, villagers ate fish for breakfast, lunch and dinner. Farmers grew several crops which could substitute for imported rice and Irish potatoes. We villagers considered ourselves poor, because we believed that only poor people worked and lived the way we did.

Living poor did not mean having nowhere to live or nothing to eat. Living poor meant the father of the house ate most of the food and, in some households, all the meat that the family was able to buy for dinner. It meant that most of our meals were starchy. Sometimes for breakfast we drank bush tea, a brew made from mint grown in the garden, along with a piece of bread without butter or cheese. Living poor meant that more than one person shared a scrambled egg and six or more people shared a quarter-pound of salted codfish for a meal. It meant lunch might be some sugared water and bread, if no cooked food was available. You gratefully ate the bread and drank the sugared water and thanked God for providing them, because other people had less than you had, or nothing at all.

Living poor also meant that instead of living in the masters' yards, as our slave ancestors did, we lived in yards owned by the matriarch of the family. It meant that children slept together on wooden floors, on bedding of worn clothes too old and torn to wear, while mothers and fathers slept in the only bed in the house, on bed linens made from the rough fabric of empty sugar bags. Children slept on the floor, separated by sex, boys with boys, girls with girls. The boys and the girls took turns dressing and undressing in the bedroom, respecting one another's privacy.

In addition, being poor meant wearing the same outfit to school all week. After returning from school, you took off the outfit and dressed in your home clothes immediately. It was customary for us to have three sets of clothing: one for school, one for church, and the other for home. Our church clothes were the newest. School clothes were those too worn to wear to church. Home clothes, sometimes patched, were those too worn out to wear to school or church. We usually walked barefoot, wearing our only pair of shoes to church—and to school if allowed by our parents, who were always concerned about wearing them out.

For those of us who went to school shoeless, we prayed to God to have mercy on our feet, especially on the very hot days when we had to traverse the hot tar of village roads. We prayed to God even more at lunchtime, when certain villagers were working at repaving the road, and the hot, black, sticky tar stuck to the bottoms of our feet, despite our efforts to avoid the burning stuff. At times, the heat was so intense that we preferred walking on the thorny grass alongside the roads, where the scorching dried grass pricked our feet like needles. Children and adults alike endured the insult to bare feet, time and time again, year after year. It was part of our way of life.

Few motor vehicles were found in St. Vincent. We walked for miles to almost every destination—mostly to visit relatives and friends and to the district clinic to see a doctor. Since there were not many doctors at the time, the government assigned some doctors to specific areas to attend to sick children and adults once a week. Lord, the doctor responsible for the area where my family lived acted as if he did not care at all about the people and their ailments. On the days he was scheduled to attend, sick people would wait at the clinic for hours before his arrival. When he finally arrived, he would stay in his office for hours before he began to examine those who had waited so long. First he saw the patients who were able to pay him a few dollars beyond his government pay. Then he saw poor patients, often prescribing the same medication for all, as if everyone suffered from the same illness. At a certain moment, he abruptly stopped seeing patients, regardless of the fact that many were still waiting and might have had life-threatening illnesses.

After subjecting ourselves to the doctor, we were then at the mercy of the pharmacist, whom we referred to as the Dispenser. He took his time dispensing the medicine, and sometimes he insulted the sick as he handed over their prescription. Then there was the nurse stationed at the clinic. We were at her mercy when she gave us injections, piercing our flesh and puncturing our buttocks with big, old-fashioned needles. She screamed and told us to shut up. We knew by her manner that she was no Florence Nightingale of a nurse. There was absolutely nothing professional about the three—doctor, nurse or pharmacist. The community respected them for their professions, but they showed little respect for the people of our community, especially for the poor ones like my family and me.

Although most of the villagers were poor, families sometimes had enough money to lend one another when there was an emergency. Villagers did not believe in banking. Some hid their money under mattresses, as did my family, while others kept theirs in cloth purses tied to their clothing Some even buried money in their garden or in the yard behind the house. Poor people always had money for emergencies; they had ways of saving regardless of their financial difficulties and the small amount they earned. You often heard them say, "No one should spend every penny they earn, because one has to put some away for rainy days."

Wanting to save money, villagers did not spend much even on necessities such as clothing. Adults took very good care of their clothing. They stored away their nightclothes, using them only when they got sick and were hospitalized. Pride and self-respect required that you look your best on important social occasions, especially hospitalizations and doctor visits. By the time they decided to wear their nightclothes and other clothes in storage, the clothes were no longer usable, being either outgrown or rotted and fallen apart. They stored children's clothing, too. If a child had a new pair of shoes, the child would be allowed to wear them only to church. If the child did not attend church regularly, the shoes would be outgrown by the time the parents gave permission to wear them. Shoes were not the only things—children outgrew their clothes, too. Some children never got to wear their new clothes, bought for them to use only in case they got sick. Some never got sick, and instead of getting to wear their nice clothes, they would watch a younger sibling wear them. Storing away clothing was a widespread tradition among the villagers, continued from generation to generation and still prevalent today.

Although most of the adults were living together unmarried as the mothers and fathers of their children born out of wedlock, they believed in God. Children may never have seen their parents in any church, but most parents required their children to attend Sunday school and church. My village had a couple of Sunday churches and one Saturday church. Our family did not attend the churches in the village—a blessing to the children in our family who attended church. We attended a church outside the village, where the Sunday worship lasted for no more than an hour and fifteen minutes. By contrast, in the churches of our village, Sunday worship lasted for hours and hours. The ministers preached all that time. I believe that most of the time they forgot their topic, wandering from one topic to another, while half of the congregation fell asleep. Children like me were bored nearly to death and could not wait for the service to end so we could go home. As children, we questioned our parents' motives for forcing us to go to church while they stayed home. I wondered if they did it to punish us, or because they wanted to get rid of us for awhile. Whatever our parents' motives might have been, some of us children benefited a great deal by participating in Sunday worship.

The teachings we learned about God built our faith and belief in Him. Most parents taught their children the twenty-third Psalm, the Our Father, and had them say these prayers before going to bed at night and as soon as they awoke in the morning. Parents also taught children to respect adults. We called adults, including our teachers, by their last names only, preceded by Mr., Mrs. or Ms. Our parents, teachers, and other adults reprimanded us and even beat us if we were caught doing or saying anything improper. Some of us endured beatings so cruel that we compared them to the beatings of our ancestors by their masters in the days of slavery.

Although there was some cruelty in the village, it was not widespread. Most people got along well together. There were few crimes other than some petty ones. Some villagers went into the fields at night and stole other people's crops. Farmers might kill other people's pigs or chickens if they threatened or uprooted the farmers' crops. Otherwise, the village was almost crime-free—or so I thought. I felt that my village was inhabited by good, God-fearing people who helped one another and looked out for one another's interests. I believed that most parents loved their children deeply.

Most of our parents had little money, but they bought their children new outfits and toys each year at Christmas. During the

Christmas season, some villagers formed a caroling group and visited homes in our village and in other villages. One would be awakened from a deep sleep by their harmonious voices. Our parents got out of their beds to greet them. Some children stayed in bed, while others joined their parents and listened to the singing. The music stopped abruptly as someone recited a story about the birth of the baby Jesus and informed the household how many days were left before Christmas. Then the rest of the group continued singing and playing their guitars and drums. When our parents gave them money, the group sang a few more carols before leaving for another house.

It was a tradition on the island that nine days before Christmas some villagers would get out of bed in the early morning to attend parties in the villages. Two days before Christmas, the villagers flocked to the grocery stores to make their largest grocery purchases of the year. The villagers baked their Christmas goodies on Christmas Eve, when a drum oven heated with a wood fire could be seen in almost every yard. Butchers in the village slaughtered more animals on Christmas Eve than they did on any other occasion. Villagers flocked to the butcher stalls to purchase meat for the big feast the following day. We also walked through the village on the night of Christmas Eve to admire the curtains hung in the windows of village houses. Unlike the American custom of having the same drapes and curtains for years, it was customary for the people of my island to buy or make new curtains for their homes each Christmas. They began decorating their houses for Christmas on Christmas Eve. The arrival of Christmas Day was quite an experience for children like me, whose parents insisted we get ourselves out of bed to attend church—but it was the merriest day for us, too. After church, we roamed the village visiting relatives, friends and neighbors and eating whatever food they offered us.

On Christmas Day our parents cooked the most food of any day of the year. Yet most of us were unable to eat at our homes, because we were so full of the food we had been given at other homes in the village. A group of men played their guitars and drums, eating and drinking as they visited home after home, with the younger children following and dancing to their music. Most of the men and some of the women got drunk on Christmas day, and some children witnessed the drunkenness of parents, as I did. Christmas Day was a day when most of the villagers, young and old alike, seemed happy, regardless of the poverty in which some of us lived.

Boxing Day, the day after Christmas, was another big holiday celebrated by the island people. They partied in the village, picnicked on the beach, or went on outings to visit some of our historical landmarks, such as the volcano, La Soufriere. On New Year's Eve, which we called Old Year's Day, our parents did a thorough housecleaning and washed every piece of dirty clothing. It was believed that if New Year's Day should find you with dirty clothing and an untidy house, your house would remain untidy for the rest of the year. After all the hard work of Old Year's Day, most villagers flocked to their churches at night. At midnight, the fervor reached a climax as people prayed and sang louder than ever, welcoming the New Year. While most people were in church, others, mostly young men, became troublemakers, walking the roads, searching for unoccupied old houses, and demolishing them with their bare hands. After all the praying and singing of the night before, as well as the mischief, most of the villagers celebrated on New Year's Day as they had on Boxing Day.

Carnival Day was another nationally celebrated holiday observed memorably in my village. Carnival Days, the last Monday and Tuesday before the beginning of Lent, were marked by fun and frolic. In each village a group of men playing drums followed a leader who was naked except for a tiny loincloth. He was painted with black charcoal on face and body to give him the appearance of a monkey, and he had a man-made tail tied to his buttocks. We called him the "monkey man." As the drummers played on, the monkey man attempted to rub his charcoal-covered body against adults, at the same time frightening the children. Some children, as well as some adults, were able to escape the monkey man, but others were not so lucky. Those who stood admiring his performance were expected to drop some money into his hands, after which he would leave them alone.

On Carnival Day, children and adults alike disguised themselves by dressing like members of the opposite sex. They covered their faces with masks, carried a closed shoebox in their hands, and approached other villagers. In disguised voices, they would ask whether the villager would like to see what was in the shoebox. Upon receiving suitable payment, the disguised person would open the shoebox and display its contents. Sometimes it contained a doll or another object, but many times there was absolutely nothing in the box. All this was done in the name of tradition and fun. Besides these national holidays for which we had our own special traditions, there were other days, like the harvest season, which were not holidays, but which still had traditional activities of their own.

Harvest season was celebrated mostly in the churches during the months of October and November. On any given Sunday, a church or two would host an entertainment program. The parishioners participated in the program with singing performances, and their children often recited poetry. Parishioners also donated baked goods and produce to be sold at the end at the program. People attended these programs well dressed in new clothing. At the conclusion, those who had attended the program, as well as those who had not, flocked to the outside of churches to places where sales were held, purchasing whatever was for sale. The money generated by sales of the donated goods went for the benefit of the church. Harvest time was another time of fun. At this time people visited different churches to participate in either the harvest program or the harvest sales, and many participated in both. Children enjoyed harvest time, too.

Besides supporting their churches, villagers also got together to support one another in times of mourning. When someone died in the village, other villagers gathered in the bereaved family's yard to give comfort to the surviving relatives. Most people died at home. One who died by nine o'clock in the morning was usually buried at four o'clock the same day. Someone in the village took the responsibility of bathing the deceased person, and village carpenters, all men, made the coffin. As payment for making the coffin, the family of the deceased provided the carpenters with food and alcoholic beverages.

After the deceased had been washed and dressed, the body was placed in the uncovered coffin. Six men carried the coffin into the yard and laid it on six chairs for viewing. The villagers gathered to view the body, their Bibles, hymnbooks, and wreaths in their hands. They sang songs like "Jerusalem, My Happy Home," expressing the sentiment that they themselves would one day meet up again with the dead person somewhere in the beyond. Stirred by these sad songs, most of the relatives of the deceased cried openly, sometimes in loud wailing voices. The people would continue with their singing until a preacher arrived from the village. The preacher would read something from the Bible, and then the men would close the coffin. Six men would lift the coffin and carry it two miles to the burial ground in the village, as the preacher and the congregation followed behind. Its final resting place was the open grave in the burial ground, dug by some of the village men. The men laid the coffin on six chairs, which formed the side of a platform beside the open grave The congregation continued with their singing until the preacher signaled for them to stop. At this point the preacher read more verses from the Bible and then signaled the men to lower the coffin into the open grave. As the men lowered the coffin into the grave, again the relatives of the deceased began to cry in wailing voices. The relatives cried and shouted, "Oh God! yo dead and me nah go see you again. Oh God! na go, na go." Some of them gave the impression of wanting to jump into the grave with the coffin, but I never heard of anyone who actually did it. Others fell to the ground in a swoon and had to be helped to their feet again. After the coffin had been lowered into the grave, the preacher read more verses from the Bible. Then the congregation, the mourners and the preacher took some sand in their hands. When the minister spoke the words, "Dust to dust, ashes to ashes," all threw the sand into the grave at the same time. The gravediggers then filled the hole with sand. Before they left the burial ground, the congregation and the preacher laid flowers and wreaths on the grave. But the burial ceremony was not the end for the relatives. I also remember, from childhood, what took place afterward.

For a period of 40 days, some villagers gathered at night at the home of the deceased to support the grieving relatives. What the support was that they gave to the grieving relatives at night was beyond my comprehension. They were there, nevertheless. It was the third, ninth and fortieth nights that were the most memorable. On the third night, more than the usual crowd gathered for a prayer meeting. This was supposedly the night when the departed would rise from the grave like Jesus, to join him in heaven. The people prayed and sang. Sometime during the commotion, the praying and singing escalated. Members of the religion, heads tied with white cloths, held lighted candles in their hands. All of a sudden, they began speaking in what were referred to as unknown tongues. They swayed their bodies in rhythm as one of the members rang a bell again and again. These rituals were supposed to indicate that the deceased person had risen from the dead and was present among them at the prayer meeting. Although the departed was supposed to be present, no one ever claimed to have seen him or her. After the prayer meeting, the participants stayed on for the food. The family fed the congregation with cocoa tea, ginger beer, bread, or small buns. On the ninth and the fortieth nights, villagers celebrated the memorial of the deceased in the same way. But those celebrations were not the final way in which the living dealt with the death of their loved ones.

On the night of November 2nd each year, the villagers weeded the graves of their loved ones prior to placing twenty or more lighted candles on them. Most of the villagers stayed at the gravesites into the night, keeping watch over the candles until they had burned to the ground. As children, we would walk through the burial ground on that night and steal candles from the graves when no one was watching. At any moment, someone might scream: "Oh! God! They thief me candle!" As others focused their attention on the screamer, leaving their own candles unattended, we stole candles from those people, too. We did this all for fun. Other relatives did not go to the burial ground, but instead lit their candles on the outdoor steps of their yards.

Those are my memories of my village from the early years of my childhood. I also remember many other things about my family and my family's yard.

My Family's Yard

During the early years of my childhood I never knew a father, and I have never in my life felt a need for a father. I was born in a small, two-room thatch house located in my family's yard. There were five single two-room houses in my family's yard: three lumber houses and two thatch houses. None of them had indoor plumbing or electricity, and had outhouses for kitchens and latrines. Like most of the villagers, we fetched water from the village pipe or spring, and we cooked and baked with wood fire.

The villagers referred to us as the Letteen family, and my great grandmother was the matriarch. Everyone in the village called her Ma Letteen after her surname, but our family called her simply Ma. We were the only family in the village, indeed in the island, with the last name Letteen, a name of French origin. My great grandfather, Ma's husband, was from Martinique, another Caribbean island, which remains even today one of France's colonies. I never knew my great-grandfather, nor do I remember hearing my family talk much about him. I think he must have died before I was born. Ma was over eighty, approximately five feet four inches tall, and light in complexion, with unblemished skin as soft as a papaya. She had grayish-looking eyes and white, soft, shoulder-length hair. She spoke in a soft, firm voice that demanded attention and respect. Because of her complexion, I often wonder whether a slave master had raped one of Ma's ancestors, making Ma a descendant of a mixed breed slave. I will probably never know for sure, but I still wonder.

As the matriarch of our family, Ma was full of wisdom. We all looked to her for guidance. My family told me that Ma named me Lola when I was born, but that name was never recorded on my birth certificate. Still, the villagers, including my family, called me Lola. For a long time Lola was the only name I knew of. Because of Ma's insistence, very few people would ever know my real name.

I was the first great-grandchild to be born to Ma Letteen in our family's yard, and I was special to my entire family. Few of Ma's children were light in complexion with special-looking grayish eyes like hers, but her grandchildren were darker—except for me. I believe that because of my lighter complexion, my family was much more attentive to me than to the other children. The other children in my family yard slept on the floor at night; I slept on the bed with Ma or my Mommy (my grandmother), who I thought was my mother. I can never remember sleeping on the floor. I knew I was special to my family. I would like to believe that I was special to my family for reasons other than the shade of color of my skin, but time has led me to believe otherwise.

Ma taught me to say the Our Father when I awoke in the morning and before I went to bed at night. Known for her cleanliness, she brushed my teeth every morning before breakfast and at night before I went to bed, and later taught me how to brush my own teeth with cane fiber. In those days, people sucked the juice from sugar cane plants and then used the fibers to brush their teeth. Ma used to fetch water from the river in a pail, and she would then give me a bath behind her house. She took care of me as a mother would have. Ma had nine living children that I knew of, and I can only imagine that she must have been a good mother to all of them.

Uncle Josey was Ma's youngest son and seemed to be her favorite child. All of Ma's sons had moved out of our family yard except for Uncle Josey. He continued to live with his mother and became very protective of her. He was a loving, kindhearted man. I believe he should have become a preacher because he prayed constantly and acted so much like a good Christian. He treated all the children well, especially those in our family yard, but I knew that I was his favorite. I was the one he would lift up and carry on his back, and I remember his throwing me into the air and catching me. Uncle Josey treated me as the fathers of the other children in my family yard treated their daughters. He would tell me how much he loved me, calling me his little princess. For a very long time I thought that Uncle Josey really was my father, even though no one told me to call him daddy. I think that was because of his fatherly interest in me. Uncle Josey taught the children in my family to love one another and to know the difference between right and wrong. The other children bonded with Uncle Josey in various ways, but I bonded with him as a child would with a parent. I knew that I meant a lot to him, but I wondered whether he knew how much he meant to me.

One day Uncle Josey lifted me up and held me in his arms, kissing me on the cheek. He began to cry. "Little Princess," he said. "I am leaving to go down South." I had no idea what he meant, being only four years old. He said that he wanted me to be able to wear pretty dresses, as I had been accustomed to do. "For you to continue to dress in pretty dresses, Uncle Josey has to find work, and there is plenty of work down South," he said to me. As he dried the tears from his watery, grayish looking eyes, Uncle Josey tried to explain that he would work to earn plenty of money so that he could buy me pretty things. He thought I should understand, but I didn't. Uncle Josey cried as he assured me he would take good care of me. Then he kissed me again, told me to be a good girl to Ma and Mommy until his return, and left. I saw him wiping the tears from his eyes as he walked away. I ran after my uncle, this well-dressed, five feet, six inches tall man, with brown complexion and soft, black hair. I begged him to let me go along with him. Someone picked me up and carried me to Ma's house, as I tried to get loose, kicking and crying. I must have fallen asleep, because I awoke in Ma's bed, screaming at the top of my lungs, "Uncle Josey! Uncle Josey! Where is Uncle Josey?" Ma heard my scream. She rushed to me, hugged me, and tried to calm me, but I kept asking to see Uncle Josey. Ma explained that Uncle Josey had gone down South to find work. I learned later that going down South meant going to Trinidad, another Caribbean island south of St. Vincent.

With Uncle Josey gone, I was attended to more by Ma, Mommy and Bulah, one of my Mommy's daughters. I missed Uncle Josey and made wishes for his return, but he never came back. He wrote and sent money to Ma and Mommy to support me, and he sent word through his letters assuring me of his love. One day my god-mother arrived from Trinidad and delivered to Ma a suitcase full of clothes from Uncle Josey. When Ma opened the suitcase, she found that most of the clothes in the suitcase were for me. I saw that Uncle Josey had sent the pretty clothes he had promised to send to me. Ma allowed me try the clothes on, piece by piece, but she insisted that they were to wear only to church. Soon after I had tried on the last piece, she packed them all away. I was then too young to walk the long distance to church, but I hoped I would soon be able to. I was anxious to wear the new clothes from my Uncle Josey.

Some of the other children in my yard were attending the vil-lage school, but I was not. I was not happy to be kept from attend-ing school. Sometimes I would sneak out of the yard, following the other children to school and into their classroom. When my fami-ly noticed that I was missing from the yard, or the teachers sent word for them to come and get me, one of them would come to the school and take me back. At these times I felt like a recaptured runaway slave. I would cry and scream, begging them to let me stay in school with the other children, but they took me home any-way. Ma would try to explain that I wasn't old enough to go to school, but I wouldn't listen. I ran away to school, time and time again. I was over four years old, but not yet five. I couldn't wait to turn five, the age at which I could begin school.

As I continued in this way, word of my persistence reached the principal of the school. This soft-spoken, petit woman made an exception for me, allowing me to attend school for half a day before I was old enough to be admitted. So I went to school prop-erly each morning, and Ma was successful in preventing me from running away and returning to school with the other children in the afternoon, even though I tried. I was happy when I reached age five and was able to spend the entire day in school. As soon as I was eligible to attend school for the whole day, Ma insisted that I attend church, too.

Walking to church was tiring. There were times when I was so tired that I could only walk very slowly to and from church. As a result, my cousins and I would be late for church and would be the last ones to return home. If I had told Ma that the distance from home to church was too much for me, I'm sure she would have kept me home. But I didn't want to stay home. I wanted to wear the pretty dresses Uncle Josey had sent me, and I was allowed to wear them only when I went to church. I believe I looked elegant in those dresses, and I felt flattered by the many compliments I received from members of the church. Although I hated the walking, I loved attending church. The songs of the congregation reminded me of the times when Uncle Josey used to sing to us children in our yard.

At this stage in my life, I enjoyed everything—people, church, school, and Sunday school. The schoolteachers taught us nursery rhymes like "Little Jack Horner." The Sunday school teachers taught us songs like "Jesus Loves the Little Children of the World," along with many verses from the Bible. The only one I could remember and repeat was a short phrase from the New Testament, "Jesus wept." I repeated the verse to my family, especially Ma, all the time. Ma did not attend church, but she was a very religious person. I think it was too far for her to walk. There were times when my family would gather in our yard and ask the children to sing and recite Bible verses. It appeared that they were counting on me to do most of this, despite my young age. I recited verses from the Bible I had learned in Sunday school and nursery rhymes I had learned in the school in the village, and I sang songs I learned from both. After each performance, my family cheered, applauded and hugged me, and I would hear them saying among themselves that I was the smartest of the children in our yard. I loved the attention and praise I received from everyone.

I remember other happy events from my early childhood. One of the villagers, a member of our church, Ms. Wallace, had become fond of me. Ma permitted Ms. Wallace to take me with her to functions at different churches, especially to harvest programs. Ms. Wallace taught me poems for me to recite at our harvest programs. When the master of ceremonies called my name, I would walk to the stage, well dressed in one of the pretty dresses Uncle Josey had sent me. Before I recited the poem, I would bow to the crowd, and I bowed again before leaving the stage. The crowd seated inside the church clapped enthusiastically. Sometimes some of them shouted, "Repeat! Repeat!" and I would then walk back to the stage and recite the poem again. Afterwards, Ms. Wallace would hug me and tell me how good my performance had been. She was very kind to me and took me other places besides church.

One day Ms. Wallace told me I had been chosen to present a bouquet to an important person who was visiting my island, maybe a Queen or a Princess, I cannot recall. That day, Ms. Wallace combed my hair neatly and tied it with pretty ribbons to match the prettiest of my dresses. I wore white gloves which covered my arms up to the elbow. Carrying a bouquet of carnations and roses, I walked to the crossroads outside my village, where a crowd of children and adults had gathered. Some of the adults were dressed up, and the children were wearing clean school uniforms. I don't know whether it was mandatory for children to wear uniforms to school, but we all did. Most of the adults, and the children as well, were waving St. Vincent's flags, singing "God Save Our Gracious Queen." I was standing beside another girl who was dressed like me, also wearing gloves and carrying a bouquet. We stood side by side before the cheering crowd. A car drove up and stopped near us. A windows of the car was lowered slightly, and I saw sitting in the back seat a well-dressed white woman, wearing gloves that covered her arms up to the elbows. She reached out and shook hands with me and the other girl standing next to me. As we had been instructed, we bowed and presented the bouquets to her. The crowd continued to sing as the car drove away. Everyone, including Ms. Wallace and my cousins, seemed excited that I had met and shaken hands with this important lady. I wasn't excited at all, and had no clue why others were. I would rather have been at home in my yard than standing in the hot sun awaiting the arrival of this white woman.

The children in our yard played well together, and our family, especially the women, took an active part in caring for us. They were very much interested in our welfare, making sure we had our breakfast every morning and were never late for school. I felt good carrying a book to school and even wrote in it when my teachers permitted me to. School was very special to me, and I got angry when school was closed for vacation.

I was only five years old, but old enough, when Ma and Mommy started to send me to the village shop to buy groceries. Almost every day, my Ma would send me to buy a drink of strong rum for her. Seeing that Ma was drinking this strong drink, I became curious about how it would taste. One day I tasted the rum before bringing it to her. I loved it. It had a cool taste that made me feel light. Because I loved the taste, I would drink a little of the rum and then stop at the village pipe or spring and add some water to fill the bottle. Ma knew as soon as she tasted it that water had been added to her rum. She accused the shopkeeper of diluting the rum, never suspecting that I was the one who had done it. I have never told her the truth of the matter. I knew that if I had told Ma that I was responsible for watering her rum, she would have given me a whipping I would not have easily forgotten. Some people accused Ma of being an alcoholic because she drank her daily drink of rum, but I never saw Ma drunk. I remember the time when a Christian lady from the village, a member of the Seventh Day Adventist Church, visited Ma at her house. She asked Ma to stop drinking rum if she had hopes of going to heaven to join God in his kingdom. My Ma was furious with the woman. She told her that the day she stopped drinking would be the day she died. Ma gave the lady a lecture about God and the Bible. She told her she expected to get to heaven sooner than the lady. My Ma was something of a character. She believed, and would often say, that it was her daily drink of strong rum that helped her to stay healthy and kept her alive so long. I think Ma was in her mid-nineties, or older, at the time.

Ma and Mommy continued to send me to do their grocery shopping at the village store. Mommy also would sometimes send her youngest son, Kyle, to buy groceries. Although Kyle was a year older than I, Mommy would have to write out a list for him of the items he was to buy, but she never needed to write a list for me. I was able to remember everything she asked me to buy. Soon other adults in my family began to send me to the village shop to buy their groceries, too. So I became a messenger for them all. I had no objection, since they would shower me with praise when I returned from the grocery store with everything they had asked me to buy. I loved the praise of my family, and other people besides my family members praised me for my fine memory, too.

The older men hanging around the village shop praised me as well. When I would tell the shopkeeper what I wanted from memory, the older men stared in amazement and whispered among themselves. They congratulated me on my memory and gave me candy. I remember that a man who was not one of the villagers bought me a book as a present, saying he was astonished that I was able to remember so many groceries without a list. He told me that I was a smart child with a fine memory. Those were indeed happy days. I experienced the happiness of a child who feels loved. I knew my family loved me, especially Ma and Mommy, and I felt that Uncle Josey loved me as much as Ma and Mommy, even though he was still living far away down South. I was also growing up and beginning to understand how I was related to all the rest of my family, especially those who were living in my yard.

Living in Ma's house was my great aunt Babe, one of Ma's daughters, and Aunt Babe's daughter, Eugina, along with Eugina's son, Wesley. Aunt Babe was dark and slender. Unlike Ma, whose hair was long, Aunt Babe had very short hair. She was a very quiet and religious woman who never missed church on Sundays. Aunt Babe was so dedicated to churchgoing that she went even when she was sick. She would walk that great distance in the rain. Every Sunday, Aunt Babe dressed up in her well-starched and well-ironed print dress. She always wore a hat to church and always carried a pocketbook, her Bible and hymnbook. At church she participated fervently in the reading of the scriptures and prayers and in the singing of hymns. When the time came for us to receive communion, Aunt Babe would walk to the altar very reverently and kneel with her head bowed. After receiving communion in the same reverent manner, she would walk back to her pew and remain in silent prayer. Aunt Babe was a good, kind-hearted Christian woman who always seemed to mind her own business. I have never heard her utter a negative word to anyone or say anything bad about anyone. She was always very attentive to Ma's needs. I have never seen Aunt Babe with a man, and no men ever came to our yard to visit her.

Unlike Aunt Babe, her daughter Eugina was rude and loud, and Eugina's son, Wesley, was the same. Wesley and I were close in age. As rude as Eugina and her son were, they showed great respect for Ma and for Aunt Babe. Ma would not tolerate anyone disrespecting her, nor would anyone in our family.

Great-aunt Bertha lived next to Ma in her own little two-room lumber (board) house. Tanty Bertha, as we called her, lived with her younger children and their father. She had only one hand, her other arm having been amputated all the way up to her elbow. According to the story, Tanty Bertha had been employed some years before in a factory where arrowroot is ground and converted into starch and other products. Tanty Bertha's hand became caught in a machine grinding arrowroot as she was loading it. Her hand was so badly damaged that the doctor couldn't save it, and he had to amputate. Tanty Bertha's handicap did not prevent her from kneading the tightest of dumplings, and she cooked some of the most delicious food I have ever eaten. As Tanty Bertha loved to cook, she also loved to eat. No one in our family loved to eat meat and dumplings as much as Tanty Bertha did. When we were young children, Tanty Bertha suffered another misfortune, losing her young son, Hudson.

Hudson was not yet five years old when he died as the result of an injection. The father of Tanty Bertha's children, who lived with her in our family yard, had been diagnosed with tuberculosis. Their oldest daughter, Sandra, was then found to have the disease as well. Both Sandra and her father were sent away to live in an isolated hospital, remaining there for years. After Sandra was diagnosed with tuberculosis, a nurse visited our yard and gave an injection to everyone living there. The nurse said that tuberculosis is contagious, and that the injection would protect us from being infected with it. After being injected, everyone who lived in Tanty Bertha's house fell asleep. Later that night, we were awaked by Tanty Bertha's loud scream. She had gotten up to check on her children and found Hudson dead. It was said that his death was caused by an overdose of the injection which he had been given. My aunt did not want to take responsibility for Hudson's burial, since she had little money to cover the expenses, so she gave Hudson's body to the government for burial. When the government men came to take Hudson's body away, I saw his corpse. There was froth covering his mouth and nostrils. They put him in a sack, carried it to a van and drove away.

The burial ground where Hudson was buried was near the hospital, from which one could view the site. At the time, one of our relatives was in the hospital and witnessed Hudson's burial. He told the family that the government had not given Hudson a decent burial, but had buried him as one would bury a dog. My family were upset and saddened by this report. My Ma scolded Tanty Bertha about her giving her grandson's body to the government to bury. She expressed her disgust, "Yes, we are poor, but not so poor that we couldn't afford to bury our own dead relatives." Everyone began to cry in wailing voices, especially the adults. For a very long time after his death, a couple of my relatives would cry every time they talked about Hudson.

Below Tanty Bertha's house was a two-room thatch house occupied by Dolly, one of her daughters, with her boyfriend and children. Dolly was slim, with hair of medium length that showed her neglect of daily combing. Dolly had buried three children, two of them twins. If there was a family member among us who was lazy, Dolly was the one. Unlike the other adults in our family yard, who took turns caring for one another's children, Dolly did not take care even of her own children, let alone the children of other family members. Dolly did not clean her house every day as everyone else in our yard did. Children other than her own did not eat from Dolly's pot, since other members of the family advised us not to eat Dolly's food. They said Dolly was too lazy to cook clean food for other people to eat.

The two-room board house situated on the right of Tanty Bertha's house at the far end of our family yard was that of my Mommy, as I called my grandmother. Mommy was of average height and dark in complexion, with black, thick, shoulder-length hair. She was a hard-working woman who labored Monday through Saturday. Most Saturdays, she worked without payment, assisting other villagers with the cultivation of their crops. Living with Mommy were my Aunt Vernice, my two Uncles, and I. She had no husband. Kyle's father came to visit frequently, but he never spent the night. Kyle and I bonded like brother and sister. He cared for me and protected me as an older brother would a younger sister. Kyle did not like school and would fake all kinds of sickness to avoid going. I did most of Kyle's schoolwork for him, and in return when we got our meals he gave me whatever portion of his food I wanted. Kyle was Mommy's youngest son.

Mommy's older son, Raymond, was tall and slender. He worked, but he did not share any of the financial responsibilities for the home. Mommy did not expect him to. Although Raymond worked and got paid, there were times when Mommy had to give him money, because Raymond would gamble and lose all of his money. I never understood why Mommy would give Raymond money when she knew that he had lost his own by gambling.

Vernice was Mommy's youngest daughter. She was of average height and had long, curly black hair. Vernice was still attending school, but she already had a boyfriend named Patrick who came to visit her. Patrick, five feet, five inches tall, with dark complexion, looked rugged. I thought he looked sneaky and felt very uncomfortable around him. I guess Ma felt the same way, because I overheard her telling Mommy that there was something about Patrick her instinct told her not to trust. She said she did not want him visiting her yard. Even though Ma made it perfectly clear to Patrick that she did not want him in her yard, he continued to visit

Vernice. He was able to do so without being detected by Ma and other family members by entering Mommy's house, located at the far end of our family's yard, where he would not be seen.

Located above Mommy's house was a two-room thatch house, the last of the five houses in my family yard. Mommy's other daughter, Bulah, Mr. Phillips, and their two children, Jerald and Marge, lived there. Bulah, of average height, with black hair and dark complexion, bore no resemblance to Mommy. I guess she must have resembled her father, but I had never seen her father, who was also Raymond's father. I heard the adults say that their father had migrated South, as Uncle Josey had. Bulah fed Kyle and me on school days when Mommy had to leave for work earlier than expected and didn't have the time to prepare our breakfast. There were times when Bulah would even prepare dinner for everyone living in Mommy's household.

Uncles Manto, Jefford, Let, and John and Tanty Cumsie were Ma's other children. Like Uncle Josey, Manto had migrated to Trinidad. I heard my other relatives talk about him, but I never knew him. I only saw the letters he wrote back and the money he sent to Ma and Mommy. Both Ma and Mommy outlived Manto, who died in Trinidad without ever returning to St. Vincent. Jefford was married and lived in another town quite a distance from the rest of the family. Although he lived far away, he came to visit Ma regularly, sometimes bringing his children with him. Mommy visited Jefford, too, and sometimes she insisted that I accompany her. I loved Uncle Jefford, but I hated the long journey we had to make on foot to visit him. Uncles Let and John and Tanty Cumsie were married and lived elsewhere in the village, nearer than Uncle Jefford. They visited Ma almost every day. Ma's children were very special to her, and she seemed to have a special bond with each of them.

Ma was special not only to her children but to the other villagers, too. Villagers came to our yard to listen to Ma's many stories about events that had occurred during her lifetime. She spoke often about the eruption of La Soufriere, the St. Vincent volcano that had erupted in 1902. Ma told stories about how our family first came to live in our village. Ma's family had lived in a village close to the volcano, but they fled the village when the volcano began to erupt. Fearing for their lives, they fled with just the clothes they were wearing, leaving all of their possessions behind. Ma said they never went back to her former village to live, because it was badly damaged by the eruption. Ma told of the people in other villages, including her own former village, who were not able to escape before the eruption of the volcano. She said that those people had perished from the hot lava and ashes which fell on their bodies. Some of them were burnt to death and beyond recognition.

Ma told us that when the eruption of the volcano had ceased, they saw a number of statue-like figures standing in various positions. These figures, which fell apart when touched, were the ashen remains of people in sitting, standing and bending positions. She said the sight of these victims, especially of children who seem to have been clinging to their parents, brought forth strong emotions from the survivors. Ma explained that there was much suffering after the eruption, because food and clean water were scarce, and many died from starvation and various diseases. She also recalled the epidemic of cholera in St. Vincent, when people were dropping like flies. Survivors were too weak to dig individual graves for the dead, so they had to bury them together in mass graves. Beside those gruesome stories, she also amused us with other stories.

Ma told about the souls of the dead, good and bad, that came back to hurt or help the living. They were referred to as "Jumby." She talked about the experiences living people walking to towns and other villages, in groups or alone. They did most of their night walking when the moon was shining. She said that some of them saw what they thought were other human beings walking behind them, and that sometimes they even heard them speak. Then suddenly they would disappear into thin air. Ma referred to them as the "Good Jumbies," being the spirits of the good people who had died. The "Bad Jumbies" were bad spirits who led the living to their deaths by asking them to follow them over embankments. Stories like these were told to us not only by Ma's generation, but also by younger generations as well. Ma seemed to me a woman of great wisdom.

Many villagers believed in bush medicine to cure their diseases more than in conventional medicine. Ma was good at telling people what type of bush preparation would cure their ailments. I remember having had a case of the measles. Instead of taking me to a doctor, Ma went into the garden and picked the leaves from some bushes, all types of different bushes, and then boiled them together in an iron pot on the wood fire. She then added fresh water to the greenish brew. She also roasted an ear of corn on the wood fire until it was burnt and soaked the burnt corn in water. She did this each day for almost a week. Each day during that week, she gave me the water from the burnt corn to drink and she bathed me in the greenish herbal preparation. Then, as she was bathing me, she took the boiled leaves and rubbed my body with them. After each bath, she oiled my body with oil made from coconut milk. Then Ma dressed me and insisted that I stay indoors out of the hot sun. She allowed me to go outside only in the evening when it was cooler. By the end of that week, Ma's medicine had cured me. The measles on my body disappeared.

Ma also cured one of my cousins with her bush medicine. Terry had mumps. Ma went to the garden and cut a couple of leaves from a plant and held the leaves over the wood-burning fire until they became soft. Then she placed the leaves in her hands and rubbed them together. She melted a soft candle and rubbed it around my cousin's neck, especially on the spot on his chin where there was swelling from the mumps. On that spot, she placed the softened leaves, tying them on with a cloth. She repeated this for several days, and my cousin's mumps disappeared, just as my measles had done.

Besides telling stories about her experiences in life to those who visited our yard, Ma was also able to cure the sickness of many of them, or to tell them about remedies which could be used. Many people, family and visitors alike, found Ma to be a most intriguing person. Ma had a wisdom which she shared with many others. We relied on her wisdom to help us make wise decisions. But Ma was not the only old person who did these things—there were others, and as a society we appreciated all of them. Unlike countries where old people are considered financial burdens and liabilities to their relatives and the government, our island valued our elders for their long lives, and the same was true for most Caribbean islands. We treated our older people with the utmost respect and care. We felt that their wisdom allowed younger generations to draw from them and make wise decisions, to the benefit of our society as a whole. There were some among them who were gifted with the ability to predict events, both good and bad, that would take place in the future. Most of these wise people were also good Christians, as was Ma herself.

With time, Ma grew old and weak. "Lola," she said to me one day, "Ma loves you but Ma is getting old and will soon die. Ma has to move on, but remember that Ma will always be with you, my child. Grow up and be a good girl." I listened to her, but my six-year-old mind failed to comprehend what Ma meant by those words. Ma did grow weaker, gradually losing her influence over the people who lived in our yard.

As Ma grew older and weaker, lots of changes took place in our yard. Many of my cousins, including my Uncle Raymond, were now adults. As adults, men and women alike had strangers visiting them in our yard. Many of the visitors came and went as they liked, as though they were related to us. But I felt they had no right to be in our family yard, Ma Letteen's yard. The visitors were a mixture of the desirables with the undesirables. Many of the adults who had never had children of their own were now having children with the visitors, and some were moving out of our yard to live elsewhere in the village with the fathers or mothers of their children. I don't remember any of them ever getting married. Bulah, my Mommy's older daughter, with Mr. Phillips and their two children, moved out of their old thatch house into a lumber house they had bought, a blue house with glass windows. The new house was situated on a separate piece of land down the hill from the family yard, next to the river that ran through the village.

When Bulah was moving, she asked Mommy's permission to have me live with them, and Mommy agreed. Before I found out about this agreement, Mommy explained to me that Bulah was my biological mother. She said the time had come for us to live together under one roof, as a mother and daughter should. "Oh, Mommy," I begged, "she is not my mother. You are my mother. I don't want to leave you, and I don't want to live with Bulah. Please, Mommy, don't send me to live with Bulah." Mommy was the only mother I had ever known. Bulah was not taking care of me as she was her two children. But Mommy insisted I had to go live with Bulah. My Aunt Vernice was pregnant at the time, and there was not enough space in Mommy's house to accommodate another person. I believe that was the only reason Mommy released me to my mother without offering any resistance.

Living with Bulah did not change much in my life. I continued to call my grandmother Mommy and to call my mother Bulah, even when Bulah insisted I call her Mommy. I was about ten years old when I finally decided to call Bulah Mommy. Whenever I did call her Mommy, I would refer to her as the young Mommy and to my grandmother as my Mommy. I loved my grandmother without limit. She was a very special person for me, and I had no doubt that I was special to her as well. I loved Bulah, too, but my love for her was like the love I had for all of the other relatives living in our yard. I continued to spend most of my time in Ma's yard, because I had bonded with that family for so many years that it was hard for me to stay away from them for long. I continued to sleep at Mommy's house more often than I slept at Bulah's, and I even went there to take my afternoon naps when I was not in school. We always had a full meal at lunchtime, and I don't know if it was the food that made me sleepy, but I would nap every day after I ate my lunch. It was during one of my routine afternoon naps in Mommy's house, in Ma's yard, that something happened to me that would change my life forever. That event robbed me of my childhood and stole my innocence, both to be forever lost, because once lost, they could never be recovered.

Innocence Lost

It happened when I was six years old, and I remember it vividly. I was taking my afternoon nap in my grandmother's house when I felt a hand covering my mouth. I awoke and saw Patrick, Aunt Vernice's boyfriend, stooping over me. He told me to keep quiet. I was frightened, but I couldn't have screamed even if I wanted to, because his hand was tightly pressed over my mouth. I was horrified, but I remained quiet. Still covering my mouth with one hand, Patrick used the other to pull off my panties. I was puzzled, wondering whether he was planning to give me a bath, but I saw that there was no pail of water around. Besides we never took our baths inside the house—we took them in the river, or, sometimes, outdoors in the yard, using the rainwater or water fetched in a bucket from the village pipe or spring. After Patrick took off my panties, I watched as he unzipped his pants, and I saw him expose his toelow (the dialect word used for the male organ). Then, he took his toelow and put it on my pumpum (also a dialect word used for the vagina). Patrick penetrated my small vagina with his large penis, moving his body up and down upon me. I felt excruciating pain everywhere in my whole body. I tried to scream for help, but his hand muffled my cries. I was frightened out of my wits—so frightened that at one point I closed my eyes and pretended to be dead. His hand partially covered my nostrils as well as my mouth, and I was afraid I would suffocate. I said some silent prayers that my Mommy, Ma, Uncle Josey or anybody of my family might come to save me. But no one came, not even my Mommy, who at the time was out somewhere in a field. She was working to support all of us, including the child that Patrick had begotten on my aunt. My family members did not come to my rescue. They could not hear my cry for help and were not aware of the danger I was in. Most of them were sitting under a tree outside the yard, talking as they shaded themselves from the blistering heat of the midday sun. My family knew that I was in Mommy's house taking my usual midday nap, and they had no reason to check on me. They thought I was safe in the yard. Little did they know that being in the yard would not protect me from Patrick, who would rape me at such a tender age.

I don't know how long the ordeal with Patrick lasted, but I have never forgotten the pain I suffered then and how scared and confused I was. I lay there in pain and gasping for air during the whole ordeal. Then he was finished. He got off me told me that what he had done was to be our secret and I was not to tell anyone. Then he pulled a knife from his pocket and said to me, "You see this? It's sharp and it cuts." Patrick threatened to cut my Mommy's throat and my own with the knife if I told anyone what he had done to me. Then he gave me a coin, as if in payment, which later I threw away. He left me there alone, in pain—lots of pain—and unable to move. I lay there, more or less in the same position as when he was assaulting me. After a while I crawled in agony under the bed, and I lay there for some time. My vagina was bleeding, and I had congealed blood sticking on my legs. When I pulled my panties up, they were soon soaked with blood. I didn't know what to do next, so I thought about it and decided not to tell anyone. Still, I hoped that someone would walk in on me, see the blood, and ask what had happened. But no one came.

I was old enough that Ma and Mommy were no longer giving me baths and dressing me. They had taught me how to do those things for myself, including washing my panties. Although I had had a bath that morning and wouldn't be taking another until the next day, I still did not show my bloody panties to anyone. I hid them until I was able to wash them the next day. I decided not to show my panties to anyone, because I was afraid of Patrick's threat to kill my Mommy and me. I was only a little girl, even if I had just been robbed of my innocence, and I was afraid to die. I wanted to live to be as old as Ma. Because I so desperately wanted to live, I kept the rape secret and bore the pain quietly. Yes, Lord, I kept the secret and the peace, but in doing so, I was condemning myself to additional pain and suffering that would seem endless.

Protected by my secrecy, Patrick raped me repeatedly. Every time he raped me, I cried and cried for pain. But I had no way of stopping him. I felt helpless and hopeless. God knows I wanted him to stop, but I'd rather have him rape me undetected than have him kill my Mommy and me. I continued to bear the suffering, but in anger, and I passed almost every day of my little life in distress.

I hoped that Uncle Josey would return. I thought that he would protect me as he had done before he went down South. But my hope was in vain, for Uncle Josey never returned. I became withdrawn and unhappy. I hoped that someone would notice my unhappiness, but nobody ever did, not even Bulah, my supposed biological mother. I wondered at times whether anyone really cared.

My mother did not have time to notice my unhappiness because she was so involved with the other children, especially her new baby. If I had still been living with my grandmother, she would have checked up on me every day and made sure that I told her everything that had happened to me. But Bulah seemed not to be much concerned about me and my welfare. Ma would have looked out for my welfare, but she was too old to help me now. I sat with her regularly, especially in the evening after I had finished my chores. God knows my love for Ma Letteen and how much I would miss her if she died before I did. But I had to keep in mind the possibility that I could die before she did. "One of these days, Patrick might kill me," I frequently thought. Anyway, Ma had already assured me that she would be with me always, and she continued to offer me this assurance. But then I wondered why she failed to be with me when I most needed her, during the rapes. I asked these questions of myself—but I never asked Ma. As it turned out, my Ma got sick and died before I had turned eight. My family said she was over one hundred years old when she died.

Ma's death and what I understood about death at the time devastated me. I knew that Ma's death meant that I would no longer be able to sit and talk with her. She would no longer call, "Lola, come, go buy Ma Letteen rum." And, of course, I would no longer have the opportunity to taste the clear cool liquid they call strong rum. I would no longer able to play with Ma's long, soft white hair and feel the softness of her skin. Most heartbreaking to me was the thought that I would no longer be able to see my Ma again, my Ma who had cared for me for all those years. "Oh, how I am going to miss Ma!" I thought. "She has been so very special to me, and I will miss the special things she did for me, like insisting that I eat part of her meals with her, even when she knew I had already been fed."

Ma was buried on the day she died. My family got some men from the village to make her coffin. They cut up a tree and from the lumber made Ma a beautiful coffin. For their payment, my family fed the men and provided them with alcoholic beverages. Two ladies from the village came to Ma's house, washed her body, combed her hair, and dressed her in her burial clothing, which had been made by a seamstress from the village. I noticed that they tied her two big toes together and stuffed cotton into her ears. They also wrapped a piece of cloth around her chin and tied it to the top of her head. I wondered why they tied up Ma's chin like that and whether they were hurting her, but I did not have the courage to ask anyone. I later learned that they had done it to keep Ma's mouth closed.

Throughout that day, people were coming and going in our yard. They talked about the good things that Ma had done in her lifetime, consoling my relatives and saying how much they would miss Ma. Some brought flowers from their gardens. Most people grew flowers in gardens in front of their houses.

At approximately 3:30 that afternoon, they moved Ma from her bed and placed her into the coffin. Six men took the coffin and placed it on six chairs in the family yard, as the congregation gathered to view her body and sing hymns of mourning. When the village preacher arrived, he prayed and read verses from the Bible. Then they covered the coffin that contained my Ma's body. Almost everyone in my family, including me, cried as they were covering the coffin. Then the six men picked up the coffin and carried it slowly to the burial ground, as the congregation, including the village preacher, followed behind singing songs of mourning. While we were following the coffin to the burial ground, I was hoping that Ma would knock on the coffin and conquer death after all, like the man I had heard of who had done just that.

There was a man living in another village who was called "Conquer Death." As the story goes, the man had died, and while he was being carried to the burial ground, the men carrying the coffin had heard a knock. They quickly dropped the coffin and began to run, with most of the congregation following them. A few brave souls ventured to open the coffin. They were stunned to see the man they thought was dead get out of the coffin and walk away. Many claimed it was a miracle, that God had raised the man from the dead. Others thought that the man himself had actually overcome death. From that day forward, they called him "Conquer Death." I was hoping that Ma would be able to conquer death as this man had done, but she never did. They carried her to the burial ground without my hearing any knocking.

They laid Ma's coffin beside the grave, while the village preacher continued to read from the Bible and another book. Then the men lifted the coffin with some ropes and lowered it into the hole they had dug to bury Ma. The preacher presided over the burial while the congregation continued singing. The Ma Letteen family, including me, cried in wailing voices. "Oh God! Don't leave us, Ma," many of us cried. The men covered the coffin with sand until the hole was filled and a grave mound had been formed. People laid flowers and wreaths on Ma's grave, and I had a wreath of my own to add to the pile. As I was laying the wreath, I knelt and cried loudly. Someone took my hand and led me away from Ma's grave, telling me I would see Ma again one day in heaven. But I knew that Ma was now buried in the burial ground, not far from our family yard.

I felt the world around me shattering. I worried about life without Ma. It seemed that all the people who loved, protected and cared for me were leaving me, one by one, leaving me unprotected and alone. Uncle Josey had left, going down South and never returning. Now Ma was dead. I wondered whether my grandmother would leave me, too, or whether Patrick would kill her because of her love for me. My grandmother continued to do what she could for me, but I feared for her life. I was afraid that something would take my Mommy away from me. I prayed to God that Patrick would not think that I had told on him and kill her. If she died, who would be left? Pondering these things, I was a confused little girl.

I visited the yard less frequently since Ma's death. My grandmother seemed to be working most of the time. Even though I lived with Bulah, Uncle Josey continued his financial support of me and would send money to my grandmother, who would give it to my mother. That's why I thought Uncle Josey was my father. My grandmother would also give my mother a dollar or two to help support me when she got paid on Saturdays. This was a lot of money for my grandmother to give just for my support, when her weekly earnings could have been no more than five or six dollars and she was the only breadwinner of her household of six people. Because of her love for me, she would have sacrificed her last dollar if she thought I would benefit.

As I grew older, I became more knowledgeable about the world and the people around me. My mother was demanding that I call her Mommy, because, after all, she said, "I am your mother." It took me a long time before I began to call her Mommy. But I never stopped calling my grandmother Mommy as well. I also became aware that my siblings' father and Patrick, my rapist, were brothers. Patrick was now a regular visitor to my mother's house and would even spend nights sleeping in the same house with me. On those nights I would go to bed fearing that he would crawl into my bed and rape me while the others slept. Many nights I stayed awake as long as I could, pondering what I would do if he were to try to rape me. I also considered telling my mother about it, but I wondered whether she would believe me. If she did not, what would be the consequences for me? My mother had started to beat me, something that neither Ma nor my grandmother had ever done. That was simply the way of life in the village, how most parents punished their children. But my mother's beatings were cruel and painful. Convinced that my mother would beat me and that Patrick might kill me and my Mommy if I told on him, I kept quiet and lived in terror. I was too frightened to utter a word about my ordeals to anyone, not even to my trusted grandmother.

Living with my mother was a daily nightmare for me. My mother trusted Patrick and would leave him to care for my siblings and me. Patrick found time to molest me even when my mother did not leave us with him for long. There were even times when he fondled me in the presence of my mother and other adults, without their being aware of it. His fondling I felt as demeaning to me, but it was his rapes that had the most devastating impact on my little life. Patrick raped me without mercy. Each time I lay there hoping for death. As the rapes continued, I began to wonder whether I was at fault. I felt dirty and ashamed. I blamed myself for everything that went wrong in my life. I prayed to God as Ma taught me to pray, saying the Our Father, hoping that God would hear me and stop Patrick from raping me. It appeared to me that God never heard my prayers, because help never came. Perhaps God did not listen to little children. Patrick continued to rape me, and I continued to live with the pain and the fear.

My aunt and my mother continued to bear children for the two brothers. One of them continued to rape me, and the other seemed not to like me. At the young age of seven, I had to wash the laundry by hand, sweep the yard every day, and wash the breakfast dishes before I left for school. My siblings' father owned pigs, sheep, goats and cows. Although I did not drink milk myself, every morning, in rain or sunshine, I had to walk to the field, three miles from home, to fetch the milk. My mother or Mr. Phillips would wake me early in the morning to go the field, while my siblings stayed in their beds asleep. Many mornings when it rained, the raindrops would soak my unprotected body from head to toe. I had no umbrella and knew of nobody who had one. Umbrellas were carried mostly by the well-to-do, and the well-to-do in my village were very few.

In spite of the many chores I had to do before I could leave, I went to school every day and made sure I was never late. School was my refuge. I felt safer at school than at home. When my mother had too much to do and was not able to comb my hair, Beatrice, eight years my senior and very quiet and kind, did my hair. She did this in order for me to get to school on time. Beatrice was not related to us, but was a member of the Polites family, friends and neighbors who lived on a separate piece of land just above our yard.

Living next to Beatrice's yard, on yet another piece of land, was Mr. James, an older man, much older than Mr. Phillips. Mr. James was one of the most respected men in the village. One morning as Beatrice was combing my hair, Mr. James came by and stood next to her. I saw him touch her breast and kiss her on the mouth. Then he whispered something in her ear and pointed to me. When Beatrice assured him that I couldn't hear, I turned and stared directly at them. Mr. James then said to Beatrice, "Little donkey has big ears. I will talk to you later," and he left.

Vicky, about twelve years my senior, short and stocky, was another one of our neighbors. She was very kind, but proved dangerous for an innocent child like me. Vicky would carry me to her house or lure me there. While I was in her house, she would take off my panties and push her fingers into my vagina. I felt pain every time she did this to me. These episodes went on for a while until one day I bit her with all my might with my sharp teeth. I bit her so hard that she screamed. She stopped what she was doing and called me a bad little girl, telling me I must get out of her house. From that day forth, she never tried her tricks again.

Vickie was not the only person who tried to do things like that to me. A few of the men who worked with Mr. Phillips ended up living with us. Most of them looked like scum, but they pretended to be trustworthy men. They would sit me on their laps pretending innocence and then fondle me. These incidents mostly took place when my mother and other adults were not around, but there were times when some were bold enough to do it in the presence of adults, and they never got caught. Besides these fondlers, two of Mr. Phillips' relatives were scum, too.

I remember when Bob and Mark came for what was supposed to be a short visit. I overheard Mr. Phillips introduce them to my mother as his cousins. He also said the men were magicians. They did perform their magic at a show at the village school, where they entertained the villagers with their performances. My mother welcomed the strangers into her home, but I was overcome by an eerie feeling when I saw them for the first time.

Instead of a short visit, Bob and Mark stayed for a long time, becoming the newest members of our household. I felt uneasy in their presence, never liking or trusting them, and more or less scared of them, possibly because of the magic I had seen them perform. As with all of the other men who came to live with us, my mother would sometimes leave us alone with them. I, of course, was the oldest of the children, with no father, and not related to them. That was perhaps why the scum continued to attack me, and the two magicians of slime, as I thought of them, were no different.

Bob and Mark began to squeeze my flat and yet small breasts soon after they began to live with us. Then Mark sexually molested me, in a way that I would never forget. I was at home with my siblings, alone in my mother's kitchen, when he entered. He pushed me into a corner and forced his tongue into my mouth. He pulled my panties off and pushed his fingers into my small vagina. Then he pushed me down on the cold, hard, dirt floor. He held my body so tight to the floor that I had difficulty moving. Then he raped me. My vagina felt as if it had been torn out of my body by Mark's over-sized penis. I tried with all of my might to push him off, but I couldn't do it—he was so heavy and strong, and I so fragile and small. I was in too much pain to defend myself and at one time may have lost consciousness. I felt as though I was floating on water. I shivered, and my body felt weaker and weaker by the minute.

The next thing I remember was seeing him standing over me. Although I thought he was finished with me, my horrible ordeal was not yet over. As I lay shivering on the floor, still feeling weak, Mark tied a rope to one of my feet and tied the other end to the ceiling. He hoisted me up towards the ceiling. leaving me hanging upside down. Mark let me know he was demonstrating how he would kill me if I were to tell anyone he had molested me. I thought this incident would once and for all bring an end to my miserable life. My heart beat rapidly and I felt breathless. When he finally let loose the rope and I fell to the ground, I thought I would be better off dying. Weakened and in pain, with blood sticking between my legs, I felt the need to urinate. After several unsuccessful attempts, I was finally able to pull myself up. I walked out of the kitchen and around to one of the sides where I could urinate. It was the most painful urinations I'd ever experienced. When I started to urinate, my vagina burned so badly that I wondered if Mark had rubbed it with some pepper. After many painful attempts, as I had to stop and start again, I urinated eventually. I crawled back on my hands and knees to the kitchen, where I lay crying. I was physically and emotionally battered.

I never thought about telling anyone. I guess Mark's demonstration of how he would kill me scared me enough that I could not think about telling anyone. Instead, my thoughts turned to Ma and Uncle Josey. I thought about the day Ma was buried and the words of the villagers who held my hand and took me away from the graveside, telling me I would meet Ma in heaven one day. "Ma, I want to meet you right now, I really, really do," I sobbed quietly. "Oh! Uncle Josey, why did you go away and leave me? Why aren't you coming to get me?" As I sat curled up in a corner of my mother's kitchen, thinking over my whole life, I continued to sob. I wondered whether these men would have held back if I had had a father. For the first time in my life I wished that I had had a father, thinking that a father might have been able to protect me from the cruelties inflicted on me. Besides, it seemed to me that because my siblings' father was with them and mine was not, their father and my mother treated them better than they did me. I was dejected, feeling like an outcast in my mother's home. I was only nine years old.

My life became worse as I grew older. I was ten years old when I suffered the most brutal whipping of my life, at the hands of Mr. Phillips. Like Patrick, he was a rugged man, about five feet, five inches tall. His hands were rough from the harshness of the fields which he cultivated. Mr. Phillips spoke very little to me except for ordering me to do chores around the house or in the fields. He was the only parent at home with us one day when my siblings ruffled the sheets of the bed and generally left the house in a mess. Mr. Phillips demanded that I clean up the mess his children had made, even though they were capable of doing it themselves. I wondered why my sister Marge had not been asked, and I hesitated. He responded by taking off his belt and using the buckle head to whip the living daylights out of me. I was beaten until my skin bled. Some of the villagers stood outside the gate and looked on as Mr. Phillips, who was not my father, nor even a member of the Ma Letteen family, beat me brutally. Those who looked on were able to see my bruised, bloody skin. As he was beating me, I wondered, "Why, why is he inflicting so many wounds on my small body and brutalizing me this way? Is it because he did not father me?" As the beating continued, he shouted at me to shut up, but I kept crying out louder and louder from the pain I was enduring. I kept wondering whether God had given up on me. "Why me, Lord?" I asked. I begged for someone in the crowd, anyone, to come to my assistance and rescue me. But no one came forward. They all just stood there and looked on.

News about my beating spread like wildfire among the villagers. I was told that my mother had heard about it before she arrived home. On arriving, she asked Mr. Phillips what I could have done that he should beat me so cruelly and brutally? "Lola na (does not) hear when people talk to um (her)," he responded angrily to my mother. My mother asked him no further questions and did absolutely nothing to comfort me. I knew that if my grandmother had been around, she would have acted differently, because she cared about me deeply.

My grandmother arrived at my mother's home shortly after. I heard her calling my name, and I ran to her. She held out her hands, took me into her arms, and hugged and comforted me. My grandmother had heard how brutally Mr. Phillips had beaten me, and she cried when she saw the welts and bruises on my body. But it was the bruises and welts that were covered by my clothing that upset her most. I unbuttoned my dress and lifted it, showing her more welts and bruises. At this sight, my grandmother held her head and let out a scream. She then shouted out, "Amondid people! Oh, Look at Lola's back. Ah yow (everyone) come look." She held her belly and continued to yell and wail hysterically. "Look what Phillips did to Lola. Look how he beat her up. This ah (is) murder and advantage! What could Lola have done to deserve such brutality? I need to take her to the police station," she cried.

The police station was located in a nearby village. My grandmother held my hand and said to me, "Let's go to the police station." But we never *arrived* there, because some of my relatives and other villagers begged and pleaded with her not to go to the police. They acknowledged that Mr. Phillips deserved some form of punishment for beating me so severely, but they asked my grandmother, in consideration of the relationship between him and my mother, to forgive him and not report it to the police. My grandmother listened to them and finally agreed, but she insisted that Mr. Phillips promise he would never beat me again. Mr. Phillips met her demand, promising he would never beat me again, and from that day forth, he never did.

But Mr. Phillips continued to subject me to mental abuse. When my mother was not around, Mr. Phillips would cook for us. He would feed all of my siblings (his own children), but not me. My sister Marge would feel sorry for me and share her food with me without her father's knowledge. There were times when I would disappear into a corner of the house to sit and cry quietly, because I felt ashamed that everyone was eating except me. At those times I wished that I had a daddy of my own around, but the reality was that I had none, and I knew I couldn't change reality.

When I was younger and living with my family in Ma's yard, I never thought of a daddy, because I knew that Ma, Mommy, Uncle Josey, and my family all loved me. I loved them, too, and everyone else around me. But those times were over, and as time passed, more changes came into my life. Instead of the loving child I used to be, I became an angry rebel. I began to hate some of the people around me, like Mr. Phillips. I hated him because he continued to abuse me mentally, and I perceived that he hated me as much I hated him. Patrick, his brother, continued to rape me, and I grew to hate him more than anyone or anything else in the world.

By the time I was ten years old, I was an emotionally disturbed child. Years of sexual abuse by the pedophiles and mental abuse by Mr. Phillips had taken their toll on me. My mother also abused me mentally and physically for every little mistake I made. Although the bruises from my mother's beatings were not as severe as those from Mr. Phillips, she left lots of them. She also cursed at me. If my mother would ask me to pass her a cup and I did not do it promptly, she would say to me in a loud voice, "I say to pass the fucking cup for me." Such foul language like that was directed at me from my mother's mouth more times than I care to remember.

Mr. James also fondled me, when I was ten years old. He used to make and sell cookies at his house. I once went there to buy a cookie, and he fondled my small breast and pushed his tongue into my mouth. At that moment, I had a flashback to what I had seen him do to Beatrice earlier, when she was combing my hair. Because Mr. James was such a respected man in our society, I was afraid to tell anyone what he had done to me, especially my mother, who I feared would beat me. All my experiences of rape and sexual molestation bothered me deeply, but witnessing what Mr. James had done to Beatrice and now did to me made my little mind wonder. It puzzled me that I hadn't heard anyone say that he had molested Beatrice, and I could only conclude that Beatrice was keeping secret what I had seen with my own eyes. If that was kept a secret, how many more secrets might there be about what happened between Mr. James and herself. I wondered whether Mr. James was pushing his hands and penis into Beatrice's vagina, too, as Patrick and the other men had done to me. I was puzzled by their behavior, and I could not tell right from wrong. It was not until I turned eleven that I realized what these men were were doing was wrong.

At eleven when I found myself questioning many things in my life, I began to look at life from a different perspective. I had questions about my father, and I wanted to know who he was. At this time in my life, I had come to realize that Uncle Josey was just that, Uncle Josey, and not my father. I also realized that I should have two grandmothers instead of just one, and I wanted to know my other grandmother. With this new awareness, I was about to take charge of my life in my own little way, thus hoping to prevent a lot of bad things from happening to me. I was also about to find answers to some other things I had heard which I had never yet thought about. It was also at this age that I developed a close relationship with one of Aunt Bertha's daughters, Sandra, who was about ten years my senior. Sandra would answer many of the troubling questions I had repressed for years, not having had the courage to ask, or rather not knowing how to ask at the time.

For years I had felt like some of my slave ancestors, who might have had many living relatives but knew nothing of their existence. They could not have known, because there was no communication between them and their families, who might still be living free in Africa or as slaves on other plantations. And what of those who had been born into slavery, some fatherless, others born as the result of rape of their mothers by their white masters. Were they ever told who their real father was? Since there was no father around for me, I wondered whether I might have been a child born as a result of rape. If so, who was this man, and why was I not told about him by any of my family? Why? Why? Those were the questions I asked myself as a little girl whose mind was now coming of age—a stubborn, inquisitive mind that would lead me to ask questions until I got answers. Unlike some of my slave ancestors, who never seemed to seek answers, I was determined to find answers to my questions.

Who is My Other Half?

Most of my eleven years of life, as I walked the streets of the village, people commented that I resembled my absentee father. Two men I had never seen before stopped me in the village and introduced themselves as my great-uncles, Charles and David. They were my father's uncles, the brothers of my father's mother, of whom I knew nothing. Then there was another lady in the village who always gave me fruit and sometime a dollar bill. One day she told me that she was my great-aunt, my father's mother's sister. Tanty Chloe, as I ended up calling her, would stress more than anyone else how much I resembled my father and his mother. She told me something that I seemed never to forget, "Yo (your) father and grandmother ha (have) to be two wicked people for then na (not) to own (acknowledge) you, and you look so much like the two ah them." I had no idea what she meant, but I would find out in time.

At eleven years old, I also realized that my godmother was Tanty Chloe's oldest daughter, and I got to know all of Tanty Chloe's other children. They acknowledged me as their cousin and always treated me well. Tanty Chloe was married, so she was not generally known by her maiden name, which was McDade. Many villagers said unkind things to me about the McDade family, and my father and grandmother in particular. Once when I asked my mother who my father was, she answered that I had no father. I also remember asking my grandmother, and she said to me, "That scamp, the vagabond somewhere in England."

When villagers would say in my mother's presence that I looked and acted like my father's mother, I perceived that she became annoyed. I was bothered by remarks that the McDade family was crazy, most of all when said specifically about my father. Time and again, other children would refer to me as the "Shaver Man Picme (child)," and even my own brothers and sisters and some of our relatives would call me by that name. I had no idea what they meant. Later, when I did learn their meaning, I did not believe that they knew what they were talking about.

The continuing sexual assaults were doing something evil to my mind. My mother continued to beat me severely more often than I wanted to admit to myself, and I continued provoking her by doing things that got me into trouble. I had come to the conclusion that since no one else was looking after me, I would have to protect myself. Once, a trusted family friend tried to molest me. Out of nowhere, I told him to go hold a goat and leave me alone. I learned that in our native dialect "holding a goat," meant raping a goat. I also learned that those were insulting words for anyone to say to another—especially to adult males. I also learned that adults would punish children with serious whippings if they heard them utter those words to grown men. I was hoping that my mother or another grownup would hear me saying those words and would question me, giving me the opportunity to expose the molester. I was intelligent enough to realize that these so-called pillars of our society would not want their crimes exposed. However, I did not realize that they would do anything to protect themselves, including telling lies. Our society would believed their lies, themselves victimizing the same children who had been victimized by these wicked men with evil souls.

I was such a child, victimized by molesters, by society, and by my mother. As the sexual abuse continued, I tried to defend myself. I would curse them and call them bad names. Some of the men would signal me to shut up by putting a hand over their mouth, and would refrain from molesting me, fearing I would expose them. Others would complain to my mother about the bad names I called them, and their complaints would be more effective if some other adult had overheard me cursing at them and would be a witness against me. Because our society trusted adults more than children, my mother would believe everything they said to her without even questioning me. Afterward, my mother would beat me with all her might, using just about anything available—a belt, a stick, a pot, a pan, or a plate. Lashes flew everywhere and would land wherever they caught me, on any part of my body. I remember how my mother once beat me so badly that I jumped over an embankment, hoping to die. But I lived, probably because I had something to live for, like going to school. In spite of all the frightful things that were happening to me, in school I felt safe and secure, even though the majority of my teachers, especially the women, were arrogant and unsympathetic. I continued to go to school even when it was raining. School was where I excelled. I had to admit, however, that the quality of the instruction was not high. Many of the teacher's aides, whom we referred to as teachers, seemed to me not qualified to be teacher's aides, let alone teachers.

There were two levels of teacher's aides. Those at the lower level, most of them with only a seventh-grade education themselves, taught the lower grades. They continued to attend classes to further their education and were tested at the end of each year. If they passed the test, they continued until they reached the level of a high school education. Those who failed the test were dismissed from the job. The other level consisted of teacher's aides who had completed a high school education. They taught the middle grades and continued to attend classes, training to become the certified teachers who taught the highest grades in our school system.

I remember that one of the teacher's aides, Ms. Campbell, once gave us an assignment to do. So as to save paper in my book, I did the assignment neatly on a half of a page left over from another assignment. Although my work was correct, Ms. Campbell marked it up without giving me a grade. She flung the book into my face, saying, "Girl, who do you think you are, giving work on half a page? You are out of your place to hand in such work to me." Yet Ms. Campbell knew that we were all poor people trying our best to get the most out of everything we had. I had done work for her on a half page before that, and she had accepted and graded it. I had no idea why she refused my work now. I assumed she was having a bad day. Perhaps she had had a fight with her boyfriend and was taking out her frustration on me.

I remember another incident with another teacher's aide, Mrs. Dick, who was pregnant at the time. My mother had given birth to one of my siblings not long before, I took some of my baby brother's powder to school, wrapped up in one of my book leaves. As children, we did things like that sometimes. While Mrs. Dick was teaching the class, I placed my chin in the powder and began to rub it on my face. When Mrs. Dick saw what I was doing, she came to where I was seated and beat me as a master might beat a mule! Then she commanded me to go to the bathroom and wash the powder off my face, and I did so. On my way back, Mr. Royal, the principal of the school, saw the bruises on my skin from the belt with which Mrs. Dick had beaten me. He called me over and asked me, "Which of the mules inside that school beat you like this?" I answered, "Mrs. Dick." A little later someone came to class to summon Mrs. Dick to the principal's office. I never knew what he said to her, but she returned to the classroom wiping tears from her eyes. Some of the teachers and teacher's aides beat us fiercely, and there was nothing we could do to prevent this cruel treatment. Some of us complained to our parents and ended up getting another beating from them for complaining. Parents seemed to believe that if a teacher or a teacher's aide beat a child, the child must have done something wrong. But it was not always true.

I had my share of beatings, from teachers, teacher's aides, and of course my mother. But I dealt out my share of beatings, too. Although I excelled academically, I could not claim the same for my social behavior. For some reason, I could not get along well with most of my schoolmates, no matter how hard I tried. The children mimicked me and called me "Shaver Man Picme" and sometimes lied about me. I thought the children were out to harm me, and so I fought with many of them. Once I felt threatened by any schoolmates, I would beat them up. I remember once when we were waiting in line to receive biscuits from the teacher. As part of a charitable program for third world countries like St. Vincent, the Canadian government provided the school children with free biscuits and milk. I was standing in front of Sundra, one of my schoolmates, when some pushing began among us, and Sundra's pen got broken. Ponda, who was standing behind Sundra, insisted that it was I who had broken Sundra's pen. At lunchtime Sundra complained to my mother, and Ponda acted as her witness. My mother, without asking me any questions, took away my pen and gave it to Sundra. I was so furious that I resolved to take revenge on Ponda.

After school was dismissed and we were walking home, I started a fight with Ponda. I beat the living daylights out of her. I tore her dress apart, sending her home in tatters. Even though I knew I would get a beating from my mother, I did not care. I would accept that beating as long as what I did to Ponda taught her not to lie about me. Not surprisingly, Ponda and her mother complained to my mother, and I received my beating. Ponda had suffered a beating from my bare hands, but there were others who received strokes from more than bare hands.

Alinda and Jose were girls my age, or close to it, but their brother Chad was much older and taller than I was. For some reason, Alinda, Jose and I were always fighting. We fought at least once a week. Although they would team up against me, I won every fight. Then one day their brother joined in the fight on their side. The three of them overwhelmed me. As Chad was beating me badly, the crowd around us cheered. I don't know which side they were cheering for, but what I did during that fight stunned the entire crowd, including the three fighting with me. I got to my feet and picked up a sizable piece of rock, stared at Chad, and flung it directly at his forehead.

He held his forehead and screamed, and I saw blood gushing over his face. I also heard the screams of the crowd as they ran in all directions. I ran, too, towards home. I jumped over an embankment, crossed the village river, and ran through fields and family yards until I was safely home. Right away I told my mother about the incident, wanting her to hear my version before the others arrived. When they and their parents came to complain, my mother listened quietly. Then she asked whether all three of them were fighting against me by myself. No one answered. For once in my life, my mother did not punish me for a complaint against me. Instead, she urged me to do it again if I had to fight more than one at a time. I took that encouragement as a sign of the approval which I so much wanted from my mother.

We continued to have our weekly fights. Why they fought me or I fought them more frequently than anyone else, I don't know. Because of our fighting, my mother and their parents became enemies, or at least that was what I believed at the time. There were always two or three of them against me. Soon, however, the situation changed. My maternal great-uncle heard about all of the fighting. He couldn't miss hearing of it, because our fights became the talk of the village. One day I went to visit my great-grandmother, my mother's father's mother. She was the caretaker of my two cousins, Iona and Shantell, who were attending the same school as I was. Their parents had migrated down South to Trinidad like Uncle Josey, in search of jobs to support the children and families they had left behind. During my visit, my great-uncle Cornell asked about the many fights I was involved in at school, especially with Alinda, Jose and Chad. He was concerned about me, and most of all that I was fighting them all by myself. He called over my two cousins, Iona and Shantell, and explained to us that we were family, good family, and that good family support one another. Uncle Cornell told my cousins that they were not to stand around watching other people fight me, especially Alinda, Jose and Chad, without joining in. He told the three of us, that if any one of us would be in a fight with more than one person, the other two of us must join in. We knew that Uncle Cornell was serious about this and took his words very seriously. That very week I got into a fight with Alinda, and the three of them were fighting me, when Iona and Shantell entered the fight. I was strong, and so was Iona

Shantell was skinny, the youngest and tallest of the three of us, but, God, her skin was hard as a rock! When she hit you, could leave marks on your skin with her bare hands. Together, we beat those three children without mercy. We also beat any others who would dare pick a fight with any one of us. Soon we were the ones to fear at school, especially me.

"Lord, I want to stop fighting other children, but I can't stop and I don't know why I can't stop," I prayed to God over and over again, night after night, after I said the Our Father prayer. "Lord, there are other things that I want to stop. I want to stop Patrick from raping me. I want my mother to love me as much as Ma, Uncle Josey, and Mommy did. I want my mother to stop cursing at me and beating me the way she does. But Lord, most of all, I want to know if I really have a daddy, and if I do, Lord, I want to know who he is and where he is. Please, lord, let somebody tell me about my daddy."

When I persisted in inquiring about my father, my mother continued to tell me that I had no father, and my dear grandmother also continued to tell me that I was better off not knowing "the vagabond." I did not know what the word vagabond meant, but it did not sound like a word used to describe a good person. The children at school continued to mimic me and call me "Shaver Man Picme." I still wondered what they meant by that, and their mimicking troubled me deeply. I wanted an answer to the mystery of my father, and I wanted to know more about the McDade family. My cousin Sandra was the only person I trusted enough to ask these questions. Because of her jovial humor, I loved Sandra more than any of my other cousins. I felt connected to her, and it was that connection that made me trust her more than the others. She was like a big sister, and I thought of her as my last hope to get answers to my questions.

I went to Sandra one day and asked her to tell me everything she knew about my father and his family, the McDade family, who lived in the next village, the ones people called crazy. I also wanted to know why people called me "Shaver Man Picme." What my cousin told me about my father and his family sent shock waves throughout my body.

Sandra told me that some of her answers to my questions would be the facts, while others would be rumors or speculations. She assured me that I indeed had a daddy like everyone else. "Don't you see you look different from your buddy and sissy (brothers and sisters)? You are lighter in complexion than they are because your father is a light complexion man." Sandra explained that my father did not own (acknowledge) me as his child and was not living in St. Vincent at the time of my birth.

My mother is much darker than my father and his mother. Because of my mother's dark complexion, my grandmother refused to accept that her light complexioned son would father a child by her, and she made it known to everyone that her son was not the father of the child my mother was carrying in her womb. My grandmother sent my father to England before I was born, preventing him from acknowledging my birth. What my grandmother did was not the norm in our society. There were many grandparents who acknowledged their sons' children, even when their sons did not, regardless of the complexion of the mother.

Sandra told me that there was a time when odd things were happening to women in some of the villages while they were asleep at night. Someone used to break into their houses and shave the hair off their vaginas, the women not realizing it until they woke up. She said there were rumors that my father was the main culprit, although no one ever caught him, and the crime continued long after he left the island. She explained to me that that was why people referred to me as "Shaver Man Picme."

For the first time in my life, I finally knew something about my father. The more I got to know, the more I wanted to know, like my father's name and what he looked like. Sandra said that my father and I looked exactly alike except that he was lighter in complexion. "His named is Gladstone McDade," she said to me. She shared my opinion that my grandmother was wicked not to have acknowledged me even after I was born and grew to look so much like my father.

Sandra continued to share with me her knowledge about my father and his family. There were rumors to the effect that my grandmother, Ms. Willis, had done many wicked things, especially to her husband. She lived abroad for awhile and returned to St. Vincent with enough money to rank her among the well-to-do in our society. She was married to Mr. Willis, the owner of many acres of land next to the new school in my village. He also claimed to be a preacher, walking about with a Bible in his hand. Rumor also had it that Mr. Willis and my grandmother had separated because she would cook, feed her household, and wash her pots as though she had never prepared a meal, leaving no food for her husband. Many believed that it was Mr. Willis' dark complexion that moved my grandmother to treat him that way and in other ways to act superior to him. Sandra claimed that my grandmother spoke to very few people and always walked with her head held up high. "She acted proud all the time," my cousin said. People referred to those who acted proud as "fresh." They called my grandmother a "fresh woman."

As to my father's family's being crazy, I knew that my great-uncle Charles, whom I had met in the village, was crazy, and he still is. He had left his children and wife in St. Vincent and spent some time overseas. Uncle Charles had not neglected his financial obligation toward his wife and children while he was away, but his wife had an affair with one of their neighbors and got pregnant by him. When Charles returned and found his wife pregnant, his life turned upside down and all hell broke loose. Although the child died at birth, Uncle Charles never fully recovered from the shock. He continued to act crazy, talking to himself and sometimes staring at people without uttering a word. As a result, everybody called him "Crazy Man." "They used to call your father crazy, too," my cousin said.

Except for what I learned about Tanty Chloe and her family, I have never heard anything good about my father and his family, absolutely nothing. Realizing that my father and his mother had never acknowledged me, I began to appreciate and love my Mommy, my grandmother, who had cared for me as long as I could remember, and even before that. I wished that I could have gone to her and told her what I had heard about my father and his family and thanked her for standing with me, beside me and around me. But I couldn't, and I don't know why. I also wished I could have told Uncle Josey how much he meant to me, but he was down South, and, besides, even if he had been around I would not have been able to tell him either. Instead, I said a little prayer to my God, asking him to bless Uncle Josey so he could retain his employment, so his breadbasket would never be empty. I used to hear Mommy pray for Uncle Josey like that, especially when he sent money for us. I guess it was a good prayer. Then I thought about Ma, my loving great-grandmother, who told me she would die, and who did die, but said she would always be with me, even after her death. Although I had never seen her since she died, I felt she was with me, because I always believed in her. "Well, Ma, if you are with me, I thank you for all that you have done for me, like making me well again when I was sick and teaching me how to brush my teeth and pray. But Ma, you said that you would never leave me and you would always be with me, Ma, so where are you? I wish you were with me, because I need you now more than ever." As I was all alone speaking to her, I felt cold even though the weather was hot, and I began to cry. I was overwhelmed with sadness, deep sadness. I felt terribly distressed. Understanding and coming to terms with the fact that my father and his mother had disowned me even before I was born made me wonder. Why did Patrick rape me and continue his rapes on me? Why did other men molest me and continue their attempts to molest me? Why was Mr. Phillips treating me as though I was lower than his dogs? After all, he gladly fed the dogs, while he refused to feed me. Wasn't my life worth more than a dog's life? Why was my mother treating me so unkindly? Was I a hindrance to her life? Did she ever want me as her child? If she did, why did I not live with her from the beginning, and why did she not tell me earlier that she was my mother? I continued to wonder whether these things were happening because my father rejected me. I had no answer, so I bore the pain and continued to live with the rage.

I also continued to clean up after my siblings. By the time I was eleven years old, my mother had given birth to five children, not including me. Whenever she gave birth to a new child, I had to baby-sit, wash diapers, and get up in the morning to go to the field and fetch the milk. I was also of the age to carry a bunch of bananas on my head, assisting with the bananas on shipment day before I went to school, and sometimes I stayed home from school to do so. My worst days were when I was out of school for long holiday periods, when my mother would compel me to go to the fields and assist with the cultivation of the crops. Fetching milk in the mornings, taking care of my siblings, and carrying bananas on my head on shipment day were oppressive and hard work for a child, but cultivation of the crops was worse. It was brutal and demeaning work for adults, let alone children. While I worked in the fields, the heat of the hot sun burned my body, my nails became soiled, and I looked more like an old tractor than a child. I hurt, but I wept within for Mommy (grandmother) when I witnessed how hard she worked, with her ulcerated foot, among the bushes and sticks.

After my conversation with my cousin Sandra, I resigned myself to the fact that I was better off without my other family. But I still wondered whether I would have been better off if my father had acknowledged me and stayed with my mother. I also wondered if my absent father had other children. If he did, I would at least want to know them. But that would never be. The only brothers and sisters I would ever know were those I lived with in the hostile household where they treated me at times worse than their dogs.

The desire to know my father's children, if he indeed had other children, rarely left my mind for long. Then one day, when I was twelve years old, I was sitting on my mother's veranda with my siblings when a light-complexioned, very attractive, well-dressed woman, who appeared to be an overseas visitor, came into the yard with three small children. She was articulate, speaking with an accent I had not heard before. She asked for Lola. With some apprehension, I told her I was Lola, since one of my siblings had already pointed me out to her. She stretched out her hand and I responded by giving her mine. As we shook hands, she introduced herself to me as Elma. She also introduced the three children to me as my brothers and my sister—Stanley, seven, Jerald, five, and Sharmaine, a baby girl less than a year old. Dumfounded, I stared at the children. I could not help seeing how much alike the four of us looked. The resemblance was most noticeable in Stanley, the older of the two boys. He and I looked so much alike that I felt a special affinity for him immediately. As Elma and my mother walked a little distance from us and chatted in privacy, I played with my newfound brothers and sister, staring at them and wondering where our father was. When Elma announced she was leaving. I hugged my two brothers and kissed Sharmaine. Elma left with the children, but she promised to return with them for future visits. After Elma left, my mother remarked that my vagabond father had sent for Elma to come to him in England, got her pregnant three times, and then sent her back home without marrying her. "That vagabond seems like he na go ever change," my mother commented. I wanted to ask her some questions about Elma, the children, and my father, but I dared not. My mother was not a woman to hold conversation with me about anything, especially my absent father, for whom she expressed such hatred and resentment.

When the opportunity arrived the following day, I went to Sandra to ask more questions. I trusted Sandra and believed that she and she alone would tell me the truth about Elma and my father, if she knew. I told Sandra about Elma's visit the day before, giving her the complete details. She was a good listener—to me, anyway. After listening for several minutes, she explained that what she was about to tell me was based on rumors she had heard. "How true the story, me na know, but me tink they ah some truth to it," Sandra said. I sat and listened attentively to Sandra. By now she was a special figure in my life, my only source of information about my absent father and his family.

According to Sandra, the rumor was that, after my father migrated to England, he sent for Elma, his girlfriend at the time, who was living in the same village as the McDade family. St. Vincent was still an English colony then, and many of its citizens left the island and migrated to England in search of work and better lives. It was my understanding that in those days women and men alike sent for partners to marry. I guess that when my father sent for Elma, she, along with her family and the society as a whole, expected him to marry her. It was what normally happened with other people in Elma's position.

But Elma's case was not the norm, according to the rumors. When she went to England to join him with hopes of becoming his wife, Elma was already pregnant by someone other than my father. People gossiped that my father deserved what Elma had done to him. They said my father knew he had fathered me, but disowned me just the same, and therefore it was only just for him to take care of "the pig in the bag" that Elma carried with her to give him. Sandra reiterated, "That was the talk at the time, but the people knew very little of that vagabond father of yours. That vagabond wasn't about to take care of nobody picme. He wasn't going to take care of a picme way nah belong to him. Me har when Elma get day, me mean England, and you poupar (father) find out she breed, he gee Elma a hard time. They say he treated her like a dog and when the picme born, them give um up for adoption or put um in ah home or something like that. That ah way me har."

In my native dialect, I asked, "How come she ha them three picme with him?" Sandra responded, "Well, people say that your poupar been really love Elma. Must ah (maybe) because ah she light skin gal. He stayed with her and breed her three times and me guess eh laws in England must be different than har because me har you can't mek lots of picme and nah get marry, yo nah see how many bastard picme ah run around har? England must be different because they say after she ha the third picme the government say, or me nah no if they say the church, say that he ha fo marry her. Yo poupar ah wa real vagabond—instead of marrying Elma, he sent her back home with she three bastard picme without marrying her."

Lord, I believed everything Sandra told me about my father. I wished it were not true, but I found out that it was, because I lived to hear other people repeat the same stories about my father. I knew the sad life I was living, and I wondered about Elma and her life, and especially the lives of my paternal half-brothers and sister. Were they about to live a life like mine? Would they endure the mocking and mimicking of other children calling them "Shaver Man Picme," as they did me? Lord, what would their lives be like? Would they be referred to as bastard picme, the name people called children born out of wedlock, but more frequently if there was also no father around? Whatever the word "vagabond" means, my father must have been a real vagabond.

Although I disapproved of the way my father had treated Elma, I also questioned Elma's morals as well. I wanted to know who was the father of the baby not my father's. I believe by now Sandra thought I was a little pest, even though she never made me feel that way. Just the same, I asked her about Elma and the child not fathered by my father. "Gal, me nah know fo sure, but me har people say eh belonged to some man who used to cut the road. They say she been day with the man. Day say yo know gal when yo poupar find out Elma breed and eh picme nah belong to him, me har em nearly go crazy. Me har things ben bad fo him, especially when he go around the other boys from home. Me har them boys used to give um some serious jokes ah no. That must been hard fo the vagabond to tek," Sandra laughed and looked at me. I laughed, too. That was my last face-to-face inquiry with Sandra about my father. At this point, I felt I had heard enough about my scum of a father.

After my many conversations with Sandra, I was shocked when one day my mother began to talk to me about Elma, my father, and their children. She stressed that my father was such a vagabond that it was not surprising to hear he had not sent any financial support to Elma for the children since their return. Because she and Sandra both spoke so negatively about my father, I became even less interested in knowing him. However, I was interested in some of the information which my mother told me about my father beyond what I had heard from Sandra.

My mother said that after I was born, my father wrote to Tanty Chloe's daughter, my godmother, Naomi, and asked her to provide him with a copy of my birth certificate. My father wanted a copy of my birth certificate to claim me as a dependent on his taxes, even though he had never acknowledged my birth. He wanted me as a financial benefit, even though he had never supported me, financially or otherwise. What a scum! My mother did not have to tell me that he did not get my birth certificate—I knew it just by her manner. Finally my mother kept silent for a moment, then said, "Poor Elma," and ended with that comment, as abruptly as she had started.

My sympathy focused on Elma and the children she had borne my father. Before, I was one bastard child abandoned by my "Shaver Man" father. Now I was no longer alone, but had three others along with me. The four of us shared a common bond—we were bastard children of the same father who had abandoned us, me before my birth and the others after their birth. Newly discovered though they were, I wanted to be close to them.

It was not long after they arrived in St. Vincent that, sadly, my baby half-sister died. I never understood what caused her death. When Stanley and Jerald enrolled in the village school, I spent much time with them, taking great interest in their welfare. After all, they were my family and I loved them as brothers, especially Stanley.

After I had met Elma and my siblings and heard more reports about my father's evil character, I was determined not to accept him as my father, if I ever were to see him. After all, he had done nothing for me. Even worse, it seemed to me that he had done more harm to his children than good. I resigned myself to having no father, just as my mother used to tell me. Then, one day—six months or a year after I had met Elma's children—I was returning to school after lunch, walking by one of the village shops, when I heard someone call my name. I looked around and saw a man standing in the doorway of a village shop pointing at me. He was light complexioned and wearing a suit. I thought he resembled me somewhat, or I resembled him. I thought he must have been from one of the McDade families from the other village. Then he called out to me, "Lola, Lola, come and kiss Daddy." Astonished and apprehensive, I stared at the man without moving. He approached me and tried to hold my hand, but I pulled it away from him. I stood glaring at him, ready to curse the hell out of him. A bystander said, "Lola, that's your father." I answered sharply, "Whose father? I have no father."

The man continued to advance towards me and tried to hug me. As he smiled, I could see that two of his front teeth were covered with gold. He spoke very properly, and I now recognized that his accent was similar to Elma's. He said to me, "I am your daddy." Speechless, I just looked at him. Other children gathered, but I left the man standing there and headed off to school. School and my punctuality were more important to me than the man claiming to be my father.

As I raced back to school, I thought about the man calling himself my father. If he was my father, what's the big deal? Where was he all these years? Why was he not around to defend and protect me from the rapists and pedophiles? Why had he not supported me financially? Did he not know I needed his support? Did he not know I walked shoeless back and forth to school, burnt over and over from the hot tar of the pitch road? What does he want with me now? Is it my birth certificate? Where was he when I needed him the most?

On my way home from school that day I again met him at the village shop. He gave me some money to take home to my mother and told me to tell her that he wanted to speak with her. I took the money to my grandmother and told her about my encounter with the man who called himself my father. My grandmother took the money from me, saying that I had grown up and did not need that vagabond's money any more. She went to the village shop and was about to throw that money in my father's face, when one of the villagers who was in the shop at the time, held her back. I witnessed this and said, "That's my grandmother, acting furious as hellfire."

I wondered whether this man would want me to live with him and ask my grandmother's permission to do so, as my mother had done. If so, would my grandmother send me to live with him? "Don't be carried away by your fears, Lola," I told myself. "Your grandmother would never send you to live with the man she called a vagabond. She had better not tell me I would be better off living with him. If she tried to force me, I would run away and go back home. On the other hand, he seemed to have lots of money, and I might be better off living with him. At least I wouldn't have to do any fieldwork, because he had no fields, and I wouldn't have to ruin my hands washing diapers." These were my thoughts after I had come to terms with the fact that the vagabond really was my father. But thoughts are not reality, and reality was that my father had shown no interest in my existence before and was not likely to change.

Living in the Lion's Den

I was being unrealistic to think that my father's presence would bring any positive change in the way I lived. In fact nothing changed in my life—absolutely nothing. I continued doing chores at home and my mother continued to get pregnant, bearing children every other year. After a while, her children seemed to be my own, being treated as my responsibility instead of my mother's. I continued to wash my stepfather's clothing and to do what I could for him, hoping that he might treat me better. But he continued the same, treating me like an unwanted dog. His brother, Patrick, was my main rapist. God, oh God, he continued to rape me, even though there was now a man in St. Vincent calling himself my father. Patrick seemed not to fear him. He continued threatening to kill my Mommy and me if I told on him, and he led me to believe that no one would believe me, anyway. So I continued to keep the secret of my rapes to myself. I was in pain every time Patrick raped me, and I had no idea what to do to stop him. Anger and rage were building within me.

Living this way was like living in a den of lions, being attacked more often than I imagined even lions would do. I had to take up different strategies, as my survival depended on my choosing a good course of action. God knows that, in spite of my pitiful life, I desperately wanted to live. Yes, Lord, I was ready to do anything within my power to fight for my life. Most of the time I could sense when an attack was imminent, especially by Patrick. I did not have to see him to know when Patrick was close by, especially when I was home alone. I would smell him. He smelled like a ram goat. There were times when I would be overwhelmed by the smell. Then who would show up but Patrick, and sure enough, he would attack and rape me—in my mother's kitchen, the bedrooms or the living room of her house, even in the outside latrine. Patrick was an evil man with a wicked soul, and he continued to prey on me. But I was growing up, and changes were occurring that would allow me to relate differently to things around me. "Watch out, Patrick," I thought, "for I am becoming a different person. The other pedophiles had better watch out, too."

I was twelve years old. The anger within me had taken its toll, and I began to act more compulsively. Some of the things I did were terribly wrong. Although I knew that they were wrong and my mother beat me for doing them, I did them anyway. Lord, I tried to do what was right, but my fights with schoolmates were becoming more frequent now. And I was not only fighting in school. I would fight with children at the river when I would go there to wash, or at the village spring and pipe where I went to fetch water, or even on the village road. My mother beat me for fighting, and she would also beat me when the men who tried to molest me complained to her. Some of the beatings were bloody.

I could not bring myself to tell my mother about the molestations. I knew she would not believe me, anyway. Instead I continued to curse the rapists and call them bad names. My cursing them, and their fear that others would ask why I was cursing them, prevented some of them from raping me. So I continued. As a result, I had to endure the agony of my mother's beatings and her threats to kill me if I did not stop cursing these men. But I preferred a beating to being raped.

My mother did almost kill me one time, probably without realizing it. It happened one day while she was beating me and swearing to kill me, at the same time choking me. It was not until I stopped breathing temporarily that she pulled her hands away from my throat. Having survived that episode, I was more determined than ever to stop the pedophiles from raping me, especially Patrick. I could never have imagined what would happen next. Everyone living in my house went into the fields, working for Mr. Phillips. I learned that he was not the owner, as I had thought, but a sharecropper and overseer of the fields, which were owned by a family of white-looking people who lived in another village. The villagers called this type of white-looking people "Portogue," which means Portuguese. I don't know whether they were descendants of white slave masters, but there were a few of them on the island. It seems that the white-looking people owned most of the land in St. Vincent, even though they were less than two percent of the population. They owned most of the farmlands and fields, acres and acres of land, stretching from the shoreline to the mountaintops. They received most of the benefit from the land without themselves ever working on it.

Mr. Phillips and the others did harsh and brutal labor on the land. With all their labor they were not able to own any big houses or vehicles. Mr. Phillips and my mother owned a board house, and the other workers lived in houses that were worse. Mr. Phillips and my mother's house was as nothing compared to the big houses which the Portogue owned—the Portogue whose lands he was cultivating and forcing me to help cultivate, even though I was still a child. I never saw the adult Portogue assisting with the cultivation, let alone their children.

One day I was home alone, intending to join the others in the fields after I completed my chores. I smelled Patrick before I saw him enter the house. Realizing that he was about to rape me, I made up my mind that very moment to bring an end to his abuse. I was tired of the rapes and was not about to take it anymore, and I knew that this was the day to bring it to an end. I determined that one of us must die, and I would not be the one if I could help it. Curiously, I did not plan it in advance, but it came to me spontaneously as soon as I set my eyes on Patrick. I decided I had to kill him before he killed my Mommy or me. He had threatened me for years, but I was not about to give him the advance warning of a threat. "No threats, just death. Death for Patrick," I said to myself. I was angry enough with that son of a bitch to kill him without remorse. I took a sharp knife from a pile of dirty dishes I was about to wash. I hid the knife without Patrick seeing me. As he attempted to rape me on that bright, sunny, hot June day, I lunged at him with my knife. Believe me, the knife was sharp, because Mr.

Phillips had used that very knife to cut off the neck of a fowl for our dinner. I told Patrick I would kill him if he moved any closer to me. "You will not rape me today, you stinking, ram goat, smelly bastard. You will not rape me today or ever again, because I am going to kill you," I said as I glared at him. There were tears in my eyes, but I was certain about what I intended to do. He seemed to understand that I was serious about it. I told him I was no longer scared of him, and I was about to go to the fields and tell my mother. "No one would believe you," he replied. I repeated myself and then took off, walking hurriedly for the field where my mother, Mr. Phillips, and the other workers were, three miles away.

As I took off, Patrick started heading there at the same time. I had to walk through some coconut groves, through other people's fields, on muddy roads, up and down hills, and over an embankment. I would run, get tired and walk, then run again, and who should be following me and even getting ahead of me, but Patrick. Then he spotted a donkey and jumped on its back, riding away. A donkey has four feet and gallops; I had only two and could not gallop. There was nothing I could do to get to the field before Patrick, so it was no surprise that he arrived an hour ahead of me.

To add insult to injury, as soon as my mother saw me she began to curse me and complain that I was lazy and should have been at the field earlier. I wondered what she would have said if I had washed the dishes first and arrived even later. She probably would have beaten the hell out of me, as she so often did. My mother's hostile attitude put me off, so I could not tell her about Patrick's attempted rape, let alone the rapes he had actually committed against me. I knew she would not believe me, because Patrick would have denied it and called me a liar, having had the hour before my arrival to persuade my mother. Convinced that my mother would not believe me, I kept my silence that day.

I must have done something right that day, for Patrick never again attempted to rape me. I often wondered whether, if I hadn't stopped him, I would have gotten pregnant by him when I began menstruating. There were times after that when I would be home alone and Patrick would show up out of nowhere, but he never again attempted to rape me. I think he was aware that I would fight back, and by then I was determined to kill him if he ever attempted to rape me again. I knew I wouldn't have cared what would happen to me after I killed him. I just wanted him dead, as dead as a slaughtered chicken, its neck chopped off with a knife sharp as a razor, and left hanging from his body by a sliver of skin tiny as a piece of thread. He had destroyed my life, and I felt that death was a just punishment he rightfully deserved, nothing less, and a cruel and painful death besides. I thought that if I killed him, my mother might realize that I needed her help and be more attentive to my welfare.

But I never had the opportunity to kill Patrick. Although he stopped raping me, he had done permanent damage to my soul, body, and mind. I was confused and troubled, consumed with so much rage that I fought even more often with other children in school. I would provoke other children just to get into a fight with them, so I could beat them up. There were also other pedophiles trying to molest me, who would squeeze and pinch my breasts, doing it in the presence of other adults without detection. These very adults would notice only when I cursed the pedophiles, calling them insulting names.

With my continuous cursing and name calling of these so-called respectable men who preyed on children like me, villagers said that my actions were those of a woman, not a child. I was in fact still a child, but the men had made a woman out of me, by doing things to me that men were only supposed to do to grown women. My cursing and calling them names was the only thing I could do to stop them. "Why don't the villagers understand," I thought, "and Lord, most of all, why doesn't my mother understand?" I questioned myself this way time and time again. Then I came to realize that I was not the only child in the village who had been raped and who suffered the aftermath.

It was Casey's situation that opened a new Pandora's box for me, forcing me to begin rethinking the village and the people living in it. Casey had been raped repeatedly by her stepfather and had reported the rapes to her mother. Her mother did not question her husband about Casey's allegation, nor did she try to help her daughter in any way. Why? Because Casey's mother trusted her husband, or was afraid of him, and she refused to believe he would commit such a crime against her daughter. But he had done it, and he continued to do it time and time again. It was not until Casey became pregnant at thirteen that her mother seemed to believe her. I say "seemed to believe" because her actions belied her beliefs.

One would have thought that the villagers, and particularly Casey's mother, would rally behind Casey and do everything within their power to punish the man for the crimes he had committed against this innocent child. The reality was that most of the villagers—it appeared to me that it was all of them—did not rally behind Casey or give her their support, not even her mother. Instead, they spread rumors that Casey had falsely accused her stepfather to protect a younger man in the village, who was the actual father of her unborn child. Even Casey's mother turned against her, supporting her stepfather when he demanded that Casey leave their house. So they put poor Casey out of the house, and for a while she had nowhere to live. She was rescued by one of her mother's relatives, who seemed to be the only one who believed Casey.

As Casey carried the baby in her womb, many villagers continued to ridicule her. They called her "the little whore" and similar names. I can only imagine the pain that Casey felt. Some of them even said that if her stepfather had raped her, she must have done something to entice him. Again, they were laying the blame squarely on Casey. Well, when the baby was born and its close resemblance to Casey's stepfather could not be hidden, all hell broke loose. The villagers began to gossip about the whole calamity, and poor Casey became the talk of the village. She became sullen and withdrawn, sitting alone most of the time. I have no idea what became of Casey after that. It was said that she suffered a nervous breakdown from the stress. I only know that she left the village to live elsewhere, or perhaps to be locked up in a mental institution.

What happened to Casey was not an isolated case. In fact, it seems that raping children was the accepted norm in my society. Lord, I began to realize that these men who appeared to be pillars of the society were raping more children than I could imagine. I heard rumors about other children who had complained of their rapes, and who, instead of being embraced by the society and helped to punish the pedophiles, were ridiculed instead. Children like me, victims of rape, were victimized not only by the pedophiles, but by the society as well.

Rape victims brave enough to tell about their rapes were called liars. Like me, many children kept their rapes secret rather than subject themselves to such public humiliation. A few children broke their silence and informed their parents, but most parents did nothing to punish the perpetrators. Most kept their children's rapes secret, fearing to expose their children to the scorn and ridicule of the villagers. Others just did not know what to do, having been themselves children in similar situations and remembering that their parents had taken no action. Lord, even children suffering from incest kept their secrets, and family members aware of the situation pretended not to know, acting as though everything were normal.

But the lives and minds of children like me, victims of rape and incest, were not normal, especially those of us who kept it a secret. Lord, I knew, because I experienced it, and, Lord, there were other wrongs taking place in the village besides the crimes of rape and incest. I looked around me, Lord, and I could not help noticing other evil things happening among the inhabitants of the village.

I grew to realize that while a few good and kindhearted people inhabited the village, the majority were evil and envious. Their souls were full of hatred, envy, rage, anger, jealousy, cruelty, and wickedness. They corrupted the minds of those they came into contact with. They exploited one another.

Mostly men exploited women. Many married men had affairs with other women, some living in the same village as their wives, some in other villages. Many of them had affairs with women as young as their own daughters. I had something in common with the children born as a result of these affairs. We were all out-of-wedlock children, born to fathers who might acknowledge our birth, or might choose not to. We were all referred to as bastard children. Many young mothers had affairs with men just for the money to sustain the lives of their other bastard children and themselves. The patterns of behavior I observed among the people seemed to me despicable.

It was mostly the women who were the victims. A man might have a child or several children with one woman, then leave her for another without providing support, financial or otherwise. Unfortunately for these women, this patterns was repeated with their many affairs with many men. The result was that the women were sole providers for their many bastard children, most of them fathered by different men.

In some cases the men took their bastard children into their own homes to live. Their wives, most of them subservient to their husbands and with no authority in their homes, took care of these children as their own. Some wives even seemed to take it as an honor to be able to raise these children as their own. There were others, like my mother, who lived together with the same man for years and bore him many bastard children. Yet these men also had affairs and created more bastard children. The cycle went on and on, and it seemed to me that there was no end to it.

I never understood why some women fought against one another, contending verbally and physically for men who showed them little love or respect. It was accepted that when a fight occurred the man would side with one of the women and that a married man would side with the other woman, not his wife. Similarly, a man living with a woman would side with the one he did not live with. Lord have mercy on some of those brave women who dared to confront their husbands or live-in boyfriends about their affairs. Many received a harsh beating as a result.

My heart went out to my cousin Sandra, the first to answer my questions about my father, who was suffering her own torment. I cried for her as I stood and witnessed Mich, the man she lived with and the father of her children, beat her severely. When she confronted him about his affair with a woman in the village, he beat her as one would beat a mule. He knocked her to the ground and pushed her into the river in the village. Like most of the women in her situation, my cousin accepted her beating with resignation. She said and did nothing, absolutely nothing, to defend herself. Adults and children looked on, many in disgust. Sandra cried for help, but no one, not even the members of her family who were present at the scene, came to her assistance.

Other members of my family had been victims of similar abuse, and there were also family members like Uncle Raymond, the gambler, who were perpetrators. Uncle Raymond lived with his girlfriend, Stage, and their children in a thatch house he had built on our family yard. I did not like the way he abused Stage by calling her undesirable names, but it was the physical abuses he committed on her that would stay in my mind forever. My uncle would gamble away all his money without providing the necessities for his children and girlfriend. Poor Stage! If other family members in the yard had not fed her and the children, most of the time they would have gone to bed hungry. My uncle would beat Stage mercilessly for failing to provide his meals, knowing that he gave her no money to buy food, having gambled it away. His beatings left bruises on her body and her eyes were so swollen that she was sometimes unable to open them.

From childhood through adolescence, I witnessed these incidents, knowing there was something wrong with this kind of behavior, but not knowing exactly what. Although I was then too young to understand it all, I knew that I did not want to become a victim like Sandra and Stage. My young mind was still developing, and as I gained more knowledge, I gradually began to understand the world around me.

I was still a sexually abused child with behavioral problems, and, even though I knew the difference between right and wrong, I continued to do wrong things. My behavioral problems got me into trouble both at home and at school. But I continued to excel in school and preferred being there to being at home. I also continued to do my many chores, and God knows that of all my chores, I hated assisting in the fields the most. I hated doing fieldwork with a passion, and why shouldn't I? After all, the fields did not belong to Mr. Phillips or my mother. They belonged to the white Portogue woman—her brother, too, so I heard. I did not see them working in the fields, nor their children, so why the hell was I doing fieldwork? I don't think Mr. Phillips could read or write. He would often ask me to write the names of the workers on a sheet of paper, along with the number of hours each had worked. I even had to calculate their weekly wages. Thank God my best subject in school was arithmetic, and thank God I loved doing calculations. I had no problem figuring how much the men should be paid at the end of each week. I had hopes that Mr. Phillips would now get to like me and start treating me like his own natural children.

At Mr. Phillips' request, every Saturday evening I took the paper on which I had written the wage records to the Portogue woman's house. I had to walk about three miles to her house. To add insult to injury, when I got to this woman's house, I had to wait outside on a bench until she came and took the paper from me. Most of the time, I sat on a hard bench and waited for hours until the Portogue returned with the wages for the men. After a while, I developed a dislike for this white woman because of the way she treated me and the other black women working as servants at her home. The two black women called her Mistress, and I even heard Mr. Phillips refer to her that way. That was the name my ancestors called the wives of their slave masters, and I was not about to call her Mistress, no sir, not me. Although I am a descendant of my slave ancestors, I am not a slave. Slavery had been abolished. I refused to give her the honor of addressing her as though we were still living as slaves. Even at that young age of twelve, I knew that

I was different from the black women who would call another woman Mistress just because of her light complexion.

Many times the Portogue woman did not give me the men's wages until it was nearly dark. As I was afraid of the dark, I took the money and hurried home to the men awaiting my arrival. I felt honored to pay the men their wages, but not honored enough to want to work in the fields. On shipment day, I went to the fields to help prepare the bananas for shipment overseas. I weighed less than a hundred pounds and had to walk more than three miles with a bunch of bananas on my head. A bunch of bananas was several hands of bananas on a single stalk, weighing over thirty pounds. On St. Vincent at the time, that was the norm. I don't think anyone there would have thought it cruel to give a young girl such a task.

But I felt differently, and for this reason reacted unexpectedly when Mr. Phillips placed a heavy bunch of bananas on my head to carry. They probably weighed not much more than thirty pounds, but it felt like one hundred pounds, and my head slumped under the weight. I'm sure that Mr. Phillips knew the bunch was too heavy for me to carry, and he could have given me a lighter one, but he didn't seem to care.

I walked down the hills away from the field. When I was out of Mr. Phillips' sight, I decided I was not about to break my neck carrying the bananas, and I threw them over an embankment. I returned to the field and informed Mr. Phillips and my mother that the bananas had fallen from my head. They were furious and began to curse and shout that I was making them lose money. My mother was so furious with me that she threatened to give me a whipping, but she didn't. Disappointed but not surprised that Mr. Phillips and my mother were more concerned about money than my safety, I felt an infusion of courage and began to think about a different kind of future for myself.

On another occasion, it was a hot, sticky day in July when I went to the field to do my share of weeding the yam crop. One has to understand that a yam field is very bushy, full of weeds and multitudes of long yam vines with sharp prickles everywhere. As I weeded the crop, the prickles stuck into my bare feet. The work was tedious, and it seemed to me that this type of work was a form of torture, not only for me, but also for the others.

After I finished my weeding, I felt itches all over my skin, as though bees were attacking my whole body. Although I saw no bees, I realized that my body was covered with welts. I was furious with anger, which then softened to self-pity. I felt like a tormented soul in hell, my mind consumed with hatred. I lacked any feeling of self-worth. I felt miserable and unhappy, I yearned for happiness in any form. Those feelings changed my life forever. They made me decide to search for a better life wherever I could find it.

After much thought, I decided that I had two choices. I could either spend the rest of my life in the same situation I was now in or try to get out by doing better. It was obvious which I should choose—to do better. To do so, I had to stay out of trouble. I had to stop fighting and cursing my fellows in school, and I could no longer let people hear me cursing at my sexual predators. Most of all, I had to stay in school and continue to do well in my studies. Then I might become a teacher and not have to work in the fields, provided I lived long enough to be an adult. So I made a pledge to myself that I would focus on my education and make it my first priority. Lord, I pledged also to be a good person like my Mommy, Uncle Josey, and Ma.

I tried hard to be the good person that I promised to be, Lord, you know I tried, but I couldn't. I seemed to have the devil within me, and it didn't matter how hard I tried to do good things—I would do bad things instead. The pedophiles were causing me to do bad things. They were still trying to molest me, and I was still cursing them in defense. I felt that cursing them was the only defense I had from them. Because I continued cursing, the villagers, especially mothers, continued to call me undesirable names. They said I was no good, forbidding their children to be friends with me. So I had no friends. These snubs bothered me because I wasn't able to explain to them that my cursing was only a means of defense against the pedophiles. I felt they should have been more understanding, but I failed to acknowledge that they could not have known if I did not tell them, and I did not have the courage to tell my Mommy, let alone them.

The villagers' scorn made me feel that I could be nothing but the bad person they perceived me to be. I felt worthless and no good, at times, overwhelmed with sadness. Many times thoughts crossed my mind of running away, far from the village, never to return. I never did, because I knew of nowhere I could run to. But I did know a place where I could go and hide for a couple of hours.

As other animals, when threatened by lions and fearing for their lives, would climb trees and hide, I too climbed trees and hid from the lions I perceived the villagers to be. When I felt overwhelmed with my troubles, I climbed up a tangerine tree and hid there until I felt safe again. It was a special tangerine tree with lots of leaves which enabled me to hide in its branches without anyone detecting me. Distressed but determined to survive, I knew of no better refuge.

The peaceful moments I spent among the leaves of that tree also led me to reinforce my determination to escape my destructive situation. As my adolescent years approached, I spent more time in that tree thinking things over. The more I thought about it, the more I came to realize that education was my only hope, the only way out of the lion's den. Education to me was independence and self-reliance. Self-reliance to me meant the self-esteem I'd had long ago when I was a child but lost when I started to live with my mother and began to be raped. I wanted my childhood back. I had been happy then, and I wanted to be happy again. It seemed natural to me that as my adolescent years were bringing changes to my body, I should want to make changes in my life situation. Now more than at any other time, I felt that I could become what I wanted to be, regardless of the threats from the lions in the den. There was no doubt in my mind that I would try to be different. If I didn't turn out to be different from the lions I lived among, at least I would know it was not for lack of trying. Lord, at least I would know I tried.

For many years I thought of ways to be different, but I was not sure how different I wanted to be. Though I felt that an education was my best way out and I tried to excel academically in school, I also had to admit that so far it had not brought about much change in my life. But I wasn't about to give up on my education. I couldn't give up on it, because I knew of no other way to bring about the change I needed. I reminded myself of a saying I had heard: If you try to do something and do not succeed, and you really want to do it, you must try until you succeed. I don't know where I heard these words, but they remained in my memory like the Our Father which Ma had taught me. Those words became the motto which guided me on my quest.

There was nothing in my life that I allowed to distract me from my education, absolutely nothing. I believed in prayer, although it often seemed to me that God didn't hear me. Both Ma and Mommy had taught me to believe that God is a good God. They said that if I needed anything, I should pray to God, for he answers prayer. I don't know what they were talking about, because when I prayed to this God, asking him time and time again to stop Patrick from raping me, nothing changed. I had to threaten to kill him before he stopped. I did it, not God. And how about the other pedophiles? I had prayed and asked God to stop them from molesting me. But God again did not stop them. I had to confront them with curse in order to stop them. I believed what Ma and Mommy had told me about God, but I felt they must have forgotten to tell me something more, that God doesn't answer the prayers of children, only those of grownups. Well, I was growing up, or perhaps I should say that I felt I had already grown up, so it seemed proper to try again. As a grownup, I believed that God would answer my prayers, so I continued to pray to Him.

I asked God to help me pass the school leavings exam, which we took when we were in the last grade in government school. Passing the exam would at least assure me of a job as a teacher's assistant, where I would assist in the classroom four days a week and attend classes once a week. God must have listened to my prayer. I took the exam when I was in the last grade in the government school and passed it on the first try. "Ma and Mommy were right after all when they told me that God would answer prayers," I thought. I was thirteen years old at the time, too young to take immediate advantage of its main benefit. Passing the exam was most advantageous for those children who were age fifteen, who were offered positions as teachers' assistants. In order to remain in that position, they had to pursue further study and pass a series of exams, being paid while they continued their education. Children like me who passed the exam before they were fifteen had two choices. They could stay in school until they were fifteen and be offered the opportunity to become a teacher's assistant, or they could take the common entrance exam for admission to high school. Each high school had its own exam and its own standards for passing it. Passing an exam for a particular school meant you would be guaranteed admission to that school if you chose to attend. In high school you could continue your education, provided you performed well and your parents had the money to pay the tuition and other expenses. Unlike the government schools, where children attended free of charge, high schools charged tuition.

Neither of the two choices suited me. I wanted to be a first-level teacher's assistant as soon as I passed the school leavings exam. I thought to myself, "Now I have passed the exams, so give me the job." But what I thought were the rules turned out not to be. It seemed that if I wanted to be hired as a first-level teacher's assistant I would have to spend two more years sitting in the classroom. The other choice, going to a high school, was out of the question. I knew that my parents would not be willing to send me to high school, even if they had the money to pay for it, which they did not. High school tuition was fourteen dollars a semester, and transportation would run about twenty dollars a month, not to mention the expense of school supplies, uniform, and lunch. The combined income of Mr. Phillips and my mother was no more than about sixteen dollars a week.

Our high schools in the islands were really what would be thought of in the United States as a combination of part junior and high. Normally, it took a child five years to complete high school. Since the majority of the people in the island were poor, most of them never thought of sending children to high school, especially not female children. I could only conclude that our society thought a female must be limited to the role of mother and homemaker, subservient to the men. There were, of course, those parents who just could not afford to send their children to high school. Other parents were willing to make sacrifices to pay for their children to have a better education than they themselves had received. But there were also parents who had enough money but refused to educate their children, especially female children. Those parents who did not want to educate their daughters argued that it was a waste of time and money to educate them beyond elementary school.

For myself, I had come to know who my father was. Even though he was not supporting me financially, it was my understanding that he had brought lots of money with him from England. My father seemed to have money, because he owned a car and had many girlfriends. "Well, Lola," I thought, "even if your father has money, his car and girlfriends are his priority, not your education. Don't even think he will help you. But, Lola, he is your father, why wouldn't he help you, and what makes you think he wouldn't? How is he to know you need help unless you ask him? Hell, no, I am not going to ask that shaver man bastard for any help. Why should I have to? He doesn't come to look for me. Why should I go looking for him? Furthermore, Mommy was right when she said that now that I have grown up, I don't need his help. No, no, Mommy was right at the time, but that was because I was not then thinking of attending high school. Forget about his helping you." That was the conversation I had with myself about my father when I was contemplating attending high school.

I also had another conversation with myself about Mr. Phillips and my mother. It appeared to me that Mr. Phillips and my mother were having serious problems, arguing regularly with one another. I heard them arguing about another woman and about money, but I really didn't understand all of it. I assume that Mr. Phillips was having an affair with another woman and giving her all his money, because my mother no longer had much. She had also stopped working with Mr. Phillips in the fields and now worked for another landowner in the village. It was the money from this new job that she used to support the household. I doubted that she made enough to pay for my high school education. Still, I pondered it, "What if she does make enough? Do you really think she is about to spend it on you? Do you think she has your interest at heart? Whose interest does she have at heart? Probably has your siblings', not yours. Are you kidding? That woman beats me too much for little reason to have my interest at heart. Interest at heart, my interest at heart! I remember her telling me she would kill me if I didn't behave myself. My interest at heart! If she has my interest at heart, how come she never asks me to tell her my side of the story when those pedophiles complain to her that I cursed them? I know she doesn't have my interest at heart, because I remember what happened to me when I had a toothache."

My sister Marge had lots of cavities and lots of toothaches. My mother treated Marge special whenever she had toothaches, cooking her special food and being extremely attentive to her. I was jealous of Marge because of the attention she was getting and because of that special soup my mother would cook for her. I wanted my mother to give me some attention and cook me some special soup, too. But I had perfect teeth, white as chalk, and strong, too. Just to get a little attention from my mother, I took a nursery pin and picked at one of my teeth until I created a hole in it. Then the tooth started to ache, and it ached for a couple of nights. Still, my mother didn't cook me any special soup as she had done for my sister. For a couple more nights I was crying in pain. Then, as I lay in bed crying, my mother said to me, "Tomorrow, you will have to go to the dentist and have your tooth pulled."

The next day my mother gave me the money to go to the dentist to have my tooth pulled. I went to a dentist I didn't know was an alcoholic. I sat in the dentist's chair while he examined my tooth. He said he couldn't understand why I had a hole in my tooth, because my tooth was strong. Instead of extracting my tooth, he put a filling in it. Perhaps he was drunk at the time, but he did something wrong when he worked on my tooth. Whatever this dentist man did to my tooth, the pain did not stop, but only grew worse. I was still crying for pain at night, as my tooth hurt more than ever. Even though I was just as sick as my sister had been when she had her toothache, my mother never cooked me any special soup or gave me the special attention I was hoping for. After several nights crying for pain, I guess I was interrupting my mother's sleep. One night she said to me, "Tomorrow when daylight comes, you better get up out of yo bed early and yo going back to that dentist to tek (take) out your fucking tooth. You ah mek (make) too much noise ah me head ah night so yo have to go and tek out yo tooth. Na come back home without taking it out." The next morning I got out of bed and went back to the dentist and asked him to extract my tooth. He did. "Girl," I said to myself, "you better not approach that woman you call your mother about sending you to some high school. You better not do it. You better forget going to high school, because you don't have anyone who cares enough for you and your damn interest in continuing your education. Besides, there is no one who has the money to pay for it."

Against the Odds

Ever since Miss English was hired as the principal of the village school I attended, she was drawn to me as much as I to her. Under her leadership our school set a record for attaining the most passes in the final elementary school examination since it first opened, ranking first among all schools that year. Because of my behavioral problems at school, some teachers were shunning me, but not Miss English. She showed her interest in me and encouraged me to try to behave myself and become a better person. Under her influence I found myself involved in fewer fights.

Miss English invited me to visit her at her home in another village, and I did so on weekends and on days when I had a long vacation from school. Many of the mothers in my village seemed jealous of my visits, resenting the fact that the same privilege had not been extended to their daughters, and they tried to defame my character. Not that I was a goody two shoes. But the mothers called me a "woman," an insulting name to call a child in our society. They advised Miss English to stop receiving me in her home. One mother went so far as to tell Miss English I was sexually involved with grown men. I don't know who these grown men were. The only grown men I was ever sexually involved with were the men who raped me. Although some of them were still trying to molest me, at thirteen I had enough sense to know they would flee if I screamed for help. It also seems that the pedophiles preferred to prey on younger children. Miss English told me she had asked the mother for the names of the men with whom I was supposed to be involved, but was not told them. Miss English recognized the story for the fabrication which it was. She encouraged me to ignore the slanders and focus on my education. "You are an intelligent child,"Miss English said to me one day. "I want you to take your education seriously and make something of yourself." I took her advice seriously, and she became my mentor.

One day Miss English saw me sitting alone under a mango tree in the schoolyard. I often sat alone when I wanted to focus on life from a different perspective. Miss English approached me and asked me why was I sitting alone and what was I thinking about. I replied that I was thinking about my educational goals. I told her that I would like to further my education. "I don't want to continue sitting in the classroom not doing anything for another two years, waiting to become eligible for a position as a teacher's aide. I would like instead to attend a high school, but, unfortunately, I can't," I said to Miss English. "Why can't you?" she asked. "My mother is poor and she has lots of us children," I said. "She doesn't have the money to pay for tuition and the other expenses," I explained. As if Miss English didn't already know that my mother was poor, that she had five children besides me and was pregnant with another. But what she didn't know was that living with my mother was like living in hell. "Go and take the high school common exam anyway," she suggested. I wanted to ask her why I should take the exam when I knew I wouldn't be able to attend high school if I passed, but I respected her too much to talk to her in that way.

I followed Miss English's suggestion and I took the common entrance examination. By that time all the high schools had already given their examinations except for Mainland High School, which had scheduled theirs for that Saturday. Without telling my mothers, I went and sat for the examination. A few weeks later I was notified that I had passed the exam and would be accepted as a new student in September. Although I knew that the school ranked very low academically among the other high schools, I felt that it would have been good enough for me to attend, if only I could find someone willing to pay my way.

Passing the exam seemed quite an accomplishment to me, and I was proud of myself. Who wouldn't be? I thought that perhaps I should tell my mother I had passed the exam, but her past mistreatment made me apprehensive. Still, I was eager to hear her response, and I decided to tell her. Wouldn't it be wonderful if she congratulated me and told me she would try her best to get money to pay the expenses? That turned out to be wishful thinking on my part. As I was telling my mother about my accomplishment, she looked puzzled. Before I had finished, she interrupted me, saying she had no money to pay for high school. Although I had expected my mother to react as she did, I still felt disappointed. But I never gave up hope and became more determined than ever to attend high school. I began to explore all of my options that might make it possible.

Previously, I had thought it out of the question to ask my father for assistance, but now I had second thoughts. I decided that it was better to ask for his financial assistance and have him refuse than not to ask at all. With that in mind, I swallowed my pride and went to my father, informing him of my accomplishment as I had my mother. By letting him know that I wanted to attend the school, I was asking him for his financial assistance in a subtle way. My father listened to me attentively and congratulated me. He promised to finance part of my education. I felt elated.

It seemed to me that financing my education was the least my father could do for me. He had never given me any financial support, except for the few dollars he gave me to take home to my mother the first day we met. I thought that he didn't deserve any gratitude from me, but still I thanked him for his offer. Knowing I would need other financial assistance besides my father's, I went as my last hope to my caring grandmother, my Mommy.

My grandmother didn't have to say it. I knew that if she could she would do anything in the world for me. Tears flowed from my grandmother's eyes and down her cheeks when I informed her of my intention to attend high school. Without my grandmother uttering a word, I knew she was proud of me. I told her about the conversation I had had with my father and his promise to assist me. I also told her what my mother had said. "Bulah said she had no money to send me to high school, so I won't be able to attend school," I said to my grandmother. My grandmother's response renewed my hope that I would be able to attend the high school. She said, "Lola, you hav brain fo high school, you will go to high school. If I have to work every day of the week until night, you hav to go to high school because you hav good brain, and you can't let good brain go to waste." My grandmother was a woman of her word, especially regarding the welfare of her first grandchild. I had no doubt that my grandmother would do everything within her power to help me make my high school dream become a reality.

From the time that I passed the high school entrance examination my behavior changed for the better. I restrained myself from fighting with other children or cursing people, even when I felt provoked. In my mother's house I was on my best behavior. I tried to do everything I was told to do, not wanting to give my mother an excuse not to send me to high school. I think my grandmother must have convinced my mother that I should attend the school, for the two of them pooled their money and purchased my school uniforms and books and paid my tuition for the first semester. Tuition was fourteen dollars a semester. This may not seem like a lot to pay for four months' tuition, but in those days, fourteen dollars was a great sum for my grandmother and my mother. My grandmother, the sole provider for her household of six, earned no more than six dollars a week. My mother's wages plus Mr. Phillips' financial support could not have been much more than my grandmother's weekly earnings, and she had five children to support and was pregnant with another. Besides my tuition, uniform and books, I needed money for my transportation to school, an expense my grandmother and mother could not afford. We lived on the windward side of the island, about 17 miles from school, an hour or more by bus. My father, on the other hand, was living in the same town where the school was located. My mother and he came to an agreement that I would live with my father while I attended school and then travel to the village to spend weekends with my mother.

Beyond the weekly lodging, my father did not provide me financial support as he had promised. Although I felt my father wasn't doing enough for me, I was still grateful for his small contribution. He could have refused to have me to stay with him, and if he had done that I would probably not have been able to attend school, since my grandmother and mother were not able to pay for my transportation.

The prospect of staying with my father wasn't something I embraced enthusiastically, but I decided to make the best of the situation, since I had no other choice. So, on the first day of the school year I began to live with my father and his girlfriend, Lacey. Their home was similar to mine in that my father and his girlfriend argued and fought with each other as much as Mr. Phillips and my mother did. But, whereas my mother cooked and fed the members of her household regularly, my father's girlfriend did not. So I went to bed many nights without having had enough to eat, and sometimes having eaten nothing at all. In spite of all that went on in my father's house, I continued to live with him, and the longer I lived with him, the better I got to know him.

My father spoke English with a British accent. He encouraged me to speak proper English, using none of our native dialect. Although he was not very well educated, having a formal education equivalent to the sixth-grade, he was a very intelligent man. I came to believe my father had been self-educated well beyond the sixth grade level, by his reading and God knows what else, probably his experience overseas. I came to know him as a very stingy man who counted his pennies. He lectured his live-in girlfriend about her spending on insignificant things like soap and toothpaste. Sometimes his lectures deteriorated into arguments, ending up with his physically abusing her. I was appalled by such mean behavior from an intelligent man. Assuming that education would bring civility to a person's life, I thought that a man of his intelligence should know that it was wrong to abuse a woman and that he would restrain himself. Having witnessed the abuses, I lost whatever affection and respect I had felt for this man I recognized as my father. I couldn't help thinking that I would have been better off not having him in my life, that I preferred how things were before. There I was in a home I thought would be different from my mother's, but again found myself in the midst of violence. I was as fed up with the cruelty I saw my father inflicting on Lacey as I had been with Mr. Phillips' cruelty on my mother. I prayed for the violence to stop.

It seemed that violence surrounded me everywhere I went. When I had to go home to my mother on weekends, I experienced two strong opposite emotions. I was happy to see my grandmother and my siblings, but with a sadness that overshadowed my happiness. I felt sad about the violence I would have to witness between Mr. Phillips and my mother and among other couples in the village. I was also sad because I would have flashbacks of my molesters and of the village women saying mean things about me. I was troubled by all of this, but not enough to prevent me from concentrating on my education. Mainland High School, the school I was attending, must have been the worst high school on the island at the time. I cannot imagine another school like it. It was a co-educational school, where the teachers and pupils were in a league of their own! The school was overcrowded, with children packed wall-to-wall in hot classrooms. Designed for about forty children, some classrooms had as many as seventy-five crammed together like bananas packed in an overseas shipping crate. The chairs were hard and uncomfortable. Most of the children seemed to have neither the ability nor the zeal for an education, so it was not surprising that they were unable to concentrate on their schoolwork, But these conditions did not deter those of us who had ability and zeal. We were highly attentive in school, did our homework, and earned good grades, regardless of the distractions from undisciplined students, unqualified teachers, and chaotic classrooms. At times a classroom would become so chaotic that the teacher was not able to distinguish the good students from the bad ones.

It was a school where teachers and students flirted with one another. Male students disrespected female students and female students disrespected themselves. I witnessed girls lifting their skirts high above their knees. With skirts lifted high, they took their books and fanned, I suppose, their hot crotches. The boys looked on their crotches, laughing. In spite of all this distracting behavior, I studied hard. At the end of the first semester I ranked tenth in my class of seventy-five students. But by the end of my first semester, I realized that the environment there was not conducive to my studies.

Living with my father presented me with yet another problem. By the end of the first semester, I knew that if I had a choice I would not live with my father the following semester. There were many times when my father and Lacey would fight and then she would stop speaking to me. I never knew why. A few days before the end of the semester they had such a fight, and then Lacey stopped speaking to me. I left my father's home without saying good-bye to her, knowing that if I should be offered an alternative place to stay, I would jump at the opportunity.

When school closed for the semester break, I returned to my mother's to live. Although it was like returning to hell, I dealt with the hell of my mother's home better than the hell of my father's. I was comforted by the thought that my grandmother lived nearby and I could always depend on her for some sort of security, whereas at my father's there was no one for me to depend on. I confided in my grandmother, telling her about conditions at my father's home, and saying I would like to avoid returning there the following semester. My grandmother knew as well as I did that I had no choice but to return to my father's home if I wanted to remain in school. We also both knew that my grandmother and my mother could not afford to pay for my transportation to school. If they had been able to, I would not have lived with my father in the first place. My grandmother, knowing all of this, looked at me and said, "You don't have to stay with that vagabond if you don't want to. God will make a way for you." Then she asked me, "Lola, do you believe in God and prayer?" I answered, "I do believe in God and prayer." Then my grandmother took my hands in her own and told me that if I believed in God and prayer, I must pray to God and God would answer my prayer. "Trust God. He is good and He has answers to all of our needs," my grandmother said to me in a cracking voice.

I trusted my grandmother, and felt that I should have faith in God as much as she did. So I took my grandmother's advice and began to pray to God every night, "God, you know I do not want to live with my father next semester. I beg you to provide me with an alternative. I know you are a good God. Please show me a way not to have to go back to my father's home. Thank you, God, for listening, and thank you for providing me with an alternative. I know you will, God, I just know that you will." I prayed to God sometimes more than once a night.

God must have listened to my prayer, for I believe that it was because of Him that I found an alternative. My Uncle Kyle had migrated to Tortola, part of the British Virgin Islands, in search of work. Before school reopened the next semester, Kyle found work and began sending money to my grandmother, saying in his letters that my grandmother was to use some of the money to help with my education. I think Kyle must have remembered all of the homework I had done for him when we attended the village school together. He must have remembered also how my grandmother used to stress the importance of education, and he must have wanted me to be educated. When we were younger, Kyle used to tell me that I had a smarter brain than he had. One day I found Kyle crying because he did not want to go to school. Kyle really and truly did not like school. My grandmother told him he had better go to school and try to do his best in school, as I was doing. She told us the story of a man in the village, the father of one of Tanty Bertha's sons. One day Tanty Bertha tried to get Thomas, her son, to go to school, and failing to persuade him, she sought the assistance of his father. His father scolded Thomas and lectured him about the importance of education. He told Thomas that while he was living overseas, an illiterate man who became his best friend would ask him to write letters to his family at home, giving him money to include in the letters. He said the man would watch him write the letter, put the money into the envelope and seal it. Then he and his friend would go to the post office and see that the letter was mailed. His friend even paid him for writing the letters. But the poor man, because he couldn't read, failed to realize that Thomas' father was sending the letters to his own family instead. After my grandmother told us that true story, Kyle showed more interest in school. Instead of having me do his schoolwork for him, he would ask me to teach him how to do it himself. As a result, Kyle was at least able to write his own letters.

With Kyle's financial assistance my grandmother paid my transportation to school the following semester. I traveled by bus daily to and from school and thanked God that my grandmother was able to pay for it. As it turned out, my father would not have been able to accommodate me anyway, since he and Lacey were no longer living together, he having relocated to another area on the island about the same distance from my school as my mother's home.

Randy was one of Tanty Bertha's sons who had also migrated to the United States in search of work. He had signed an agreement with a company which allowed him to enter the United States as a migrant worker to pick fruit for the season. Kyle and Randy were both proud of my desire to be educated, and they were not the only ones. Everybody in the Ma Letteen family was proud of me as the first in the family to pursue a high school education, and they all contributed to my education in one way or another, even if only by a word of encouragement when I felt discouraged. Randy sent money home to my mother to save for him, as well as some to assist with my education. I wrote them letters thanking them. After a while, I was the one who would take care of their banking. I believe that God intervened on my behalf, allowing my uncle and cousin to migrate to these countries and help me obtain an education. I felt that God had listened to my prayer.

During my first few days in high school, I started my period, and it came with a vengeance. I had unbearable stomach cramps and would vomit the first few days of each monthly cycle. There were days when I was so ill that I would either have to stay home from school or be sent home. While I lived with my father there had been no problem. My problems began when I started travelling to school by bus each day. When I had my period and was too ill to attend school or was sent back home in agony, some villagers, most of the mothers in particular, started rumors that I was pregnant. How could I have been pregnant every month without my stomach getting big? When they saw no bulge in my stomach, they spread the rumor that I had had an abortion. How many abortions could I have had in a year? Although I knew they were only rumors, I still would feel hurt when I heard them. Sometimes I would cry and try to console myself. Eventually I learned not to get too emotional about rumors, ignoring them instead. I was also encouraged in this by a few of the villagers.

I will always remember the encouraging words of Sarah, Elitha and Leeann, three mothers living in my village. Whenever Leeann heard a rumor about me, she would encourage me to ignore it and concentrate on achieving my education. Elitha comforted me by saying that she understood my pain. "I have lived among these people longer than you have, and me know them better than you," she said. "Them nah like yo because them jealous ah yo. Them always wish the worst on people like you because they believe you go be better off than them. Ignore them and concentrate on yo school lesson. If yo do that yo go be all right," Elitha advised me as she sat on a step in her yard that led to the entrance of her board house. Elitha's yard was different from my family's. Her house was the only house in her yard, with concrete steps from street level to the front door. She grew beautiful roses, carnations and other flowers in a garden in front of the house. On my way to school I would often smell the sweet aroma coming from her kitchen, set apart from her house about five yards.

Sarah, the most soft-spoken of the three women, would tell me that jealousy was the reason why some villagers were speaking ill of me. "Yo nah see yo different than them young gals in ah the village. Yo different because yo ah try to make something out of yo life and na gae breed up and havin all the picmies like the other young gal ah them. That ah way them envy you fa," she often said to me. She would always tell me how proud she was of me, especially when she learned of my promotion in school. Sarah was a kind and caring person. She had been taking care of her two nieces, my age, whose mother had migrated to Trinidad, from the time they were young children, while also caring for her own three children.

The Staddards were a married couple who lived outside the village, having lived overseas for many years before returning to St. Vincent with their four children, who were older than I. They appeared to me to be decent people. The Staddards must have known, since everybody else did, the difficulties I faced with some villagers, for they were always kind to me, offering words of encouragement and encouraging me to concentrate on schoolwork. Miss John, who lived just above the village with Mr. Allen, was another who would tell me to ignore the rumors and strive for academic excellence. Although Miss John was not originally from our area, I felt she understood my situation as much as the others did.

Because of the many wrongs I had suffered, I continued to believe that many of the villagers were wicked and envious, especially when I saw Mr. Horn lying in a gutter one day. Mr. Horn, who lived in the village with his common law wife and children, was the most knowledgeable carpenter in the village. I never knew that he had enemies in the village, but obviously he did. Mr. Horn was found lying in the gutter, his tongue pierced with an ice pick. He had been left in such a position as to suggest that he had fallen over the bridge, but that was not so. Mr. Horn died in the hospital several weeks later. Had he lived, he would have been unable to speak because of the puncture wounds to his tongue. The villagers said he would have been like a vegetable. Although there were rumors about who might have committed the murder, no one was ever taken into police custody for questioning. Like the rapes against children, this crime became yet another secret among the villagers. And it was not the only deadly crime in the village.

One of my great uncles from the McDade family in the village was also murdered. According to the rumors, Uncle Sammy had been a thief, and a good one, too. They say he was so good at it that he could be talking to you while stealing your fowl without your ever noticing. Uncle Sammy's final theft was harvesting and stealing someone's entire yam crop. Uncle Sammy was probably not seen in the act, since most thieves committed these crimes after people had left their fields. They probably suspected him because of information from one of Uncle Sammy's friends or from the buyer of the stolen yams. It seems that two nights before Christmas that year, some men of the village lowered him into a pit used for butchering cattle. Since the shed was not wired for electricity, the owner would light the shed by connecting an electric wire to an outlet from his house above. The murderers gave Uncle Sammy the electric wire to hold in the rain and plugged in the other end. Benup, as they referred to him, was electrocuted. After burying him, they decided it would look suspicious, so they dug up his body and laid it on the ground where it could be seen. So Uncle Sammy, thief that he might have been, lost his life for it. Those involved never broke their code of silence, and no one was ever punished for it.

One thing I learned about the people of my village as I lived among them was that they could not be trusted, neither men nor women. I was about fourteen when my cousin Randy returned from America, his contract with the fruit company having expired. He brought back items of clothing for almost everyone in the family, and many for me in particular. I felt once again the favored person in the family. Nightgowns and pretty panties were some of the items Randy brought back to his favorite cousin. Although I didn't think I was my mother's favorite child, if she had a favorite, she and I slept together in the same bed with one of my younger siblings, while my other siblings slept on the floor. Every evening before dark, we would close all the windows, especially in the bedroom. One night, as I slept close to the window, in the same bed with my mother and a sibling, I was awakened by a cool breeze, as if from an open window. Afraid, I opened one eye slightly and peeped towards the window closest to the bed. It seemed to be open. I immediately thought that a ghost must have opened it. The adults told us ghost stories, saying ghosts are the wicked dead who come out of their graves at night and do bad things to the living. I feared that a ghost was about to injure one of us.

Although I was afraid, I kept my eyes slightly open and continued to peer at the window, but I saw no ghost. The window I knew I had closed before dark was now wide open. I was too scared to move, so I screamed, "The window is open! The window is open!" My screams awakened everyone in the house. My mother saw the open window, fussed at me, and accused me of not having closed it, even though I swore to her that I had done so. She cursed and said I was unreliable and a damn liar, because if I had closed the window as she had instructed me, it could not have been open in the middle of the night. It was useless for me to try to convince my mother. From then on, she closed the windows herself before dark each night.

On the following Sunday I attended church, wearing one of the new pairs of panties that my cousin had brought me from the United States. They were a little tight around my legs, but they were pretty and new, so I wore them anyway. I wore the panties all day and went to bed wearing them that night, a night I will never forget. My experience that night will have a chilling effect on my life forever. As I again slept close to the window in the same bed with my mother and a sibling, I felt yet another cool breeze. Afraid, I opened my eyes again and saw the window open. Frozen in my position, I screamed, "The window is open! The window is open!" Again my screaming awakened everyone in the house. My mother shouted, "I closed that window before dark! I am sure that I did!" Mr. Phillips entered the bedroom and checked the window. Frightened by the commotion around me, I continued to lie in bed, feeling frozen in time. I needed to urinate desperately, but was too afraid to move, so I continued to lie there, even when the others went around the house to check the window from the outside.

Because we had no electricity, my mother carried a lantern as she followed Mr. Phillips around the house, checking, for what and for whom, I didn't know. I was still lying in the bed unable to move when I overheard my mother say to Mr. Phillips that someone had tried to break into the house. He agreed. They had found muddy footprints on the window ledge. I felt helpless and weak, and I began to tremble with fright. We had no indoor plumbing, but in each bedroom we had a potty used to urinate in at night. These potties were emptied and washed each morning. There was a potty on the floor at the foot of the bed in the room where I lay, but I was still too afraid to get out of bed. Finally, my need to urinate became so unbearable that I stepped nervously out of bed to locate the potty.

Having found the potty, I lifted my nightgown to pull down my panties, but I couldn't find the pretty, new, tight panties I had worn to bed that night. My panties seemed to have disappeared into thin air, and I had no idea why or how. Horrified, I continued to search my body and discovered what was left of my panties on my flat chest below my small breasts. "Lord, how did my panties get there?" I wondered in fright.

When I tried to pull my panties down from under my breasts, I was astonished to discover the crotch of my panties cut. Confused and frightened, I screamed, "Mommy, Mommy, they cut me panties crotch!" I was so terrified that I urinated on myself. My mother came into the room screaming, as terrified as I was. My sisters Marge and May were screaming, too, while my other siblings looked on with fright. My mother asked me to take off my panties, or what was left of them, for her to examine. With trembling hands, I took off my panties from my now shaking body and gave what was left of them to my mother. It became clear that someone had cut the crotch of my panties with a sharp instrument. Lord, someone unknown to me cut my panties while I lay asleep in the same bed with my mother and a sibling that night!

After the commotion, everyone in the house went back to sleep, except me. I lay awake in bed, reflecting on my life and sobbing quietly, until daybreak. Yes, I thought about Patrick, my former rapist. Was he the one who had committed such an awful act against me? If so, was he trying to kill me? He had threatened me before. Was he trying to do it that night? Was he trying to rape me again? Oh! I was hurting. That night, I hurt deep within my soul and felt that I should have died with Ma—then these awful things would not have happened. I continued lying in bed and wishing for death. I felt I would be better off dead and at least be in heaven with Ma. Then I thought about my Uncle Josey. I wanted Uncle Josey to appear that very minute and take me away. I felt very sad.

To me, the life I lived had to be the worst there ever was. I began to believe that nobody cared for me, that I lived in the worst place and among the most envious, devious people on God's created earth. I was a confused little girl who needed someone to hug me, tell me they cared, and assure me things were going to be all right, but no one did, not even my mother. I felt so unwanted as a child that I pledged, if I ever grew up to be a woman, never to bring a child into this world.

In the morning my mother informed my grandmother what had happened in the night. My grandmother held me in her arms and asked if I was all right. She was crying as she listened to my mother. I did not want my grandmother to worry about me, so I assured her I was all right, even though I knew I wasn't. Friends and relatives chatted about the incident and puzzled over who could have committed such an act, and why. They commented that I was still a child and wondered what wicked soul could have committed such an unspeakable act against a child. They concluded that someone might have been trying to rape me. No one bothered to ask me if I had ever been raped. No one asked me that question, not even my mother. They didn't know that I had been raped time and time again and that I lived in the fear of someone raping me again, or even killing me. No one observed that I had a tormented soul and a confused mind resulting from the rapes. They couldn't have known because I never told anyone. I now began to ponder whether I should break my silence and tell about the rapes committed against me by men who were looked on as the pillars of our community. What would happen to the men and to me if I exposed them to the community? Would the community scorn me? In fear, though I don't know what I was so afraid of, I chose to maintain my silence. Yes, I chose to remain silent, just as my ancestors had done in the days of slavery. Even though I chose to remain silent, I would never forget the rapes committed against me, just as I would never forget the happenings of that night.

I would forever remember that night vividly. I relived that night every day. Thoughts of that night would come to me, and I would panic. Fear would rush through my body and send cold through every vein. I would remember how helpless I felt and the terror I felt deep within on that night. The puzzle of that night would remain with me for the rest of my natural life. Not knowing who had done me such an evil haunts my soul to this very day, as I continue to live with the trauma of that night.

Before the day was over, the news had spread through the village. Some of the villagers came by and spoke with my mother, each voicing an opinion about the incident, wondering who could have done such a thing. I became uncomfortable. I felt too ashamed to talk about what had happened and did not want to listen to anyone else talking about it. I noticed people staring at me, and I wondered what were they thinking. I wondered if the perpetrator was among the crowd of people. I became angry and depressed when I heard rumors that accused me of being the one who opened the window to the unknown perpetrator.

As I was growing up in the village, I had heard many villagers speaking ill of others, so I knew there were not many kind people among them. However, I did not think there was a single soul in the village who would have said such an unkind thing about me when it came to such an incident as this. How could they accuse me of letting someone in the window with my mother and sibling lying next to me? Why would I welcome someone to commit such a heinous crime against me? I had no motive. My education was my only interest. I had never had a boyfriend, nor had I ever given anyone permission to touch my body, though there were those who had more than touched it by force. Still emotionally distraught over the incident of that night, I felt even more devastated by the remarks and insinuations of mindless people. I wanted to get away from them and stay away for good. I felt I could not tell the evil ones from the good, if there were any good ones. I felt like committing suicide. I felt death would release me from all of my emotional pain, which had become unbearable. I just wanted to be released from it all and to be free.

I contemplated killing myself, but I could not do it. I remember the time my mother had beaten me and I had thrown myself over an embankment in hopes of breaking my neck. When my attempts at suicide failed, I began to pray to God for death, but for some reason God never answered that prayer. I concluded that God must have wanted me to stay alive for reasons unknown to me. "Whatever your reasons are for keeping me alive, God, please don't let anyone else rape me and please, Oh God, please, don't let anyone else come into the window to cut my panties, because the next time, they might cut my throat instead. God, even though I want to die, I don't want to die a painful death. I think if someone were to cut my throat, that would be a painful death, so don't let my throat be cut. Just let me die as Ma did, peacefully lying in my bed." As I said, God must have had some reason for keeping me alive, because I lived to attend a new high school to pursue my educational goals.

Ever since I had started attending the Mainland High School, I had known that I would not be spending all of my high school years there. I knew I could do better. With the financial help from my uncle and cousin, I decided it was time for me to move on to a better school. I wanted to attend a more academically reputable school, so at the end of my first year at Mainland High, I sat for another exam to attend a different school. I was interested in one school and one school only, a school that ranked high in academic excellence and had rules that students obeyed. That school was St. Joseph's Convent, an all-female Catholic school operated by an order of nuns. While the nuns were strict disciplinarians, they were loved and respected by the students and the island's people because of the school's good reputation.

My acceptance into St. Joseph's Convent was one of the best things that ever had happened to me. I hoped and prayed that Kyle, my grandmother, and my mother would continue to finance my education, including my transportation to and from school. Lord, I knew my grandmother would do anything to assure payment of my tuition and the cost of my books, and I hoped my mother would do her part as well. My mother began to show interest in my education, and I believed she would assist me financially, but I was worried about Kyle. I needed his continued support to pay for my transportation, because my grandmother and mother would not be able to. As for that damn no good father of mine, he had not given me a penny to help with my tuition since I had begun high school. There was nothing else I could do except to do my very best in school, if I could attend, and to keep praying to God.

When I began to attend St. Joseph's Convent, I had to walk approximately two miles to and from the crossroads outside the village for the bus that took me to school. If I were not there in the morning at seven, I missed the bus and was likely to miss school that day. School was approximately seventeen miles from the crossroads. On school days, I awoke by five and prayed before going to the river to bathe. Taking a bath in the morning in the cold water was no joke. With chattering teeth, I stooped on a rock and stretched out a hand to test the temperature of the water. After soaping my wash cloth and gently washing my body, I jumped into the bone-chilling water. I became so thoroughly chilled that every other feeling in my body seemed to disappear in those first few minutes in the water. Bathing early in the morning in the river was quite an experience for all of us children. After my bath, I returned to the house, put on my school uniform, and ate my breakfast, at least on days when breakfast was available. Breakfast usually consisted of bread and butter and a cup of tea brewed from mint leaves from our garden. If a fowl in the yard had laid some eggs, I might have an egg with the bread instead of butter. But there were times when my mother did not provide me with any breakfast at all. Knowing that she did not have the means to do so, I went to school without complaining.

St. Joseph's Convent had strict rules for its students, including a dress code. The uniform consisted of a white blouse, white shoes and socks, and a blue pleated skirt with a hem four inches below the knee. Our hair had to be neatly combed at all times, and we were not allowed to wear nail polish or make-up. We were to respect our teachers and others in authority, as well as our peers and ourselves. Since people of the island identified us by our uniforms, we were told to respect our uniforms by obeying all the rules of the school.

The classrooms at St. Joseph's were much larger than the ones at Mainland High, with no more than thirty students to a classroom. There was a large schoolyard with benches located under the trees, two mangoes, a nutmeg and a few others, along with an area where we practiced sports like track and field and net ball. On the grounds, yards apart from the school, there was also a convent, a large house used as living quarters for the nuns. It was mandatory that we attend mass once a week at the Catholic church located within walking distance.

"Lord, I needed something like this in my life to regain my self-esteem," I thought. The discipline of the rules was good for me. It was trying, but I did everything within my power to obey, because I felt proud of being part of that school. I was no longer fighting, and I refrained from swearing, even when I was provoked. I knew I could not afford to have any negative comments about me reaching the nuns. I was able to be good, as I wanted to be.

Lorraine was another student who had taken the entrance exam with me, and she and I were placed at a higher grade level than the other children we had outscored on the exam. We were placed in Form 2A (ninth grade) instead of Form 1 (eighth grade). There were two ninth grade classes, Form 2 and Form 2A. According to my understanding, Form 2 was the class with the smarter children. Wanting to be a part of that smarter class, I resolved in that first semester to dedicate my whole effort to my studies. I succeeded in being placed in the class with the smarter children. Lorraine seemed to have similar determination, for she too was placed in Form 2.

After being placed in Form 2 with the supposedly smarter children, I realized that my present classmates were more competitive, but not necessarily smarter, than my former classmates. It was the competition for academic excellence that motivated each of them to do her best. On our exams, a student with an average score of 4.00 ranked first, 3.99 second, and 3.98 third. The difference between the student ranked first and the one ranked tenth was a mere nine hundredths of a point! I never ranked first, but most of the time I ranked in the top ten. Perhaps I could have done better with more favorable conditions, but I did my very best under the circumstances. It was a daily struggle for me to stay in school and do well. I believe no other child in the class lived under the conditions I did. Traveling to and from school an hour each way was one thing, but living in my mother's home and among the villagers was quite another. Most of my schoolmates lived among friendly people and in peaceful homes without having numerous chores assigned to them. When we had had discussions during our free period, they would talk about their parents and villagers. I, on the other hand, lived among people consumed with envy and in a home filled with violence. Mr. Phillips and my mother still argued and fought all the time, violence often erupting when I was doing my homework. Sometimes I went to bed without completing my work and had to get up even earlier the next morning to finish it. I could start my schoolwork at night only after assisting my siblings with their schoolwork and preparing them for bed. My sister Marge did some chores around the house and did her own schoolwork, but she did not assist the others. She seemed not to have much interest in her own education, let alone our other siblings. Jerald, five years my junior, May, Sonia, Rox and Marge attended the elementary school in the village, and Tyrone and Nikki were too young to attend school. Since we had no electricity, we used oil-burning lamps for light. There were times when the lamps would give off soot that got into my nostrils. When I cleaned out my nostrils the next morning, I removed soot as black as the ceilings of the kitchens where a wood fire was used for cooking. I also had to iron my uniform with an iron heated by coal. I had to clean the bottom of the iron before using it, rubbing it with a piece of cloth to make sure that no black coal remained to soil my uniform, especially my white blouse. Many times I washed my only pair of socks at night hoping that they would dry before morning. If they didn't, I wore them to school the next day, wet as they were. I was also bothered by false rumors that some of the villagers continued to spread about me. I spent many sleepless nights worrying that the rumors would spread to my school, ruining the good reputation I tried so hard to build there. These were some of the many difficulties I faced in my first year attending St. Joseph's Convent. It was a rough year, but I survived it. At the end of the year, I was promoted to Form 3, the next highest ranked class.

I was more determined than ever to stay in school. I was not about to be like Helena, a former student at my school. Helena was the first child from my village ever to attend St. Joseph's Convent. I was the second. Rumor had it that Helena had been expelled from school because of her behavior, but I never knew for sure. After her expulsion, Helena was accepted at a technical school and attended there, but apparently her behavior did not change. I was determined not to follow in her path. My intention was to obey the rules, strive for academic excellence, and graduate. Although my first year in school had been difficult, I had overcome the difficulties and managed to stay in school. But I knew there would be even more difficulties ahead.

During my second year at St. Joseph's, Kyle wrote to say he had to stop his financial assistance, as he was now unemployed, but he promised to resume his assistance as soon as he found work. It was some time before Kyle was able to find employment again, but my grandmother managed to come up with extra money to replace Kyle's contribution. Instead of working in the fields with the other villagers, my grandmother began working for the government repairing the village road. She had an ulcer on her foot that caused her excruciating pain, especially at night, when she would cry out in her sleep from the intense pain. Always in pain, my grandmother would bandage her ulcer and go to work. She had to carry a container of sand on her head, walking barefoot all day, as she helped in the mending of the road. My grandmother undertook this work as a means of supporting her household and herself, but mostly to finance my education. Although I was grateful to my grandmother for her support, I felt guilty that she had to do such hard work for my sake. I knew she wanted me to succeed as much as I wanted to myself, and I felt I couldn't let her down.

By the time I was fifteen years old, my mother had given birth to eight children, including me. She seemed to be having more financial difficulty at that time, and I came to understand why she and Mr. Phillips argued and fought constantly. Mr. Phillips had a new girlfriend, as young as I was, or perhaps even younger. His girlfriend had been a student at the village school I had attended, where she had been in a lower grade than I. When Mr. Phillips began his relationship with this other girl, he started to neglect his financial responsibility at home. Consequently, there were times when my mother had no money to buy enough food for her children. Knowing the circumstances, I went to school many times without asking her for lunch money.

God bless my friend, Jennifer, who shared her lunch with me on days when I didn't have money to buy my own. Jennifer lived on the other side of the island. She befriended me when she learned I lived in the village where her father had been born. Jennifer, shorter than I, was light-complexioned and had beautiful, sleepy-looking eyes. I did not smile or speak much at school, but Jennifer was friendly and smiled constantly. She was one of the kindest people I have ever met. Jennifer's father, Mr. Bobb, was a soft-spoken man, and a religious one. Jennifer and he looked alike. Mr. Bobb earned good wages as a professional builder, and he gave Jennifer and me equal amounts of money to buy our lunch whenever he met us on our way to lunch. Mr. Bobb treated me like his own daughter. He seemed to me the ideal father. There were times when I wished he were my father, or that my father were like him.

My lunches usually consisted of bread and butter, with an eight-ounce mauby drink, a beverage made from the bark of the mauby tree, boiled in water with added sugar. This drink cost less than a soda and for me, with hardly any money, buying a soda was out of my question. Jennifer seemed to be financially well off. Her daily lunch consisted of bread and cheese with a soda, at twice the cost of my own lunch. On days when I had no money for lunch, Jennifer would buy two portions of bread and butter with two mauby drinks for both of us. She was a kind-hearted and caring friend to me, and throughout our school years we were not just school friends, but more like inseparable sisters.

I continued my progress in school, inspired by teachers who showed great interest in our educational goals. God bless those teachers! I remember once not having textbooks for two of my classes, my family at that time not being able afford them. Miss Stage noticed that I had no textbook for her French class. It so happened that the other textbook I did not have was for Geography, which she also taught. At the end of French class, she asked why I did not have the textbook, and I told her my parents could not afford the textbooks just then, but I hoped they would be able to soon. When she asked what other textbooks my parents were unable to buy, I told her about the Geography book. Miss Stage promised to get the books for me, and when she returned from lunch that day, she gave me the two textbooks free of charge. I accepted the books gratefully and thanked her, saying that the cost of those two books was one expense my grandmother and mother would not have to worry about. Needless to say, I did my very best in Miss Stage's classes, and I ranked high at the end of the marking period. I felt this was another way of showing my appreciation to Miss Stage for the generosity she had shown me.

Mr. Cato was another teacher who motivated us to do our very best in his classes. He certainly got the utmost out of me in his English literature class. Mr. Cato was an excellent teacher who used his teaching techniques very effectively. I consider him the best teacher I ever had in high school. His assignments usually were to write about and critique chapters we had read for class. After grading our assignments, he would read them out in class, in the presence of all of our classmates, criticizing them and pointing out their weaknesses. We students felt humiliated when he pointed out the incorrect grammar we had written. I remember feeling such humiliation when I had written "could of" instead of "could have." Mr. Cato stood in front of the classroom, lowered his eyeglasses, and informed my classmates that he was about to read my essay. At one point, he lowered his glasses even more and stared at me. He asked how I could have written "could of" and where on earth I had ever seen such a verb. "I am sure you have seen sentences with 'could have,'" he said, "but I am equally sure you have never seen 'could of' written anywhere as proper English. You should have known better than to write a sentence like that." I felt deeply ashamed that day. I wished I could have become invisible to my schoolmates. Nevertheless, in spite of my embarrassment, I learned a valuable lesson that day and never again wrote "could of" in the future. I came to appreciate Mr. Cato's criticisms, and I am quite sure many of my schoolmates did, too. Most of the teachers gave us fair grades for our work, but some teachers seemed to give grades based on the social status of students' families rather than on their actual performances.

We lived in a society with a subtle class structure. There were teachers who believed that students whose parents were politically connected and held high positions in the white collar professions were smarter academically than children like me, whose parents worked as laborers in the lowest of jobs. As a result, these teachers tended to grade our work unfairly. They would often give children like me an average grade for superior work, and we dared not question them and risk being perccived as being disrespectful.

Being disrespectful of a teacher was cause for suspension from school, or even expulsion. Children who felt they had been graded unfairly talked about it among only themselves, fearing it was not in their best interest to challenge their teachers.

Dealing with unfair grading was nothing compared to what I had to deal with when two new girls from my village started to attend St. Joseph's Convent. For my first year in school, nothing from my home or village had followed me to St. Joseph's Convent. No one there knew anything about me except what I told them, which was very little. Then the next year Winnet and Judith came. They were both in lower ranked classes than I, even though Judith was older. I feared sharing a friendship with girls from my village, so I did not speak to Judith and Winnet, and I assumed they wished to keep their distance from me as well. Although I was the girl who had cursed and fought with other children, I now no longer had the anger within me that had caused me act that way. I felt that I was now able to contain myself and refrain from doing the destructive things I had done before.

My behavior at home was quite different. In school, I behaved like any other student, but, God, in the village I had to struggle to contain myself. As much as I tried not to be part of the goings-on in the village, many of the villagers were involving me without my consent! They continued to accuse me of getting pregnant and having abortions, and I found that Winnet and Judith were spreading those same rumors about me at school. These two girls became my worst nightmares. Fortunately, I had schoolmates who could support me. My schoolmates would tell me what the two girls had said about me, and some of them even heckled the girls in my defense. In spite of it all, I continued to progress academically in school, much more than my two nemeses. While they were failing and had to repeat their forms, I passed and was promoted, reaching Form 4 by the end of 1972.

The girls and even some of the mothers in the village seemed to resent my academic progress, and a few of the mothers even tried to get me expelled from school. Sister Agatha, the principal of St. Joseph's Convent at the time, although a very strict disciplinarian, was fair above all. I remember the time when miniskirts became fashionable and many students, including myself, hemmed up our skirts above our knees. Sister Agatha warned us that our skirts were to extend four inches below the knee and that any of us with shorter skirts should hem them to the proper length. Many of us did not heed the warning and continued to wear short skirts. After lunch one day, she ordered us to stand in line in the schoolyard. It was a hot, sticky day, with steam rising from the paved area of the schoolyard where we stood. We were sweaty from the blistering heat of the sun, and the steam from the paved area penetrated the soles of our shoes and made our feet hot, but we stood there obediently. Our teachers, all prim and proper, applied tape measures to our skirts to see which were too short. Those girls with skirts of proper length were sent back to their classrooms, while the majority, including me, remained standing in line in our short skirts, fearing our punishment. At last Sister Agatha, with her hands or her hips, ordered us to rip apart the hems of our skirts. Some students had two or more hems in their skirts, and they had to rip out all of them. Many of us now suddenly found ourselves sporting skirts to our ankles. Many of us had to walk to the school buses parked a mile from the school, and others a greater distance home, while children from other schools mocked us and called us "grandmother." As ordered, we returned to school the following day with our skirts hemmed to the correct length. That was Sister Agatha. She meant business, and we knew it.

Whenever Sister Agatha called you to her office, you could assume you were in trouble. I had never been called to her office before, so when I received the summons I was surprised and could not imagine what I had done wrong. I entered her office in fear, wondering what I could have done. She told me to have a seat in the chair across from her desk. I was nervous, even though I knew I had not done anything wrong. When Sister informed me of the contents of an anonymous letter she had received from someone in my village, I got even more nervous and felt a chill throughout my body. The letter described me as a woman (a bad name to call a child) and a whore and accused me of being pregnant at that time. She also told me that two mothers from the village had visited her at the school and told her that I had had several abortions. Sobbing uncontrollably the whole time, I denied it all. Surprising myself, I broke my long silence, telling Sister Agatha the true facts of my experience, including being raped many times by pedophiles in my village. I even told her that there were days when I came to school without having had anything to eat, believing that my only hope for a better life was a sound education. I also confided to her that I had never been able to tell anyone before, because I was afraid no one would believe me. Sister listened to me very attentively until I was finished talking. Then she got up from her chair, walked to where I sat, and placed one hand on my shoulder. With the other hand she wiped the tears from her eyes with a handkerchief. "Pray my child," she said, "pray. Child, we cannot wipe away all of the evil and envy of the world, but we can pray about them." I listened to her, and I knew I was about to do some serious praying to God. After all, religious education was part of our school curriculum. We were at least as serious about religion as we were about our academic studies. Sister continued to console me as I cried. She encouraged me to continue striving for academic excellence, telling me to feel free to come to her if I ever felt a need. Sister's words of comfort and her belief in me gave me the strength to carry on in the difficult times to come.

I was fifteen or sixteen years old. As my body was changing, so were my thoughts and my understanding of my environment. In school, some girls talked about their relationships with boys they called their boyfriends. Whenever we had a free class period, we would sit under one of the mango trees in groups, with books in our hands, pretending to be studying, but instead conversing with one another about our boyfriends. I had no boyfriend and was not sexually active with anyone. Having been raped repeatedly as a child, I was much too afraid of men to get involved with such boy-girl relationships as my peers talked about. Nevertheless, I participated in the conversation, pretending that I too had a boyfriend. I said I was doing whatever the other girls claimed to be doing, because I wanted to be part of the crowd. I wonder how many other girls were like me, saying things that were not true just to impress the group.

In the village, girls my age and even younger were having relationships with boys that resulted in pregnancies. Some of my schoolmates got pregnant and had to leave school without graduating. I did not intend to have children, so the idea of getting pregnant seemed very remote to me. I wanted to graduate high in the class and be employed in a job with a good salary, perhaps becoming a teacher. In no way was I about to risk my future prospects by getting involved with some man and having him get me pregnant. Although I continued to wrestle with those thoughts, time brought about some changes in me.

It appeared as though the relationships between young ladies and young men varied a great deal. Sometimes a young man would ask the parents of a young lady for permission to have an intimate relationship with their daughter. If the parents granted permission, the boy and girl would have an open relationship—the boy would not have to hide and sneak around to talk to or be with the girl. The parents, in return, expected him to marry their daughter at a later time, especially if she were to become pregnant. Needless to say, many young ladies got pregnant, but far fewer marriages resulted.

In other cases, a girl had to keep her relationship with her boyfriend secret. She had to speak to her boyfriend surreptitiously, fearing that if her parents knew about her relationship, they would either throw her out of the house or beat and curse at her. I was not about to have this kind of relationship with a boy, in part because my mother would beat me, but most of all because I feared getting thrown out of the house and not graduating from high school. As a precaution, I would curse at any boy who tried to start a relationship with me. But, oh, how time and age can change things and they certainly changed me! Lord, time and age completely changed my way of thinking.

One young man in my village in particular, Andrew, was pursuing me. I cursed him as I had cursed the other boys, but unlike the others, he did not leave me alone. After a while, I gave in to Andrew and decided to start a courtship with him. Before Andrew, I had been friendly with Kenneth, who lived in another village. Kenneth would come to my village or meet me at the crossroads outside the village, where we would stand and talk. Some people spread rumors we were having an intimate relationship, but we were only friends. With Andrew it was different.

Andrew was well-built, tall, with a chocolate-colored complexion and smooth skin. Had he been a girl, there was no doubt in my mind that he would not have been able to grow long hair, because his hair was nappy looking. He spoke with a speech impairment. Andrew had graduated from high school and was already working as a teacher at the school in the village where we both lived. I heard rumors that he was having an intimate relationship with a female teacher who worked there with him, but he denied it. As he began to pursue me, I continued to question him. Instead of answering my questions, he would ask me why he would want to spend time with me if he had another girlfriend. Because of my distrust in people, especially the villagers, I did not believe the rumors about Andrew. Being naive, I saw no problem in starting a relationship with him.

I liked Andrew because he would always inquire about my school. He sometimes helped me with my schoolwork, encouraging me to do my best so that I could graduate and find a good job. The nuns at school warned us about the dangers and evils associated with boys and the sweet nonsense they talked. They told us to stay away from men and concentrate on our studies. Andrew did talk lots of sweet nonsense, trying to make me believe I was the only woman in the world for him. Although I knew such talk was deceitful, I was flattered by the things he said to me, and I loved to have him repeat them. Andrew and I were not yet doing the things other girls in school claimed to be doing with their boyfriends. Although we were becoming close, I was afraid to go beyond friendly conversation. I had my own reasons to fear men, and I focused more on my education than on romantic relationships.

I wished that school would never close for vacation, because it was the best place for me to be. Jennifer and I continued our sisterly friendship. Saline also became our friend, but she was closer to Jennifer than to me. Saline was the shortest and most attractive of the three of us, academically accomplished, too, but quite a character. She loved men and money. She was someone you would not leave for long in the same room with your boyfriend, for fear that your boyfriend would become hers instead. The three of us lunched together every day, and we confided in each other. I told them that my education was a financial burden to my grandmother and my mother and that my mother's relationship with Mr. Phillips saddened me.

Mr. Phillips was continuing to mistreat my mother, and his physical abuse of her had escalated. It troubled me that she stayed with such an abusive man and continued to bear his children, a newborn every two years. Neither Mr. Phillips nor his girlfriend had any respect for my mother. He spent many nights with his girlfriend, in an old house not far from where my mother lived, and he fed her food which my mother had cooked. My mother continued to take out her frustration on me and my brothers and sisters, but I got the worst of her abuse. Lord, my mother would curse at me as though I was nothing, and she continued to beat me for the simplest of things. I did what I could for my siblings because I wanted them to be like me and pursue their education, assisting them with their schoolwork every evening, regardless of how much work of my own I had to do. I also continued to make academic progress, knowing that my grandmother and my mother had to make daily sacrifices to finance my education. I went to school wearing shoes with holes in their soles. I had no problem wearing them outdoors on sunny days, but on rainy days my shoes and socks would get wet. Sometimes I would wear those wet socks all day long, letting them dry on my feet as they would. I needed new shoes, but since I knew my mother and grandmother couldn't afford them, I didn't ask for them.

It often seemed that I would have to drop out of school for financial reasons, but thanks to Mr. Samson, who had a store in the village, I was able to continue. The villagers patronized Mr. Samson's store more than other stores in the village. On Saturdays, many villagers filled the store, each waiting an hour or more to purchase their groceries for the week. On one such Saturday, as I stood among the other villagers waiting my turn, Mr. Samson asked me to step behind the counter and help him with the orders. Hesitantly, I did so, and remained until nighttime, when most of the customers had departed with their supplies.

Mr. Samson asked that I return the next day to assist him again, and I did so, working until midday, the closing time for all stores on Sundays. He offered me a regular job working in his store on weekends, and I accepted. I never knew what my wages were, because he gave the money directly to my mother, and she never told me how much I earned, nor did I ever ask her. I also never asked her for as much as a penny of my wages, because I knew she was helping to support my education.

Mr. Samson and Ms. Freda lived together with their children. Like Mr. Phillips and my mother, they were not married, and Mr. Samson spent time with other women. Their oldest child, Lorraine, who was the same age as I but attended a different high school, began working with me in her father's shop a few weeks later.

I immediately sensed Ms. Freda's disapproval of me. Noting that she pretended not to hear me when I said hello to her and sensing her resentment of me, I stayed away from her. I discovered that Ms. Freda and my mother were not on speaking terms, but for what reason I did not know. Whenever my mother came to the store, the two would ignore one another. Ms. Freda would roll her eyes at my mother, acting as though she hated the very ground my mother walked on. I concluded that she resented me simply because I was the child of her enemy.

Mr. Samson praised me for my skill at arithmetic and asked me to audit his book of creditors. After I showed him my findings, he patted me on the shoulder and said, "Smart, you should do well in life." Lorraine saw her father praise me and appeared to resent it, even though she remained friendly with me. Ms. Freda told Lorraine in my presence that her father was acting as though he were my father. I wanted to tell my mother about her remark, but I didn't do it, as I did not want to be the cause of their cursing each other.

I had nothing but the utmost respect for Mr. Samson, who encouraged me to study hard in school and to be the best person I could be. I was therefore devastated by the rumors spread by Ms. Freda that I was having an affair with him. I wanted to quit my little weekend job, but I knew I could not afford to lose the money I earned. I was confused. I failed to understand why Ms. Freda would intentionally make up and spread such a falsehood about me. At that time I needed a friend to confide in but was afraid to trust anyone. Somehow, Andrew became the trusted friend that I needed.

Our friendship led to a deeper relationship between us. On many evenings he would wait at the crossroads outside the village for my arrival in the school bus, and then we would walk to the village together. After several months of courtship, he would wait for me to get off from work on Saturday nights and walk with me until we neared my mother's house, where we would steal a kiss in the dark before I hurried home. I knew my mother would beat the hell out of me when she found out about my relationship with Andrew, and that is exactly what happened.

My mother was sitting on her veranda when I returned from school one evening. I knew something was wrong when I said hello and she did not respond. "Let me tell you something. Me har that you hav a man, and if you hav a man that mean that you ah a woman. Two woman can't live in one house, and me ah the only woman in this house," my mother said to me in an angry voice Before I knew it, she was pounding my face with slaps. I would have liked my mother to ask me about my relationship with Andrew instead of cursing and slapping me, but we had never spoken even about my anatomy, let alone about having a relationship with someone of the opposite sex.

I remember that when I started my period, she said with sarcasm that I could go and tell my friends if I wanted to. I knew she meant that I shouldn't tell my friends, but I told my friends anyway. My friends were the ones who educated me about my periods and the other things I was sure most of the mothers, like my own mother, would never discuss with their teenage daughters. There was nothing I could say or do to my mother that evening when she cursed and slapped me, and I wondered why she didn't fight back and slap Mr. Phillips in the same way when he abused her. After all, I did nothing to her that warranted this type of treatment, but Mr. Phillips did. He was the one who continued to abuse her, and it appeared that he was spending more time with his other woman than he was spending at home with her. Arlene, the other woman, seemed to have power over my mother, because she was now appearing at my mother's gate to curse her. I wondered why my mother didn't slap her as she had slapped me.

Mr. Phillips was renovating the house where we lived into one with walls and glass windows. When the men began their work on the house, we spent the days there, but my mother, my siblings, and I slept with Tanty Inis in her house until our house was completely renovated. Tanty Inis was a family friend not related to us. She was light complexioned, short, soft-spoken, and very religious. She had been our Sunday school teacher for many years, the first to teach many village children about God and the Bible. Tanty Inis lived alone near my family, and she was more than happy to have our company during the nights. It was at her house that I met her sister, Edna.

Edna, who resided in the United States, was on vacation in St. Vincent and visiting Tanty Inis when I met her. The two looked alike, even in the glasses they wore, and both were religious. When we were all introduced to her, she seemed more interested in me than in my siblings. When she inquired about my grades in school, I showed her one of my report cards. No one had ever congratulated me about my grades as Edna did that night. Before the end of the week I heard her talking to my mother about adopting me.

"Adopting me?" I thought. "Does she think I am an orphan? Why does she want to adopt me? I don't want to be adopted by her." These thoughts went through my mind as I overheard the conversation between Edna and my mother. But when I heard Edna say something about my immigrating to the United States, my attitude quickly changed. "Well," I thought, "if she wants me to live in the United States with her, that's a different matter." I had heard people say that America offered lots of opportunities, particularly for an education. If I were to immigrate to America, I would attend a university and become a lawyer, and then I could come back to St. Vincent and prosecute pedophiles who raped and molested children. I liked the idea of being able to put those suckers in jail, where they belonged, locked up and kept away from children. I had heard that jail cells were hot, sticky, and smelly and that the jailbirds were confined by iron bars and were not allowed to bathe frequently, their meals consisting of dry bread and sugar water. I also heard that there were lots of rats, big as cats, that crept all over the jailbirds' bodies when they slept. Sending those suckers to jail would be the best thing I would ever do in my life, and it would be no more than fair.

I answered yes when Edna asked me whether I would like to live in America with her. I even answered yes when she asked if I would like her to adopt me. The truth was that I was no damn orphan and I really did not want to be adopted by anyone, but I would readily agree to Edna's adopting me if it were the only opportunity for me to get to America. Although I would hate to leave my grandmother and my siblings behind, I wouldn't miss repeated verbal and physical abuses of my mother, and I certainly wouldn't miss living among the wicked, devious, envious people of this village. I wanted to get as far away from them as I could.

Edna explained to me that I should keep working hard in school because good grades would make it easier for me to get into a school in America. Edna claimed that she wanted to help me so I would be able to help my family and myself. She said Ma Letteen had been very kind to her family when she was a little girl, and her sending for me in America was a way of showing her gratitude. She said it would be easier for me to immigrate in to America if she adopted me. After my conversation with Edna, I was full of enthusiasm and was even more motivated than before to excel in school.

School meant everything to me. When I was in school, I felt I could become the person I wanted to be. I wanted to be a good student, and that I was, but I wanted to have fun as well. That was why I participated in a class play where I portrayed the relationship I had with my great-grandmother, Ma Letteen. I played the role of Ma, portraying her teaching me the Our Father and brushing my teeth. I made sure that I included the episode of her sending me to buy rum. At the end of the show my classmates congratulated me on my performance, and I was happy. But it was what Sister Agatha said to me when she congratulated me that I would always remember. She told me I would be a great actress and that I should become involved with drama and theater. I had no idea what she was talking about, and I didn't ask her to explain.

Jennifer, Saline and I remained the best of friends and continued to confide in each other. Because our school was for girls only and we went from form to form with practically the same girls from the day we started school, we three got to know one another well. We were all young ladies, but each with a different view of our lives. We would sit and talk about the good and bad in our lives and confide our hopes for the future. Many of the other girls were in serious relationships with their boyfriends, hoping to marry and have children in the future. I felt I couldn't say much about my life, since I knew my life was no Bible story. I couldn't tell even my best friend Jennifer about the sexual abuse I had endured, let alone my other classmates. Then when Amy got pregnant, I realized that I was not the only girl in our school who had been sexually molested.

Amy's mother had immigrated to England in search of a better life, probably before Amy began attending high school. In those days people went to England without their children. After they found work and were able to send for their children, most of them did so, especially the mothers. Amy's mother had left Amy and her younger sister in the care of an aunt, sending home money to support them. Amy's aunt was married to an unscrupulous man who repeatedly raped Amy, as the scumbags in my village had raped me. But Amy did not keep her rapes secret, as I had. She reported her molestation to her aunt. The aunt defended her husband, called Amy a liar, and did nothing about her complaint. After Amy got pregnant, it became apparent that Amy's uncle had raped her younger sister, Jose, as well. Poor Amy had to drop out of school, and it was said that she wouldn't be able to conceive another child because of the damage done to her reproductive organs.

Amy's story spread rapidly through the school and the community. We all felt sympathy for Amy, and I wondered how many others had been victims of sexual molestation. I knew about myself, but I wondered who else might be like me, with the same thoughts and fears going through their minds. These new hormones were changing our bodies and our lives. From what I heard in school and saw happening in the village with girls my age, I could only imagine the effect these changes might have on our bodies. The girls in school talked more about sex and many became sexually active. It must have been the same for the girls in my village, for many who were younger than I were having babies. I was no different from the other girls my age, going through the same hormonal changes.

I blame the hormonal changes in my body for the fact that I no longer ignored Andrew's pleas for us to become sexually involved. He taught me about condoms and the other precautions he would use not to get me pregnant, but I was still afraid. I was haunted by the childhood memories that tormented my soul. Some of my schoolmates talked about how enjoyable having sex was to them, but I couldn't imagine what was enjoyable about it. My sexual experiences had been crude and painful and I wasn't about to endure such pains again. Andrew was persistent about our having sex, just as he had been persistent about our having a relationship, and I never told him why I was afraid to have sex.

Jennifer confided to me that she had had sex once, and our friend Saline was already sexually involved with a former boyfriend and her present boyfriend. Lorraine, Mr. Samson's daughter, told me she had had sex with a couple of young fellows, and I was dumfounded when she told me of her sexual relationship with an older man, one of her father's friends. This man drove a passenger bus. He would pick up Lorraine from school and drive her to his home, where they would have sex together. Lorraine's account of her relationship with this man old enough to be her father bothered me a great deal. "Yes," I thought, "I have a boyfriend, but Andrew is not as old as my father, and he certainly is not my father's friend.

Andrew continued to await my arrival on the school bus at the crossroads outside of the village, and we continued to walk to the village together. We also saw each other on the village road every Saturday night after I got off from work, where we continued to kiss each other in the dark. As Andrew continued to press me to have sex with him, the time came when I could no longer refuse. I met him at his friend's room, as we had planned, where he was patiently waiting for my arrival. I was scared as hell. Andrew and I kissed passionately. When I saw him unzipping his pants, I began to tremble and cry. I wanted to get up and flee, but I didn't. He told me not to be scared because he would take care of me. He assured me he would never get me pregnant, not now anyway, not until I graduated from high school and we were married. By this time, the hormones in my body had already assumed control of my emotions and my sex organs. Although my mind told me not to do it, I couldn't resist the urge, so I did it. I lay motionless in the bed the whole time. Although he was gentle, I cried through the entire ordeal. I can't say whether I enjoyed it or not, because I was more concerned about not getting pregnant than about pursuing the pleasure my friends had told me about. I closed my eyes just as I had done during my rapes. Andrew, on the other hand, seemed to have enjoyed himself. But I was still crying when he finished.

The rapists had left me crying after they finished, but Andrew did not. He stayed with me, hugging me and wiping the tears from my eyes. Andrew assured me that I was not pregnant because he had used a condom. He apologized to me for doing this "sex thing" with me and said I did not have to do it again if I didn't want to. He promised he would never force me. He never got the opportunity to force me, because my life changed that day. Before then, I had been afraid of sex and of men. Now, I grew to love the man who called me his girlfriend and whom I called my boyfriend. Because I trusted him, I would give my body to him freely.

From that day on, Andrew and I continued to have sex. Although school was still my first priority, I found time to be with him. I fell in love with him, or so I perceived it, and I discussed my deepest thoughts and feelings with him—but not my childhood sexual molestation. He was a good listener and I found in him a true friend and lover, to whom I would give my body as often as he needed it. I was doing it not so much because I wanted to, but because I thought he would stay with me forever if I gave him my body. I was happy with him and didn't want to lose him, at least not then. It was for this reason that I did not respond to Edna's letter when she wrote to me asking if I was still interested in immigrating to the United States. When Edna wrote another letter asking the same question, I replied without answering her question, telling her instead how well I was doing in school. This letter she did not answer. The fear of my mother's physical abuse no longer kept me from being seen openly with Andrew, and I was glad not to have to be sneaking around with him. Our friendship grew and we were seen as a couple, friendly with other couples in the village. Through this friendships with other couples, I became friendly with two sisters in the village, Lynette and Jasmine.

Lynette, the older of the two sisters, was secretly having an intimate relationship with one of Andrew's friends. The relationship that Jasmine was having with her boyfriend, Randy, probably twelve years her senior, was no secret. Randy had requested and received permission from Jasmine's mother, Miss Curtis, to have a relationship with Jasmine. In granting him permission to date Jasmine, I am sure Miss Curtis was expecting Randy to marry Jasmine should she become pregnant. Jasmine, Lynette, and I went out with Andrew, Randy and other couples. Without neglecting my schoolwork, I enjoyed this period of my life, partying and drinking lots of alcoholic beverages. I realize it was all an effort to escape the pain I suffered from the violence between Mr. Phillips and my mother. When they started to curse and fight, I would walk to the village looking for Andrew. He was my refuge.

When I returned home, my mother would sometimes beat me. One day I became fed up with my mother's physical abuse and decided to take a stand. It happened when she began to beat on me after I had returned from seeing Andrew. I told her to stop and she didn't. I was furious. "Stop hitting me! If you don't stop, I will hit you back!" I shouted at my mother, and I was serious. Believe it or not, my mother stopped hitting me, and she never beat me again after that day. After that I began to spend more time with Andrew, thinking that if I spent more time with Andrew and had sex more regularly with him, he would love me more. I was looking for someone to love me and thought Andrew was the one to do it. I couldn't wait to get back to school to tell Jennifer and Saline what had transpired with my mother. When I told them I had threatened to hit my mother back if she ever hit me again, Jennifer became angry. She said that I had been disrespectful to my mother, and she urged me not to do it again. Saline only laughed and asked whether I thought my mother would beat me again.

Jennifer also had a boyfriend she would sneak off to see, but Saline played a different game, having two boyfriends at the same time. Although we both warned Saline not to get involved with two men at the same time, she did not listen to us. Other girls in my village who attended other high schools were having intimate relationships with boys, too. Some of them did it secretly, while others were more open about it. Some girls were said to leave home dressed in their uniforms as if they were going to school, then spend the day with their boyfriends instead. That was something I vowed never to do. I loved Andrew, but the idea of spending time with him when I should be in school was abhorrent to me. I knew that Andrew was not the kind of guy who would encourage me to do such a thing.

One day Mr. Samson confronted me about my relationship with Andrew, telling me that education should be my first priority, not boys. A few weeks later, he fired me for reasons unknown to me. I can only assume it was because he did not approve of my relationship with Andrew. Little did he know that his own daughter was having a relationship with one of his best friends and was also sexually involved with another guy. Even though I wondered what he would say to Lorraine if he found out about her goings-on, I knew he would never hear these things from me, in any event.

In due course, Lorraine got pregnant and was thrown out of school and her father's home as well. She was not the only girl in my village to get pregnant while attending high school. Lorraine's cousin got pregnant, too. Then one of my classmates got pregnant and was expelled from school. It was the rule that girls who became pregnant while attending school were expelled. That was the law of the land. But the law protected the guys. It took no account of the guys attending school who got these girls pregnant. There was nothing in this world I feared more than the prospect of getting pregnant while attending high school. Every time I discussed my fears with Andrew, he assured me it would never happen as long as I was with him. His word was good enough for me.

It seems that some of the mothers in the village continued to wish the worst for me. I remember Miss Freda cursing to my mother that my turn was near at hand (to get pregnant). I often related to Andrew that most of the mothers in the village did not like me, as shown by their character assassination of me. Andrew and I would take pleasant walks together almost every Sunday. One Sunday he seemed to be behaving differently. After we walked silently together for awhile, he stopped and stared at me, saying, "Believe me, I will never get you pregnant while you are still in school. I promise I will never do that." "Why are you saying these words to me now?" I asked, having noticed a difference in his tone and demeanor. He seemed worried and spoke with some sadness. "What's wrong, Andrew?" I pressed him. He took my hands in his own and assured me of his love, saying, "I want you to graduate from high school as much you want to." I was confused, seeing no point in this conversation, since we had discussed it all before.

"Andrew, tell me what's bothering you," I pleaded. Then he told me about Miss Freda and Mrs. Thompson.

Andrew had been on his way home from his bath when Miss Freda lured him into the house of Mrs. Thompson, who was known as a mean woman and a troublemaker in the village. Miss Freda was one of the very few people friendly with her. Once they had him inside the house, they told him I was too stuck up and it was time for him to get me pregnant. They patted him on the shoulder and said he had a job that he must do right and soon. Though I was not surprised that these two women would wish me such evil, I felt numb at Andrew's tale. He said that he had walked away from Miss Freda and Mrs. Thompson without uttering a word. As he continued to hold my hands, he assured me that these women's wish for me never would become reality. I later discovered that Miss Freda would go beyond encouraging Andrew to get me pregnant.

When Lynnette, Jasmine, their sister Tammy, their cousin Brenda, and their mother, Miss Curtis, went to another village to visit one of their relatives, I accompanied them there. A few days later, a rumor was spread that we had gone with knives in our hands to fight Lorraine and her two cousins. Suddenly we were "the five tyrants with five knives." I found out that these serious allegations had been made by Miss Freda. When the people in the village would spread rumors that I had been pregnant and had an abortion, when they called me a whore and other names, I was hurt, because I Knew I was no whore. But these new allegations left me devastated. It is true that while I was a student at the village school I had fought with other children. But things were different now. I was a student of this very prestigious school, and with the guidance of my beloved nuns and teachers I had regained some self-esteem. Except for having a relationship with Andrew and living a sociable lifestyle, I was focused entirely on my education. To be accused of fighting someone with a knife could jeopardize my standing at St. Joseph's Convent and my entire future. With a criminal record, no one would hire me as a teacher, and to become a teacher was what I wanted most of all. I was so devastated by this character assassination that I couldn't restrain myself from doing what I best knew how to do. After thinking about what could happen to me if Sister Agatha, the principal, were to hear what had been said about me, I went into my mother's bedroom and began to pray. I prayed and cried so loud that some of my sib-

lings cried with me as they looked on, and my mother began praying for me, too.

A few days later, it became public knowledge that Miss Freda
was the one who had made up the allegations, and thank God, Miss
Curtis was with us the evening we had gone to the other village.
As soon as Miss Curtis became aware of the allegations, she went
about proclaiming our innocence, and the villagers believed her.
She told the villagers that Miss Freda's allegations were a fabrication and that she had accompanied us that evening. Had Miss
Curtis not vindicated us, we might have been in trouble with the
law. Although we were vindicated, I am still puzzled about why
Miss Freda had made up such a story that could have done such
serious damage to all of us. I was even more puzzled when Miss
Curtis remarked that Miss Freda should not have gone so far as to
drag her own children's names into such mischief, as much as she
had wanted to hurt me. I wondered what grounds Miss Curtis had
for believing that Miss Freda wanted to hurt me and why Miss
Freda might want to do me harm.

Lynnette, Jasmine, and I remained friends. Lynnette and
Jasmine continued their relationships with their boyfriends, as I
did with Andrew. Our little group continued to attend parties and
to have a good time drinking and dancing. Then Jasmine got pregnant. Since Miss Curtis had approved of Jasmine's relationship
with Randy, I was taken aback by her reaction. It was the norm for
girls to get pregnant by men with whom they were supposed to be
having those approved relationships. It was also the norm that
most of the men never married the girls, and Jasmine became part
of that group. Miss Curtis had said that Jasmine would never have
gotten pregnant if she had not been friendly with me, and so I felt
partly to blame.

Miss Curtis would not be the only mother to blame me for her
daughter's bad behavior or misfortune. Mrs. Jackson was one of
my mother's friends, and I became friendly with her daughter,
Susan, five years my senior, who went to high school in a different town. Susan was quiet but very sly. Mrs. Jackson may not have
known that Susan was having a relationship with Dwayne, one of
her schoolmates. Susan never told me about this relationship, but
I was aware of it.

One Sunday evening, Susan suggested that we walk together to
the crossroads outside the village. On Sundays, lots of young people, mostly young lovers, took friendly walks together to the vil-

lage crossroads. I agreed to walk with Susan to the crossroads, and, as we were walking, I saw two guys on a motorcycle riding towards us. They stopped when they reached us. I recognized one of the guys as the boyfriend of one of my schoolmates, Joslin. I assumed the other was Susan's boyfriend, since I hadn't met him before. The four of us stood talking for a few minutes before Susan told me she would be back soon. She insisted that I not return to the village until she came back. Then she jumped onto Dwayne's motorcycle, and they drove away. Joslin's boyfriend and I walked the rest of the way to the crossroads together, having a friendly conversation about Joslin, school, and other topics of a humorous nature. We passed more than two hours in this way before Dwayne and Susan finally returned. As we walked back to the village, Susan made me promise never to tell anyone what she had done that afternoon. "Susan, girl, I pledge I won't tell anyone what you just did," I told her. "It is none of my business. Let your fears rest in peace because, baby, your secret is safe with me."

It was not unusual for Mrs. Jackson to be visiting my mother, but I felt uneasy when I saw her sitting on the veranda with my mother one evening as I arrived home from school. I entered the now renovated house, saying hello to both of them. Then Mrs. Jackson said to me, "Lola, ah way you and Susan bin Sunday evening?" "We walked to the crossroads," I replied. "Ah yo walk to the crossroads?" she questioned. "Me har ah yo bin go meet two man Sunday and ah yo bin way pon motto bike with the two man," she said with hands on her hips, staring at me. "I don't know where you got your story, but I stood at the crossroads until we were ready to walk back to the village," I replied. I considered telling her that Susan had gone away with her boyfriend, but I didn't. I still believed that what Susan had done was none of my business, and it was surely none of my business to tell on her to her mother. Mrs. Jackson kept talking and I kept ignoring her, while my mother more or less looked to me to confirm or deny the whole story. I did neither. I went into the house and left both of them standing there. Rumor had it that Mrs. Jackson had said I took Susan to meet some man. So it seems that I was the one to be blamed for Susan's actions, even though I had not been aware of her plans for that evening. Had it not been for Andrew, I don't know what I would have done. I needed him to talk to. I depended on him to comfort me in those troubling times, and he did.

I was grateful to God for answering my many prayers. I believe it was through God's divine intervention that my grandmother and mother were able to finance my education. God had also blessed my Uncle Kyle and my cousin Randy, who found work and were able to contribute financially to my education. I was blessed to have met Jennifer, who fed me when I was hungry, not to mention Sister Agatha, who encouraged me to pray when I was troubled. She could have expelled me from school when those ladies went to her and defamed my character, but she listened to me and understood my pain. I was also grateful to Mr. Samson for hiring me; the wages he paid my mother for my work helped finance my education when assistance was most needed. The negatives in my life while I attended school sometimes overshadowed the positives, but I remained in school and continued to excel academically, and for that I was truly grateful. I continued to attend church on Sunday. That was my way of showing God how grateful I was for making the impossible for me possible.

The Wrath of Betrayal

There were things I would have liked to discuss with my mother but could not, so Andrew became the friend in whom I could confide. We talked about education, relationships, and our anatomy. I felt that I could trust him with my life. He pledged he would not get me pregnant before I finished school, and he honored his pledge. But later when I discovered that Andrew had betrayed the trust I had placed in him, our relationship changed beyond our comprehension. We broke up and vowed never to make up again. But then we resumed our relationship, even though we no longer trusted one other. We faced difficult decisions, and mine were more difficult than his.

Before starting a relationship with me, Andrew had denied having had any involvement with Dawn, a female teacher who worked in the same school as Andrew, and I believed him. After we began our relationship, I had no reason to believe he was having a relationship with another woman. Or maybe I trusted him so much that I could not imagine he would do such a thing. Eighteen months into our intimate relationship, rumors began to spread through the village about his relationship with Dawn, and I became concerned.

I went to Andrew and demanded that he tell me nothing but the truth.

I pressed him until he admitted that he was in a relationship with Dawn, claiming, however, that this relationship was nothing serious. He apparently felt I should be grateful that he had admitted to this relationship and even more grateful that he had assured me that I meant more to him than Dawn or any other woman. "Well, Andrew," I thought, "you betrayed my trust and you will have to pay a price. I will be damned if I am going to sit around like my mother and the other women in this village who stay with their men, or lovers, or whatever you call the sons of bitches, while they have affairs with other women. Some of the stupid asses of women even fight with one another over the men. Are they out of their minds to fight over men who disrespect them all the time?" As to my mother, Mr. Phillips continued to abuse her physically, and I was fed up with all that damn violence. He caused nothing but confusion in our household, and I did not understand why she did not get rid of him. Sadly, every time he abused her, she abused us, her children. Thank God, she no longer beat me, but she continued to curse me and call me names. She would have done better to focus on getting rid of him. Even though he continued to abuse her, she still gave him the biggest piece of meat and the most food when she cooked, and she was not the only woman who treated her abusive man that way. I heard of cases where abused women would give their men all the meat they cooked, while they and their children did without. If I had been in their situation, I would have fed those men doses of their own poison instead. I would have gotten rid of them all, or at least would have fought back. I wondered why these women stayed with their unfaithful men. I would have given them a dose of their own medicine and would have been unfaithful, too. "Well, Andrew," I thought, "I am not about to be part of the statistics in my mother's league of women. I am different from those other women, and I am about to show you how different I am."

"I am different," I thought, " because I am more educated than most of the others living with those cheating men. Andrew, if you can have another woman, I sure enough can have another man, and I don't have to go far looking for him." At that time in my life, a few other guys were interested in having relationships with me. I at first showed no interest in them. Then, when I found out that Andrew was being unfaithful to me, I wanted revenge on him. I felt it was my turn to deal him the hand of unfaithfulness and betrayal that he had dealt me. It might not have been the right way to deal with it, but I knew no other way at the time. So I began a courtship with David, who at the time had a job and a car. Andrew and I used to walk together to the village crossroads on Sundays, but I stopped that after I found out about Dawn. There was a certain time on Sundays when Andrew and his friends would be sitting on a wall in the village, congregating and socializing as they would in a clubhouse. When David asked if he could visit me and take me for a drive one Sunday, I told him to pick me up at a time and place such that Andrew and his friends would be sure to see me. Andrew's friends recognized me in the car with the other man, and from the car's rear-view mirror I could see them laughing at him. I can only imagine what they were saying, but there was no mistaking the sad expression on Andrew's face. I knew he was hurting, but I felt no compassion for him.

That evening, after David had left for home, I was returning to the village when I saw Andrew. He came up to me and asked if he could have a word with me. I stood listening as he asked me questions about David and complained about what I had done. Without remorse, I reminded Andrew that the Bible says, "an eye for an eye and a tooth for a tooth." I let him know that I would see anyone I chose to see. "I am just giving you a dose of your own medicine," I said to him, "and I will continue to see as many men as I please as long as you continue your relationship with Dawn." I walked away, leaving him standing there dumfounded in the shadow of the trees.

When I arrived on the school bus the following day, I was surprised to see Andrew standing at the crossroads. Knowing he had been awaiting my arrival, I began to walk towards the village without acknowledging him. He began to walk along with me, questioning me about David and begging me to stop seeing him. I told him I would stop seeing David on the condition that he stop seeing Dawn. He assured me that Dawn meant nothing to him, claiming that she was the one pursuing him. I listened to him talking all that sweet nonsense to me, that I was the one he was in love with and on and on and on, but I was still so angry I couldn't accept any of it. I had trusted Andrew more than anyone else in the world, and he had hurt me deeply when he betrayed that trust, so I was unwilling to forgive him. I told him it was over between us and walked to the village ahead of him.

The news that Andrew and I had broken up spread quickly through the village. Breaking up with Andrew turned out to be painful for me. I missed him. I don't know why I would miss such a cheating liar of a guy, but I really did. He had been there for me when I needed a friend and had been a good listener. To help fill the void, in my spare time I began to read any book I could get my hands on. I found several books listing the name, age, sex and address of girls and guys seeking friends to correspond with. I began corresponding with several of them who lived on other islands. I was intrigued with the letters I received, and corresponding with my overseas friends became a favorite hobby.

Mr. Phillips seemed to know I was no longer seeing Andrew and must have supposed I was looking for a man, for he began to bring home some guys he was friendly with. He would disappear, leaving me alone with these friends of his, who were all older than I. I couldn't figure out what was going on until one of his friends, Daniel, informed me that Mr. Phillips had given him permission to have a relationship with me. "Holy smokes, you mean to tell me Mr. Phillips gave you permission to start a relationship with me, without my knowledge?" I asked Daniel. Daniel was not a guy who would interest me. I don't think he had ever finished elementary school, and I felt that I was above going with some damned illiterate man. What did an illiterate man have to offer me? The environment surrounding me was full of illiterate folks. The men worked in the fields or did some type of laborer's job, and the women did the same kind of work and had babies almost every year. For me to become one of these women, I would have had to be out of my mind, and I knew I wasn't out of my mind. "Daniel, I don't know what Mr. Phillips told you, but I am not looking for a man," I said to Daniel. "I love you and I will take care of you and we will have a good life together. I will build you a house," Daniel said to me. When he wouldn't stop, I lost my cool and told him I didn't like him and didn't want him to build me a damned house and that he must get the hell out of my damned face. But Daniel was not discouraged. He would send me little gifts like fruit, and one time he even gave me money. I surprised myself by taking it. "If Daniel is stupid enough to give me his money," I thought, "I am smart enough to take it." But I still did not want him. I guess Daniel finally understood that he and I would never have a relationship, for he stopped coming around and sending me gifts.

I couldn't understand why more and more guys were becoming attracted to me, or at least saying they were. I wondered if they were becoming attracted to me because they knew I had given my body freely to Andrew, and they wanted me to give my body freely to them as well. I wasn't about to do that, not even with the guy I was dating.

Andrew was trying to make up with me, but I was now dating Jim, a student in another school less than a half mile from St. Joseph's Convent. We would meet for lunch at one of the many small restaurants less than mile from our school. We would sit at a table for two, and Jim would flatter me, saying my lips were charming and I was more precious to him than gold. His letters were even more flattering. In them Jim would write that he would like to make love to me, caressing and kissing me from the crown of my head to the soles of my feet. Jim had a way with words, making me feel as though he were right there doing these things to me as I was reading his letters. I loved Jim, but not as much as I had loved Andrew. I could not discuss with Jim the things I had discussed with Andrew. Somehow I found him to be immature. Like Andrew, he wanted sex. Jim's pressuring me to have sex with him and my determination not to do so caused me to break up with him and make up with Andrew. My sex drive had not diminished while I had been away from Andrew. Those damn hormones were still around more than ever, controlling my body, driving me to have sex. Poor me! Although my mind was telling me not to do it, I couldn't resist.

Even though I knew that Andrew was continuing his relationship with Dawn, I was comforted that he had pledged not to get me pregnant. So far, he had not broken his promise. Although I felt I could not trust him as before, it was still better to have sex with him and not get pregnant while I was still in school than to risk getting pregnant with someone new. I had heard that women could protect themselves from unwanted pregnancy by inserting some sort of loop into their vagina, but I also had heard that some women had died from it. I had also heard about taking a daily pill to prevent pregnancy, but that only adult women could take the pill. The thought of getting pregnant and not achieving my goal of graduating from high school gave me chills. "If I were to get pregnant," I thought, "I would be doing my grandmother, mother, uncle, and cousins who had struggled to finance my education, an injustice. I could not do that to them, nor could I do it to myself."

I chose instead to make up with Andrew, and, believe me, it pleased him more than it pleased me. This time it was a changed relationship, because I never regained my trust in him. So I never gave him my body freely as I had before, but only when I could not control my urge. I yielded to my own urge, not his.

Somehow, the villagers had ways of knowing other people's business. They were some nosy suckers. I understood that they saw Daniel when he came to visit me. But how the hell they knew I was dating Jim, I'll never know. Jim never visited me in the village; we only saw each other in town. The village girls who attended school in town must have seen me with Jim and come back to the village to spread the news. After the villagers became aware that Andrew and I had made up, all hell broke lose. The mothers and daughters in that village, who despised me for some reason, went out of their way to make my life miserable, some of them calling me a whore. Living among them and the vicious rumors they spread about me was like living with the devil in hell. There were times when I just had to get away from the village and its people.

Our local beach was approximately three miles from the village. Many villagers visited the beach on holidays, and young people my age visited the beach more often, especially when schools were closed for vacation. I used to visit the beach because it was my getaway place, where I loved to watch the waves breaking. Because I could not swim, I did not bathe, but would spend most of my time reading. On arriving at the beach, I would climb a rock where I could sit and observe the ocean as far out as my eyes could see. I would read my book until I couldn't read anymore, and then I would still sit on that rock and look far out into the ocean. In the evening, I would watch the sun sinking peacefully into the horizon, wishing such peace for myself. I would notice the birds flying freely over the horizon, and I would wish to be as free as they were. I would even wish I had their wings, so that I could fly as they were flying, far away, never having to return to the village. Knowing that I was not a bird and would never grow wings, I just continued to sit on the rock and stare at the horizon. I would be overwhelmed by a peaceful feeling deep within me, and I would feel completely free. Then I would find the courage to get up from the rock and walk back to the village to face the envious people again. Sometimes I looked at the villagers and could not help comparing them to those who lived in the cities of Sodom and

Gomorrah. According to what my Sunday school teacher taught me about this Bible story, these people committed so much sin that God finally destroyed them and their cities. "God, the people in this village are sinners and they are evil," I prayed and prayed, time and time again. "They are worse than the people of Sodom and Gomorrah, and God, they are liars and they inflict pain on people without mercy. Lord, they have caused me so much mental stress and anguish. God, destroy this village and its people. Destroy them and the village as you destroyed the people who lived in Sodom and Gomorrah." But God never destroyed the people or the village, and I had no choice but to continue to live among them.

I was seventeen years old when I began to look at my mother's situation from a different perspective. I was beginning to understand her. I could not help feeling that she loved me in spite of all her physical and verbal abuse of me. Instead of hating her, I was beginning to love her and sympathize with her. When I witnessed the abuse that Mr. Phillips committed against her one evening in July, I felt even more sympathy for her.

It was on this evening that Arlene, Mr. Phillips' other woman, came to my mother's gate and began to curse at her and call her names. My mother cursed back, using some of the same language Arlene had used on her. They called one another whores and sluts, each accusing the other of being unfaithful to Mr. Phillips. They even taunted one another by each saying that the other needed to bathe more frequently. Mr. Phillips was not there during this exchange, but I had no doubt that he would hear about it. Later that day, my mother had prepared food for dinner, and Mr. Phillips tried to take some of it to Arlene. My mother tried to prevent him from taking the food, saying he had not given her any money that week to take care of the home. They began to argue, and Mr. Phillips took up an object to strike her with, although I only realized what was happening when my mother began to hold her head. When I saw blood gushing from her head, I realized that Mr. Phillips had clubbed my mother on her head. My mother began to cry. I don't know if she was crying because of the pain or from the humiliation of having that beast of a man had strike her. My mother was pregnant at the time, and my eight siblings and I stood crying as we looked on in horror. I cried for my mother's pain, but most of all because I was unable to do anything to help her. I wished I could have protected her, or at least assisted her to battle against this man. But I was still only a helpless child. From that day, I was more determined than ever not to let myself wind up in the same position as my mother and so many other women like her.

It was my determination not to repeat their experiences that kept me focused on my education. Some girls in my village dropped out of school because of their inability to perform well academically or because they became pregnant, I remained in school and continued to excel. Winnet and Judith did not become pregnancy statistics either, but both of them dropped out for academic reasons. Unfortunately, my success in school brought me more pain, because my enemies in the village did whatever they could to undermine me. One night I dreamt that two black birds had picked out both of my eyes and left me blind. When I awoke from the dream and found my two eyes intact, I was delighted. As a blind person living among my enemies in the village, I could not be expected to survive for long. No doubt if I had turned up blind some of them would have been happy and probably would have given me feces to eat. I had the same dream again every single night for an entire week. I told Jennifer and Saline about my dream and asked whether they might know its meaning, but neither of them had a clue. I told my cousin, Sandra, but she was clueless, too. She said it was not a good dream and that I must stay alert at all times in case some wicked soul was planning to do bodily harm to me. Sandra remained my ever caring and trusted cousin.

On Saturday of that week, my mother asked me to go to town to conduct some business for her. During the week I wore my uniform while attending school in the town, but Saturday was not a school day, so I had to dress in civilian clothes. I did not own much in the way of clothing, but I dressed very neatly at all times. Planning to wear a blouse and skirt to town that day, I searched my mother's house for my blouse, but could not find it anywhere. My mother looked also, and when she could not find it either she panicked. She believed in a superstition that a person could cause harm to others by burying pieces of their clothing in the burial ground. It was supposed that the person whose clothes were buried would get sick, lose a lot of weight, and then die. For that reason, no one left clothes outside at night, and some people even took their wet clothes inside at night instead of leaving them outside on the lines to dry. I had never given this superstition a thought, not until I discovered that my blouse was missing. Now I wondered whether someone had taken my blouse in order to harm me.

Looking further, we realized that my blouse was not the only item missing from my mother's house. Another piece of clothing and some of my books were missing, too. We wondered who could have entered our house and stolen these things. We did not believe it was a mere coincidence that my things were the only ones taken. I began to fear that I would get sick and die.

At that time, I would have welcomed death, because the turmoil in which I lived seemed unbearable. Winnet, Judith, and other girls in the village made fun of me because of Andrew's continuing relationship with Dawn. Andrew would tell me to ignore the gossip and concentrate on my schoolwork, as he always did. It was easy for him to say that to me, but hard for me to do when I knew he was the cause of it all. Yet I loved him more than any other. Among the girls who made fun of me, Judith stood out the most, cursing at me whenever she met me in the street and even threatening to beat me up. I failed to understand Judith's motive, but her behavior towards me seemed similar to that typically shown by a woman of my village towards another women in a relationship with the same man. As far as I knew, I was not in a relationship with the same guy as she was, but there was more there than I knew about. It turned out that Andrew was indeed involved in some sort of sexual relationship with Judith. When I heard the news through the grapevine and felt it had to be true, I had a better understanding of Judith's hostility toward me. Knowing Andrew would never admit to what I had discovered, I broke up with him without confronting him about it. I grew to realize that, except for his not beating women, he was no different from Mr. Phillips and the others.

I began dating a guy named Charles Harding, who lived not far from my mother's house. For the first time in my life, my mother seemed to approve of my having a relationship with a guy. Charles was very mannerly. He asked for and received permission from my mother to talk to me. As Andrew did, he encouraged me to do well in school, but unlike Andrew, he brought me many gifts. Although Charles and I kissed passionately during our three-month relationship, we were never more sexually involved than that. He wanted to wait until I graduated. That was one thing I liked about him, but it would not do for me to stay with him for long.

A talent show and dance were to be held in the village one Saturday night. Some of the guys from another village that rode in the same school bus with me planned to attend. I used to have fun with these buddies of mine, sitting with them in the back of the bus, teasing the girls by pulling their hair and untying their ribbons without their knowing which of us had done it. I looked forward to having fun at the show with these buddies, and most of all to indulge my love for music and dancing.

I told Charles on Friday night that I would be attending the show the following night, but he insisted that I should not go. I felt that I was Charles' girlfriend, not his wife, and even if I had been his wife, I would not have allowed him to tell me what to do. I sensed that he had a strong need to control me, and I was determined not to allow him to do so. "I will go to that show whether he likes it or not," I said to myself.

Charles was dressed for the show and on his way there when he visited me that Saturday night. After he left, I got dressed and went to the show myself. The entertainment hall where the show was being held was packed with villagers. Most performers in the talent show sang various selections, and others who called themselves comedians did comic routines, after which the band began playing calypso, raggae, and soca music. Charles and I ignored each other throughout the entire show, but that did not prevent me from enjoying myself in the company of my school bus buddies, dancing, joking and generally having fun. When the show ended, Charles offered to walk me home. Although my instinct told me to decline his offer, I allowed him to accompany me.

On our way home, he stopped abruptly, stared into my face and said coldly, "I want to know why you attended the show tonight when I told you not to." "Who the hell is he talking too, not me for sure. I'm not his child," I murmured to myself. I ignored his question. I must have made Charles angry, for he held my hand tight, pulling and squeezing it hard as he repeated his question. I answered that being neither my mother nor my father he could not tell me what to do, that I was not a piece of property and he did not own me. I was pretty good at using my tongue to tell people what I thought of them. Well, my words offended Master Charles. I thought of him as Master because he acted like one in authority over me instead of my boyfriend. As we approached my mother's house that night, Charles announced that I was about to suffer the consequences of disobeying him. Before I could respond, he placed his hands around my throat and began to choke me.

"If you won't do what I tell you to, I will kill you," he repeated. He covered my mouth when I tried to cry out, and this brought back memories of how Patrick used to cover my mouth to prevent me from crying out while he raped me. I tried to get away from Charles, but I could not overcome him, and for a moment I thought he would kill me. Suddenly he released me and tried to kiss me, proclaiming how much he loved me. Fearing for my life, I responded to his kisses. In fear and disbelief, I realized that Charles was a monster capable of killing me. And no one would have known for sure that this crazy bastard was the murderer. My mother, who always said he was a good person, would not have believed that he could commit such a heinous crime. When he stood there asking me to come back to him, I saw my chance to run away and raced into my mother's house, thereby probably saving my life. Although I heard him calling my name, I never looked back. Everyone in the house was asleep. I walked quietly to my bed.

I hardly slept at all that night. I kept having nightmares about Charles and his abuse of me. I reflected that I loved Andrew more than Charles, and Andrew had never abused me physically. I wasn't even sure I loved Charles. He was the first guy I dated to abuse me physically, and I was determined he would be the last. When Charles came to visit me the next day, I stayed inside my mother's house. He stood at the veranda waiting and waiting for me to come out and talk to him, but I never did. Finally he left. That was the end of my relationship with Charles, and I vowed never to get involved with him again. I have never spoken to him since.

It seems that Andrew would always be waiting for me when I broke off a relationship with another guy. He must have heard about my breaking off with Charles, because I received a message that he wanted to see me. I ignored his messages for a week or two before I agreed to meet with him. Sure enough, he asked me to give him another chance, and, foolish as I was, I agreed. Even though I knew he had betrayed my trust, there was something about Andrew that I hated to lose. I believe he felt the same about me, even though I purposely did things to hurt his feelings.

My mother no longer gave me beatings over my relationship with Andrew, but she still did not approve of my seeing him. I guess that was why she encouraged me when I was sixteen years old to accept a marriage proposal from Sidney, who lived in Calgary, Canada. In spite of his poor penmanship, I managed to read his letter, in which he proclaimed his love for me and asked me to migrate to Canada and marry him. My mother also received a letter from him asking her permission or her blessing for our marriage. I never understood what he was asking, since it seemed to me that one cannot ask for a marriage blessing until there is an acceptance of proposal. I couldn't remember ever knowing a guy named Sidney, let alone one who lived in Canada, or even knowing of a place called Calgary. I did not think my mother knew him, either. After some inquiry, I learned that Sidney was one of the guys who had worked on my mother's house when it was being renovated.

I vaguely remembered the man, of medium height and dark complexion, who did not talk much. Whoever he was, I knew just from his penmanship that I was not about to get hooked up with him. Under no circumstances would I marry a man who could hardly write. I wondered what his level of education could be and why he was interested in me. Even though my mother could hardly remember Sidney herself, she encouraged me to accept his marriage proposal. I was still in high school and had less than two years before graduation.

"Well, mother dear," I thought, "I know it is hard on you to finance my education. I've heard of the men and women like Elma who migrate to England to marry their lovers or even to marry men or women they never met before. At one time I could even have thought of myself doing the same, in the days when I was a still child. But now I am a young woman. I am not pregnant, even though I am sexually active. I also know you don't like Andrew, but I like him. He has kept his promise not to get me pregnant. Andrew is good compared to other guys who get girls pregnant. In short, mother, I am not migrating to Canada to marry Sidney, even though you think I should be grateful for the offer. I have no intention of getting married, especially at such a young age. There is a bright future for me when I graduate from school. At least I can then get a job and support myself. That will give me independence. My independence is something I am working hard to achieve. I need to be independent of you, and I sure don't want to end up in a situation like your own. I get the feeling that the only reason you are in this abusive relationship with Mr. Phillips is because you are depending on him for his financial support. If you were financially independent, you would have left him long ago. As to Sidney, I thank him for asking me, but no thanks, I don't want to marry him." With these words, I told my mother I intended to decline Sidney's marriage proposal. She heard me out and then began cursing me. She said that my relationship with Andrew was the reason why I didn't want to marry Sidney. She continued to curse at me for many weeks. I think my mother was hoping that her continued verbal abuse would make me change my mind and accept Sidney's offer, but I never did. Sidney would not be the only one my mother would encourage me to marry before I graduated from high school.

Vernon, a native of Barbados, was one of my pen pals. Like Andrew, Vernon was a teacher. He had heard about the possible eruption of La Soufriere, St. Vincent's volcano. Fearing for my safety, he wrote to ask if I would like to travel to Barbados until after the anticipated eruptions. Vernon assured me that his family would like to have me and would assist with the cost of my airfare. Since I had never traveled out of St. Vincent, I found his offer appealing and was inclined to accept it, even though I had never met Vernon. The only idea I had of him was from the photos he had enclosed with his letters. Nevertheless, I decided to accept his offer, not only to avoid the danger of a volcanic eruption but also to see another island.

My mother encouraged me to accept Vernon's offer. Besides being an opportunity for me to visit another Caribbean island, it would also allow me to surprise Uncle Raymond, who had immigrated to Barbados a few years earlier, with a visit. "She must want to get rid of me," I thought. Exactly two days before my seventeenth birthday, I boarded the small plane that flew me to Barbados. After approximately 35 minutes the plane landed in sunny Barbados. I claimed the suitcase carrying my clothes and walked out of the terminal. I spotted him. He looked exactly like his photograph, tall, of dark complexion, wearing glasses. He was carrying my photograph, with the help of which he had spotted me, too. Vernon walked up to me and said, "You must be Lola." I told him I was, and he welcomed me to Barbados. He took my suitcase from me and escorted me to a waiting car. While we sat together in the back of the car, Vernon commented that I looked exactly like my photograph. I told him that I thought the same about him from the moment I saw him standing at the airport. He gave me the same pleasant impression of himself as I had gotten from his letters. We chatted until the car pulled into the unpaved driveway of Vernon's family home. When I entered the house through the front door, his entire family greeted me, and it didn't take me long to feel at home. I spent the next six weeks with Vernon and his family.

Uncle Raymond was not aware of my visit to the island. A few days after my arrival, I told Vernon about my uncle and asked him to take me to see him at the address I had written down on a piece of paper. It so happened that Andrew's mother had also immigrated to Barbados and was living in the same apartment building as my uncle, although I did not know it at the time. When Vernon and I visited Uncle Raymond, I was surprised to find Andrew's mother, Madeline, right in his apartment. Madeline told us she was returning to St. Vincent that very day. As Uncle Raymond, Vernon and I were sitting across from her in the apartment, she asked whether Vernon was my boyfriend. I told her he was just a friend. I watched the expression on her face and the manner in which she stared at Vernon. It was not a friendly stare. I knew she was not pleased to see me with Vernon, nor did she believe me when I told her he was just a friend. I examined her reaction from the corner of my eye. I wanted to say to her, "Madeline, you can think whatever you want. I have the right to be with any guy I choose. The relationship between your son and me, which you never approved of anyway, is over." Vernon and I were still at my Uncle's apartment when she said in a voice heavy with sarcasm that she was leaving. Then she left for the airport.

Just over a week had passed since I had begun living with Vernon and his family. It was the happiest week I had ever experienced since Ma's death eleven years before. Vernon's home was peaceful, and his family members treated me well. Vernon's mother, Miss Laurel, a single mother, acted as though I were part of her family. She and Vernon's brothers and sisters inquired about my family. God knows I did not want to deceive them, but I felt I had to lie. Also living in the house were two sisters older than Vernon and also some younger siblings, three brothers and one sister. Vernon told me that he also had an older brother, living in Canada at the time, who helped support the family financially. Miss Laurel did not go out to work. The contributions to the family income from Vernon's older sisters and his brother in Canada and from Vernon himself made his family a little better off than mine. Still, both families would be considered poor. Unlike my family, Vernon's family seemed fun loving and kind to one another. I did not want to portray my family as any less happy than theirs. I told them I was the first born of my mother's eight children, soon to be nine. I lied and said that Mr. Phillips and my mother were married to each other. I told them that Mr. Phillips treated me the same as my half-siblings, even though he was not my father. I also told them that my stepfather and mother lived lovingly together, worked as farmers cultivating many different crops, and did their very best for us, their children. I wish I had not felt the need to lie to them, especially to Vernon, who had been so kind to me. But it seemed to me I had to do what would serve my best interest, even if it meant lying.

Vernon took me to visit many sights of Barbados, trying his best to accommodate my interests. Almost every day we went to the beach. Although he was not a dancer and disliked parties, he took me to a party when I told him of my love for music and dancing. Because he was so attentive and generous to me, I was not surprised at the contents of a letter he slipped into my hand three weeks after my arrival. I waited until I was alone to read his letter. Vernon had written that he was falling in love with me and asked whether we could be more than just friends. Like Andrew, Vernon was full of sweet nonsense rendered in an extensive vocabulary. I had to resort to a dictionary to find the meanings of some of the words he used. I read his letter over and over again. Instead of responding directly, I just told him my priority at the time was my education and graduating from high school, and I was afraid that having him as my boyfriend would interfere with my studies. Vernon wouldn't accept my excuses. Like Andrew, he pursued me relentlessly. I ended up caring for him because of his kindness and generosity toward me.

Although Vernon was not wealthy, he earned a good salary as a teacher. He showered me with gifts and even money. There was nothing I needed that he would not give to me if he could manage it. Vernon and I slept in separate rooms. We were alone together only when he took me on sightseeing visits and to the movies. While we were out one such visit, he confessed to me that he had fallen in love with me the very first time he had seen me at the airport. Miss Laurel also told me that Vernon was in love with me and expressed her wish that we would marry some day. Marry? What was Miss Laurel talking about? I wasn't thinking about marriage. I cared for Vernon, yes, but marriage at this young age before graduating from high school was out of the question. Vernon had his education. Did she not think I wanted my education too? "Miss Laurel, I know Vernon loves me and I love him too, but I can't think about marriage until I graduate from high school," I said to

Miss Laurel one day. Miss Laurel said that she agreed I should wait until I graduate before getting married.

I had already spent five weeks with these kindhearted people who had so fully accepted me, a stranger, in their home. Vernon had paid for my airfare and now was paying all my expenses in Barbados. I felt more comfortable living with him and his family than in the home of my mother, and I was relieved not to be around the envious people of my village in St. Vincent. I wish I could have stayed with them forever, but such was not possible. I knew I had to return home for school, which had already opened for the semester. The eruption of our volcano, which had been the pretext for my visit, had not occurred.

Vernon and I had become very much attached to each other. His family was as fond of me as I was of all of them. When I told Vernon I had to return home for school, he and his family did not want me to leave. Miss Laurel suggested I stay with them and attend school in Barbados. Vernon said that if I decided to stay he would pay my tuition and other expenses. I was struck by the kindness of his offer. Enticing as it was, I felt I had to decline. I was grateful that Miss Laurel and Vernon thought so highly of me and wanted me to stay, but I wasn't ready to sacrifice my independence for that type of living arrangement. Having a man take care of my every need was not part of my plan. I gratefully and regretfully declined the offer, but I promised Vernon I would return to stay sometime in the future, after I graduated from high school. Vernon understood.

I found I had become attached to the Broadwaite family as much as they to me. Some nights we would sit in the living room imitating one another. The night before I departed for home, they invited a few of their friends to a farewell party for me. Their friends wished me good luck and expressed their hopes of seeing me again. It was quite an emotional experience when I hugged Miss Laurel and the rest of the family as I said my good-byes to them the following day before leaving for the airport. Everyone was crying as they flocked to the front of the house. They all waved good-bye as I entered the car that took me to the airport, with Vernon accompanying me. On our way we talked and made plans for our future together. Six weeks ago, he had been a stranger to me. In this short time he had become a very special and caring friend. Time, oh time, with time there are so many possibilities. My friend, Vernon, wanted to be more than a friend to me. It was while we sat together in the back seat of the car on our way to the airport, that he informed me of a letter he had written to my mother. "Why did you write to my mother?" I asked. "I wrote to tell your mother how wonderful a daughter you are and of my wish to marry you some day," he replied. Dumfounded, I stared at him. He appeared to be quite serious. On his face I saw an expression of happiness. I felt I had no choice but to reassure him that I would return to him as soon as I graduated. "I will miss you Vernon, but do I really want to marry you?" I asked myself.

When I checked in at the airport, I learned that my flight was delayed. As Vernon and I walked about the airport, we came to a platform at one side of the airport terminal. I couldn't help noticing the big airplanes, some at the gates, others on the runaways. I had never seen such enormous airplanes, since my island did not have the landing facilities to accommodate them. I listened to the announcements about departures to places like England, Canada, and America. Looking at the passengers boarding planes, I wished I were among them, on my way to one of those big and far away countries. I immediately thought of Edna, wondering whether she would still be interested in adopting me. I felt a yearning to go to America, feeling disappointed to be heading for old and familiar St. Vincent. I was about to resume living in my mother's violent home among the envious people in my village. As I pictured in my mind my mother's home and those envious people, I questioned whether I had made the right decision in declining Vernon's offer to stay in Barbados. I wondered whether I might not have been better off living with Vernon and his family.

"Vernon's mother was so kind to me," I thought, "and oh! Vernon, Vernon, you were so good to me. I love you so much, but I don't know if I love you as much as I love Andrew." As I thought of these two men who had entered my life, I felt sad and suddenly began to cry. Vernon hugged me and used his handkerchief to wipe the teardrops from my face. I knew I would miss this beautiful island of Barbados. I already missed the mimicking of Miss Laurel at night and waking up to her friendly smile in the morning, the peacefulness of her home. Most of all I would miss Vernon. He had given me the opportunity to see a place different from the one I lived in. Because of him, I had flown on an airplane for the very first time. I wondered how I could ever repay him for his kindness. With these thoughts in my mind, I kissed Vernon, holding him tight. I was already missing him. When we heard the announcement, I knew it was time for me to board my small airplane to St. Vincent. We kissed passionately as we said our good-byes. Again, I promised him I would return. I left him standing there watching me go, while I walked to the plane for my departure. It was sunny and bright in Barbados. Even brighter in my mind was the idea of boarding one of the other bigger airplanes some day. I knew it would only be a matter of time before I would be a passenger on one of them. This I felt deep within my soul.

The small plane lifted off, and I cried as it ascended into the air. Beautiful, sunny Barbados, with its white sand beachfronts, receded from my view. As the plane began to descend to St. Vincent and landed on the island 35 minutes later, I had mixed feelings. I took a taxicab from the airport to the village, and it took an hour to get there. I was glad to see my grandmother, my siblings, and even my mother. But when I entered the village the sadness within me was overwhelming. It came to me that I was once again in the lions' den among the people I called the lions. "Oh, Andrew," I said to myself, "your betrayal of my trust makes it even worse. I wish I had stayed in Barbados." But in reality I was back home. I had no choice but to face reality and make the best of it. That was what I was firmly determined to do.

A Light in the Tunnel

Ever since I began attending high school, especially after I enrolled at St. Joseph's Convent, I pictured myself travelling through a tunnel in stages, at each stage facing many unforeseeable obstacles. There were times when these obstacles discouraged me and I questioned whether I could complete the journey. When I felt overwhelmed, I prayed, and I believe that God intervened in my behalf, giving me the courage to go on when I was most discouraged. Somehow, I had been able to get almost to the end of the tunnel, but I knew I was not yet there. I refused to give up, becoming more determined than ever to get to light at the end.

I had only a year and a half of school before graduation, less than half the total. Being so close, I was determined that, come what may, I would finish.

I was excited to be back in school among friends, and more than ecstatic to see Jennifer and Saline again. I could not wait to tell them of my experience in Barbados. I missed Barbados and Vernon's family, but most of all I missed Vernon, more than I would like to admit. "Vernon, I know I am in your thoughts and you are in mine, too, but school is what I want to concentrate on

131

right now," I would say to myself whenever I questioned whether I had made the right decision in returning to St. Vincent. Since I was already two weeks late for school, I had to explain to Sr. Agatha the reason for my absence and get her permission to enter my classroom, which I did. I had to spend extra time doing the schoolwork my teachers had assigned during my absence, but it did not take me long to catch up. I told Jennifer and Saline all that had taken place during my visit to Barbados. I told them I felt I had fallen in love with Vernon. Jennifer was skeptical. She had always liked Andrew. When she asked about him, I would tell her it was over between Andrew and me. But she knew as well as I did that Andrew would always be special to me.

I thought it strange that I had not seen Andrew since my return the week before. Since my village was small and had such a knack for spreading other people's news, I was sure he had heard of my return. But why did I care whether he had heard of my return? Even though we had broken up before I left for Barbados, I guess I still cared for him. Then one evening, five days after my return, I saw him standing there before I stepped off of the school bus, and I wondered whether he had another girlfriend on the bus and was awaiting her arrival. I thought he might have been waiting for Dawn, because she attended a typing class some evenings, and she had to pass the crossroads on her way home. I decided to ignore him and began to walk to the village alone.

I had walked only a short distance when he called my name. He said he had come to the crossroads to wait for me. I wondered why he would do such a thing when we were not on speaking terms. He knew I had gone to Barbados, even though I had not told him. Andrew acted as though we were still in a relationship and began to question me about Vernon, expecting me to answer his questions. Andrew said his mother had told him she had seen me with another guy in Barbados. "I thought you went to visit your uncle, not to meet another man," he said. Where he had heard that, I did not know, for I had not told him whom I was going to visit in Barbados. "It's none of your business whom I went to visit in Barbados. It's none of your mother's business either," I said to him as I walked away.

When Andrew followed, I stopped and we had a civil conversation. As usual, he proclaimed his love for me and for the first time he cried. He begged me to forgive him and asked that we make up and be friends again. Andrew swore he loved me enough to break off with Dawn, and he uttered again those words of sweet nonsense. Young, foolish, and in love, so I guess I was at the time. I was foolish enough to believe him when he said he had broken up with Dawn because of his love for me. Although I was young, I was not too young to be in love, or at least to think so. So I decided to go back to this liar and cheat of a boyfriend, who I thought was in love with me as much as I was in love with him.

After we made up, I heard a rumor that his mother did not approve of our relationship. Madeline would never answer me when I would meet her or say hello, and eventually I stopped saying hello to her. My mother must have heard Madeline speaking ill of me, because they soon began cursing each other. My mother would curse his mother and tell her that I didn't want her son, and his mother would curse my mother and tell her that her son would never marry me. Their feud soon became public knowledge.

Andrew lived with his mother and three other siblings in a two-room thatched house. There were times when I would hear some villagers say that Andrew was too poor for me. They said he was so poor that he attended high school wearing patched pants. Because his family could not afford the cost of transportation, his grandfather would walk with him half the distance to his school, about four miles away, leaving before dawn to get there on time. Although we were all poor people, Andrew was considered by many even poorer, because of the house he lived in and having to walk to school. I was not of the same opinion, considering all of us simply to be poor people, and I had previously thought that everyone else felt the same. As I grew older, I realized that the society in which we lived had their ways of classifying some people as better than others. I wondered how some could be better than others, when we all ate the same food, walked the same roads, and lived in the same environment under the same conditions. But that was how things were. I never knew how my mother felt about Andrew, since she never told me, but I found that her continuous verbal abuse of me escalated as I continued to see him. Her insults would remain vivid in my mind for the rest of my life. When she threatened to cut off my education, I became frightened and decided to be more discreet in my relationship with Andrew, asking him not to meet me any more at the crossroads in the evenings.

As Andrew and I continued our relationship, Madeline continued her crusade against it. She would tell anyone who was willing to listen that Andrew would never marry me. I don't know who told her I wanted to marry her son. I didn't. At that time in my life, I had no interest in marrying anyone. Then I heard she had said that Dawn would make a better daughter-in-law and wife than I, because I had nothing to offer Andrew.

She must have been brainwashed by the society to think so. Like me, Dawn was born into this world a bastard picme, as the villagers would say. At least I knew my father, if only from his brief appearance when I was twelve, but Dawn never knew her father. It was rumored that her mother had become pregnant by some unknown man on shipboard.

The idea that a person's value was based on material things seemed to me a destructive force in many relationships. Such was the case with Lawrence Peters, Susan Rose and Viola Payne. Susan Rose was a teacher's assistant, whose parents lived in the United States and whose family owned many acres of land in another village. Viola's mother also lived overseas, but her family did not own much land. Viola and Susan both got pregnant by Lawrence, and he felt that he had to marry one of them. Lawrence confessed to some of his friends that he loved Viola more, but had to marry Susan because the family's money would enable him to immigrate to America, where there were lots of opportunities. It was for this reason that he married Susan instead of Viola. Needless to say, his marriage to Susan did not last long. Susan had two children within a year, and she filed for divorce before the birth of the second child. Lawrence confessed to his friends his deep regret over his decision to forsake love for money. Because I believed that marrying for anything other than love was wrong, I could only hope that, if I were to marry, it would be for romantic love. Then again, why should I hope? Marriage was not on my list of things I hoped for in life, even though I had promised Vernon I would marry him. My educational goals and my independence remained my top priorities.

Looking forward to our graduation, we encouraged one another to study hard to achieve the academic requirements. We had discussions among ourselves about our hopes for the future. For the most part, our views on what we wanted to achieve in life never changed. I remember Maureen Jack standing among a group of us and saying, "Well girls, how many of you would like to join the convent and become a nun?" No one wanted to be a nun. Then Maureen said, "How many of you would like to experiment with sex by changing boyfriends every three months?" No one wanted that either. But when Maureen asked how many would like to get married and have children, all other girls except for Saline and me were hoping to get married and have children. Joan Scott planned to marry someone wealthy, and she planned to have only one child, because she did not want the stretch marks on her body which one gets from having kids. We burst out laughing. Joan was the kind of girl who would have led us to believe that she did not use the bathroom, let alone emptying her feces in it. Jennifer wanted to marry and have four or five children, and Saline did not say much of what she wanted to do. For myself, I was firm against having children. True, I did promise Vernon I would return to Barbados after graduation and marry him, but I had no intention of doing so. If I were ever to marry him, it would certainly not be right after graduation. I felt I was too young for a life of breeding for a man, having legitimate children instead of bastard ones.

I received a letter from Vernon almost every week, and at the end of the month, when he got paid, money was enclosed. I was pleased with the money he sent to me, most of which I was saving at the penny savings bank in town, where I had opened an account. I thought that Vernon must really love me to send me money, and I had no doubt that he would make a good and caring husband. Sometimes I thought I probably would return to Barbados and marry him. Then I would say to myself, "Hell, no, girl, you are too young to get wrapped up in the marriage business! I thought you said you wanted to be independent. Marriage is dependence, not independence. How about immigrating to America? Yes, if Vernon lived in America rather than Barbados, I would marry him. At least America promises opportunities. The only opportunity in Barbados would be a teaching job, and I could do just as well here in St. Vincent. I just don't see why I have to go to Barbados." Still, I continued to write to Vernon, assuring him of my love and promising to return and marry him after graduation.

Vernon wrote to say he missed me and that he would like to visit me in St. Vincent. He wanted to know whether my parents would allow him to come and stay with them. "No way will you be visiting me in St. Vincent, Vernon. Are you crazy?" I said to myself, wondering what I had wrought by misrepresenting my intentions toward him and misleading him about my family. Now that Andrew and I were back together again, I could not possibly let him come to visit. Vernon had no idea that I had a boyfriend or that I lived in a violent home. I pondered over how I could get out of the mess I found myself in. I replied that my mother welcomed him, but my stepfather—I was appalled to find myself referring to Mr. Phillips as my stepfather—had overruled my mother and said no. I told him to take into consideration that the house belonged to Mr. Phillips, and that he was not my father. "Why do I allow myself to say Mr. Phillips owns the house?" I asked myself. "How can he be the sole owner of the house when my mother contributed towards building it?" I must have been as confused as the other people of the village, for whom it was understood that men were the owners of everything that their legal or common-law wives had worked for and earned, including lands they purchased and houses they built. Women owned nothing, absolutely nothing.

Vernon wrote back to say that even though he was disappointed, he accepted my explanation. I was relieved that he believed my lies. He asked me to return to Barbados for two weeks during my summer vacation, but I convinced him I couldn't because I planned to attend typing classes in the summer. He wrote to me again, this time to ask if I would be kind enough to check on the cost for hotels in St. Vincent for some friends who were planning to visit. It was a lot cheaper for me to get the information in person than to have his friends telephone St. Vincent for it. I hoped he was not planning to visit with his friends, but I felt obligated to meet his request. It was the least I could do for my generous, caring, loving Vernon. Because I attended school during the week, I went back to town on Saturday to check on hotels.

At the Island View Hotel, I introduced myself to the receptionist and told her I would like to speak to the person in charge, hoping I would be able to negotiate a price with him. That was my first encounter with Mr. Randell Ralston. After keeping me waiting in the hotel lobby for about twenty minutes, he introduced himself as the owner and escorted me to his office. Mr. Ralston appeared to be middle aged, but age had done nothing to his tall and slender, handsome form. Unlike the middle-aged men in my village, he seemed to have taken good care of himself. He seated himself behind his desk and I sat on one of the two chairs on the other side. As I was telling him the purpose of my visit, I could not help thinking that he hadn't heard a word, even though he appeared to be listening attentively. He was gazing at me with such piercing eyes that I began to feel uncomfortable. After I stopped speaking, Mr. Ralston asked, "Where in this town are you living?" "I am not from town. I am from the country," I replied. Some people, especially those who lived in the town, called where I lived "the country." "You can't be from country," he said. "Yes, I am from Amondid Village," I responded. "You mean you are from Brother Roy's country? I did not know Brother Roy's country had such smart and articulate young women as yourself," Mr. Ralston remarked. Brother Roy, as everyone called him, was a member of my church. He owned and operated a shop in the village where I lived. His also owned one of the few wall houses in my village, and lots of businessmen from throughout the island would gather at his place when they visited the village, and Mr. Ralston must have been one of them. I assured Mr. Ralston that I was indeed from Brother Roy's country, but I attended school in town. He asked which school I was attending, and before I knew it the conversation was more about me than about hotel rates. Mr. Ralston finally did give me the information I needed, but not before he had extended an invitation to me to join him for lunch later that day, and I politely accepted. I returned at noon after I had walked about town shopping for some window curtains my mother had asked me to buy.

In those days, poor families like mine did not set the table when we had our meals. We would eat with a spoon, but no knives or forks. The first time I had eaten a meal using a knife and fork was at Miss English's house. Because using a knife and fork was new to me, I tried my best to hold them the same way Miss English and her family did, but I was quite uncomfortable. When I visited Barbados, there were times when we ate our meals using knives and forks, but it seemed to be optional in Vernon's house, so I ate with just a spoon most of the time. Sitting with Mr. Ralston in his private dining room at the Island View Hotel, using a knife and fork, I felt uncomfortable. In the Caribbean, the knife is held in the right hand and the fork in the left, which is also used to carry the food to your mouth. Eating this way when you are not used to it can be a difficult task. Mr. Ralston noticed I was having difficulty, but he did not laugh at me, as others might have done. Instead, he taught me how to do it. "Look at me, and try to do exactly as I do," he said. Normally I would have been embarrassed, but his manner was reassuring, teaching me as a father might have done. He wanted to know more about me, including how I was doing academically. I told him all about school, that I loved St. Joseph's Convent but hated the long skirt that I had to wear as my uniform. I told him I thought my school was the best school in the island because of the well-rounded education one received there. I was always enthusiastic about the school to anyone who inquired. I even told him about my friendship with Jennifer and Saline and that we had most of our lunches at a restaurant a block away from his hotel. When Mr. Ralston suggested that my friends and I join him for lunch the following week, I told him I would talk it over with my friends. Before we parted, he told me not to be a stranger, to come and visit him sometime. I promised him I would.

When I left Mr. Ralston that day, I could not help thinking how kind he had been to me. He had invited me to a very good lunch, and it was the first time I had ever been served a meal by a maid. Mr. Ralston appeared to be someone who would be characterized in the island as a big shot with money. I could not wait to be back in school on Monday, when I could tell Jennifer and Saline all about this Ralston man and our invitation to lunch. I thought that Jennifer might hesitate to accept, but not Saline, who loved to mingle with men who had money. She would jump at the opportunity to have lunch with this big shot. When I told them about Mr. Ralston's invitation, sure enough, Saline wanted us to have lunch with him that very day, while Jennifer hesitated a while before agreeing to accept. We decided among ourselves to go the following day. On my way to the bus stop that evening, I went back to the hotel and left word with the receptionist. The next day Jennifer, Saline and I joined Mr. Ralston for lunch in the private dinning area. In the course of the conversation, we were surprised to learn that he had done business with Jennifer's father and knew him well. He encouraged us all to do our best in school. As he was speaking, Jennifer began to pinch me, an indication that she wanted to me to be aware of something, but I had no clue what she meant. Saline did not say much except to answer Mr. Ralston's questions about her grades in school, but I noticed her penetrating stare at him. When he left us for a brief moment, she remarked that I was lucky to have met Randell, but she would not elaborate. After lunch, we shook hands with Mr. Ralston, thanking him for the lunch, and then left the hotel. It was to prove only the first of many lunch meetings with him, sometimes with Jennifer and Saline and other times alone. On one of those days when we had lunch alone, he told me he thought I was a very attractive and articulate young lady, and he believed he was falling in love with me. I was so shocked I knew not what to say when he asked whether I felt any love for him.

"In love with me?" I asked myself. "How could such a man, old enough to be my father, and with money, be in love with me, dirt poor me? Besides, he has children older than I and also two other daughters younger than I who attend my school. He's married, so he can't be in love with me. I probably misunderstood what he was saying." When he repeated himself, I realized I wasn't imagining things. Mr. Ralston told me to call him Randell and said he would provide me with anything money could buy. "Think about it and we'll talk about it, but know that I am serious. I fell in love with you from the very first time I laid eyes on you," he said to me. "Come to me if you are ever in need, and I will help you." He tried to kiss me before I left to return to school.

I thought about what Randell had said to me. I wanted to tell my best friend, Jennifer, but I decided I would wait until the next day. Knowing Jennifer, I wasn't surprised that she discouraged me from getting involved with him, because she was partial to Andrew. Of all the guys who wanted to be my boyfriend, Jennifer liked one guy for me and one guy only, Andrew. "Jennifer, girl, you are my best friend and have been like a sister to me," I thought, "but I can't rule out seeing this older man who seems to have so much interest in me. Oh, God, no, he is married! I can't afford to be with a married man, let alone fall in love with him. But rumor has it that he and his wife are separated. So what if he and his wife are separated? What? They are still husband and wife. You are right, Jennifer. I should stay the hell away from him." Even though a part of me was telling me not to get involved with this married man old enough to be my father, I did it anyway, not telling anyone else, not even my best friend, Jennifer.

I met Randell for lunch several times during that semester. Like Andrew, he encouraged me to do my very best in school. Although he treated me well and gave me money to buy the things I needed, and I learned he was separated from his wife, I was still concerned about his marital status. Because of that concern more than any-thing else, I refrained from kissing him and would not see him as often as he wanted me to. I realized that I had entered a path of deceit, misleading Vernon by not telling him about Andrew and going against my moral beliefs in seeing Randell. To have had sex-ual relations with a boyfriend didn't bother me much, because for-nication was accepted in my society. But committing adultery was another thing. Ironically, it was because of Vernon's inquiry that I had crossed paths with Randell, and after all was said and done,

Vernon wrote to say his friends had decided not to visit St. Vincent after all.

Vernon and I continued our correspondence and I continued my relationship with Andrew, but nothing, not even my relationships with men, was allowed to interfere with my education, especially at that time. As the end of the semester drew near, and my classmates and I looked forward to our last year in school, we resolved to spend less time with boyfriends. "Let's concentrate on our schoolwork so we can be promoted to our last class together," we would encourage one another. One more year and we would be out of St. Joseph's Convent for good. No more long skirt, and no more saying "Hail, Oh Mother Mary" forty times a day, we would then be able to laugh and make fun of the prayer we had to repeat each morning at the beginning of school. We had been in school together from the beginning and we were hoping to leave together. When I had worked for Mr. Samson, I had begun to take weekly typing lessons, saving half of my lunch money to pay for them. After Mr. Samson fired me, my mother continued to give me the same amount for lunch and I used part of that money to pay for my lessons and I saved some of it as well. When Randell came into my life, he paid for my typing lessons. Randell had been extremely generous to me, and I wished I could be generous with him in the way he wanted me to be, but I was afraid.

During the vacation before the beginning of my last year in school, Andrew and I were back together again, but he also got more involved with Dawn. I saw him walking her to the crossroads, and he even attended church with her, things that he had never done before. I was devastated. "I am breaking up with you for good, Andrew, and I swear that I will never make up with you even if my great grandmother, Ma, comes back from her grave and asks me to," I told Andrew when we met at a village corner road one evening. I was distraught, feeling just an inch away from insanity. Andrew just looked at me and said, "You and I love each other too much. Don't you see? There is no end to our relationship. It doesn't matter that you might be having a relationship with another, or that I might, for ours will never cease." I just glared at him and walked away. When I got to my mother's house that evening, I found that Mr. Phillips had just beaten her. As I witnessed her crying, I began to analyze her situation in a new way.

For years I had witnessed the abuses that Mr. Phillips committed against my mother, and I wondered why she stayed with him.

I couldn't imagine that she stayed with him out of love, so it must have been for his financial support, which she so desperately needed to take care of us. Having realized what her situation really was like, I began to feel more sympathetic towards her. Although none of us children had never heard her say she loved us, it was obvious that she must have loved us to stay in such an abusive relationship for our sake. I began to recognize what I needed to do to help her.

I realized that my mother had lost her self-esteem, and I wanted to help her regain it. Recovered self-esteem would bring self-empowerment, which would bring independence, so she would not to have to depend on this Mr. Phillips man for anything, not money and surely not love. I was sure he hadn't shown her any love in quite a long time. I saw myself as my mother's only hope of becoming independent.

Although my mother had stopped abusing me physically, she continued to abuse me verbally, and I saw her beating my siblings, though not as severely as she had beaten me. One of my sisters had bad breath, so my mother would tell her to get away from her with her fucking stinking mouth. I had never heard my grandmother using such foul language, and sometimes I wondered if my mother really was my grandmother's daughter. My poor sister would walk away from my mother looking like a stray dog. Later we found out the poor child was sick with a head cold, suffering with it for years before a doctor diagnosed it correctly. Still, although my mother was not the best of mothers, she did the best she could for us, and I knew of many mothers in the village who treated their children worse. Because I realized that her cursing and beatings were her ways of punishing us, I tried for the first time to understand her. I thought that whatever wrong mother had done us she had done because she had had a rough life and had lost her self-esteem. Understanding my mother from that point of view, I felt indebted to her. I wished my siblings could understand my mother's situation in the same way, but I doubted that any of them would be able to. My siblings and I had never talked about the goings-on in our home or about my mother. I had almost lost my sanity because of Andrew's behavior toward me the summer before my last year in high school, but my new outlook on my mother had given me a sense of purpose in life. With my financial help, I was certain my mother would be able to regain her self-esteem, and it would only be a year before I would be able to help her. In just a year I would graduate and find myself a job to support her and my siblings. In this frame of mind I awaited the beginning of my last year in high school.

The Education Department was offering free night classes that would benefit students in their last year of high school, but those classes were only offered in the town where I attended school. Most of my classmates planned to attend, but I couldn't because I had to travel home to the village in the evening. Jennifer and Saline were travelling home to their villages, too, but they made arrangements to stay in town on the nights when those classes would be held. I very much wanted to do the same, but I didn't know where I could stay. Although I had not seen my father since I stopped living with him, I had heard that he was living in the town, so I went looking for him. He looked the same as he did on the day when I first met him in the village, except that he now wore short pants and a short-sleeved shirt rather than a suit, and I found out he no longer owned a car. He did not seem like a man with money. He did arrange for me to stay with Alma, a friend of his, who lived in a two-bedroom apartment with her two sons and a boyfriend, a policeman, who was hardly ever at home, because rumor had it that he had another girlfriend. On school mornings, Alma would prepare my breakfast and lunch before she left for work.

After school, I had to walk two miles to Alma's place. It was no difficulty to walk there, as I walked slowly with other school children through the town, stopping to buy roasted peanuts or a lollipop from the street venders, and at times rushing to buy a pen at a bookshop before it closed. Alma lived half a mile up a hill, and we children would sometimes try to run up the hill, only to become breathless half way up and have to walk slowly the rest of the way. When I got there I did my schoolwork and assisted Alma with preparing dinner and various other tasks. Then I would meet Jennifer and Saline in town and together we would walk to the classes. The instructors did what they were paid to do, but it seemed to me that most of us were inattentive, feeling we had already been taught these things in school, and the classes were often used as an excuse for dating. I began to behave differently, in a way that I noticed also in many of my schoolmates, including Jennifer and Saline. Most of us were now open with our relationships with boyfriends, cuddling up with them after classes at night. Jennifer had a new boyfriend, Jeffrey Harry, and she even fell into the trap of leaving home for school but instead spending the day with her boyfriend. I was so furious with Jennifer when I found out that I threatened to tell her father if she ever did it again. Saline had a couple of men, as usual. Although most of my classmates were sexually active, we were discreet about it. But not Saline.

Saline changed boyfriends faster than we changed our exercise notebooks. She went to bed with all of them and would go with any man who offered her money. I remember Saline dating our school bus driver and how ashamed I was, knowing that other children on the bus knew and called her a whore behind her back. Then one day Saline invited Jennifer and me to have lunch with her and her new boyfriend, Jason Tucker, who was a policeman. Two days later, Jennifer and I were summoned to appear in Sister Agatha's office. We knew we were in some sort of trouble, and I began to tremble. Sister told us to be seated in the chairs in front of her desk and she sat on the other side. "Belitha and Jennifer," Sister Agatha said, "Mrs. Tucker came to school this morning to inform me that Saline is having an affair with her husband. She also said that Saline and the two of you had been seen having lunch with Mr. Tucker. You must understand that I do not expect my students to be involved in such behavior and I will not tolerate it. This behavior warrants an expulsion from my school." Speaking to us with authority, Sister Agatha said that she wanted us to tell her the truth and nothing but the truth. There was a short pause while Sister answered the telephone , during which Jennifer and I had a brief discussion. Jennifer thought we should deny everything and protect Saline, but I told Jennifer that I could not tell Sister the truth and protect Saline at the same time, and I was not about to get thrown out of school. I thought of how the villagers who had wished me harm all those years would react to hearing that I had been expelled from school, and I also thought of Elitha, Leeann, Miss John and the Staddards, who had encouraged me to persist. I felt I couldn't let them down. Most of all, I did not want to let down my family, especially my mother and grandmother. Furthermore, I was so close to graduation, and I so much wanted to graduate and walk with our class on graduation night. Besides, I felt that we had warned Saline over and over again about her indiscreet behavior with men, and it was now only fair for her to accept the consequences. To save Jennifer and myself from expulsion, I admitted to Sister that we had had lunch with Saline and the man, but that Saline had told us he was her uncle.

"Had we known the man was Saline's boyfriend, we never would have gone to lunch with them," I told her.

I wondered why Saline had ever arranged that luncheon. Perhaps she had done it because we had had lunch with Randell, but Randell was different. Around my friends he never acted as though he was interested in me, treating us as a father might treat his daughters. "You stupid ass, Saline," I thought, "you can't differentiate between what will get you into trouble and what will not." My explanation to Sister saved Jennifer and me from expulsion. Sister allowed Saline to take the final exams, but she did not allow her to walk with the class on graduation day. That did not prevent Saline from carrying on with her men, and it surprised neither Jennifer nor me when, a week before graduation, Saline told us she was pregnant. The biggest shock came when her baby was born and Saline told us she did not know who the child's father was. Jennifer and I thought that at least to some degree Saline's mother was to blame. Although she might not have encouraged Saline to carry on this way, she must have known about it, since Saline gave her mother most of the money she got from these men, and her mother accepted it, knowing that Saline had no job. Thinking about Saline's promiscuity, I wondered whether she might have been a victim of childhood rapes, like me.

I was determined not to be like Saline, having sex for money and getting pregnant. I was about to get even with men, or so I thought when I was seventeen. I would date any guy who expressed an interest as long as he could offer me gifts and money, but I vowed not to go to bed with any of them. After all, guys had raped me and scared the hell out of me when I was a defenseless child, and that bastard, Andrew, had hurt me so much when he betrayed my trust by having relationships with other women. During this time, still living with Alma in the town, I got to know Alston and Derrick, who were also attending classes at night. Alston, a soft-spoken young man who always sat next to me in class, one night as we were leaving the classroom asked if he could have a talk with me. I agreed, and as we walked out of the two-story government building and stood on the green lawn outside, he asked whether I was dating anyone. I lied and said no. "I have been admiring you since the first night of class, and I was wondering if you would give me the opportunity to get to know you better." "Why do you want to get to know me," I asked, and he replied that he would like to be my boyfriend. We could have lunch sometimes, I told him. A week after our conversation, we met for lunch and made plans to attend a movie together. Alston lived in a rented board house in the town with his mother and a younger sister. When I inquired about his father, he said that his father had immigrated to England when he was five years old. His mother was a nurse, and they were able to survive on her salary. Besides, his father would send them money now and then. Still in school at eighteen, Alston did not have much to offer me beyond paying for the lunch and movie. I dated him for a month, but I stopped when I realized that he could not offer me money or gifts. That was when I began dating Derrick, a tall, handsome man two years my senior, with a chocolate complexion, who had a job as an accountant. I noticed that Derrick would be standing under one of the two-story buildings in town almost every evening when I was walking from school to Alma's place. Sometimes Derrick would wink at me, and I would immediately turn my face away from him. Then one evening he walked up to me and asked my name. Before I knew it, Derrick was asking me for a date. The following week, Derrick began walking with me as soon as I got to the building. "I have been admiring you for a while, and I would like to get to know you," he said to me. From that day, Derrick would buy me roasted nuts or a lollipop, walking with me until we came near Alma's house. I introduced Derrick to Jennifer, who said she liked him for me. Jennifer liking any guy other than Andrew for me was quite a turnabout. I dated Derrick for about two months, and during that time he showered me with small gifts like perfumes and handkerchiefs, and he gave me money. Three weeks after we began dating, I asked Alma's permission for him to visit me at her house. He visited me frequently there, and Alma would disappear whenever he came to visit me.

Five weeks after we had begun dating, Derrick suggested we become sexually involved. "Derrick, I like you," I thought, "but I do not love you, and there is no way in this world that I would get sexually involved with you. You are not going to pump up my stomach with some damn picme. No way! The man who pumps up my stomach with a picme has not yet been born, and his mother has already died. I just have the feeling that if I ever let you on my stomach you will pump it up with a picme. I'll never make a picme, not now or ever." I thought these things time and time again, but still I continued to promise Derrick sex. If I thought we were about to meet at a location where he could subdue me, I would wear a sanitary pad. I had heard that men stay away from their women during their periods, and that many wouldn't even allow women to cook for them, let alone have sex, during that time. Derrick continued to pressure me for sex. One night when we were alone at Alma's house, Derrick was about to force me to have sex with him when Alma came home unexpectedly, and I broke up with him a week later. Jennifer felt I had treated him badly, saying I should have stayed with him because he had treated me kindly and was in love with me. "Sorry, Jennifer," I thought, "I can't be with all the men who love me and want to get into my crotch."

Derrick was only the first who sought me out as their prey. In those years, between seventeen and eighteen, I got the attention of lots of guys. Tony, for one, was a mechanic who showered me with gifts and money and even promised to buy me a car. I would be in a store, at a restaurant, or on my way home, when Tony would show up unexpectedly. He seemed to want the world to know we were dating. Then there was Joel, a policeman, who even bought me clothes, which unfortunately I was not able to wear. My mother did not notice money and small gifts like perfume and handkerchiefs, but clothes would have been too obvious. All the guys wanted sex, but none of them got what they wanted. I became a master of my trade, which was to get as much money and gifts as I could from my pursuers, giving them nothing in return but a broken heart. To fulfill my sexual desires I went back to Andrew, who troubled me the most, yet whom I loved the most. Immaturity has a way of playing with young minds like mine. I was almost at the end of my school years, and Andrew had lived up to his promise not to have unprotected sex with me. Although I cannot say I trusted him fully, since he had already betrayed me, I felt secure with him in avoiding pregnancy.

It bothered me that Andrew was still seeing Dawn, but I continued to go back to him. The villagers knew I dated other men, and their name-calling escalated to calling me a whore. Thank God, I was whoring only with Andrew, while some of their daughters, like Lorraine, were out whoring with men I would not even look at, let alone have sex with. While they were minding my business and leaving theirs unattended, their own daughters were getting pregnant and having babies as if in competition with one another. I remember Tina Lynch, probably seventeen at the time, who had gotten pregnant and carried the baby full term, without her parents suspecting anything until she was rushed to the hospital. It was said that the doctors had to cut away three girdles to deliver her baby boy, who was born deformed. Many of the mothers were disappointed that I wasn't yet pregnant, and even more so that I was about to graduate from high school. Many of their own daughters had already dropped out of high school due to pregnancy or academic failure. Some mothers were so devious as to spread rumors that I was sexually involved with men I had never even spoken to. It was undoubtedly due to these rumors that some men for whom I had great respect began hitting on me.

I had always respected George Saunders, about fifteen years older than I, who was one of my former teachers at the village school. He was aware of my relationship with Andrew, and I am sure he had heard the gossip about us. One Sunday evening, George, one of the few people in the village who owned a car, invited me to go for a ride with him. Knowing that Andrew would hear about it and be upset, I accepted George's invitation as a means of getting back at Andrew. George and I visited Georgetown, a town approximately four miles away, where he took me to Louise Hideaway, a place where couples hang out drinking and dancing. The Sunday tradition of rest and worship was now changing. Although many people attended church and rested, many others, especially young people, had begun to have parties on Sunday evenings. Such a party was taking place that Sunday evening at Louise Hideaway. Normally, I would not attend parties on Sunday, even though I loved music and dancing. That evening George and I each had a few drinks at the party, but I refused to dance with him. I suspected that George was up to no good when he kept ordering drinks for me, even when I told him I didn't want any more. There was loud music, and the crowd, half of them drunk, had been there for hours, dancing and making loud noise. I had seen many guys kissing girls, holding them tight as if they were about to have sex with them right there on the dancing floor. I had the feeling that George was trying to get me drunk so he could take advantage of me. "George, you are much, much older than I am," I thought, "but I am much, much smarter than you think I am." When George was not watching, I poured away most of the drinks. Finally, we left the place to drive back to the village.

On our way home, George began to speak ill of Andrew, saying he was no good and I shouldn't waste my time with him. "An attractive and intelligent girl like you should date someone of more intelligence than that boy Andrew," he said, implying that he had more intelligence than Andrew. I wanted to tell him to shut up, but I was afraid to argue with him. All I wanted was to get back to the village safely. Approximately two miles from Georgetown, George stopped at Mt. Greenan, another village, where we entered Richie's Lounge, a place similar to Louise Hideaway. I was standing among the small crowd of people when George said, "I will be right back." He went to the bar and brought back a drink for me. While George was speaking to someone in the crowd, I walked over and poured the drink out of a window. I continued to pour out drinks when he wasn't looking, just as I had done at Louise Hideaway. By this time it was getting dark, and I wanted George to take me home. Instead, he drove me to his sister's wall house in Mt. Greenan, where he had been spending his nights. When we got there he said, "I guess you know why we are stopping here." I told him I had no idea. That was when George suggested we have sex. I told him I was not about to have sex with him, and he had better forget it. George got angry and told me in that case I would have to walk home.

It was after seven that Sunday night, and George's sister's home was a little over a mile from my village. The distance was one thing, but darkness was another. The road from George's house to my village was surrounded by banana trees and there were no lights. The entire area was pitch dark. I remembered stories about the ghosts wandering on dark roads who supposedly blinded you and led you over the embankment of a cliff to your death. I decided I would rather risk death by some ghost than allow a living man like George to force himself on me. That was the choice I was faced with that night, and I chose to walk. The days when men could take advantage of me and rape me were over. I left George sitting in his blue Volkswagen, an angry man, and I began to walk the pitch-dark road back to my village. I think George was surprised by my decision, because he drove up to me and told me he would take me home, but I refused, walking on until I reached my village. Since most villagers went to bed early, the village was already dark, but prayer meeting was still going on in one of the churches, where I entered. I cried when the minister began his prayer, asking God to bless the sinners. I felt as though God had blessed me that night, and I was proud of myself. The following day, I heard a rumor that I had had sex with George that night, and I had no doubt that it was George who started the rumor. I came to realize that many of the men spread rumors that they had had sex with young women like me as a form of bragging and revenge, especially when those young women had rejected their sexual advances. I came to ignore much name-calling and rumors as I did this latest one.

Daymond was another one of my predators. He seemed much older than George, and I thought of him as my friend. He would visit me a few evenings each week and fill me in on the village gossip, and would even talk about other girls. Daymond lived in Chapman Village, and we attended the same Anglican Church. One afternoon he invited me to a gospel show, saying that other church members would be there, so I accepted his invitation. When we got there Sunday evening, I was surprised to see that he and I were the only church members in the audience. Understanding that he had lied to me, I did not enjoy the show and was glad when it was over. We chatted about church and even about my school. Although I told everyone I wanted to be a teacher when I graduated from high school, for years I had had a secret ambition to become a lawyer. When Daymond asked about my future plans, I was surprised to find myself telling him my secret aspiration. I felt uneasy while Daymond and I were engaged in conversation, keeping my eyes on his every move. When we got close to my village, he left the road to my village and turned into a dark winding road leading to an area surrounded by banana fields. I was able to see a few houses at a distance, and only the sounds of nature broke the dark silence. He stopped the car and tried to hug and kiss me. I sensed that he wanted sex even before he had made his advance. I told him I could not have sex with him because I was dating Andrew. "What's the big deal?" he asked. "Doesn't he date other girls besides you, and you other boys besides him?" "That doesn't make any difference, and I am not about to have sex with you. You had better take me home before I run to the nearest house and cry for help." He took my threat seriously. I said to him that I would have sex with him only after Andrew had had sex with his woman, knowing she was as attractive as an old mule. He was insulted and then became angry, saying, "Let me take you home." He drove me home and when I said good night to him, he drove away hurriedly without responding. I felt proud to have kept another of those sons of bitches off of my stomach.

I would normally see Daymond driving through the village, but that entire week I did not. So I was surprised when he came to my mother's house the following Sunday to offer me a ride to church. I was not planning to attend church that Sunday, and I would not have accepted his offer even if I were. Later, when I was walking to the crossroads outside the village, I saw Daymond driving towards the village. As soon as he recognized me, he stopped, but I kept on walking. Only when he said he wanted to apologize to me for his recent behavior did I stop and listen. "I am sorry I acted the way I did, and I am asking for your forgiveness," he said. He said he had thought that I was a different kind of person, based on the rumors he had heard about me saying I was "easy to get." He now realized the rumors were malicious lies, saying he thought that I was a very good person, and encouraging me to continue to strive for academic excellence. Most islanders felt that the legal profession was not for women, but Daymond encouraged my aspirations, telling me I would become an attorney one day and lending me books about the law. He and I became closer friends, and as a result rumors were spread that we were sexually involved.

In spite of the continuing malicious rumors about me, I pursued my educational goals relentlessly. During my last year of high school I confided to my father that I intended some day to fly in one of those big airplanes travelling to America, Canada or England. My father discouraged me from immigrating to England, explaining that England could be a cruel place for a young woman like me. He said that when he lived in England he had seen the many difficulties experienced by the young women who immigrated there. Having gone to England in hope of a better life, they found themselves in worse conditions than those they had left behind. My father told stories about the men sleeping on railroad tracks, and the women, especially the younger ones, selling their bodies in order to survive. Many of the women survived by marrying men they would not otherwise have considered. He described how wealthy English people having parties would throw food out the window, watching the poor immigrants catch the scraps like dogs. He asked me whether I knew the true meaning of Boxing Day, the day after Christmas, celebrated as a holiday in most of the Caribbean countries that once were colonies of Great Britain. My father explained that the English did not give their maids the day off on Christmas because they needed them to cook and serve their guests at the traditional Christmas parties. So the rich packed the Christmas party leftovers in boxes and gave them to their maids the day after Christmas. So the day after Christmas, the maids' day off, came to be called Boxing Day and celebrated as a holiday. After hearing all of this about England, I deleted it from the list of countries I would like to travel to.

That was the first meaningful conversation I had had with my father since his return to St. Vincent from England six years ago. I learned much about England, but not about the relationship between my mother and my father around the time I was born. I wanted to ask him why he had abandoned my mother and me. When the time seemed right, I asked him straight out, and I expected him to give me straight answers.

I also wanted to ask my father about Elma and my half brothers, who I had heard had immigrated to Trinidad five years ago. Elma had not brought them to say good-bye to me, and they had not written to me. The opportunity came when I went to visit my father in the two-room board house he was renting, where he had just the basic things: a bed, a table, three chairs and a pumping oil stove. My father seemed no older than when I had seen him for the first time. He was not well dressed, and I thought he must have already spent most of the money he had brought back from England. Since I knew he had not spent it on me, what he had done with his money was the least of my concerns. Sitting across from him, I began to ask him questions about Elma and her children, my English-born brothers and the baby sister who had died shortly after their arrival in St. Vincent. I wanted him to clarify or confirm what Sandra had told me. He confirmed that Elma was pregnant by another man when she went to England, that the child was put up for adoption, and that he could not forgive Elma and so did not marry her. I asked whether he was keeping in touch with my brothers in Trinidad and was disappointed to learn he was not. I assumed that he was no longer sure where they were and therefore would not be supporting them financially. My father also told me that I had two other brothers still living in England.

My father talked about another woman he had loved while in England, a white girl, either English or Irish, who was sixteen years old when he first met her. It made me sick to my stomach to hear him brag that the girl was only sixteen. I could not help thinking that, even though he said he loved her and she was the mother of two of his sons, he must have raped her as the pedophiles had raped me. "Why didn't you marry her?" I asked. "After Elma's

betrayal I couldn't marry any woman," he answered. I asked my
father if he was keeping in touch with these two sons. When he
answered that he was not, I concluded that he was a vagabond, a
bastard who abandoned his children, something lower than a dog,
possibly a pedophile and rapist as well.

Sad and angry, I asked him why he had abandoned my mother
when she was pregnant with me and why he had disowned me. My
father told me he was never my mother's boyfriend, but had only
visited her and had sex with her one night while my grandmother
was selling nuts and sugar cake (a candy made from sugar and
peanuts) at a village party. A few months later, when my mother
told him she was pregnant, he told her another man had to be
responsible, since he had had sex with her only one time. He left
St. Vincent a few weeks later. "Yeah, you left St. Vincent " I said,
"because your mother thought you were too good for my mother
and she sent you away." He said sadly that he hoped that I understood, but I refused to accept any of his sorry excuses. I thought,
"It's lucky that ass of a mother of yours is dead now and I never
knew the bitch until I saw her with sores all over her lips and nose.
The bitch is dead now and I never had to call her grandmother.
Grandmother, my ass, I would never have called her grandmother.
She wasn't a grandmother to me!" My father protested that he really and truly did not believe himself responsible for my mother's
pregnancy, speaking as though he were trying to convince me, but
he failed. I looked my father directly in his eyes and asked him
why he had never acknowledged me as his child, since everyone
in the village believed he was my father from the close resemblance between us. He told me he had never heard any comments
about our resemblance. I knew he tended to lie to me, so I asked
him calmly—and it took a lot to remain calm at the time—why,
then, he had tried to get my birth certificate quite some time after
my birth. He said that he had never done so, which I knew was a
lie. I became more angry with him, crying and repeating my question over and over again, "Why did you disown and abandon me,
knowing I bore such resemblance to you? Didn't you know I was
hungry and needed your financial support for food? Didn't you
know I needed shoes to wear to school? Didn't you know my feet
suffered from the heat on the pitch roads? But most of all, didn't
you think I deserved to know I had a father who cared about me?"
Asking those questions made me realize that the man sitting across
from me was no damn good. He had abandoned all his other chil-

dren as he had abandoned me. My brothers and I were all victims of his neglect. I had heard that he fathered three more children in St. Vincent, one of whom had already died from starvation, undoubtedly because the mother could not afford to buy food without my father's support. I thanked God that of the nine children I knew he had fathered, seven of us were still alive. After all was said and done, I concluded that I was better off not knowing this man while I was growing up. This vagabond who called himself my father had been nothing more than a sperm donor to my conception, and for once in my life I felt damn lucky to have had some good people in my life. I thought of people like my Ma, who loved and cared for me until her death, and my Uncle Josey and my grandmother, who continued to support me financially and otherwise. I came to appreciate Bulah, my mother, who, in spite of all her abuse, was still present to me. I knew I would never call my father daddy, because I felt he never did anything for me to deserve that name, which should be considered an honor reserved for a good father. My father was not a good father.

My mother continued to fight my battles in the village, cursing those who were defaming my character, but she was fighting battles of her own, as well. This Miss Freda woman and my mother despised each other, each hurling insults and unkind names at the other. I still do not understand why. Besides, Mr. Phillips' girlfriend had become bold, cursing my mother more often now, sometimes even being joined in cursing by her mother. If all that were not enough of a cross for my mother to bear, Mr. Phillips continued to abuse her. "Well, mother," I promised myself, "all that will stop soon after I graduate and find a job. I will assist you in regaining your self-esteem with my financial support." Yes, my high school years are coming to an end.

I also remember some inspiring moments in my life and the few kindhearted and generous people, beyond my family, who had made them possible. Randell was one of them. I continued to see him on and off, and he continued to support me financially, but it was his sincere encouragement that had the most effect on me. Randell spoke to me as a father would to his daughter. He boosted my ego, saying I was a smart person and could be whatever I wanted to be, could even climb the highest mountain. At times when my spirit was low and my hopes and dreams almost abandoned, Randell's words of encouragement would renew my spirit. Although he wanted us to have a sexual relationship, we had never gone beyond kissing, and he had yet to make another sexual advance towards me, assuring me he would never do such a thing before I graduated. Like Randell, I must also remember Leeann, Elitha, Sarah, the Staddards and Miss John, the ones who never seemed to believe the rumors about me.

Most of the mothers in the village were against me, and I despised them as much as they despised me. I must be grateful to Mr. and Mrs. Steven, who must have known, as everybody else did, the difficulties I faced with the villagers. They were always kind to me, offering words of encouragement and telling me to ignore people and continue to strive for academic excellence. Their encouragement would forever stay with me, even though I never let them know how much they meant to me in those troubling days. Miss John, who lived just above the village with Mr. Allen. was another supporter who used to encourage me. Once when she met me in town, she had given me a dollar and I bought my lunch with that money. Although I thanked her at the time, I hope she realized how grateful I was to her. Whenever they saw me, Sarah, Elitha and Leeann, all of whom lived in my village, had an encouraging word to say to me. Had it not been for the encouragement of those wonderful people, I wonder if I could have made it through school. They lifted my spirits when they were sinking into despair over the rumors of the envious villagers, giving me the strength and will power to carry on when I thought all had been lost. I wanted to thank them from the bottom of my heart.

When I walked to the platform to collect my diploma from Sister Agatha, I knew I was at the end of the tunnel and seeing the light on the other side. Lord, I was surrounded by all of my classmates, except poor Saline. Happy for myself and my classmates, I was also sad that Saline was not with us at the graduation which we all had looked forward to for so many years. Dressed in white dresses, shoes and stockings, we sat in the four adjoining classrooms that had been converted into a single large space, with our parents and teachers seated behind us, all facing the platform. The graduating class each sat with a male escort, a brother, uncle, father or boyfriend. Our team song was "Bridge Over Troubled Waters" and, oh, how I cried as we were singing. A few teachers made their remarks on the platform before Sister gave her commencement speech. Then she called out our names to come up for our diplomas. Each of us walked to the platform with our male escort, bowing to Sister Agatha after receiving the diploma. My mother, of course, was sitting in the audience. Although she had not said anything about it to me, I believe she looked forward to my graduating from high school. I wondered if she knew how much I had longed for this moment, not so much for myself as for her. I felt obligated to help her and resolved to do everything within my power to ease her burdens. I wished she could have shared her thoughts with me and I could have shared mine with her, but we did not have that kind of relationship. Without her saying anything to me, I knew she was counting on me for help, since that was the norm in our society. Children were expected to assist their parents financially when they were old enough to find work, and I assume that was why most of them had so many children.

I had now entered into a new phase in my life. I now had lots of decisions to make, and looking for a job and returning to Barbados were just two of them.

After Graduation

I had promised to return to Barbados and marry Vernon, and he sent me my plane ticket a week before I graduated from high school. Since all of the schools would soon be closed for vacation and I planned to seek employment as a teacher when they reopened, I decided to go to Barbados until the start of the new school year. Two weeks before flying to Barbados I went to Randell to inform him of my plans and my intention to seek employment as a teacher. He insisted that I spend some time with him before I left, so I had lunch with him several times. It was during one of these luncheons in his private dinning room, overlooking the flower garden of lilies and carnations, that we spoke openly about having a sexual relationship. "Randell, you have been so kind to me and I appreciate it, but I am concerned about this sex thing between you and me," I said to him, conscious of talking to him like a woman, not a girl or a teenager. Randell asked if I was afraid of him, but I assured him I was only afraid of getting pregnant. Randell pledged that he would use protection and would never get me pregnant. "Randell," I thought, "I believe you would, but you are a married man and too damn old for me. I question the morality of having sex with a married man, but your case is sort of different, since you are separated from your wife, and it is said that the separation is a result of her infidelity. Even though you had been unfaithful to her for many years, you could not accept her being unfaithful to you. Holy shit, Randell, you are too much for me to deal with. But you have been so generous and kind to me. You have never let me down, and you waited until I graduated from high school before you pursued this sex talk with me. What the hell, Lola, Andrew hasn't done shit for you except cause you pain and heartaches, yet you continue to have sex with him. I don't see the big deal in having sex with Randell, who has done so much for you." With these thoughts flowing rapidly through my mind, as the river below my mother's house flowed when there was a heavy rainfall, I decided I had nothing to lose if I had sex with Randell.

A few days before my departure for Barbados, we met for lunch and had a few drinks, as we had planned. By now I had acquired some class; Randell no longer had to show me how to use my knife and fork. He introduced me to some of his big shot friends, one of whom was trying to hit on me by asking me for a date. The old men loved to mingle with young girls like me, and they referred to us as young papayas. After lunch, Randell escorted me to his private room, and, girl, that room was gorgeous. The walls of his private bathroom were painted in a bluish color, and his bedroom set was of mahogany, with bed properly made with blue sheets and spread. Blue draperies decorated the windows, from which there was a lovely view of the garden of roses, daffodils, and carnations.

Entering the room and thinking about what was going to take place between this older man and me, I felt scared out of my boots. It was not his age but his marital status that bothered me the most. When he opened the door to answer his maid's knock, she entered carrying a tray of alcoholic drinks, which he must have ordered ahead of time. We were sitting on the bed when he began kissing me passionately, but I wasn't enjoying it because of my fear. I never liked anyone looking at my naked, bony body, so when Randell undressed me, I hurriedly covered myself with the bed covers. Randell was ready to have sex with me when he noticed my sobbing and trembling. He took me in his arms and asked if I were getting sick. I replied, "No, just scared." He held my body tightly to his and reassured me of his love. "I understand your fear. I am not about to have sex with you if you don't want me to. I will wait until you give me permission," he said, and he helped me get dressed. After both of us were dressed, I lay in his arms in bed and he comforted me. I told him all I could about my relationship with Andrew. I guess he gathered from my conversation that I didn't trust many men, because he insisted that I could trust him. He said I was special to him and promised to do everything in his power to protect me. What Randell didn't know, because I didn't tell him even when he asked me directly, was that he was becoming special to me, too. This special feeling overwhelmed me as I kissed him good-bye and walked away. I visited Randell again the day before my departure for Barbados. Kind and generous as always, he gave me a hundred dollars, a great sum of money to me, and told me to take good care of myself while I was away. His voice was soft and sincere as he said, "I love you."

Vernon was waiting for me when I arrived at the airport in Barbados. It was a sunny day, and the smile on Vernon's face was full of excitement as I hugged him. Before leaving the airport terminal for the car that Vernon had hired, I noticed again those large airplanes, much larger than the seventeen-passenger plane I had flown in from St. Vincent. I was more determined than ever to be a passenger on one of these planes some day. When we entered Vernon's home, his family was sitting in the living room. They greeted me with excitement, especially Miss Laurel, who referred to me as her daughter-in-law. Vernon seemed to be in love with me more than ever, and he asked whether I had decided on a date for us to get married. Thoughts went through my head, "Vernon, I care for you, love you, whatever, but not to marry you. Marriage is not a big deal for me. After all, I am only eighteen years old. Would I be thought ungrateful to you if I told you that I was not ready to get married? How would Miss Laurel feel about me if I refused to marry you? Why, Vernon, why do you want me to marry you at my young age? You only know what I have told you about me, but you don't really know me. Even though I say I love you, I am confused about love. What is love, really? Is it possible that a woman can love more than one man at a time? It must be possible, because I love Andrew, I have a special love for Randell, and I love you, too, Vernon. Although I think I am in love with all of you, I have no intention of marrying any of you, at least not now." Vernon's asking me to set a date had led me to question the whole idea of love and marriage. The more I questioned love and this thing that society called marriage, the more I objected to marrying at all.

I remembered, of course, that I had promised Vernon I would marry him after I graduated from high school. But that was then and this is now, and between then and now I had changed my mind. At that time in my life, I believed marriage was a commitment between a man and a woman, in which both vowed to love each other until death did them part. I remembered from wedding ceremonies I had attended a phrase about "for richer or poorer." But never was anything mentioned about the babies, and I knew that married people do have babies, and not one or two, but lots of babies, lots of picmies, as my mother had. Hell, yes, I was too young for all that marriage stuff. The things I didn't like about marriage outweighed what I liked. I felt I couldn't promise any man to love him until death. Suppose he abused me as Mr. Phillips abused my mother. Could I still love him? Not likely. And if my man became poorer while we were married, I'm sure I wouldn't stay married to him just for marriage's sake. I would more likely divorce him, live on my own, and do better without his dragging me down. As to having babies, or picmies, the man who would breed me and let this belly of mine get big hasn't been born yet, and his mother and grandmother have already died.

I didn't know how to tell Vernon I wasn't going to marry him. It had nothing to do with love, because I loved him well enough. But marrying him or anyone else at the time was not something I wanted to do. My top priority was to get a good job to assist my mother financially. My siblings, soon to be nine of them, since mother was pregnant again, needed me more than any man ever would. In spite of my not giving Vernon an answer, he continued to treat me well, taking me on sightseeing trips and buying me small gifts. Vernon also would give me 20 or 25 dollars when he got paid. Vernon trusted me so much that when I told him I wanted to visit my uncle alone, he even showed me how to catch the bus to his house.

It was on the bus one day when I went to visit my uncle by myself that I met Reggie. We rode the bus from St. Michael, the capital and one of Barbados' parishes, to Christ Church, another parish. I guess it was a coincidence that both Reggie and I got off at St. Lawrence Gap, close to my uncle's residence and not far from the hotel where Reggie worked. Sitting across from me, Reggie never took his eyes off me, and I could tell he was interested in me. I normally didn't speak to strangers, but when Reggie asked me where I lived I told him I was staying with friends while visiting the island. We talked for a while and then exchanged telephone numbers.

When I realized that I had just given the telephone number of Vernon's family to another man, I rationalized to myself, "What the heck, it's only a telephone number, and he's just someone I met casually. Nothing will come of it." Yet I knew that I should never have given him the number. As it turned out, Reggie became more than just someone I met casually, for I began dating him. Reggie took me to the racetrack, the movies, lunches, dinners, and even to the beach. Whenever I had a date with Reggie, I would tell Vernon I was visiting my uncle. Sometimes Vernon wanted to accompany me on these visits, but I would persuade him not to. Like Vernon, Reggie treated me well financially and otherwise, providing me with so much that I didn't have to ask him for anything. He introduced me to his friends as his girlfriend. I don't know what it is about Barbadian men and marriage, for it didn't take Reggie long to tell me he wanted to marry me. Then it was that sex thing again.

I was not about to get involved with Reggie sexually, so I told him I was a virgin, that sex before marriage violated my religious beliefs, and that I personally felt it was morally wrong. Young as I was, I felt that we women could deceive men better than they could deceive us. After all, we gave birth to them. In this case I was right, for Reggie believed the lies I told him. I overheard him telling one of his friends that he was in love with me, that I was only eighteen years old, attractive and smart, a high school graduate, and was still a virgin. "Boy, she is untouched. She believes strongly in religion and has lots of morals, too," he told his friend, not knowing I was listening. I felt good about myself, thinking it was about time I had some power over men. I don't know whether it was because of the crimes the rapists and pedophiles had committed against me as a child, but I developed a hate-love relationship with men, even with Vernon.

Vernon was still asking me to marry him, and I knew the time had come when I couldn't keep him in suspense any longer. We were returning from the beach that day in August 1973 when I told him that I was not ready to commit myself to marriage. I tried to explain to him that I loved him but felt I was too young and immature for such a serious commitment. After we got back to his house, Vernon told Miss Laurel about our conversation and asked her to have a talk with me. Although I knew Vernon was hurt, I felt I had made the right decision, not only for myself, but for him as well. If I had wanted a good man at that time in my life, there is no doubt in my mind that Vernon would have been the right one.

He was such a loving and caring person that I felt I had to let him go. Vernon deserved a woman who was as caring and loving to him as he was to me, and I knew that I was not that type of woman. I would like to believe I did it for the sake of my love for him, or at least because I cared for him.

When I told Reggie I was returning home, he pleaded with me to stay, without success. Vernon was still trying to convince me to marry him, but he could not persuade me to change my mind, either. I wanted to return to St. Vincent. I felt sad when I had to say good-bye to Vernon and his family. Vernon accompanied me to the airport, and again my flight was delayed. I sat watching those big airplanes, one of which some passengers had been boarding, and I wished that I could have been boarding it too instead of waiting for the small plane that would fly me back to St. Vincent. After Vernon and I had said our good-byes, he assured me of his love and said I was to let him know if I changed my mind. "I love you, too, Vernon, and I will always love you, but at this time, I have to do what I have to do," I said to him. I kissed him good-bye as I took my handkerchief and wiped away the teardrops from his eyes. Then I boarded my small plane, soon ascending into the air. I viewed the big planes until they were out of sight, the thought of someday being a passenger on one never leaving my mind, not even when the small plane was descending to land in St. Vincent.

It was the middle of August when I returned, three months after I had left St. Vincent, time for me to begin my search for a teaching job. There were several reasons why I wanted to be a teacher. I thought as a teacher I could become a source of inspiration for poor, discouraged children like me. Teaching was also the only job I knew that offers three vacations a year, at Easter, summer and Christmas. Besides, the pay was fairly good. I went to the Education Department and applied for a teaching position and was disappointed when the Education Officer, Mr. White, who had been the principal of the village school I had attended, did not make me an offer. I soon found out that to get a job as a teacher, or a comparable government position, one had to be politically connected or know someone in a high position. I further learned that men with authority to hire would hire young girls like me only if we were willing to give them sex in return. I looked with disgust at some of the old crows of men, old enough to be my father or grandfather, some of them looking as though they hadn't washed their beard or brushed their dirty-looking teeth for days. Others sat haughtily at their desks seeming to think they were God on the throne, expecting you to bow down and worship them for a job. "Well," I said to myself, "I might be hungry for a job, but I'm not starving, and I'm not about to throw away my education by putting myself at the mercy of these bastards. Hell, no, I would rather starve to death. Lord, you know I am poor, and I know it, but the idea of going to bed with any of these men to get a job is out of the question. Why are the people in this society so backward? Why do they vote these politicians into power, knowing how corrupt they are and how much they exploit their children, especially the girls?" Like the rapists who continue to rape women and children, most of our politicians continued to exploit the young, and it seemed to be considered acceptable behavior in our society. As I looked at the whole scenario, it seemed that it was mostly poor girls like me who would be exploited, girls whose parents could hardly maintain us through high school, and who finished high school with hopes of repaying our poor parents. Yes, they exploited young girls like me, whose parents had no political connections, working as laborers and maids. Yes, these bastards of men would try to exploit young girls like me, and we made up the majority of our society. This experience of seeking employment at the tender age of eighteen made me more aware of my society as a whole, and I was able to analyze things in a new way.

Although I had applied a month before the reopening of the school year, I was never offered a teaching position. I was able to find a temporary position at the Banana Association as an accounting clerk, mostly balancing the accounts of the banana farmers. Except for my transportation and lunch money, I gave all my wages to my mother, and as a result she seemed to change her attitude towards my siblings and me. She began to treat us more humanely. My mother did not curse me or beat any of my siblings from the day I began working. Unfortunately, my job lasted only two months, and after that I was unable to continue my financial support. I searched for another job.

My cousin Laura was a nurse at the Kingstown General Hospital, the main hospital in the island. She encouraged me to try nursing. "Laura," I thought, "nursing is not for me. Only special people with a little Florence Nightingale personality can be a nurse, and I am not special. I have not got as much as an iota of Florence Nightingale in me, and I'm not interested working at that smelly hospital." I remember accompanying Jennifer to the hospital when she visited her sister, who had broken her foot. That hospital was so damn smelly that it made me sick to my stomach, and I had to cover my nostrils with my handkerchief. I couldn't wait to get out of there. Then I thought that if I became a nurse, I would have to work on Sundays, as well as Christmas Day, Boxing Day, New Year's Day and all of the other major holidays. After thinking it over, I told Laura I wasn't interested in a nursing career. Seven months after my return from Barbados, still needing a job to give my mother the financial support that she so desperately needed, I thought of Randell. As a businessman, I knew Randell would have connections, and I remembered that some of his friends were men in high positions. I knew Randell would help me if he could, and so I went to him for assistance.

I hadn't visited Randell since my return from Barbados six months earlier. He was surprised when I visited him in his office at the hotel, but he seemed happy to see me. I lied, saying I had returned only four days earlier, and then I asked him to help me find a job. "What type of job are you looking for?" he asked me. "A teaching job," I replied. "Teaching job? You can do better than that. How about a job with the government or the bank?" He arranged an interview with Mr. Jordan, a friend of his working in a high position at the Public Works Department. When I informed Mr. Jordan's receptionist that I was there to see Mr. Jordan, she escorted me to his office. There I found a middle aged man sitting behind his desk, hands clasped under his chin, who asked me courteously to be seated. Mr. Jordan asked when I had graduated from St. Joseph's and how long I had known Mr. Ralston. When he asked if I liked working with figures, as the job would require, I told him that mathematics was my favorite subject in high school. "Well, the job is yours. You can begin working in two weeks, the first day of February. Tell Randell to call me," Mr. Jordan said as I was leaving his office. We shook hands and I thanked him for offering me the job. By the time I returned to Randell's office, he had already spoken to Mr. Jordan. Randell offered to rent an apartment for me in town so I would not have to take the bus back and forth to work. Surprised by his offer, I told him I would think about it.

"Randell," I mused "if you were to rent a place for me, you would be my sugar daddy, as the people say, and I would be your woman. Most young women in my position, especially my friend Saline, would accept this offer faster than they would a ticket to heaven. I don't know how old you are, Randell, but you look old enough to be my father. Your offer is tempting. If you were to pay my rent and expenses, it would leave me more money with which to assist my mother and grandmother. Some young girls would reason that way, and I have heard a few say that they would rather be an old man's darling than a young man's slave. I am tempted myself to jump at the opportunity. But, Randell, I am not like Saline and those other young girls. The only thing they and I have in common is the poverty we were born into, and, as my grandmother would say, poverty is a hell of a thing. Poverty causes people to do things they would not normally do otherwise. Randell, renting an apartment for me and paying my expenses would mean you own me, and I don't want any man owning me, let alone a married man like yourself. So I most definitely have to reject your offer." Although these were my thoughts, I never had the courage to convey them to Randell. Instead, I politely told him I would consider his offer. I left Randell's office that day confused, not knowing what I would do.

I decided not to take the job, even though it would have paid much more than a teaching position, and I desperately needed the money to support my mother, grandmother, siblings and myself. It was an offer that not too many poor, young girls like me would have refused. But I felt that if I accepted the job I would have to accept Randell's offer of an apartment, so I decided to reject both. I was not about to compromise my pride and morals, even for a job that could bring an end to my poverty. So I continued to live among the devious people in my village and with the continuous domestic violence in my home.

Years of physical abuse were taking a toll on my mother. She had more marks on her body than a road map, and Arlene, Mr. Phillips' other woman, continued cursing at her. Then Arlene tried to hurt me physically, and I decided I would not tolerate any of that. I was walking back to the village from the crossroads with a cousin one evening when Arlene spotted us. The moment she recognized me, she began to curse at me. I ignored the woman, telling myself I was not my mother and would not stoop to her level by getting into a verbal confrontation with her. When she saw that I did not respond to her cursing, Arlene grew more angry. I could not understand why she was angry with me in the first place, since I had never done her any harm. Arlene began throwing rocks, almost hitting me with one. My cousin warned her that if any of the rocks hit either of us, we would beat the hell out of her. Arlene stopped throwing the rocks, concentrating her energy instead on cursing me. My cousin and I decided to ignore her curses and continued to walk towards the village. I said nothing about it to my mother. I knew I could have filed a complaint against Arlene at the district police station in Colonarie Village, but I decided not to. I had heard that the policemen at the station tended to ignore complaints from women, so I felt they would not have taken my complaint seriously. But I still wanted to teach Arlene a lesson. I wanted her to learn not to provoke me as long as both of us lived in St. Vincent and that she would pay the consequences if she did. As another option, I thought I could report the incident to the main police headquarters in town, and not to just any police officer, but to the chief of police himself. I did not know whether I would be able to see the chief but I decided to try.

I could hardly wait for the following day. I awoke early and walked to the crossroads for the bus to town. I planned to lodge a complaint against Arlene with none other than the St. Vincent police chief, the highest-ranking police officer on the island. I went directly to Mr. Ashton's office at the police headquarters and told his secretary I wanted to speak to him. As I sat waiting, other policemen walked in and out, some seeming not to notice me, others staring at me, probably wondering what I was doing there. After 15 minutes, I was escorted to Mr. Ashton's office and seated across from him. I gave him a vivid description of Arlene's attack on me the evening before, emphasizing that I feared for my life. I cried, wiping tears from my eyes as I spoke. When I told him I was a graduate of St Joseph's Convent, I could tell that a chord was touched in him. I thought he probably had children of his own attending there. After listening to my complaint, Chief Ashton comforted me and assured me he would take care of the situation. He told me to come back to him immediately if Arlene ever came near me or threatened me in any way. I was satisfied with what I had done and with the chief's response.

That evening, Mr. Phillips came home in a rage, cursing and shouting at my mother that I had to leave his house. "He's about to throw me out of this house," I thought, "the house my mother helped him build with her toil in the fields. It seems the house is all his, not hers." The society in which we lived at the time allowed men to claim entirely everything they rightly should have owned jointly with women. Seeing the pain in my mother's face, I decided to spare her the agony of asking me to leave and left on my own. With my mother and siblings crying as they looked on, I walked away from the yard and went up the hill to the home of Tanty Inis. I told her what had happened at home and asked if I could stay with her. Tanty Inis said that as long as she was living in her home, I was welcome to come and stay with her.

Elitha, the lady in the village who had told me not to bother with the villagers and that I must continue to do my very best in school, encouraged me again. "You will be all right," she said. She told me not to worry about not living with my mother, as long as my mother hadn't turned her back on me, which she never did. My mother continued to send me my meals, and the only difference between living with her and living with Tanty Inis was that I now had a bed to myself instead of sleeping in my mother's bed with her and my sister.

I still did not have a job. I was surprised one day while I was walking to the crossroads, when Mr. White, the Education Officer, saw me and asked me why was I not at work. "What work?" I replied. "Are you not working as a teacher?" he asked. When I told Mr. White I had never been hired, Mr. White said that he thought I had been. He promised he would hire me as soon as a teaching job became available nearby. I knew he did not mean what he said, and I was tempted to tell him he was a hypocrite, but I thought it would not be wise to offend him.

Nine months after I had graduated from high school and six months after I had returned to St. Vincent from Barbados in hopes of being hired as a teacher, I was still unemployed. Discouraged and confused, I wondered if I had made the right decisions. Would I have been better off staying in Barbados and marrying Vernon? Had I been foolish in declining the clerical job at the Public Works Department and Randell's offer of a place in town for me? I began to have doubts about my judgment. I thought that perhaps I should have done this or that instead of what I had actually decided to do. "Oh, Lola," I told myself, "what you think you should have done is all in the past. Concentrate on what you can do now and make your plans for the future." I remembered that during my last semester in school Edna had visited St. Vincent. Recognizing me from across the street, she called me to her. Edna told me she was still interested in helping me in immigrate to America and gave me her address. I told her I was still interested in immigrating to America, even though I really wasn't at the time. Unfortunately, I must have thrown away the paper on which she had written her address. "If only I had her address," I thought, "I could write to Edna. I would do better to immigrate to America than to sit around in this damn island waiting for Mr. White to offer me a teaching job." Suddenly, it occurred to me that Tanty Inis must have Edna's address. Saying I felt like writing to Edna, I asked her for the address, and she wrote it on a piece of paper and gave it to me.

The next day, I sat at the table in Tanty Inis' house and wrote to Edna, informing her that I had graduated from high school but had not yet found a job. I explained to her how and why Mr. Phillips had thrown me out of my mother's house, and I asked for her assistance in immigrating to America. My grandmother was the only one I told about my letter to Edna. Because my grandmother's house was where Patrick had first raped me, it was like a haunted house to me. Otherwise I might have been living with her instead of Tanty Inis. Whenever I was in my grandmother's house, I would have flashbacks of those frightening experiences. The memories of my rape were still tearing me apart, and the pain I suffered within was unbearable at times. Still, I kept it all secret.

My grandmother always encouraged me to pray to God, especially in times of need. I continued to pray, asking God to provide me with a job, but there were times when I couldn't help wondering whether God had forgotten me. Almost a year after my graduation, I was still out of work. The more I lived in the village among these hateful people, the more I felt I needed to get away from them. I felt there was something destructive about most of the people in my village, and I knew that whatever it was, I didn't want to be a part of it. I didn't want to be part of the malicious gossip-mongering, and I certainly didn't want to become one of the young girls my age or younger who were having many children, most of them fathered by different men. And, oh, my mother! My mother! I was absolutely, positively sure I never, never wanted to become a victim like her. Oh no! No! No! I would never allow a man to beat me as she was allowing Mr. Phillips to beat her, let alone allow a man to stuff up my belly with a kid almost every year. Then I thought of what I could do if I immigrated to America. My mother would not have to worry as long as I had a job. I promised myself to take care of all of her financial needs if I could. I would make the necessary sacrifices for my siblings and for her. And I could not forget my grandmother, my Mommy. "Oh, Mommy," I thought, "I wish I could hug you and tell you how much I thank

God for you." But it was not the custom in our village for members of a family to show affection to one another.

Edna replied to my letter stating she would assist me in immigrating to America, and I asked God to bless her even while I was reading her letter. She asked me to call her as soon as I received her letter. There were only two homes in the village with telephones. I could have gone to the Jeffersons and asked to make a phone call, but I wanted to speak to Edna in private and I was afraid that they would want to listen in. I decided to go to town the following day to Cable and Wireless, the main office of the telephone company. I told the receptionist that I wanted to place a call to America and paid her for a thirty-minute call. She directed me to a private telephone booth within the building.

During our conversation, Edna outlined to me the procedure for getting a visa from the American Embassy. I needed a bank statement and a current passport, along with a letter from an employer or a school stating that I was obligated to return to the island to fulfill an employment or educational commitment. Edna promised to send me a letter stating she was inviting me to spend a vacation with her and that she was willing to accommodate me during my stay. I would send all these things along with a cover letter to the American Counsulate in Barbados, asking them to grant me a visitor's visa.

I already had a passport that was valid for the next seven years, and I received Edna's letter of invitation within seven days of our conversation. But I had to think of how to obtain a bank statement and a job or school letter. I was no longer in school, and I felt I could not ask Sister Agatha to make false statements for me. I was not employed, so I could not get an employment letter. And the two hundred dollars I had in the bank was not sufficient for a bank statement. It occurred to me that my mother had a good sum of money in the bank, having saved it for Mr. Phillips and herself. In our society, it was the custom for people to save some money, no matter how poor they appeared to be. Whenever Mr. Phillips sold a pig or a cow, she would put the proceeds in the bank. I thought she could use that money to get me a bank statement. All she would have to do would be to transfer some of the money into an account in my name. After I received my bank statement, I would transfer the money back into her account.

I went to my mother and explained what Edna had told me. When I asked my mother to transfer some of their money to my name, one would have thought I had asked her to commit a felony. In a loud, defensive voice she said, "The money that me ha in the bank a no fo me money, ah Phillips money and me can't touch um fo ewe." I was dumfounded and ashamed. Although I was disappointed, I had to admit that my mother had the right to refuse me. After all, it was her money, or as she said, Mr. Phillips' money. My grandmother had taught me not to hold a grudge against other people for what they owned, because one never knows what they might have gone through to get it. So, disappointed as I was, I held no grudge in my heart towards my mother.

Although I had reservations about asking her, I went to Sister Agatha for a letter stating that I had a school commitment for which I must return to St. Vincent. I had heard a saying somewhere that the tragedy in life is not in trying and failing, but in not trying at all. I reasoned that Sister didn't really have to lie for me since I was signed up to take some extra subjects in May. She could write a letter stating just that much, and it wouldn't be a lie. I was nervous entering her office. When I explained the purpose of my visit, Sister Agatha smiled and typed the letter for me without hesitation. As she handed me the letter, she wished me good luck and encouraged me to stay in America if I could. She said that I would be better off there than in St. Vincent, emphasizing that America had lots of opportunities and that, with my determination, she had no doubt I would be successful there. Then she asked God to bless me, praying, "Bless and guide Belitha, Dear Lord! Take care of this child, God. Let her realize that with you all things are possible if she only believe. I pray for her safety, God. In Jesus' name, Amen." After thanking her, I looked around the office which I had once so dreaded venturing into. Looking at the picture of the crucified Christ hanging on the wall, I felt a peace within me. "Yes, God," I said to my self, "you have already blessed me, but I need more blessings. I need a bank statement."

When I got back to the village that day, I went looking for my grandmother. I found her sitting on a bench under a breadfruit tree next to our family yard. I told her about my meeting with Sister Agatha and about how disappointed I was with my mother. My grandmother seemed to have one piece of advice, one answer to all of my troubles: to pray and to believe in what I prayed for. She told me that believing is receiving. "Lola, when you pray to God, believe that you go receive way yo pray for and you go receive it," my grandmother said to me. I walked away from her believing that if I prayed to God and asked him to provide me with a bank statement, I would receive one. I believed in my grandmother.

I went back to Tanty Inis' house, locked myself in one of her bedrooms, and began to pray. "God, you know all of my needs. If it is possible, please show me a way to get a bank statement." I continued to pray and began to cry. I must have fallen asleep, because the next thing I heard was Tanty Inis calling me. She was concerned that I had been locked up in the room for such a long time without making a sound. I assured her that I was all right. That night I dreamt I was drowning in a deep and rapidly flowing river. Then, out of nowhere, Randell swam up to me and saved me. When I awoke, I knew that the dream was telling me to go to Randell, and he would be able to help me get a bank statement. I realized that this advice was coming from a voice deep within my soul.

I had not spoken to Randell since declining his offer to rent an apartment for me. Although he acted at times like my father and at other times like an adviser, I knew he was a married man, so I had stayed away from him. But when I thought of the prospect of a better life, I said to myself, "What do you have to lose if you go to him and ask him for assistance?" "But, no," I answered myself, "I couldn't do that. I never even gave him a reason for refusing his offer of an apartment, let alone the job that he used his position to get for me. That was rude of me." "Yes, that was rude, but he is your only hope now if you want the bank statement. Who else would be able to give you one? Surely not Andrew, even though he has a job. As far as you know, his ass is poorer than you are. Why do you keep going back to him when he can't give you much anyway?" "It's because I love him." "Love, my ass, how could you love a man who betrayed your trust? Girl, your concern is not about Andrew and something you call 'love.' Your concern is to get yourself a bank statement and the only person who can help you is Randell. Girl, swallow your pride and go to him and ask him for his assistance. Apologize to him for not coming to see him sooner. Come up with some damn explanation of why you did not accept his offer, some lies that won't hurt his feelings or bruise his ego." This was my internal dialog as I lay in bed in the dark. I decided to swallow my pride and ask Randall's help. The following day I went to town to visit him.

I entered his office at exactly 8:15 a.m. Randell was sitting at his desk, but he jumped from his seat to embrace me as soon as I walked in. I returned his embrace, and we sat facing one another across his desk. I apologized for not getting back to him, and I lied about my reason for not accepting his offer or the job. Randell said he understood and listened attentively as I told him about Edna and my plans to immigrate. When I asked him to help me get a bank statement, he said "No problem. I am more than happy to assist you." Then he telephoned a bank manager he knew and instructed him to transfer ten thousand dollars of his money into an account in my name and to provide me with a bank statement. The manager was to transfer the money back to his account in three weeks, by which time I should have received a response from the American Consulate. Randell told me to go directly to the bank and ask for the manager, Mr. Stanley, who would give me the bank statement. We agreed to meet again at noon for lunch.

I walked into the bank and asked for Mr. Stanley. Some of the tellers looked puzzled when Mr. Stanley escorted me into his office, as this was a gesture usually extended only to the well-to-do in our society. Some of the tellers had been schoolmates of mine, and they knew the impoverished condition of my family. Mr. Stanley and I chatted while a member of his staff prepared my bank statement. Handing me the bank statement, he wished me good luck, and I thanked him and left.

While Randell and I sat together having lunch in his private dining room, he expressed apprehension about my immigrating to America on the advice of a woman I hardly knew. Randell thought I was too young to immigrate to such a large country, but he said he wouldn't discourage me if that was what I wanted to do. He asked me to promise to seek his assistance for another job if the American Consulate did not grant me a visa, and I promised that I would. As I was about to leave, he gave me fifty dollars, and I thanked him for everything. I left the hotel thinking how generous he had been to me.

Riding the bus home, I thought about what I should do next. I needed to write a cover letter to send to the consulate, but I had never written a letter of that kind before. I was sure I could do it, but I thought it would be a good idea to have someone else review it before I sent it, someone well versed in national and international affairs. Andrew was a possibility, being a teacher, but I didn't think he was well versed in national affairs, let alone international affairs. The only person I knew who possessed those skills was Oscar, a man I first met about five years ago when he came to my village to live.

Oscar's family was originally from my village, but they had all relocated to town. Oscar had gone off to a seminary to study to become a priest. Afterwards he came back to live in the village. I never knew why Oscar left the seminary before becoming a priest, but he did more for the people in the village than any priest I knew of had ever done. He was slender, bearded, soft-spoken, and always very reverent. He was kind to the people, visiting the old, poor, and downtrodden and he encouraged the youths to stay in school. There was nothing Oscar had that he would not give to you if you asked. I gathered my passport, bank statement, and the letters from Sister Agatha and Edna, and I went to Oscar's house to seek his help. I met him sitting on the veranda of his two-bedroom wall house, and I asked him to assist me with the cover letter to the American Consulate. He agreed, and the two of us sat on the veranda composing the letter. Gathering the letter and the other documents into an envelope, we addressed it to the American Consulate at the American Embassy in Barbados. The next day I bought the appropriate stamps at the post office in the village and mailed the letter. There was nothing left for me to do but wait for a response from the American Consulate.

The response came exactly fifteen days later. When I saw the envelope with its return address from the American Consulate, I was too scared to open it. With trembling hands, I finally tore open the envelope and inside found a letter informing me that I had been granted a visitor's visa to travel to America. Also enclosed was my passport, stamped to indicate a three-month visitor's visa. I felt ecstatic that I was on my way to the Promised Land, America. I went looking for my grandmother and mother to tell them the news. "I am so happy to leave all these devious people." I thought. "But wait, girl," I told myself, "you are forgetting something, You still need money to buy your plane ticket. Edna has already told you she could not afford to pay for your ticket, and the little money you have in the bank isn't enough to cover it. And you would feel ashamed going back to Randell for more assistance so soon."

I went to my close friend, Jennifer, who had a job, and she lent me a hundred dollars, but it was not enough for my plane fare. So I decided I had no choice but to go back to Randell for more help. When I informed him about my visa, he expressed his happiness for me and encouraged me to stay in America if I could. Randell advised me to do whatever I could, even scrubbing kitchen floors, to get a green card. "What the hell is a green card?" I wondered, but I never asked Randell. He encouraged me to enroll in school soon after I got the green card. He also said I should always remember my mother and her position and never forget where I came from. He stressed the importance of my helping my mother financially whenever I could. Then he brought up the subject of men. Randell warned me that America is a big country, much, much bigger than St. Vincent, and I must be careful of the men who would try to get into my crotch. "Your priority is to do better in life. Let no one come between you and that," he stressed. It was a long discussion which we had that day. I couldn't help thinking of all he had done for me and was continuing to do for me even at that moment. He seemed to have come into my life for a reason, and I felt connected to him in a unique way. For once, I put aside my moral scruples. I felt compelled to be with him in a sexual way, so I promised that I would return to spend an entire day with him before I left St. Vincent. Without my asking him, he gave me one hundred and fifty dollars. Added to my savings and the hundred dollars I had borrowed from Jennifer, it was enough for my plane ticket to America. My grandmother and mother together gave me another two hundred dollars to take with me to America. I bought my plane ticket and was scheduled to depart St. Vincent in exactly eight days. I telephoned Edna and she promised to meet me at Kennedy International airport on my arrival.

When I got back to the village, I told my grandmother about my plans, except for the part involving Randell. I also met Andrew at the village road and told him of my date of departure. Andrew and I were once again on friendly terms. Of all the men who had come into my life, Andrew seemed to be the one I loved most. Although he had been disloyal to me, I kept a place for him in my heart that would allow him to come in and go out of my life as he pleased. "Are you really going away?" he asked. "What will I do without you Lola? In spite of the differences between us, I love you more than any other. Believe me, I really, really love you," he murmured sadly. Then he held my hand and told me to look at him in the face. I saw how sad he looked when he said that he would never forget me, and I turned away. "I never told you about the sleepless nights I spent thinking of you whenever we broke up," he said, "especially if I heard you were dating someone else. Girl, there is no word in the dictionary to describe my feelings for you. It's something beyond my control, and I will always love you." Sitting there on the front steps of Tanty Inis' yard, three nights before my departure, I was touched by his many expressions of affection. I could not help thinking that our connection was beyond our control, and that was why we had so many times mended our relationship, even when we had vowed not to. Both of us had our faults and to a degree we each did things to get even with the other. I still wanted to blame him for some of my own lapses, like taking gifts and money from men who were hoping to have sex with me. If Andrew had been faithful to me, I would never have dated any other. But then again, I was lucky as it turned out, because I was blessed to have met Randell.

Two days before my departure, I went to spend the day with Randell. At that moment, Randell became my intimate lover. He was kind and gentle and, Lord, I loved him in a unique way. He was a unique man to me, and he was the only man ever to lay naked in bed with me without our having sex. He didn't do it because I didn't want him to. That's what you call respecting the other person, and his respect for me granted him a special place in my heart forever. "If the going gets rough for you in America and you want to return home, I am just a phone call away. I will pay for your return ticket and find you a job. I love you and I want you to be happy," Randell said to me as he caressed my body. Under the dim lights of his private bedroom in his own hotel, he touched my body tenderly. I was overcome by a sweet sensation throughout my body as he whispered, "Sweetie, I love you and I'm going to miss you." Randell wanted to come to the airport for my departure, but I persuaded him not to. My mother did not know about him, and I had already arranged for Andrew to accompany me to the airport. We kissed and hugged as I said my good-bye to him. Then I left him sadly, knowing he would miss me. I wondered whether he knew how much he meant to me and how much I would miss him. But I had never been able to express that to him.

Even though I was eager to leave, I thought about how I would miss my family, especially my grandmother. I consoled myself by reasoning that they would be better off financially when I found work in America. Lord, I hoped my support would be enough for my grandmother to stop working in the fields and the village road, work that brought so much pain from the ulcer on her foot. I considered my mother's situation with Mr. Phillips, and I wondered whether she would be able to leave him if I sent enough money for her to take care of my siblings and herself.

The night before my departure, my grandmother, mother, siblings and relatives gathered in the living room at Tanty Inis' house to have a small prayer meeting. They knelt with their heads bowed, one after the other praying for my flight to be a safe one and for God to bless me. My grandmother and my cousin Sandra counseled me to be grateful to Edna for her kindness and to obey her. I promised them that I would respect Edna and seek her advice. That night I couldn't sleep, and I lay in bed anxiously awaiting daybreak. Since we had no clock, I knew it was dawn when the cocks began crowing. I got out of bed, took a bath behind the house, and dressed myself in the pants and shirt that Vernon had bought me when I visited Barbados. My grandmother, along with siblings and relatives, gathered around me and cried. One by one they hugged me and wished me the best. Jasmine, Andrew, and my mother accompanied me in the taxi to the airport, and my best friend, Jennifer, met us there.

I checked in my luggage with one of the airline personnel, who tagged it to the United States. As we waited for the announcement of my departing flight, I could not help noticing my mother sobbing and wiping her eyes with her handkerchief, and at one point she cried hysterically. My mother had never said she was going to miss me, but I knew she would. I looked again and again at her, especially at the scars on her body that showed the abuse she had suffered from Mr. Phillips' hands. I wondered how long she would stay with Mr. Phillips, and I realized that I was her only hope. If she were ever to leave Mr. Phillips and set herself free, I was her ticket to freedom. I felt more than ever indebted to her, and I promised myself that I would do everything I could to help her.

I spent some time with each one who had accompanied me to the airport. Jasmine and I talked about the time we had spent having fun together, and we talked about how we were going to miss each other. Then I started to cry. Jennifer was my best friend, the one who never turned her back on me, who had offered me lunch when I had none. We had shared and kept our small secrets. "Jennifer, oh Jennifer, I will miss you," I told her, and I said I would miss my green bananas too, because she knew how much I loved green cooked bananas. Jennifer and I hugged for a long time, and, oh, how I wished she was boarding the plane, too. Jennifer knew that I would miss her as much as she would miss me. I promised to write to her.

Andrew looked sad, and I noticed the tears in his eyes as I was walking towards him. We hugged and kissed each other. "Never doubt my love for you. Never doubt how much I love you and how much I am going to miss you. I will miss you more than you can ever imagine," he said to me. Andrew said he had a feeling deep within that he was about to lose me forever. I told him he would never lose me, because I would always love him. I promised I would send for him if I were able to stay in America, and he promised he would wait for me to do so.

I said one more good-bye to my loved ones before I left them in the small airport lobby, looking on as I walked to the plane. Again, it was my mother I was most concerned about, and she was sobbing louder than ever. But I was also leaving my three other friends, and I wondered how soon I would be able to see them again. The thought of not seeing them made me cry as I stepped into the plane and took my seat. From there I could watch them from the window. Then the plane lifted off and I saw the clear, bright, blue sky above and the birds flying over the clear, blue waters of the Caribbean Sea below. For the first time in my life, I felt free, free from the vicious rumors and lies of the devious people living in my village, as free as the birds flying over the waters below. I felt like Jonah coming out of the belly of the whale. Sad though I felt, I was at peace with myself. The plane flew towards Barbados, where I would board one of the big airplanes that would take me to America, the Promised Land.

Going to the Promised Land

Approximately thirty-five minutes after I left St. Vincent, I arrived in Barbados at the Grantly Adams International Airport, where I was to board one of the huge airplanes that would take me to the Promised Land, America. My scheduled midday departing flight was delayed until late evening, so I spent the day visiting Vernon's family and some of my other Barbadian friends. It was a gorgeous April day in sunny Barbados, the only other land I had ever walked on besides St. Vincent. I had fond memories of my visits, and this one was no different. When I arrived at Vernon's house, Miss Laurel and other family members rushed to the door. We hugged and chatted for a while. As I was leaving, Miss Laurel was overcome with emotion as she hugged me and said, "I wish you all the best, Lola." "I will miss all of you," I said as I embraced Vernon and began to cry. I promised each of them that I would write and kissed them again before I left for the airport. I felt sad leaving them and the beautiful island of Barbados behind, but I was eager to board the big airplane that would take me to New York. I eagerly anticipated entering a land which I had heard offered many opportunities, even to poor people like me.

At about 7:30 that evening I boarded a huge Pan American plane for my departure to America. Taking my seat in this large airplane was quite an experience for me. Compared to the 24-seat airplanes that I had flown in from St. Vincent to Barbados, this airplane had more seats than I was able to count. As the plane lifted off and began to ascend, I thought fondly of my friends, wondering whether I would ever cross paths with them again. Then I began to cry quietly, as the plane soared higher and the beautiful and sunny island of Barbados faded out of view.

I sat next to two white American tourists, Bob and Lisa, who were returning to America from their vacation in Barbados. They were friendly and chatted with me throughout the flight about their wonderful vacation in Barbados and the warm and friendly hospitality of the Barbadian people. They seemed to have enjoyed themselves in Barbados as much as I did when I first visited there. When they asked if I lived in New York, I noticed an accent I did not recognize, presumably regional American. I told them this would be my first visit, and they, thinking I was a Barbadian, said they hoped I would enjoy their country as much as they had enjoyed mine. When the plane was about to land at Kennedy International Airport, Lisa told me about the spectacular view over New York City at night, and she changed seats with me so I could sit next to the window and enjoy the view.

I was amazed. Never before had I seen anyplace with so many lights shining so magnificently. As I admired the scene below, I wondered whether New York might be the gateway to the heaven, lit with bright and shinning stars, that my Sunday school teacher had told me about. Gazing at the magnificent brightness I saw below, I wondered whether the lights were like the lights of the gateway to heaven or only like the streetlights I had left in St. Vincent. As I anticipated landing and walking with my feet on the ground in America, I was filled with happiness.

After the plane landed, I shook hands with Bob and Lisa, and I thanked Lisa for allowing me to see the spectacular view she had suggested. Saying good-bye to them, I left the plane and went to stand in a line at a counter marked "Immigration, Non U.S. Citizen." When my turn came, I gave my passport to an Immigration officer behind the counter, who was dressed in a uniform like a police officer. In an accent similar to that of Bob and Lisa, she asked me how long I wished to stay in the country. I told her four weeks. She stamped my passport for four weeks and handed it back to me. I was looking forward to embracing Edna, who was supposed to meet me in the waiting area.

I left the Immigration counter and headed to the customs area to claim my luggage, a single suitcase less than half full with what little clothing I had brought with me. Edna had informed me that there was no need for me to bring all of my clothes to America, and I also heard Tanty Inis say that clothing was less expensive in America than in St. Vincent. After retrieving my suitcase, I walked to the waiting area to look for Edna. There were hundreds of people awaiting the arrival of loved ones, but I did not see Edna among them. I looked carefully through the crowd for some time, but saw no one who seemed to be looking for me. Realizing that Edna had failed to meet me, my happiness turned to sadness. and I was a frail, five feet, seven inch young girl, weighing one hundred six pounds, and I felt scared. I sat in a chair in the lobby, searching my pocketbook for her address and telephone number. After I found her number, I began looking for a public telephone. Then I suddenly realized that I had no American coins. Since I could not place a phone call, I would have to take a taxi to Edna's house.

When I walked out of the crowded, noisy airport terminal, I heard a man shouting, "Taxi, taxi, Miss, do you need a taxi?" I nodded, entered the taxicab and gave the driver the exact address in Corona, Queens. It was now past midnight. The friendly, Indian-looking taxi driver conversed with me through the whole trip. Before letting me out of the taxi, he asked me for the name of the person who was supposed to meet me at the airport, and I told him, "Edna." I looked out of the window and saw for the first time houses that were joined together in rows, and I wondered whether Edna lived in such a house. The driver got out of the cab, walked up to one of these houses, and pressed what I would later come to know as the doorbell to an apartment. A black old lady opened the door, and I told the driver she was not Edna. He then turned to the lady and asked if she knew an Edna. The lady informed him that Edna was living upstairs. The driver pressed the bell for the apartment upstairs, and I recognized Edna's voice when she put her head out of one of the windows of the second floor apartment and asked who it was. I told the taxi driver she was the woman I was looking for, and I stepped out of the taxi and onto the sidewalk. When Edna recognized me, she came downstairs and opened the door that led to her apartment. "Oh! It's you, Lola," she said. The taxi driver retrieved my suitcase from the trunk of the taxi, and I paid him ten dollars in American currency, seven of which was the cost of my trip. He thanked me and wished me good luck. Then he drove away.

I followed Edna up the narrow stairs to the second floor. I was waiting for her to ask me about my flight and to welcome me to America. I expected her to apologize for failing to meet me at the airport, as she had promised to do, but she never mentioned any of those things. She asked me for my passport and whatever American dollars I had brought with me. Without asking her what she wanted them for, I handed her my passport and two hundred and thirty dollars, all of the money I had. Then I asked her why she hadn't been at the airport to meet me. Edna said that when she called the airline for information about my flight, she was told that my flight was delayed. Not knowing any better, I accepted her explanation without questioning her further. I had hoped to reach America safely, and now I was here, so why pursue the matter further. I was in America, where I hoped to find work and go to college. If I could accomplish those things, I knew that I would be able to assist my grandmother, my mother and my brothers and sisters, making their lives as good as my own or better. I felt happy to be in America, even though I was hungry and Edna had yet to ask if I wanted as much as a drink of water. It was to be the first of many nights that I would go to bed hungry while living with Edna. Ever since I was a child of three, Ma and Mommy had taught me to pray to God before I went to bed at night, and that night not even my hunger prevented me from praying.

I prayed to God and thanked him for a safe flight to America and my arrival at Edna's home. I asked him to bless Edna. I cried when I prayed for my Mommy, my mother, my younger brothers and sisters, and the other poverty-stricken families I had left behind in St. Vincent. Although I had only been in America for a few hours, I missed my home. I thought of Barbados and the wonderful people I had met there. I missed them, too. I missed all of them so much that I cried myself to sleep, as a baby would, lying on a single bed in the small bedroom of Edna's apartment.

I had a restless sleep on the first night I spent in America. When I awoke the next morning, I prayed again. Then I peeped through a window and saw that it was sunny outside. The scene was completely different from St. Vincent. I noticed two women walking hurriedly down the street, but there was no one standing outside talking to a next-door neighbor. The front doors of the houses were shut, and I wondered whether most of the people around there were still asleep. After I had finished looking at the strange world outside the window, I walked into Edna's living room, where she sat in a chair rifling through my suitcase. I said good morning to her. Before I could ask Edna why was she searching my suitcase, she volunteered her answer, telling me she was searching my suitcase for a suitable outfit for me to wear to Manhattan that day. "Where the hell is Manhattan?" I muttered to myself as I accepted her explanation.

After we ate our breakfast of tea, toast and eggs, Edna said in a condescending manner, "Lola, go and take a shower, then dress in these trousers and the blouse I found in your suitcase." She informed me that it was cold outside and that I needed to wear a sweater over my clothing. She gave me an almost-new-looking sweater to wear, but took it back before I put it on, claiming her daughter would be upset if she saw me in the sweater. "Why the hell did she give me the sweater in the first place if she knew it belonged to her daughter?" I asked myself. This was the first time I was aware that Edna had a daughter. I was grateful when she gave me another sweater to wear, even though it was shabby. Edna and I got dressed and left the apartment to go to a place she called Manhattan.

We caught a bus a few blocks from her apartment and took it to Junction Boulevard. At Junction Boulevard, we boarded the No. 7 train and rode it to Manhattan. It was a new experience for me since it was my first time riding a train. I was scared, because the train was running high above the street, and it was going fast. It was also crowded with passengers, blacks, Asians, and more white people than I had ever seen in my life in one place at the same time. Most of the passengers buried their heads in newspapers or books. I noticed that no one said hello to anyone else, and I wondered why these people acted so differently from the people I had left at home. They all seemed to be minding their own business.

By the time the train arrived at 42nd Street Station, we were underground. We got off the train onto a platform, along with what seemed to be hundreds of other passengers, who all appeared to be rushing somewhere. I wondered where they all could be rushing to, as many hopped onto escalators, and others walked hurriedly up stairways. Edna was middle aged, short and stocky, and she could hardly walk, let alone keep up with the other passengers. I wanted to rush along with the other passengers, but I had to walk along with Edna. We slowly walked up the steps that led to the street above.

Emerging at street level, I saw another crowd of people, most of them walking as briskly as those in the station. I stared at the tall buildings and the endless crowds of people, more than I had never seen before. I walked with Edna to one of these tall buildings, where we entered the lobby. "We have to take the elevator," Edna said to me. She pressed what seemed to be a lighted doorbell next to the door of an apartment. Other people entered the lobby and pressed the same doorbell and stood waiting with us. When the door was opened, people who were standing behind it walked out to the lobby. The people waiting in the lobby, along with Edna and me, entered what Edna informed me, at that moment, was the elevator. It was my first elevator ride. We stepped off of the elevator at the thirty-sixth floor. I had never before been in a building with so many floors. I was very much impressed with this new adventure. Edna and I entered an office. Standing behind her, I overheard her telling the receptionist that I was her niece and was looking for a housekeeping/nanny job. That was my first inkling that Edna had taken me to Manhattan to look for a job—and not just any job, but a housekeeping/nanny job. I felt furious at having her seek such a lowly position for me. Still, I thought it better to say nothing. If it had been in St. Vincent, I would certainly have asked Edna where we were going before we left her apartment that morning, but here I did not. Dumfounded as I was when I heard her telling the receptionist I was looking for a housekeeping/nanny job, I still did not question her. The receptionist handed me an application to complete. I sat on a chair next to Edna, while she assisted me in completing the application. In answer to one of the questions, she wrote that I had experience doing jobs of that kind. After completing the application, I handed it back to the receptionist. After a short wait, a well-dressed black woman, with a short afro-cut hairstyle, walked out of a private office and called my name. She introduced herself to me as Ms. Faya and asked me to follow her. Edna followed close behind me.

Ms. Faya told us to have a seat on the chairs on the other side of the table, and Edna informed her I was new to America and was looking for a housekeeping/nanny job. Ms. Faya questioned me about my childcare experience. I told her my only childcare experience was assisting my mother with the care of my nine siblings.

Edna was trying to interject something, but Ms. Faya told her she would like to speak to me alone, and Edna left the room. Ms. Faya continued to question me, and I answered her questions to the best of my ability. She wanted to know if I had worked as a housekeeper before, and I told her no. Nevertheless, she scheduled an appointment for me to meet with a Mrs. Silverstein for an interview. She explained that Mrs. Silverstein was looking for someone to do housekeeping and serve as a nanny. Mrs. Silverstein lived somewhere in New Jersey with her husband and three children, two boys aged seven and five and a three-year-old daughter. If I got the job, I was to live with the Silversteins from Tuesday mornings until Sunday mornings, and I was to be paid sixty dollars a week. After Ms. Faya explained all she could about the job, she asked me if I were interested, and I told her I was. Ms. Faya instructed me to take a bus from 42nd Street to somewhere that I couldn't remember in New Jersey and telephone Mrs. Silverstein when I arrived at the bus terminal in New Jersey. She wrote the time I should arrive for the interview with Mrs. Silverstein the following day on a piece of paper, along with the directions she had given me. Then she called Edna back to her office and repeated what she had told me about the job. Edna thanked Ms. Faya, and we left her office, out through the receptionist area to the elevator, down to the first floor. We walked back to the 42nd Street subway station, where we took the train back to Junction Boulevard in Queens.

While riding the train back to Junction Boulevard, I had second thoughts about the job. I thought it odd that Edna seemed so excited about it that one would have thought that she was the one about to be interviewed for the job instead of me. Certainly, I was grateful that I was about to get a job. After all, I had been born in St. Vincent, went to high school there for five years, and I graduated. I had high hopes of finding a teaching job, but my hopes had been shattered when I refused to go to bed with the old cronies of men who could have helped me. Now, one day after I arrived in America, I was about to be employed without having to fulfill anyone's sexual desire in return. Nevertheless, I was about to be employed in a job cleaning a stranger's house and taking care of her children. This is a maid's job, I said to myself. Then I began to reason with myself, "You mean to say, after spending all those years getting an education, I still have to do what the dirt-poor girls back home did for a living—cleaning other people's houses and taking care of their children?" Jobs of that kind were good enough for those girls, because most of them did not finish elementary school, let alone high school. In St. Vincent and other Caribbean Islands, only the uneducated did those kinds of jobs. I found it hard to believe the same kind of job those girls did was what I was qualified to do in America. The more I thought about that, the more upset I became. Payment for the work seemed the only good thing about the job offer. I would be paid more money in one week than maids were paid in a month back home, and I was sure to be paid more money in a month than most of the civil servants and teacher's aides were paid in a month back home. Nevertheless, the job was a housekeeping/nanny job, and I was angry that Edna had taken me to seek such a job. I would rather have earned less money as a teacher's aide or some other white-collar job than do the maid's job for more money.

As I pondered these things, I wondered about Edna. Edna had not consulted me about this maid's job beforehand. I felt she had betrayed me and that I could not trust her. When Edna had invited me to America, she had told me that she wanted to adopt me. I was motivated to come to America because Edna told me I would have the opportunity to further my education here. She had not yet said anything to me about continuing my education. I questioned her motives for bringing me to America. If Edna had told me that a housekeeping/nanny job was the only job I was qualified to do in America, I might have stayed home in St. Vincent and accepted Randell's offer to find a job for me and rent me an apartment. I considered returning to St. Vincent. I looked at Edna with anger, and the more I looked at her, the angrier I became. "How dare you, Edna?" I wanted to shout at her when we got off the train at Junction Boulevard. "How dare you invite me to America to work as a maid?" But I kept my silence, because I thought that if I spoke out, she might threaten to send me back to St. Vincent. In spite of my anger, I did not want to return to St. Vincent—not yet, anyway.

Edna suggested that we walk home instead of riding the bus. While we were walking home, all Edna wanted to talk about was my upcoming interview and my prospects of getting the job. She had made plans for the money I would earn if I got the job, and she reiterated that the salary was not at all bad. "After all, Lola," she said, "you would be making more money than I made when I first came to America. I worked all these years cleaning white people's houses, even cleaning their shit, and still I haven't accomplished much in life. I never could save much on the salary I made over the years." When I had met Edna for the first time in St. Vincent, I thought she was rich. My mother probably thought the same, and that was undoubtedly why she was eager to listen to Edna and agree to her adopting me. But from what I had seen so far, Edna was not rich. By American standards, she must have been as poor as my family was back in St. Vincent. Edna kept talking about the job until we got to the home of the Canners, some friends of hers whom we visited before going home.

Edna introduced me to the Canners when we were welcomed into their home. Millicent Canner appeared to be older than Edna, who I thought to be in her late fifties. Aunt Millie, as I would later call her, was a native of Barbados. Although she appeared to be in her late sixties, age seemed not to have affected her beauty, because this lady was one good-looking black woman. She had a light complexion, with smooth, soft skin and long, curly, grayish shoulder-length hair. When she saw me for the first time, she complimented me on my white teeth and my thin figure and continued to smile at me when we made eye contact. She seemed to take a liking to me, and the feeling was mutual. She was married to an African American man with a deep southern accent, appearing to be in his mid fifties. After we were sitting for about half an hour with the Canners, Mrs. Canner offered us something to eat, which I graciously accepted. I was very hungry, having had nothing to eat since breakfast at 8:00 that morning.

Mrs. Canner made tuna sandwiches for us, and she and Edna chatted while we ate. As Edna and I were leaving the Canners' house, Mrs. Canner told me not to be a stranger to her. In the presence of Edna, she told me to visit her whenever I felt a need to get out of Edna's apartment. While Edna and I walked the remaining block back to her apartment, Edna said I should not visit the Canners without her being along. When I asked her why, she explained that Mrs. Canner was jealous of other women when they were around her husband. "If you visit her alone, she might think you want to have an affair with her husband," Edna said to me. I listened to Edna speaking ill of the friend who had just fed her, and I said to myself that Mrs. Canner didn't need an enemy if Edna was her friend.

Edna planned to accompany me to the interview with Mrs. Silverstein in New Jersey, and Ms. Faya telephoned before we left the house instructing me to tell Mrs. Silverstein that I had worked as a housekeeper/nanny for a family in New York for two years until they relocated to California recently. Ms. Faya also told me that if Mrs. Silverstein asked me for the telephone number of the family, I was to tell her that the family hadn't contacted me since relocating to California.

Here I was on my second day in America, on my way to New Jersey, where I was to be interviewed by this Silverstein woman for this housekeeping job, and I was expected to lie to her if she asked certain questions. When Edna and I left the apartment to catch the bus to Junction Boulevard, it was sunny outside. Unlike St. Vincent where it was always hot on sunny days, here it was cold. We rode the train to Manhattan and the bus to New Jersey, as we had been instructed by Ms. Faya. I felt I would rather be going to interview for Ms. Faya's receptionist's job than for this maid's job in New Jersey that I felt was demeaning to me. I thought Ms. Faya's job would have suited me better, because I felt that I had the intelligence, education, and qualifications to do it. I was angry. But a voice within told me to be prudent and forget my anger. That voice was saying I should accept whatever job would be offered to me and stick to it until I made enough money to be able to do better. Then I could quit the job and look for something better suited to my qualifications and abilities.

I told myself that later I should be able to find a job in a bank and act like a bigshot, like those people working in the bank in my homeland. I reasoned that I could do even better by becoming a brilliant lawyer, fighting in the courts for justice for the poor. As a lawyer, I would be able to expose those damn pedophiles and rapists and put them behind bars, locked up in jails where most of the time their only meal would be bread and sweetened water. I could picture them spending the rest of their lives there, sleeping with the rats in the dark, dirty, hot cells, urinating on themselves and smelling worse than the latrines at home. People would call them jailbirds, and I hoped to God they would rot in jail, never seeing sunshine again, and never have the opportunity to rape another child. I remembered that I had had some of these same thoughts back in St. Vincent. I realized then that an education could give me the power to protect people and bring justice to dirt-poor people like myself.

Edna and I stepped off the bus at our destination in New Jersey. Mrs. Silverstein, a white woman appearing to be about thirty, had neatly combed blonde hair and well-manicured nails that I thought

made her look like a doll rather than a human being. She arrived
at the bus stop in a white Cadillac approximately twenty minutes
after Edna telephoned her. Edna sat beside her in the front seat, and
the two of them conversed while I sat in the back without uttering
a word. Then Mrs. Silverstein pulled up in the driveway of what
seemed to be a small hotel. I could not imagine that it was Mrs.
Silverstein's house. When we got out of her car and walked into
the house, we found it well furnished, with floors covered by wall-
to-wall carpeting except for the kitchen. When we entered the
large kitchen, Mrs. Silverstein offered us some lemonade before
she and I sat at the kitchen table and talked about the job.

When Mrs. Silverstein asked if I had any housekeeping/nanny
experience, I told her everything Ms. Faya had said I should tell
her about the family I supposedly had worked for in New York
before they relocated to California. I had an answer for every question she asked me. She seemed impressed with my answers, as I
could tell by her expression. She offered me the job, told me I
would be paid sixty dollars a week, and promised to increase my
wages after three months. I was to arrive at the bus stop no later
than 9:30 every Tuesday morning and leave every Sunday morning, because my days off were to be Sundays and Mondays. She
asked if I wanted her and her husband to "sponsor" me. Before I
could answer, Edna said, "Yes, she was told that you would be
willing to sponsor her and that was the main reason why she came
for the interview." Mrs. Silverstein then asked me how long was I
willing to work for her, and I told her, "Forever," because I
assumed that was what I was supposed to say. At the same time, I
thought that if this woman believed that I would work for her forever doing this maid's job, then she was not a smart woman. I was
afraid she might think that I lacked the intelligence and ambition
to do better.

Mrs. Silverstein was pleased to know that I was single and had
no children. In response to her question whether I had any plans to
return to St. Vincent any time soon, I told her I had no reason to
do so. She said that I would be very happy with her family, and she
told me that I would begin working on Tuesday of the following
week, at which time I would meet the children. That Tuesday
would be exactly eight days since I had left my tiny homeland of
St. Vincent and immigrated to big America, where I was about to
be employed as a maid, cleaning house and taking care of children
who were not related to me. I was not pleased about the job, but I

needed the money to support my family at home and myself in America. I also needed money to pay Edna whatever she would charge me for the weekends I would be spending with her, even though she had not yet said anything about that.

Edna seemed ecstatic when Mrs. Silverstein offered me the job. She continued to express her gratitude to Mrs. Silverstein while we were riding back to the bus stop. On the bus back to Manhattan, Edna said, "Lola, I will save your money for you because you don't have a Social Security number, and you will not be able to open an account of your own at the bank." "What the hell is a Social Security number and why couldn't I open up my own bank account?" I wanted to ask her, just as I wanted to tell her not to make plans for my money. But I kept quiet. I also wanted to call Edna a liar, since she had promised to assist me in going to school as soon as I immigrated to America, but she had only found me a housekeeping/nanny job. Although I thought of calling Edna a liar and telling her that I felt I could not trust her, I didn't do it. I remembered that I had promised to be grateful to this wolf in sheep's clothing, as my grandmother, mother and cousin had begged me to. They thought that she was doing me a great favor in helping me to immigrate to America. For my family's sake, I agreed to everything Edna wanted me to do. But God had given me some sense when I was born and also the ability to use it to my advantage. I would use my sense, Lord, because Ma Letteen used to say common sense was made before books. Ma Letteen had also told me one could overcome many obstacles if one knew how to use one's common sense. "Ma, I hope I can overcome all of my obstacles with only my mind to help me," I said silently and secretly to my invisible Ma.

Edna and I again stopped at the Canners' house on our way home from the interview. When Edna informed Mrs. Canner that I had gotten the job, Mrs. Canner congratulated me and expressed her happiness for me. She told me to stop by her house on Friday of that week, because she would like to give me some things to take with me to the job. Edna said nothing at the time. When we returned to her apartment, she reminded me that I should not look at Mr. Canner when I visit their home. I felt that what Edna was saying to me made no sense, and I wanted to tell her to shut up, but I didn't. She rambled on about Mrs. Canner's jealousy of her husband until she finally decided to stop talking.

Edna attended the New Testament Church of God, located on the same street as her apartment. It was the only church in the block of row houses. Compared to the church of the same domination in my village, this church was larger and more modern. There was to be some sort of prayer meeting at the church that night. When I told Edna that I didn't want to go, she insisted that I attend the meeting with her. When we entered the church, the congregation of over one hundred people was singing, clapping, and doing some sort of dancing. One woman played the piano while others played guitars and shook tambourines. Some of the congregation threw their bodies about and shouted, "Praise the Lord! Alleluia!" The scene in the church was chaotic, reminding me of the church in the village back home.

I remembered what happened one night when I was attending a prayer meeting at the church back home. I was clapping and dancing like the other church members, when one of the members, seeming to appear out of nowhere, grabbed my hand and led me to the altar while whispering in my ear. Then he shouted, "Come with me. God sent me fo yo because he loves you and wan to save yo soul." As I stood at the altar, other church members shouted, "Jesus! Alleluia!" and I felt the preacher's hands and the hands of other church members on my head and shoulders. The preacher shouted, "God, rebuke the devil from this soul, cleanse her body and set her free! Save this sinner tonight, God! Save her, Lord Jesus!" Then others whispered and shouted, "Jesus! Jesus!" The congregation was carrying on around me and I was mimicking them, shouting, "Jesus! Jesus!" At the time I wondered whether the actions of the members of the church were sincere, or whether they were faking, as I was. I wondered the same thing as I sat with Edna in her church. I continued to wonder as she introduced me to the preacher and some of the members of the congregation, and even when Edna and I went back to Edna's place later that night.

Before I went to bed that night, I prayed to God. But this time, instead of asking him to provide me with a job, I told him that I had gotten a job I didn't want. I told God he knew the reason why I had accepted the job. I asked God for his guidance and begged him to assist me in finding a better job. Tears flowed from my eyes and down my bony cheekbone as I prayed to God that night. "God, my life and everything about me is in your hands. Please be my guidance, Lord," I prayed to the God in whom I believed.

The next day, before I visited Mrs. Canner, I wrote to my family and friends, including Andrew and Randell. I asked Edna for directions to the Post Office, but she offered to mail my letters for me instead. Then, before I left to visit Mrs. Canner, she advised me again not to look at Mrs. Canner's husband. Mrs. Canner was excited to see me, as I was to see her. After I ate the tuna sandwich that she offered me, she and I left for Junction Boulevard, where she took me on a shopping spree. Mrs. Canner bought me a toothbrush and some toothpaste, two sets of bath towels, soap, deodorant, feminine napkins, skin and face cream, and a comb and brush. When we got back to her house, she packed all of these items in a little suitcase and gave it to me, saying the suitcase and its contents were mine to take with me to my job.

As I was thanking her, Curtis got up from his chair in the living room. He took up his wallet from a table next to his chair and handed me a twenty-dollar bill. "Take this to buy your bus ticket to the job in New Jersey," he said to me. Both Millie and Curtis advised me not to tell Edna about the money. I promised not to. Aunt Millie remarked that I was a well-mannered and attractive young lady and should do well in America if I remained that way. I thanked her for the compliment and both of them for their kindness and generosity. When I was leaving their house to go back to Edna's apartment, they told me that I was welcome to visit them any time. I promised them that I would, and I left with the suitcase and, of course, my twenty-dollar bill.

When I returned to Edna's apartment, I showed her everything the Canners had given me except the twenty-dollar bill. Edna seemed astounded and said that I should be grateful to the Canners. I told her I was. I detected some resentment in Edna's tone of voice, as she warned me again about Aunt Millie's jealousy over her husband. I wanted to ask Edna why was she talking about Aunt Millie in such a negative way, but I didn't. Instead I prayed and asked God to stop her from speaking ill of people who were so kind to me.

On Saturday, I helped Edna clean her apartment, and on Sunday I went to church with her for almost the entire day. We arrived at church at about 8:30 a.m. and returned home about 4:30 p.m. We went back to church around 6:00, and returned home about 10:00, shortly after services ended for the day. I thought, "If this is Edna's Sunday routine and the way she chooses to worship her God, good for her, but it won't be my routine and the way I choose to worship my God. As soon as I know my way around America, I won't be going to church with Edna nor remain here with her even when I am hungry. According to the scriptures, God had already died on the cross and suffered for my sins. He never told me to suffer for Him in return and to stay in church all day listening to a minister preaching, and a congregation responding to his sermon as though they were having a brawl. That is a form of suffering that I am not going to endure for long." I also questioned the number of times they passed around the collection bowls. I understood that there must be a collection to maintain the church and to pay the minister, but I wondered about a collection for the minister's birthday and wedding anniversary, and for his son who was about to go to college in North Carolina. I questioned why the people in the church gave the preacher so much of their money, when he appeared to be financially better off than most of them. I was sure he was financially better off than Edna. I did not give them as much as a penny. I could not understand why the members of the congregation continued to give their dollars to the minister. I was glad when the service was over and I was out of that church.

On Monday, Edna took me to a clothing store that I later learned was a thrift shop, where she bought me a pair of high-platform shoes. I was dubious about the shoes, hoping I would be able to walk in them without breaking my bony legs. I couldn't help wondering why Edna would buy me shoes that I did not need, especially shoes I would probably not be able to wear. "What the hell is she thinking?" I wondered. "Is she buying something for me because the Canners have bought things for me?"

After we left the thrift shop we walked to the Laundromat, Washing clothes at the laundromat was a new experience for me. I welcomed the new idea of machines to wash clothes instead of doing them by hand. I couldn't help thinking how much easier it would be for people back home if they had washing machines like these. When I saw the dryer I remembered the many days I wore wet socks to school, not having sunlight to dry them and thought about how I could have avoided wearing those wet socks if only we had had dryers. As Edna and I folded the clothes and packed them into the laundry bag, I marveled at how easy it is to do laundry in America. I wished my mother were in America to enjoy this easy way of getting her laundry done. I hoped one day I would be able to make these things possible for her. I thought about these things again before I went to bed that night. When I awoke the next day, I was on my way to begin my first job in America.

With Edna's directions, I had no problem catching the train to Manhattan and the bus that took me to New Jersey. I was sure that Edna had given me perfect directions, because I knew she wanted me to be on that job. When I got to the bus stop in New Jersey, I telephoned Mrs. Silverstein, and she picked me up in the same car she had used when I met her for the interview. She drove me to her house, which in my mind I had nicknamed the "Mini Hotel." Then I changed to calling it the "Mansion," as it was clearly not a place bustling with visitors and tourists. Mrs. Silverstein escorted me to the room where I was to sleep and keep my belongings, after which she showed me the rest of the house, Then she handed me two handwritten pages listing my duties and the manner in which I was to get my work done.

The Silversteins' house had three floors, with more rooms than I could remember. Most of the rooms were carpeted, including Mrs. Silverstein's bedroom. She explained that after I vacuumed her bedroom, I was to rake the rug, as one would rake up fallen leaves from a yard. Besides vacuuming the house, I was to clean the four bathrooms, six bedrooms, the bar and the kitchen. I was to dust and polish all of the furniture, scrape the dishes before packing them into the two dishwashers, and make sure that I understood which dishes went into which dishwasher. One dishwasher was used to wash the utensils and dishes used for meat; the other, those used for fish. Mrs. Silverstein also expected me to assist her in preparing meals, and I was to play with the children and read to them when they were at home. I was to bathe the children and dress them for bed every night I was there. I had not yet met the children or her husband.

After I changed into the white uniform which Mrs. Silverstein handed me and told me to wear while I was on the job, I began the task of cleaning the house, working my way from the third floor down to the first. It was my first time using a vacuum cleaner, so I had to read the instructions first. The noise bothered my ears as I vacuumed the carpet and used other attachments to vacuum the steps. The work was tiresome and sometimes strenuous, but I did my very best. Around midday, Mrs. Silverstein suggested I take a break and make myself a corned beef and cheese sandwich for my lunch. After I was finished eating, she told me to clean up the cereal, pancakes, syrup, toast and scrambled eggs the children had made for breakfast that morning. I did as I was told. As I was packing one of the dishwashers, I consoled myself that the job was not too bad, because I didn't have to wash all of the dirty dishes by hand. After cleaning the kitchen, I resumed dusting and vacuuming and by 5:00 p.m., I had vacuumed the entire house. At that time Mrs. Silverstein said she needed me to help prepare dinner.

I couldn't help noticing that Mrs. Silverstein cooked differently from the way I was accustomed to. She did not wash or season the beef when she took it out of the wrapped package, but instead placed it into a pot with some water. She chopped an onion and a few celery stalks and added them to the pot with the meat and boiling water. While the meat was cooking, she sampled it with a spoon, putting the spoon into her mouth and then back into the pot without washing it. I was shocked. I had never seen anyone in the island taste food like that. Whenever we tasted food while cooking in St. Vincent, we would take the food out of the pot with a spoon and put it into the palm of our hand before tasting it. If we ever did taste the food directly from the spoon, we would always wash it before returning it to the pot. If Mrs. Silverstein had been seen tasting food that way in the island, most people would never eat from her pot. Frightened of catching her germs, I was determined not to eat the food she was cooking.

After we finished cooking the steak, mashed potatoes, and mixed vegetables, we made a salad of lettuce, cucumbers and tomatoes. I then got my first glimpse of Mr. Silverstein as he arrived home from work. He walked directly into the kitchen and said to Mrs. Silverstein, "Hi, Honey," and she smiled at him while he kissed her cheek. Then she said to him, "This is Lola, our new housekeeper," and said to me, "Lola, my husband, Mr. Silverstein." Mr. Silverstein said, "We are happy to have you, Lola." Mrs. Silverstein asked me to set the dinner table, and the two of them walked into a room adjacent to the kitchen. Thank God for Randell, I thought. Because of him, I had learned to set a table by observing how his maids did it when we had our lunches together in his hotel. As I was setting the table, I heard a vehicle coming into the driveway. I peeped through the window and saw a yellow school bus, and, at the same time, three children walking towards the front door. The doorbell rang, and Mrs. Silverstein rushed to the door and opened it. One after the other, the three children entered the house—seven year old Paul, five year old Eric, and three year old Stephanie. Mrs. Silverstein brought them into the kitchen and introduced them to me. She told them that my name was Lola and I was their new housekeeper/nanny. Eric said hi, but Paul and Stephanie looked at me and walked away. Before leaving the kitchen, Mrs. Silverstein informed me that I would eat my dinner after the family members had finished eating theirs. Since I had no intention of eating the food she had cooked, I wondered whether she intended for me to eat their leftovers as though I was their dog. In St. Vincent, dogs were the only ones who ate after other people. I went to my room and stayed there for an hour and twenty-four minutes until the Silversteins had finished eating dinner. When they finished eating, Mrs. Silverstein called me and told me that I could eat as much as I pleased of the food they had left on the table. After they retired to the family room, I made another corned beef and cheese sandwich for my dinner, as I did on all the other nights I spent in the Silversteins' house. I threw their dirty leftovers into the garbage disposal. After I had finished cleaning the kitchen, around 8:00 p.m., it was time for me to assist the children with their bath, read them bedtime stories, and tuck them into their beds. Paul and Eric took their baths without my assisting them, but I had to assist Stephanie, who screamed at the top of her lungs as I put her into the tub of lukewarm water and washed her body before dressing her in her pajamas. Then I read a story to each of them before tucking them in bed. I retired to my room about 9:30 p.m. This was the first day that I spent in the Silversteins' home.

After I took a shower and dressed for bed, I knelt and prayed. Never before had I felt so tired, not even when I was assisting with the bananas and the weeding of the crops in the fields back home, toiling in fields of bushes with thorns that left prickles in my fingers. I ached from the top of my head to the soles of my feet. Groaning in pain, I tried to fall asleep. I considered leaving the job the following day, and I quickly fell asleep. I awoke in the morning fully aware that I needed money, so I decided to continue.

I had two slices of buttered toast and an eight-ounce glass of orange juice for my breakfast, and the children left in the school bus. Mrs. Silverstein left the house shortly after nine o'clock that morning, telling me she would return in the afternoon. Relieved, I planned not to work as hard as the day before. I was sitting at the kitchen table, reading the newspaper, when the telephone rang, I answered, "Silverstein residence." The voice on the other end of the line asked my name and what island I was from. Because I recognized the voice as belonging to another West Indian woman, I told her my name and that I was from St. Vincent. "Girl, me ah Lucille and me com from Jamaica," she said. Then she asked if the bitch was at home. "Who bitch?" I inquired. "The bitch, Mistress Silverstein," she said. I told her that Mrs. Silverstein was not at home and would not return until three o'clock. "Good, because ah want to talk to yo dough you na know me. All ah we come from the island whether yo com from St. Vincent and me com from Jamaica, all awe ah one and hav fo look out for one another and na mek them white people tek advantage ah awe and treat we like some fool, fool." Lucille rambled on, informing me that the Silversteins had until recently lived in a smaller house and had had a housekeeper named Angela, whom they fired after moving into their new house two months before. The Silversteins paid Angela sixty-five dollars a week, and they were sponsoring her to get her a green card. When they moved into the bigger house and the job became more demanding, Angela asked the Silversteins for an increase in her salary. Instead of agreeing or simply refusing her the raise she requested, the Silversteins fired her. They also stopped the processing of the green card that she would otherwise have gotten in six months. According to Lucille, Angela paid a lawyer in New York two thousand dollars to assist her with the processing of the paperwork for immigration. Angela not only lost her job and the opportunity to get her green card in six months, but she also lost the money she had paid the lawyer. Lucille said that what the Silversteins did to Angela was unfair, since Angela had worked for them for two years at the same salary. I knew little about sponsorship and green cards then, but I agreed with Lucille that what the Silversteins had done to Angela was unfair.

When I informed Lucille of the salary the Silversteins were paying me, she was outraged and cursed that the bitch was under-paying me. She was also furious when I told her the amount of work I had done the day before. She gave me some tips on easier ways to get things done. She suggested that I quit the job without giving notice if I thought the job was too demanding. Lucille informed me that she worked within walking distance of the Silversteins' home and would visit me one day soon.

Mrs. Silverstein returned promptly at 3:00 o'clock, a half hour before the children were to arrive home from school. She walked around the house inspecting what I had done while she was out. She told me she was pleased with my work. "You are very thorough with your cleaning. You have done a great job," she said. I detected some sincerity in her compliment. Before I went to bed that night, both Mr. and Mrs. Silverstein approached me. I did not know Mr. Silverstein's profession, but I thought he must be paid well, because Mrs. Silverstein did not work and they seemed to have a lot of money. They each complimented me, telling me I was doing an excellent job. Then they told me that they were willing to sponsor me to get my green card, if I wanted them to. According to Edna, I would have to work two to three years for them, because that was how long the processing of the paperwork for a green card took. Even though I knew that I would not be working for the Silversteins for a year, let alone two or three, I told them that I would very much like them to sponsor me. I guess they were happy to hear that, because Mr. Silverstein shook my hand and told me that he was willing to start the process as soon as possible.

The next day, I overheard a telephone conversation in which Mrs. Silverstein told one of her friends that I was a very hard worker and an excellent housekeeper, and that she and Paul, her husband, had decided to start the processing of my green card immediately. Mrs. Silverstein confided to her friend that she did not want to lose me. She bragged that I had vacuumed the entire house in one day and that I was educated, because I read to the children every night. I think Lucille must have had some sort of special intuition, for as soon as Mrs. Silverstein ended her phone call and drove away, Lucille telephoned me.

Lucille and I spoke on the telephone for more than an hour, mostly about what I could remember that had happened since our last conversation. I gathered that Lucille knew most of the duties of my job without my having to read her the list Mrs. Silverstein had given me. After my conversation with Lucille that day, I decided that working for the Silversteins was too overwhelming. I could not imagine how I could keep up with the work I was expected to do. Nor could I endure eating bread and cheese for dinner every night, as I was doing so as to avoid consuming Mrs. Silverstein's saliva as part of my dinner. Under no circumstances would I ever bring myself to eat the food that Mrs. Silverstein cooked, let alone the family leftovers. Besides, I imagined that I would die from exhaustion if I were to stay on the job. So I decided to quit. I telephoned Edna and told her that the job was too much for me, stressing to her the amount of work I had to do.

Surprisingly, Edna advised me to walk out with all of my belongings when I left for my days off the following Sunday. On my fourth day on the job, Mrs. Silverstein asked me to let the exterminator into the house if he came while she was out. Only minutes after she left, someone rang the doorbell. When I opened the door, standing in front of me was the exterminator, as I could tell by his blue uniform that had "pest control" marked on the front of the shirt. I opened the door to a fat white man with blonde hair, balding at the crown of his head. Upon entering the house, he asked for Angela, and I told him that Angela was no longer working for the Silversteins. I proceeded to show him several areas of the house that Mrs. Silverstein had specified he should spray. When we descended into the basement, the exterminator withdrew his wallet and began to count twenty-, fifty-, and hundred-dollar bills. He counted the money over and over as if trying to get my attention, but I pretended not to watch him. Then he flashed the money in front of my face and asked if I needed any money. I told him no. "Angela and I had some good times down here, and I gave her lots of money," he said. I eyed him as he stood in front of me flashing his money. All of a sudden, he unzipped his pants and pulled out a large, pale penis with no skin on the head and asked me to suck it. He told me that if I did what he asked, he would give me lots of money. "Don't be afraid. Angela did it for me all the time, and I gave her lots of money for doing it," he said. I looked at him in disbelief. I wondered how Angela could have done such a despicable and nasty thing as putting a man's penis into her mouth, and a white man no less. I don't know if I would have thought better of Angela had she done it to a black man. I had never heard of people doing such things. The idea sounded sickening to me. It was beyond my comprehension. I looked scornfully at the exterminator for a few moments and thought what nerve he had to ask me to commit this act. Just his asking me seemed to upset my stomach, and I began to feel I would vomit. Then I became overwhelmed with fear that the exterminator was about to rape me. I ran upstairs, leaving him standing in the basement.

I ran through the house, bumping into walls, tables and whatever else was in my way, until I got to my room on the third floor. I locked the door and hid under the bed for what seemed an eternity. It was actually only twenty minutes later when I heard Mrs. Silverstein calling my name. I went down to the second floor, where I met her in the kitchen. She seemed not to notice that I was

trembling, and I wondered whether I should tell her about my
ordeal with the exterminator. When she asked me if the exterminator had done a good job, I told her he had. I did not utter a word
about his sexual solicitation of me. I kept silent about the exterminator, just as I had about the pedophiles and rapists who assaulted
me as a child back in St. Vincent.

Mrs. Silverstein informed me an hour later that she would be
joining her husband for dinner in Manhattan that evening. She told
me that I should bake some chicken, cook some rice, and make a
green salad for the children's dinner. She asked me to assist them
with their homework before I gave them their baths and tucked
them into bed. After the children arrived home from school and
greeted their mother, Mrs. Silverstein told them she was joining
their father for dinner. Then she kissed Stephanie and went outside
to the car. Stephanie ran after her, and I had to run outside to get
her and bring her back into the house. I was dressed in a short-
sleeved white uniform and wearing slippers. It was sunny but cold
outside.

Later that evening, I prepared dinner for the children and
myself, so that I would be eating cooked food for dinner for the
first time that week. The children and I sat around the table and
had dinner together. "Lola, your food is tasty," said Eric, eating as
though he had not eaten all day. "I need more juice," said Paul, as
he jumped from the chair with his glass in his hand. He went to the
refrigerator and poured juice from a container. Stephanie was picking at her food, not eating much, when Paul noticed and told her
to eat up. An hour after we had had our dinner, I assisted the children with their homework, gave them their baths, and read them
stories out of the books they each had in their rooms. Then I
tucked them into their beds. I fell asleep at about ten o'clock.
Sleeping soundly, I opened my eyes slightly when I felt someone
touching me. I saw a little white, blond-haired thing with blue eyes
standing beside my bed staring at me. Not realizing that it was the
Silversteins' three-year-old daughter, Stephanie, I began to scream
at the top of my lungs. As I screamed, the thing jumped into the
bed with me and began screaming, too. Poor Stephanie was so
frightened that she held me around my neck for dear life. Our
screams awoke Eric and Paul, and they came running into my
room, frightened themselves. After the commotion had settled, I
calmed the children's fears and tucked them back into their beds. I
could not do as much for myself, for I remained shaken.

When I awoke the next day, Saturday, I had a headache. My nose was congested, my eyes were watery, and my throat felt sore. I felt very cold and began to shiver. Without taking my temperature, I knew I had a fever. I thought I must have caught a cold when I ran outside after Stephanie the day before. I felt so sick that I wanted to stay in bed. I wished it were my day off, so I could stay in bed as long as I wanted to. Since it was not my day off, I had to work. When I entered the kitchen that morning, Mrs. Silverstein asked me to polish the silverware. She was having guests over for dinner the following night, and she needed the silverware for that occasion. She also told me that I would have to polish the silver again when I returned to work on Tuesday.

I did not know, since Mrs. Silverstein had said nothing about it, that I should have worn gloves to protect my hands from the harsh silverware polish. My hands were burning, and I was feeling sicker by the hour. Mrs. Silverstein noticed my discomfort and suggested that I take a break. She gave me some Excedrin to take. I went to my room and fell asleep. I resumed my duties after I awoke and then went back to my room about at 10:30.

That night, while I was showering, I thought about the four nights when I had eaten bread and cheese for dinner, refusing to finish the Silversteins' leftovers. Then I thought of how large the house was and what an overwhelming job it was for me to keep it clean. I reasoned that I was poor, yes, and I needed a job, but this job was too much for me. I couldn't see myself doing it for one year, let alone the three years I would need if I wanted the Silversteins to sponsor me. I was afraid I would die from overwork before receiving the green card. Although I had endured some difficulties in my life, I loved life and was not about to bring an end to my life for a green card. With these thoughts in my mind, I decided not to return to the Silversteins' house after my days off, which were about to begin. I went to bed feeling at peace with myself, believing I had made a sound decision.

Sunday was another sunny day. I awoke eager to leave the Silversteins' home. I felt sicker than the day before, but I managed to take a shower and get myself dressed. I felt extremely cold, even though I was wearing a sweater, an old one Edna had given me which made me look like a homeless person. At that moment I was grateful for the sweater, because I needed to wear something heavy over my blouse. After dressing and gathering my belongings, which I packed in the suitcase Mrs. Canner had given me, I went into the Silversteins' kitchen, where I waited for Mr. or Mrs. Silverstein to drive me to the bus station. They came into the kitchen together, said good morning to me, and emphasized how pleased they were with my work. They also expressed again their willingness to start processing the papers to sponsor me for my green card. I listened and thanked them for their compliments and their offer. I told them that I wanted them to start the process of sponsoring me for a green card, knowing all the time that I was about to leave their home intending never to return.

I remembered Randell telling me that, even if I had to scrub floors to get a green card, I should do it. "Well, Randell," I thought, "you didn't tell me that I might have to eat people's leftovers, seasoned with a rich white woman's saliva, and clean a mansion every day to get that card. Randell, those are the things they want me to do in America for a green card. You know what, Randell? I am not willing to do those things for a green card, no matter how I might benefit from having one. It is one advantage I am willing to forego, because no way in high heaven will I subject myself to doing these things for a green card. Sorry if I let you down, Randell, but I will not do these things." I wondered what was taking the Silversteins so long to come and pay me my damn money and drive me to the bus stop. I was eager to get to hell out of their house and out of their sight. Mrs. Silverstein returned to the kitchen and announced that Mr. Silverstein would pay me and drive me to the bus stop. He came to the kitchen shortly after and asked me to follow him to the car. Suitcase in hand, I followed Mr. Silverstein, who was dressed in a white tennis outfit, to his car, a black Cadillac.

I sat in front next to him. Mr. Silverstein again said what an excellent job I had done and reiterated their willingness to sponsor me. Upon our arrival at the bus stop, he handed me some rolled-up dollar bills, stating that they were my week's salary. Saying he would see me on Tuesday, he drove away. After the car was out of sight, I counted the bills and discovered that he had paid me fifty-five dollars instead of the sixty his wife had agreed to. I was upset that he had underpaid me. Five dollars might not be a lot of money to them, but it was to me. I felt I deserved to be paid the correct amount because of the hard work I had done for them that week. I was astonished that a man as wealthy as Mr. Silverstein would rob someone as poor as I was of five dollars. Even though I had no proof, I believed that Mr. Silverstein had underpaid me deliberately. I consoled myself by thinking how Mrs. Silverstein would be waiting for my call on Tuesday, not knowing that I had quit. I felt that she would be more disappointed with my not showing up for work than I was over losing the five dollars out of which her husband had cheated me.

Edna was getting ready to go to church when I arrived at her apartment that Sunday, and I let her know that I was too sick to attend church. I saw the expression on her face and knew she was not pleased. Before Edna left for church, she asked me if I had been paid, and I said yes. Then she asked me to give her the money. Foolishly, I gave it all to her without asking why she wanted it. Then Edna announced that she was borrowing ten dollars of my money to pay her church dues. I wondered what money Edna would have used to pay her church dues if I had not gotten paid.

Edna had not given me a house key, nor did she allow me to make calls on her telephone—not that I knew anyone to call. She locked the dial on her rotary phone whenever I was home alone, so I was able to answer calls but not initiate any. While Edna was at church, I had the urge to call Aunt Millie and visit her, but I could not. I just stayed in bed in the apartment until Edna returned about 4:30 in the afternoon. An hour later, she announced that it was dinnertime. My mouth was tasteless and so was the food that Edna served me in a margarine bowl. I thanked God that I had no appetite. The food she gave me in that little plastic bowl would not have filled the stomach of a three-year-old child. I ate very little of the food, but I drank the four ounces of fruit drink which she gave me in a small plastic glass.

After dinner, I told Edna that I had quit my job because it was too overwhelming for me. I told her about the work I had done that week and the long hours I'd had to work. I also told her that Mr. Silverstein paid me five dollars less than his wife had agreed to pay me. That upset Edna, and she agreed that I should not return to the job. She suggested that I contact Ms. Faya at the employment agency the next day, which would be Monday, and ask her to assist me in finding another job.

Although I was sick on Monday, I contacted Ms. Faya and informed her that I had quit the job at the Silversteins' home. I explained that the job had overwhelmed me, and I asked her to assist me in finding another job. Ms. Faya understood. She told me not to worry and promised that she would find me another job. She suggested that I telephone her as soon as I was well and ready to work again. Aunt Millie called to check on me while Edna was out. She did not know that I was sick and said that if she had known, she would have cooked me some soup. She wanted to bring me some medication, but I told her that I could not let her in because I had no house key. She was quite upset that Edna had not given me a key to her apartment. Aunt Millie took a personal interest in my welfare, and I trusted her because my intuition told me that she was a good person.

I found in Aunt Millie the caring qualities of my great grandmother and my grandmother, and I developed a loving feeling for her. When we chatted on the telephone that morning after Edna left the apartment, I told her everything that had taken place on the job that week: my telephone conversations with Lucille, the incident with the exterminator, and the Silversteins' willingness to sponsor me for the green card. I did not forget to tell her I had quit the job, and why. After listening to me, she educated me on the immigration laws of America.

Aunt Millie told me that if I stayed in the country beyond the four weeks I had been granted I would become an illegal immigrant. She said I had already violated the law by working for the Silversteins, that I was ineligible to work, being neither a citizen nor a permanent resident. According to Aunt Millie, I was not the first to violate those laws, and I would not be the last. People from all over the world were living in America as illegal immigrants, most of them working and violating the law. She said the government did not have the personnel to crack down on illegal immigrants who violated the law by working. She informed me that I could attain legal resident status if a permanent resident or an employer sponsored me or if I married an American citizen. She advised me that I could pay a man to marry me, or I could marry any man interested in marrying me, even if I would not otherwise be interested in him. "That no big deal," she said, since I could divorce the person soon after I attained a permanent resident status green card. Aunt Millie explained that during the processing of the green card, many employers treated their employees unfairly, seeming to feel that the employees were indebted to them. Aunt Millie explained that most of the employers overwork and underpay their employees. Some employees, unable to endure the oppression of their employers, leave their jobs without getting a green card. Most of those who stay long enough to get a green card leave their jobs soon afterwards. At that point there is nothing those oppressors calling themselves employers can do to prevent them from leaving.

She warned me not to tell anyone, especially people from the West Indies, that I was in America illegally. "Don't trust too many people. Once they know your business, you are at their mercy," she warned. "Although all of us came here to achieve our own goals, educational, financial or otherwise, people get jealous of one another, and it is the jealousy they build up within themselves that leads them to report other illegal immigrants like themselves to Immigration," she commented. She explained that when anyone reports illegal immigrants to the Immigration authorities, the authorities would come looking for them. If found, they would be locked up in prison until being deported to their country of origin. Illegal immigrants in America, she said, have to be careful in choosing their friends, because friends are the ones who know their friends' immigration status, and they are the ones who are most likely to report them.

Before Aunt Millie ended her conversation with me, she told me that if anyone were to ask me about my immigration status, I must never tell the truth. "People are nosy, especially other West Indian people, but you are never to tell anyone that you are in America illegally. It is none of their business," she emphasized. She told me that if anyone asked me about my immigration status, I was to say that my father had sponsored me and I was living with him in Queens. "Some of them are so nosy that they will ask all kinds of questions," she commented."Tell them your father works as an engineer for New York Transit."

Aunt Millie also explained to me about Social Security numbers. She said I would need a Social Security number in order to apply for jobs and pay taxes. Until a few years before, illegal immigrants had been allowed to apply for Social Security card, but then the government prohibited it. When the economy in America was bad and lots of people were out of jobs, she said, the public blamed illegal immigrants for the high unemployment. They would say that the immigrants, legal and illegal, were employed in jobs which should have gone to Americans.

Aunt Millie disagreed that immigrants are the cause of high unemployment among American citizens, since most immigrants are employed in the unskilled, low-paying jobs which citizens refuse to do. She said immigrants are used as scapegoats. "We are blamed for high unemployment, crimes, and God knows whatever else goes wrong in America," she said. Then she told me I could not open a bank account in my own name without a Social Security number. But I was not to feel discouraged. With time, everything could change. I listened to every word Aunt Millie uttered to me that day, and I stored as much of the information in my memory as I could. I analyzed her words throughout our conversation, and I knew they would become my Bible while I remained in America. I ended the telephone conversation when I heard Edna's footsteps on the stairs.

I was lying in bed pretending to be sicker than I really was, when Edna entered the room where I lay. She asked if I was all right, and I told her I was still feeling sick. I was grateful for the soup she warmed for me, but I had no appetite because of my illness. I remained ill for the two weeks that followed. Aunt Millie telephoned almost every day to check on my progress, and when my illness had persisted for two weeks, she began to worry. Reluctantly, Edna allowed me to spend a day with her. Millie was happy to see me, but she remarked that I looked pale and was coughing too much. She was furious that Edna had not taken me to see a doctor. Aunt Millie cooked me some soup and gave me some medication. When I was leaving her house, she gave me some additional medication in a bottle and said that she would have to take me to a doctor if I did not show signs of improvement within two days. "Don't worry about the doctor's fee. I will pay it," she said. I was grateful that this stranger I had adopted as my aunt was more concerned about me than was Edna, who once had expressed a wish to adopt me.

I was home alone one day in the second week of my illness when the telephone rang. It was Herman Powell, who had lived in the same village as my father's family. Before he immigrated to America, Herman had been a teacher at the village where Andrew taught. His father and Mr. Phillips were good friends, and I knew his mother. Herman had heard that I was in America and had gotten Edna's phone number from one of Edna's nephews. I was happy to hear a familiar voice. We spoke for more than two hours.

Herman asked about his family back in St. Vincent, and he was particularly curious to find out how I had gotten to know Edna. I was surprised to find out that I was not the first person Edna had promised to adopt and assisted to come to America. According to Herman, there were two others. Edna had found both girls housekeeping/nanny jobs and insisted on taking their wages away from them. When one of the young ladies refused to turn over her money, Edna reported her to Immigration authorities, and she was deported. The other young lady left Edna without telling her she was leaving. Herman warned me to be careful. He said that Edna might seem to be concerned about me, it was just a pretense to mask exploitation.

He said he was not surprised that Edna had taken the money which I had brought to America with me as well as my wages from the Silversteins. When I told him I was looking for another job, he advised me strongly to go to the agency without bringing Edna along and that I should not give Edna the name, address, or phone number of anyone who might employ me. He warned that Edna would report me to Immigration if I did not do everything she demanded. Herman recommended that I pay Edna for room and board when I got a job and not give her any more of my money. He said I should save my money on my own. "If you give her money to save for you, I guarantee that she will never give it back to you," he said. Herman had nothing positive to say about Edna.

When I was well again the following Monday, I went to the employment agency alone, as Herman had advised, and I spoke with Ms. Faya. She scheduled an appointment for me to meet with a Mrs. Newman on the Wednesday of that same week. When Edna inquired about my job search, I told her about the scheduled appointment Ms. Faya had arranged for me. Before she volunteered to accompany me to the appointment, I informed her that I would go alone, because I had better learn now rather than later how to travel alone. She agreed, and I went for the interview alone. I took the train from Queens to Manhattan and a bus from Manhattan to New Brunswick, New Jersey. I called Mrs. Newman when I got to the bus stop, and she came to pick me up and drive me back to her house, where she interviewed me.

Mrs. Newman, a former schoolteacher, wanted a housekeeper/nanny to clean her house and assist her with her two children. Jason was five years old and Joslyn was three. She showed me around the house, which was much smaller than the Silversteins' house. Then we sat at a table, where she questioned me about my experience with children. I told her I was the first of ten children and I had assisted my mother with the care of my siblings. During my interview, Joslyn dropped her pacifier onto the floor. I picked up the pacifier and asked Mrs. Newman if I could wash it before giving it back to Joslyn. After I washed the pacifier and gave it back to Joslyn, Mrs. Newman offered me the job, because she said that I seemed to be good with children.

She told me my salary would be sixty-five dollars a week and I would work from Tuesday through Saturday. I was to arrive on the job Tuesday mornings and leave on Sunday mornings. I accepted the job, thinking I could manage this smaller house and that the pay was higher than at the Silversteins. I hoped she would not shortchange me on my pay, as the Silversteins had done, and that she would not expect me to eat leftovers. While she was driving me to the bus stop, Mrs. Newman said that she would inform Ms. Faya that she had offered me the job. When we arrived at the bus stop, she gave me money to reimburse me for my transportation to New Jersey. I thanked her and thought how kind she was.

Since I did not have a key to Edna's apartment and she was not at home when I returned from my interview, I went to Aunt Millie's house and waited there until Edna came home. While waiting for Edna, I told Aunt Millie about my new job. She was happy. For reasons unknown to me, Millie recommended that I wait until Friday to tell Edna about the job, and I agreed. When Edna called Millie to find out if I was there and to inform me she was home, Millie questioned her about not giving me a key to the apartment. Edna said she did not have an extra key, but she promised to have one made. Not believing her, Millie called her a "damn liar."

As soon as I returned to Edna's apartment, she asked if I had gotten the job. Remembering what I had promised Millie, I told her I wouldn't know until Friday. Edna said she had prayed that I would get the job because I needed the money. That night I heard her praying, asking God for his divine intervention to assist me in getting the job. God, of course, had already answered my prayer. Many thoughts entered my mind as I lay in bed that night. I questioned whether I had made the right decision in coming to America. I could not see myself working as a housekeeper/nanny for a year, let alone the three years for the Newmans to sponsor me for a green card. The idea of marrying someone that I didn't love was beyond my comprehension, and I was no more interested in marriage than when Vernon had proposed to me. Since I could not imagine doing either of those things for the sake of a green card, I supposed I wouldn't become a legal immigrant any time soon. I drifted off to sleep with those thoughts racing through my mind.

Edna shouted, "Praise the Lord" when I told her Friday that I had gotten the job and that I was to begin working on Tuesday. She did not ask me for the name, address or phone number of my new employer, and I did not volunteer them. Ever since I had spoken with Herman, I realized that Edna was not a person to be trusted, and I did not trust her. I accompanied her to church that night and on Sunday, too, but I was looking forward to Tuesday when I would start my new job. Not that I expected to like the job, but I was eager to get out of Edna's apartment and away from her.

As planned, I began working for the Newmans on Tuesday, and the work was not as hard as it had been at the Silversteins. Mrs. Newman suggested I take a midday lunch break and taught me how to cook hamburger by taking the frozen patties from the freezer and setting the oven to broil before putting in the hamburgers. She also pointed out some cold lunchmeat and suggested that I have some for my lunch if I wanted to. She conversed with me more on my first day on the job than Mrs. Silverstein had done the entire week I worked for her. Although Mrs. Newman seemed friendlier than Mrs. Silverstein, they bore many similarities. Both expected me to eat the family leftovers for my dinner. I refused outright, eating hamburgers in the afternoon so that I did not need to eat dinner at night. As a matter of survival, so as not to eat their leftovers and not to starve myself, I cooked rice and ate it with hamburger during the day while Mrs. Newman was out. Although I was not sure whether Mrs. Newman had contaminated the food with her saliva, I found it demeaning to eat the family leftovers.

Mrs. Newman would leave her used sanitary pads unwrapped on the bathroom tank for me to throw into the wastebasket. She also left her dirty underwear wherever she took them off and expected me to pick them up. I felt all of this demeaning to me, and I wondered whether Mrs. Newman thought I was less of a human being than she was. In my country, women's underwear was so personal to them that they would never leave it around, clean or unclean, for others to see, let alone their used sanitary pads. Women in my country were secretive about their periods and felt embarrassed going to the store to purchase their pads, taking them home hidden in their pocketbooks. Before I had worked long for her, Mrs. Newman changed my days off from every Sunday and Monday to every Monday off and Sunday off every other week. When I questioned her, she said those were the days off we had agreed upon when I accepted the job. That was a lie. She stressed that they were comparable to what other housekeepers in the area had. Considering her lies about what we had agreed upon when I accepted the job, I thought of quitting, never to return, when I left for my days off that Sunday. When Sunday came, I packed my things and waited in the kitchen for Mr. or Mrs. Newman to drive me to the bus stop. Mrs. Newman came in and announced that Mr. Newman would be driving me. Then she handed me sixty-five dollars in cash and gave me an extra five dollars for my transportation to New York. Shortly after she paid me, I followed Mr. Newman to his black thunderbird, and he drove me to the bus stop. As I was stepping out the car to wait for the bus to New York, Mr. Newman said, "Have a nice weekend, and we will see you Tuesday."

I had many thoughts about the job as I rode the bus to New York. I loved taking care of the Newmans' children because they were well-behaved and manageable, and I was not overwhelmed with my duties. I took breaks for a couple of hours each day, and the salary was good, too. Those were the good things about the job. But then I considered how Mrs. Newman did nasty things like leaving her dirty panties and used sanitary pads for me to pick up, which I found demeaning. Yet she was kind and generous to reimburse me for my transportation. Her generosity and my fondness for the children were the major factors in my decision to return to the job on Tuesday.

Edna was getting dressed for church when I arrived at her apartment. I wondered whether she would have gone to church without me had I not arrived when I did. She waited until I had put on a dress which she had bought me at the thrift store. Then she remarked that the clothes I was wearing were not free and I owed her twenty-five dollars for them. I felt that I had heard enough about her not giving the clothes to me free of charge. I told myself she need not worry about the twenty-five dollars she claimed to have paid for clothes I had not asked her to buy and that I would reimburse her the inflated amount. I realized that Edna's motive in assisting with my immigration was so she could take my money. I was resolved not to allow her to take all of it, planning to leave her apartment as soon as I had earned enough. I wished to share my earnings with my family back home, not with Edna, who was able to support herself and, after all, was not a close friend or relative.

I went to church with Edna that day, as I did on all the other church days. The minister preached a long sermon, and the church members screamed and shouted as usual while he preached. I was glad when it was over—I was tired and needed to go back to Edna's place and rest. Soon after I got there and changed into a housedress, I fell asleep. Edna shouted, "Lola, time for dinner," and I woke up. Peeping through the window, I realized that the sun had already set. After dinner she asked me whether I had gotten paid and how much. When I answered, she demanded I give her all of my money except the ten dollars I was to use to pay my way back to work.

I immediately thought of my conversation with Herman, who had told me, "Go to the interview alone and don't tell her the name of your employer if you get the job. Don't give her your employer's address and telephone number. Ask her how much she charges for your room and board, pay her that amount, and don't give her all of your money." I told Edna that I would like to pay her for room and board if she would tell me the cost, and I would also like to reimburse her for the clothes she had bought me. She replied that her charge for room and board was twenty-five dollars a week and an extra ten dollars a month to assist with her gas payment, reiterating that nothing is free in America. I paid Edna fifty dollars that night, and she accepted it even though she already had forty dollars from my previous pay and the money I had brought from home, over a hundred and fifty dollars. I looked at Edna and muttered that she was like a wicked witch. I had no doubt that I would move away from Edna without giving her notice, and the sooner I moved, the better off I would be. I recognized the possibility that Edna might report me to Immigration authorities for deportation if I did not give her my money, so I prayed to God that night and asked for guidance.

Aunt Millie telephoned while Edna was away from the apartment on Monday, and I told her what had transpired between Edna and me the night before. Millie said Edna was a witch and should not have brought me to America intending to mistreat me. Then she informed me that she had my passport. The previous week, Edna had given her my passport to hold. Edna told Millie she had paid someone two hundred dollars to write the invitation letter she had sent me in St. Vincent, and I would have to pay her back the two hundred dollars before she would give me back my passport. Millie said she was quite sure no one had charged Edna for the invitation letter and that Edna had written the letter herself. "Edna is evil, and you will have to get away from her and stay away from her. If you don't, she will report you to Immigration," Aunt Millie warned me.

Millie advised me to pay Edna the two hundred dollars because it was important for me to have my passport. She was furious and shouted that Edna and people like her should not be going to church claiming to be Christians. "I will give you the two hundred dollars to pay Edna. You can pay me back after you get yourself together," she said. She told me to pass by her house on my way to work the following day for the money. I could not help crying as I thanked her for everything that she had done for me since we met.

It seemed as though Millie and Herman always sensed when I was home alone and they could phone me without Edna overhearing the conversation. Soon after I hung up from speaking with Millie, Herman called. I told him about my conversation with Millie and her advice to me. "Millie is right," Herman said angrily. "You will have to get away from that witch." He advised me to look for a room to rent. He suggested that if I would meet him in Brooklyn on my next day off, he would assist me in finding a room. I agreed. I hung up the telephone when I heard Edna's approaching footsteps.

Edna said a not-so-friendly hello to me when she entered the apartment. Then she said to me, "I paid two hundred dollars for the invitation letter that I sent to you and you will have to pay me back my money." I pretended not to know what she was talking about, even though Aunt Millie had informed me about her intention. "What invitation letter?" I asked. She reiterated that she had paid one of her male friends two hundred dollars to write the invitation letter that she sent to me in St. Vincent. She said that if her mysterious friend had not written that letter, I would not have been able to immigrate to America. Not knowing that I knew she had given my passport to Millie to hold because she was afraid that I would find it in her apartment and not pay her the money, she said, "I will keep your passport until you pay me the two hundred dollars." I looked at Edna with disgust. God knows how much I wanted to curse her, but I could not do it just then. So I told her that I would pay her the money as soon as I was able to.

On my way back to work at the Newmans' house on Tuesday, I stopped by Aunt Millie's house and, sure enough, she gave me two hundred dollars in an envelope. While handing me the money, Aunt Millie said that it was a gift from her because she wanted me to get my passport from Edna right away. Millie had given back my passport to Edna during the week and had told Edna that she did not want to get involved with her blackmail of me. Millie said, indignantly, "Edna brought you here for you to support her. You are not her child and you shouldn't be giving her all of your money. Get away from that wicked woman as soon as possible." I took the envelope with the money, thanked her for it, told her that I would call her sometime during the week, and left for the bus. I thought how kind and generous Aunt Millie had been to me, and I wondered what I would have done in the first weeks in America if I had not met her.

Herman had my telephone number at the Newmans, so he called me on the job that week and again we talked about Edna. I informed him that I could not meet with him as planned because I had to go and pay Edna so I could get my passport back from her. Herman was angry enough to suggest that I should "beat the living daylights" out of Edna, then leave her apartment. He knew as well as I did that I could not do that. All I wanted was my passport and to leave Edna as soon as I was able to save enough money to rent a room at some distance from the neighborhood where Edna lived. Herman promised he would inquire about rooms or apartments for rent and would call me if he heard of any that were suitable and I could afford. As soon as I hung up, Aunt Millie called, and from the tone of her voice, I knew something was upsetting her. I had a feeling that Edna had something to do with it. That was when she told me that Edna had told her I had not given her the name, address, and telephone number of my new employer and that I was rude and unmannerly. "I did not give her the information about my employer because she could not be trusted," I said. Aunt Millie called Edna a snake, and a very dangerous one at that. She said that I had done the right thing.

Soon after I entered Edna's apartment the following Monday, my only day off that week, Edna said she wanted to have a talk with me. She told me the period the Immigration authorities were allowing me to stay in America had expired. "You could stay longer if you want, but you wouldn't be staying with me, because I don't want the Immigration authorities to come knocking on my door looking for you. As soon as you pay me the money for the invitation letter, I will give you your passport. Then you can leave," she said to me. In essence she was putting me out. I was frightened and hadn't a clue as to what I should do next. My body felt numb and I trembled with fright. Nervously, I took the two hundred dollars from my pocketbook and handed it to Edna. She smiled and seemed pleased that I had given her the money. She left me in the living room and went to her bedroom. She returned a few minutes later and said, "Here is your passport." Then she suggested that I call my employer and ask if I could return to the job that day. My gut instinct told me Edna was trying to trap me. Following my instinct, I dialed a telephone number in New Jersey pretending to be calling my employer. When someone answered, I disconnected the call by pressing the button in the cradle and pretended to be talking to my employer. Edna looked on and listened. After I ended my pretended conversation with my employer, I told Edna my employer had said it was all right for me to return to the job that day. I packed the few belongings that I had with me into my travelling bag, thanked her for whatever she thought she had done for me, and left.

Unbeknownst to Edna, I went straight to Aunt Millie's house. When I told Aunt Millie what had transpired between Edna and me, she cried and said that Edna had not treated me well and had done me wrong by telling me that I could not stay with her any longer. Aunt Millie knew that I did not have to go back to work until the next day, so she suggested that I spend the rest of the day and night with her. She called Edna and signaled me to pick up her other phone and listen in. "I just kicked her out of my apartment," I heard her tell Aunt Millie, "and soon after she left, a man by the name of Herman called for her. Lola has been in this country less than a month and she has already picked up a man! If she had not paid me the two hundred dollars, I would have reported her to Immigration for deportation." She went on to say that I had not given her the phone number of my employer, but she would get it from her next phone bill. Then she told Millie she had suggested I call my employer from her phone. "She was stupid enough to make the call that will list the number of her employer on my next telephone bill," Edna explained. I covered my mouth with my hand to prevent myself from laughing at her thinking that she had outsmarted me.

Edna told Millie that if she reported me the Immigration authorities would be able to find me by tracing the telephone number where I was working. After this remark I didn't want to listen any longer. Aunt Millie was so upset by that same remark that she told Edna she was not the Christian she pretended to be, but a woman with a wicked soul. She had helped me immigrate for her own self-ish reasons, not to help me, as she claimed. "You brought Lola to America thinking you would be able to exploit her as you did the other two girls before her," she said. "You should go and find a job and try to build a friendship with your daughter and leave Lola alone. If you are a God-fearing person, you will do what is right!" Then Millie slapped the receiver down.

After Aunt Millie got off the phone, she began to tell me more of what she knew about Edna. She confirmed what Herman had told me about the two other girls Edna had assisted. She said Edna found them domestic jobs, took away their earned wages, and intercepted their letters from their relatives and friends. It then struck me that Edna might not have mailed the letters I asked her to mail for me my first week in America. Aunt Millie said Edna had also treated her daughter unkindly, and the daughter had moved away without letting Edna know her whereabouts. Millie was so upset that she referred to Edna as "that bitch." Curtis, Aunt Millie's husband, was in the living room with us at the time, lis-tening to the entire episode. He was upset with Edna, too, espe-cially when Millie repeated what Edna had said to her on the phone.

Both Aunt Millie and Curtis consoled me that night. They said I could have stayed with them on my days off, if they weren't liv-ing so close to Edna. However, they promised to do everything within their power to keep my whereabouts secret from Edna. Since Edna had told Millie I had telephoned my employer from her phone, Millie was worried about what Edna would do once she got the number from her phone bill. I told Aunt Millie not to worry, that I had merely tricked Edna into thinking I had made the call. Aunt Millie said, "I knew you were smart and articulate, but I did not imagine you were that smart. You have outsmarted the witch!" Aunt Millie suggested that I return to work the next day, when I was expected, and she promised to contact her cousin in Jamaica, Queens to ask if he knew of anyone looking to share or rent a room. The next morning, after I ate the fried plantains and fried Red Snapper fish that Aunt Millie made me for breakfast, I gath-ered my belongings. She came into the bedroom and told me she would do everything she could to help, and I believed that she would. We embraced as I told her to relate my good-bye to Curtis, who had already left for work. Sadness overcame me when I noticed her crying as she closed the front door behind me.

When I returned to the Newmans' home in New Jersey, I must have looked sad and worried, because Mrs. Newman detected something about me that wasn't quite right. When she asked if I felt ill, I told her Edna had thrown me out of her apartment and I did not yet have another place to stay on my days off. Mrs. Newman suggested that I stay with them during my days off and offered to take me to and from the bus stop if I wanted to go to New York. She said that if I decided to spend my days off with them, I would not have to do any work around the house on those days. I expressed my gratitude for her offer, but before accepting it, I called Aunt Millie to discuss the matter with her. Aunt Millie encouraged me to accept, because I would be safer at the Newmans' home than living in an apartment alone, and I could visit her when I went to New York. I also telephoned Herman and told him about my living arrangement with the Newmans. He did not think it was a good idea. "I do not trust white folks in America," he said. "They could turn on you, too. But I will support you in whatever decision you make." He, too, suggested that I visit him when the opportunity arose.

I accepted the Newmans' offer. I rode the bus to New York almost every Monday. I shopped, and I alternated visits between Aunt Millie and Herman. Both of them were very kind to me. Aunt Millie always prepared special meals for me when I visited her, and she gave me enough food for another meal to take back to work. She expressed her concern for my welfare, even though, as she herself would say, she believed I had enough common sense to keep myself from getting into trouble. When she spoke that way, I found myself comparing her with my Grandmother, because I believe that my Grandmother would have expressed her concern about me in exactly the same way.

Herman knew I loved to eat West Indian food, especially fried or broiled red snapper fish, and he prepared those foods every time I visited him. At first, Herman treated me like his little sister, but I had the feeling he wanted our relationship to go beyond that. On one of my visits, as we sat in chairs across his table in his kitchen talking about my status as an illegal immigrant, Herman said, "I am legal. Marry me. I could help you get your green card. It would be a business marriage." I politely declined. Although he said our marriage would merely be a business marriage, I could not see myself marrying one of Andrew's close friends, even though Andrew was in St. Vincent and we were in America. I felt that marrying one of Andrew's closest friends, for business or otherwise, would be wrong. I still considered Andrew my boyfriend, even though he was in St. Vincent and I was in America. However, Herman and I remained friends.

After Edna threw me out of her apartment, I began financially supporting my grandmother, mother and siblings. I was able to increase their support, because I made a good salary working for the Newmans, living with them all week, and I did not have to pay them for room and board. The money my grandmother and mother each received from me each month was more than the monthly income of some civil servants and teacher's aides back home. Since I did not have a Social Security number and could not open a bank account in my own name, I sent money to my mother to deposit in my account at a bank in St. Vincent. I did not like the work I was doing, but it took care of my financial needs. Most of all, it gave me the chance to accomplish one of my goals—supporting my grandmother, mother and siblings. I had even thought of sending Andrew a little money, too, until I received his second letter, less than two months after my arrival in America.

Andrew wrote lots of his usual sweet nonsense in his first letter, which I received the third week I was working for the Newmans. It was the kind of sweet nonsense that sent pleasant sensations through every bone in my body, so I could not resist reading the letter over and over again. I read that letter more times than I would ever admit. That was why I was so eager to read his second letter. I tore the letter open and began to read. "My dearest Lola: You are a wonderful and intelligent lady, and please believe me when I say that I love you. I love you more than I will love anyone else or anything in this whole wide world and I will always do so. Please do not believe otherwise or ever doubt the love that I hold within my heart for you. Regretfully, Lola, there comes a time in a man's life when he has to make decisions. It's hard for me to explain why I have made the decision that I have made, but it is a decision that will help me in the future. I have decided to marry Dawn on August 4, 1974." I could not read on, but I noticed that he ended with, "Will always love you, Andrew." After I saw the ending, I began to cry, and I threw the letter on the table in disgust. When the letter arrived, I was in the kitchen about to eat lunch. Now my appetite vanished. I tried to drink a glass of juice, but I could not swallow it, nor could I swallow water. I hurt so much that I was unable to chew or swallow. As the night approached, my throat hurt and my stomach hurt even more from starvation. A few weeks later I was still vomiting everything that I had been able to swallow, and I had begun to lose weight.

I hurt when Uncle Josey left home and went to Trinidad, because I missed him. I also hurt when Ma died, because she meant so much to me and I missed her, too. I hurt every day from the aftermath of rape. I hurt when I left home to come to America, missing my family. But never before had I felt so hurt as when I read Andrew's letter. Andrew was special to me in a unique way. It was hard for me to explain why he was so special to me, even after he had betrayed my trust. Our intimate relationship, of course, had had its ups and downs, but our shared connection would cause us to make up many times after we had broken up and vowed never to make up. I guess that I was hurting more than ever before because I realized there would be no more making up between Andrew and me. I went to bed that night with pain in my heart, tears on my pillow, and Andrew on my mind.

Mrs. Newman had a way of detecting when I was unhappy, and sure enough, her antennae worked this time, too. When she confronted me two days after I had received Andrew's letter, I broke down and told her about Andrew. She was very sympathetic and told me that I was young, beautiful, and intelligent and would meet someone someday who would appreciate me and love me even more than Andrew did. She encouraged me to forget about Andrew, to consider him part of my past, and to look to the future. "Yes," Mrs. Newman, I thought, "but that is easier said than done. I can never forget Andrew. You don't understand, and I can't explain to you, because I don't understand myself why I love him so much." Although my heart continued to ache, I knew I had to go on with my life without Andrew being a part of it. I had to concentrate on my goals, the financial support of my family and to have my green card and enough money to attend a university some day. I told Mrs. Newman that I would like her to sponsor me for a green card. Mrs. Newman had no previous knowledge of how to proceed, but she knew that the Sterns, the Newmans' neighbors and friends, were sponsoring their housekeeper. Mrs. Newman introduced me to Cynthia, the Sterns' housekeeper, and encouraged me to ask Cynthia the procedure for obtaining a green card.

Cynthia, a native of Jamaica who had immigrated to England and lived there for many years before coming to the United States, was ten years my senior, at twenty-nine years old. She was married, but her husband was still living in England. After Mrs. Newman introduced us, we visited each other on evenings after we had finished our work for the day. Cynthia said she would file for her husband's green card soon after she received her own, so I told her that the Newmans had expressed willingness to sponsor me and asked her how I should proceed. Cynthia informed me that I needed a lawyer and gave me the address and telephone number of Mr. Shutter, a lawyer in Manhattan. She advised me to call his office and make an appointment to see him, and I did.

On the day of my appointment, I entered Mr. Shutter's office, on the thirty-eighth floor in a building on 42nd Street. The receptionist, a white woman dressed in a blue suit, escorted me to a door, knocking before entering a large office. She introduced me to Mr. Jeffrey Shutter, a short, skinny white man sitting in a well-upholstered chair behind a large mahogany desk. Mr. Shutter, seeming from the wrinkles in his face about sixty years old, told me to sit opposite him and asked the purpose of my visit. I told him I was there for a consultation about the processing of my immigration papers for a green card, saying that Cynthia Thomas, one of his clients and a good friend of mine, had referred me. Mr. Shutter listened attentively as I told him that I worked for the Newmans as a housekeeper/nanny and that they were willing to sponsor me. When he asked me my country of origin, I told him St. Vincent. Then I told him that I would like to retain him as my lawyer to handle the processing of the immigration papers.

Mr. Shutter agreed to serve as my lawyer, but he made me aware that I would have to work for the Newmans eight to ten years before I could get a green card. "Cynthia told me that I could get it in three years," I said, stunned at this bit of bad news. He explained to me that Jamaica had gained its independence from Great Britain, but because of St. Vincent's colonial status, it would take me much longer to get a green card. Then Mr. Shutter asked if I would be willing to work for the Newmans for that long. Mr. Shutter agreed with my assessment that I would not. He explained that I would be able to get a green card in two years if I were to marry a legal immigrant or an American citizen. Then he changed the tone of his voice from business to personal, saying that he believed I was still a virgin and implied that, if I went to bed with him, he would process the immigration papers without charging me a fee. "You are attractive and young, and I am sure that you are still a virgin," he said. Then he rose from his chair, walked to where I was sitting, and placed his hands on my shoulders, staring into my eyes in a seductive way. He tried to kiss me, but I refused, pulling myself away from him. As I turned to leave, he repeated that he was willing to assist me free of charge if I would to cooperate with him. Without responding, I yanked the door open and walked away, never looking back.

As I hurried to catch the bus back to New Jersey, I thought about Mr. Shutter. His offer was tempting, and I might consider it if I were desperate for a green card. A green card would enable me to get a better job, save some money, and go back to school. But there was no way on earth, come hell or high water, that I would give in to the sexual advances of that white man who was old enough to be my grandfather. Rather than have sex with that bastard, I would go back St. Vincent and live among those evil villagers, eating bananas and breadfruit every day, without any fish or meat. He must be out of his cotton-picking mind if he thinks that I would have sex with him for a damn green card. I wondered whether Cynthia had made such a deal with him. If she had, she must be just as crazy as he is. I wondered what Mr. Shutter would do to a man as old as he was if he knew that the man was making sexual advances to his granddaughter. I kept wondering these things all the way back to New Jersey.

Mrs. Newman picked me up from the bus stop and, as she was driving me back to her house, asked me about my meeting with Mr. Shutter. I told her that according to the lawyer I would have to work for her for eight years before I could get a green card. I saw the happy expression on her face when I told her that. Then she said, "It's nice to know that you will be working for us for a long time. We'd love to have you work for us that long, because you interact well with the children and we love you." "Love me, my ass," I thought. "You love what I am doing for you, not me. Rich white folks like you don't love poor black folks like me. You love the dirty work poor black folks do for you. I'm not a fool to believe you when you say that you love me. You love it when I pick up your dirty underwear and dispose of your sanitary pads." As these thoughts drifted through my mind, I heard Mrs. Newman offer to pay the lawyer's fee for processing the papers.

I should have been grateful for her offer to pay the lawyer, but I was not. I thanked her anyway. "Well, Mrs. Newman, I have news for you," I thought. "Nowhere on this earth—even if this earth were to turn into heaven—am I about to work for you for eight years, let alone eight years doing housekeeping/nanny work. You would have to be crazy to think I would." I calculated that eight years from that time I would be twenty-seven years old—too old to go back to school, or so I thought. Then thoughts of Mr. Shutter and his proposition came back to me, and I became angry about the nerve of this old-ass white man to suggest that I go to bed with him for a green card. Just the idea of it made me sick to my stomach.

I glanced at Mrs. Newman sitting next to me in the front seat of the car, and I wondered if she was thinking that I had no other choice but to work for her for those eight years. I believe that she did, for from that day on, Mrs. Newman demanded that I do more for her, and even asked me to babysit Joslyn on my days off. Because I was living with her for free, I felt obligated to comply, so I babysat Joslyn whenever Mrs. Newman asked me to. As a result, I spent more time on my days off babysitting Joslyn and less time doing the things I enjoyed doing, like visiting Herman and Aunt Millie in New York. I felt that Mrs. Newman was taking advantage of me. I lost a lot of weight, partly because I was still hurting over Andrew and wasn't eating enough, and partly because I became more disenchanted and dissatisfied with the job. I considered quitting, but I would not quit a job before finding another one and a room to rent where I could spend my days off.

Needing to confide in someone, I telephoned Herman and told him I was considering quitting my job. Herman listened and then suggested that I telephone Ms. Faya and ask her to help me find another job. Before contacting Ms. Faya, I telephoned Agnes, a long-time friend of my relatives back home, who had immigrated into the United States many years before. Agnes had visited St. Vincent after I left. When my mother told her that I had immigrated to America, she gave my mother her number and told her to have me call her. I had not called her, but I felt a need to call her that day. Most of her family members, and she herself, lived in Philadelphia. During our conversation, I told her that I was thinking of quitting my job. Agnes suggested that I move to Philadelphia. She promised to assist me in my search for employment and have me live with her until I was able to rent a place of my own.

Always valuing the advice of Aunt Millie, I telephoned her and asked her opinion. Aunt Millie encouraged me to move to Philadelphia, saying that the change in location might do me some good, but not before reminding me not to let anyone know of my immigration status no matter where I might find myself. She repeated what I should tell anyone who asked whether I was a legal resident, and I told her that I would remember to do that. It seemed that I had Aunt Millie to look out for my best interests, as Ma and Uncle Josey had done when they were alive, and my grandmother while I lived in St. Vincent. When I contacted Herman and told him about Agnes and her suggestion that I move to Philadelphia, he was not thrilled. He said it was a decision I would have to make myself. "Who knows, things might work out better for you there," he muttered in an uncertain tone of voice. I thought it might make him unhappy if I decided to relocate. In August, 1974, four months after landing in New York, I boarded a train to Philadelphia's 30th Street Station. I hoped to start anew my search for all that I had heard the United States of America promised for people like me.

Renewed Hope

Agnes, a brown complexioned woman with soft curly hair, was very attractive. Her teeth, as white as cotton balls, grabbed everyone's attention when she smiled. Living with Agnes in her four-bedroom row house in the Germantown section of Philadelphia were her four daughters, Donna, Hilda, Alice and Charlotte, and also her mother, Miss Lizzie. Miss Lizzie, a short, older lady with soft shoulder length gray hair, appeared to be a descendant of the Portuguese people back home. Agnes was also a single parent who worked very hard to support her household. A few days after I relocated to Philadelphia, Agnes took me to the Social Security office to apply for a Social Security card. Like most of the people who knew me, Agnes thought Lola was my real name, so I applied for the Social Security card under the name of Lola instead of my real name, Belitha. I could not have imagined at the time how beneficial it would turn out for me to have a Social Security card under the name Lola.

I got the Social Security card, but I still didn't have a green card, so the only job that I could apply for without being asked to show my green card was a housekeeping/nanny job. Agnes assisted me with my job search. She telephoned Mr. Bullock, who owned and operated a domestic employment agency, like the one Ms. Faya worked for in New York, and asked if he had any jobs available. I didn't have to go to Mr. Bullock's office, as he came to Agnes' house to interview me. Then he took me to the home of the prospective employer, Mrs. Wessler.

Mrs. Wessler appeared to be in her late twenties or early thirties, but her posture made her look like a crooked old woman. Although she looked frail and unhappy, she managed to smile while interviewing me for the job. She hired me on the spot. Mr. Bullock must have expected this outcome, because he had suggested that I bring some working clothes with me. Mrs. Wessler had two children, a four-year-old daughter and a baby. A nurse was taking care of the baby, but she left the day after I was hired. My duties were similar to my previous two jobs, mainly house cleaning and taking care of the children. After the nurse left, I was solely responsible for the care of the two children, especially the baby. I noticed Mrs. Wessler's lack of attention to the baby. Even when the child cried, she would tell me to take care of her and stop her crying. Then she would walk away as if she didn't want to be close to the baby. I wasn't making a big deal of it, not yet, anyway, since I was being paid twenty-five dollars a week more than I had been on my previous job. "She pays me well, so why complain? And there are fewer people in this household than in my last job," I said to myself. I saw no husband, but I noticed a wedding portrait. Mrs. Wessler mentioned that her husband had moved out of the house four months before I was hired.

It was only my second night on the job when, about midnight, I heard some crying. I got out of my bed, tiptoed across the hallway and followed the crying sound to the closed door to Mrs. Wessler's room. I stood at the door for a while, listening quietly, as she continued to cry. Then I tiptoed back to my room. Not long after that I heard the baby crying at the top of her lungs. I knew her mother must have heard her, since their rooms were next to each other. Then I heard Mrs. Wessler's footsteps walking towards my room, and she knocked on my door. She asked that I please go to the baby's room and take care of her. I pulled on my robe and hurried to the baby's room, where the baby was still crying, seeming to be in pain. I tried to comfort her, but she kept crying the whole night. I was quite sure her mother heard her crying, but she never came to check on her, let alone comfort her. This behavior puzzled me, and I wondered whether Mrs. Wessler had any motherly love towards her baby. After the baby fell asleep about 5:30 a.m., I went back to my room and fell asleep myself. My sleep was interrupted by the knocking on my door at 7:15 a.m. I had only slept for a few hours, but I had to jump out of bed at Mrs. Wessler's request that I prepare breakfast for four-year-old Laura.

I took a shower, and then I went to the kitchen to prepare Laura's breakfast. I found her sitting there alone. I spent the rest of the day cleaning and taking care of the children, while Mrs. Wessler spent most of the day locked up in her bedroom. That night when the children were asleep, I again heard her sobbing uncontrollably. I became frightened when I heard the baby screaming at the top of her lungs again, and I jumped out of bed and rushed to her room. I took her in my arms and comforted her, knowing that her mother seemed not to care about her, and I only went back to my room when the baby fell asleep. As I was lying in the bed, I couldn't help wondering whether Mrs. Wessler's constant crying at night meant she had lost her mind. I was afraid that she might come into my room and harm me, so I began to think about ways of defending myself.

By my fourth day on the job, lacking sufficient time to rest, I felt tired and overworked. Taking time to rest would have meant neglecting the children, and I didn't want to do that. They needed someone to care for them, as their mother had withdrawn herself from them almost completely. I felt sorry for the children, especially for the baby, who needed more of her mother's care because of her age. One evening while I sat in the living room with the children, Mrs. Wessler called Laura to the dining room. I saw her dial a number and give Laura the telephone. I listened as she told Laura to ask her daddy to come home. "Tell him that you miss him and ask him to come home," she instructed Laura. I guess that Laura did what her mother instructed her to do, because about 6:00 p.m. that evening, a man came to the house and introduced himself to me as Mr. Wessler. He was a handsome white man with red hair and freckles on his face. He spent some time talking to his wife, but mostly playing with Laura. Then he left. As Mr. Wessler walked to his car in the driveway, Mrs. Wessler began her sobbing again. She sobbed uncontrollably throughout the night. Afraid to sleep, I prayed to God for tomorrow to come quickly. It would be my fifth day and my last night in Mrs. Wessler's house before leaving for my days off. I thought I probably would not return.

The next day I was happy. I met Mrs. Wessler's mother, Mrs. Harte, a short, friendly white woman, who sat around most of the time watching me take care of the children. She commented that I was doing an excellent job with them, saying that her daughter was lucky to have someone like me. Mrs. Harte explained that her daughter had been in a state of depression ever since her husband had left her and moved in with his secretary. Mrs. Harte complained that Mr. Wessler was more interested in his secretary than in his children and that her daughter should concentrate her energy on her children and herself instead of the unfaithful husband. Mrs. Harte was saddened by the situation, but she said there was nothing that she could do to change it. I sympathized with Mrs. Harte and her concern for her daughter, but I was looking forward to the following day, when I would leave Mrs. Wessler's house. I couldn't wait.

When I left that day for what was supposed to be the beginning of my two days off, I knew I wasn't coming back. I hugged the children, saddened by the fact that I wouldn't be seeing them again. I felt guilty that I had to leave the baby with an unloving mother, but I reasoned to myself that the baby was Mrs. Wessler's and not mine, so I shouldn't feel guilty. My concern for the welfare of the children made me cry as I left the Wessler's home.

When I got to Agnes' house, I described my experiences on the job that week. I told her that I was concerned about the welfare of the children, and I couldn't help thinking about them. Agnes told me to worry less about the children and more about myself. "If that woman is in a state of depression and she kills herself while you are there, the police would question you, and you don't want to be in that mess," Agnes said. She advised that I quit the job, because Mrs. Wessler was unstable and might do things that she wouldn't do if she were normal. Agnes was afraid that if Mrs. Wessler did harm to her children or to herself, I would be a suspect, causing me serious problems as an illegal immigrant. She felt that although Mrs. Wessler paid a good salary, the money was not worth the risk. Unlike Edna, who was only interested in my making money so she could take it away from me, Agnes was concerned about what was best for me. She even refused the rent money I offered her, suggesting that I should wait until I got settled on a job before I thought about paying her rent. She even contacted Mr. Bullock for me, informing him that I was quitting the job and explaining my reasons.

Two days later Mr. Bullock came to Agnes' house again and took me to another interview, with Mr. and Mrs. Fisher, who lived in a beautiful neighborhood in Cherry Hill, New Jersey. During the interview, they informed me that Mohammed Ali owned a house close by. Having no idea at the time that Mohammed Ali was a famous boxer, I couldn't understand why they acted so proud to live close to him. At the end of the interview, they offered me the job, which I accepted without hesitation, especially when they told me that my weekly salary would be ninety-five dollars. I stayed with them that night and began working the following day. This job was my fourth live-in housekeeping/nanny job in five months.

I had only one child to care for, and I was now being paid more money and seemed to have less work to do than any of my previous jobs. Not until they showed me my room, which was located in the basement, did I have any apprehension about the job. I had a phobia about house basements, let alone sleeping in one. Although the room in the basement was quite livable, sleeping down there bothered me every night when I went to bed. I feared that I would burn to death down there if the house were to catch afire. I was paranoid.

Mrs. Fisher was a very attractive woman, short with wide hips. Mr. Fisher owned a car dealership in the area, and I wondered why Mrs. Fisher had married him, because he was shedding flakes from his skin, like a dog shedding hair. The flakes that dropped from Mr. Fisher's skin could be found everywhere, in the bathrooms, his bedroom, and all over their bed sheets. I had to use a hand vacuum to vacuum the sheets on their bed, and cleaning their bathroom was a task in itself, particularly the shower. At times I got sick from just looking at these sheddings scattered all over the house. Mr. Fisher said that the shedding was caused by a disease. He assured me that his disease wasn't catching, but I took precautions by wearing gloves whenever I was cleaning. Unlike his wife, who was boastful, Mr. Fisher was a humble and caring man. He would give me an extra five dollars every week with my salary. I was able to send more money home to those who needed my financial support and more to save for me in the bank at home.

Agnes suggested that I open a savings account in America, and she took me to a bank and had me open an account in the name that was on my Social Security card. Besides saving money every week when I got paid, I was now paying Agnes for room and board. I planned to quit the Fishers' job and find another that would enable me to work in the day and attend school at night, but this could only be after I saved enough money to pay for a couple of years of college tuition. I was determined to achieve the educational goals that I had set for myself before I left St. Vincent.

I met Rita one evening when I was taking the Fishers' daughter, Ashley, for a walk. Rita worked as a housekeeper for the Golden family, who lived in the same neighborhood as the Fishers. A native of Barbados and eighteen years my senior, she hoped to benefit from Goldens' sponsorship for a green card. She had lived in England for several years before immigrating to America a couple of years ago. Rita talked about her children in Barbados, especially her only daughter, Sheila, who was attending high school there. She hoped to file for her children's green cards, enabling them to immigrate to America as legal residents. Rita and I became good friends, and we took turns visiting each other every evening at our employers' home after we were finished working for the day.

I was stunned by what she told me when I visited her one night. Rita seemed upset that night and appeared to have been crying. When I asked her what was upsetting her, she said that Mrs. Golden had demanded that she clean up her feces which had overflowed onto the floor from a clogged toilet. I told Rita that if I had been in her position I would never have done it, because that was a job for a plumber, not a housekeeper. I asked her why she had cleaned up the feces. Rita explained that she really needed her green card and she was afraid that Mrs. Golden would fire her and stop the processing of her green card if she had refused. "Rita girl, better you than me, because green card or no green card, I would never have done what you did," I said to Rita in anger.

Rita explained to me, as an older sister would to a younger sister, that she had to do it because of her children. She said that I was lucky not to have children of my own. "If my children weren't depending on my help, I would have walked away from this job today, Lola. Believe me, I would have walked away from this job. But I am a mother. I care about my children and their future, and I want them to have lives better than the one I had. I need the green card to give them that opportunity. That's why I did it," she cried.

I began to compare Rita's situation working for the Goldens to mine working for the Fishers. Mrs. Fisher would annoy me when she would complain that I vacuumed the rug too hard and I should be careful with the walls, but Mr. Fisher told me to ignore it when he overheard her one day. He confided to me that his wife was born into a poor family and was not accustomed to the finer things in life until he married her. Sleeping in the basement was like sleeping in hell, especially when they had their friends over and I was kept awake by the noise they would make walking back and forth on the floor above. Then there was the time that Ashley had a diaper rash, and Mrs. Fisher blamed me for it, saying I must have hit Ashley to leave such a mark on her skin. After she took Ashley to the doctor and he confirmed that it was diaper rash, she apologized to me. These were some things I considered bad about my job, but I had to admit it was not as bad as Rita's. And Rita was to have yet another humiliating experience.

Rita would always go back to New York on her days off. I planned to spend my days off with her that weekend, so I went to meet her at the Goldens' house. From there we were to take a cab to the bus for New York. Rita appeared to be upset again and when I asked she told me what was upsetting her. The Goldens kept many packages of frozen meat in their freezer, and Mrs. Golden apparently suspected Rita of stealing some, for Rita caught her searching the bag she had packed to take to New York. It was one thing to have Rita clean her feces, but it was another thing to accuse her of being a thief. Rita was furious, and she wanted to curse Mrs. Golden, but she had to restrain her anger because she didn't want to risk getting her green card.

I came to find out that there were lots of West Indian women in America in the same position as Rita. Some of them gave up their teaching, nursing and civil servant jobs back home to immigrate to America. Others came to America as I did, having heard that America was a promising land, giving everyone an equal opportunity. Many came because they wanted to provide a better life for their children. Once in America, they realized that housekeeping jobs were the only jobs that were available to them. They did these jobs and accepted their employers' offer to sponsor them for a green card. Like Rita's employer, most of their employers treated them like slaves, overworking and underpaying them. Many paid men to marry them. Others got married to men that they would not otherwise have associated themselves with, let alone marry. They did these things for the green card that would give them the legal right to stay in America as permanent residents, thus allowing them to apply for any jobs they were qualified for and to sponsor their families to immigrate to America legally. Although I knew of all the benefits I could gain by having a green card, like sponsoring my mother and all of my siblings, I wasn't willing to do any of the things that would make me eligible for one.

I wasn't willing to pay a man to marry me or to marry a man I didn't love, and I had already declined the offer of an employer sponsoring me. I had no plans to bring my relatives to America, so there was no need for me to endure the exploitation of any employer for the sake of a green card. That was why I quit the Fishers' job when she demanded that I go out to the yard and rake up the leaves that had fallen from the trees.

It was in October, 1974, when I quit the Fishers' job. Before Mrs. Fisher left the house that day, she said that I should go outdoors and rake up the leaves. I knew that I had been hired as a housekeeper to take care of the house, not as a yard boy or a lawn caretaker. So I didn't rake up the leaves as Mrs. Fisher had requested. The following day, when Mrs. Fisher demanded that I go outside immediately and rake the leaves, I cursed at her. I said that she was born as poor as I was, and she should go outside and rake the damn leaves herself. I dropped whatever I had in my hands and went down to my room to pack my belongings in my bag. I told her that I quit and left. I went to the Goldens' house to call a cab to take me to the train station and to inform Rita what had happened. I swore to her I would never work as a housekeeper again. "I don't know what I am going to do, Rita, but I am through cleaning white people's houses and taking care of their children," I said.

I took the train to Philadelphia and the bus to Agnes' house. Agnes was not at home when I got there, and I wondered what she would say to me when I told her that I had quit the job. I was comforted on reflecting that, unlike Edna, who treated me unkindly and took most of my money, Agnes treated me well and encouraged me to save my money. She took me to the bank to open an account of my own, and she waited until I was on the job for several weeks before she took money from me for room and board. She was kind and generous, but I didn't want her to feel that I was taking her for granted and to think that I quit my job because I didn't want to work. I knew I would have to tell her that I quit my job and the reason why, but I wondered if she would assist me in finding another job or would think that she had already done enough for me.

When she came home, Agnes was surprised to see me. I informed her that I had quit the job and gave my reason for quitting before she asked. Agnes commented that Mrs. Fisher should never have asked me to rake the leaves. "She was out of her place to ask you to rake her yard, and I am proud that you stood up to her and didn't do it," she fussed. She reasoned that the job was good, but there could be a better job somewhere out there for me. She said that I would just have to look until I found such job. That was exactly what I did.

I got out of bed the next day and decided to go searching for a job, but I didn't know where to go. Agnes' oldest daughter, Donna, had worked at the McDonald's restaurant that was located nearby, and I remember her saying that the manager at the restaurant was a native of Trinidad. I wondered if he would ask me for my green card if I were to apply for a job there. "Lola, you won't be able to answer that question unless you apply for the job," I told myself. So I went into McDonald's and completed an application for a job as a cashier/waitress. The young lady that took the application from me said that the manager was not available, but she would give him my application. She assured me that the manager would call me for an interview if he was interested in hiring me. Bazil, the manager, called me a few days later to schedule an interview. Bazil wore his hair in an Afro style and spoke with a thick Trinidadian accent. He did not ask me for my green card, without which it would be illegal to work in America. He telephoned me a few days later, informing me that I was hired. I began working at McDonald's about the end of October, 1974, as a cashier/waitress at an hourly rate of two dollars, working forty hours most weeks. These earnings allowed me to continue paying Agnes for my room and board, to send monthly financial support to my mother and grandmother, and add to my own savings. I was still working at McDonald's and living with Agnes during the Christmas season of 1974, my first Christmas season in America and away from home.

Although I was part of Agnes' household and she treated me well, and even bought me several gifts for Christmas, I missed my mother, siblings and grandmother. Most of all, I missed Andrew. The Christmas season reminded me of him and the happy times we had spent together on holidays gone by. On Christmas day, while everyone in Agnes' house was joyous, I was sad, crying like a baby. I felt lonely, even though I was surrounded by lots of people who were having fun eating, drinking and dancing. Agnes did her best to cheer me up, but I was sad, feeling I should be home instead of in America. Boxing Day, the day following Christmas, was a national holiday back home, and people did fun things together like partying and visiting the national landmarks. Others had picnics on the beach or at their homes. That was back home, but in America the day following Christmas was not a holiday, and I was scheduled to work. I went to work, even though I wished that I didn't have to. I was happy to know that Americans celebrated Old Year Night, although here called New Year's Eve, many in the same way we celebrated New Year's Day at home. There were lots of parties and cabarets to attend, and Agnes invited me to attend a party with her. I loved music and dancing, so I was happy.

I noticed that the people at the party dressed as if for a wedding ceremony. That was new to me, because back home we didn't dress up for parties. I would have felt out of place if I hadn't worn an elegant pants suit that fit me well. It was a West Indian party, with soca, calypso and raggae music. We West Indian people were dancing our behinds off, as many of us moved our waists up and down, swayed our bodies and wound down to the ground. When the slow music began, the atmosphere changed, and men and women grabbed their partners and danced close, to the rhythm of the soft love tunes. The dancers seemed as caring, tender and loving to their partners as the words of the soft love tunes they were dancing to. I didn't have a significant other, but I remembered the many parties Andrew and I had attended together, dancing to some of the same songs that were being played that night. My thoughts were on Andrew, and I was missing him as I sat admiring the couples who danced together that night. Then I noticed a man looking at me while I sat at the table. We made eye contact, but I wondered why was he looking at me that way, whether he was someone that I had met in the past. Someone at my table asked me to dance with him, and while I was dancing I saw this other man still staring at me, his gaze seeming to penetrate my body. I felt uncomfortable. I was sitting at the table with Agnes and some of her friends when he walked over and asked me to dance with him. Even though he was a stranger to me, I accepted his invitation.

"My name is Simeon. What's yours?" he inquired. I told him my name and we conversed with each other while we were dancing. I learned that Simeon was from St. Vincent, like myself, and that he had lived in a town approximately four miles away from my village back home before immigrating to America to attend school. He also told me that Andrew and he were classmates in high school and had graduated in the same year. Simeon volunteered to tell me that he worked a full-time job during the day and attended school at night. We exchanged telephone numbers and he promised to call me. I told him that I worked at McDonald's, informing him of the best time for him to call me.

I continued to work at McDonald's, although that was not the ideal job. Still, it was a step up from the housekeeping/nanny jobs I had done since my immigration to America. Ha! I was moving up, and I hoped to move up even further, taking the opportunity to attend college like Simeon. But sometimes I would wish that I were like most of the young men and women who worked with me on the job. Many of them were working part time while attending high school, but there were others who had graduated from high school and had the opportunity to continue their education but weren't doing it. I wondered why they were not taking advantage of the educational opportunities which would enable them to find better jobs. Unlike them, who were legal residents or American citizens, I was an illegal immigrant, lucky that the manager had hired me without asking me to prove my immigration status. I wasn't living with my parents and I sure didn't have the educational opportunities that they had. If I were in their position, I would not be working at McDonald's. I would be attending college. Since I wasn't in their position, I had to be grateful that I had a job, and Agnes was not a bad person to live with.

Everyone living in Agnes' house, including myself, got along well together. Then Agnes sponsored her sister, Ann, along with her five children, to immigrate to America. Because she was financially responsible for them, they came to live with Agnes. The number of people living in that four-bedroom row house increased from seven to thirteen, and the chaos began soon after they moved in. Agnes' and Ann's children fought with one another, and the mothers and grandmother sided with one set of children over the other. Although Miss Lizzie was the mother of both Ann and Agnes, she always favored Ann and her children. Miss Lizzie would join Ann in speaking ill of Agnes in her own house, and there were even times when Agnes' own children would join their grandmother and aunt in speaking ill about their mother. Agnes' brothers and her other sister, who visited the house when Agnes was not at home, also all sat around and spoke ill about Agnes. I loved Agnes and felt she was a kindhearted individual who did more for people than she received in return. I failed to understand why her family was saying such bad things about her when she was doing so much good for all of them, and I began to feel uncomfortable living there. I felt sorry for Agnes, but there was nothing that I could do to help her, except to tell her what her relatives were saying about her. For this, her relatives, including Agnes' children, resented me.

Alice, one of Agnes' daughters, left the house one day to go to school, but she spent the day with her boyfriend instead. Agnes' older daughter, Donna, found out what Alice had done, but she did not confront her sister, nor did she inform her mother. Instead, she told the grandmother, Miss Lizzie, who advised them not to tell Agnes. I was dumfounded that they wanted to keep it a secret among themselves and not share it with Agnes, the single parent who was the sole provider for the entire household. I knew that if Alice had gotten pregnant that day, Agnes would have had to take responsibility for her, and I believed their decision not to tell Agnes was a betrayal of trust. I refused to be a part of the conspiracy. I broke the code of silence and informed Agnes about Alice.

Agnes was furious when I told her, and she began cursing at Alice. The others suspected that I was the one who had told Agnes, and life was never again the same for me in that household. Miss Lizzie, Ann and Agnes' two older daughters, Donna and Hilda, began to taunt me. They cursed at me when Agnes was not at home, telling me to get to hell out of the house and find another place to live. They called me all sorts of undesirable names and several times threatened to beat me up. Even though Agnes cursed at them when I complained to her, they continued their harassment. There were times when Simeon would call for me and they would tell him that I wasn't at home, even though I would be there. They would even listen in to my conversations on the phone.

Ever since the night that Simeon and I exchanged telephone numbers, he called me regularly, and we also dated several times. I felt that Simeon and I had become connected, in a way. He was an intelligent man, and we had similar goals and ambitions. Simeon wanted to know if I had a boyfriend, since he wanted me to be his girlfriend. I asked him if he had a girlfriend, and he assured me that he hadn't. When I questioned him about the woman I saw him with at the party, he said that she was just a friend. I told Simeon what I could about my relationship with Andrew. I let him know that I wasn't looking for a boyfriend, because I was incapable of being in love with another. I had the feeling that if I were looking for a boyfriend, Simeon would have been good for me, but at the time I wasn't. My mind was set on my educational goals and my obligation to provide my folks back home with financial support. In spite of all my disappointments, I had not abandoned the goals I had set for myself, and I was as determined as ever to attain my independence. Even though I told Simeon that I couldn't be his girlfriend, he continued to telephone me. We saw each other as often as we could, and this gave me the opportunity to get away from the miserable people living in Agnes' house. Besides, I liked being in Simeon's company. Simeon noticed that when I went on dates with him, I wore usually a new outfit. He commented on it one day, suggesting that I shouldn't be spending so much of my money on clothes, but should be saving it instead. Simeon reasoned that it would be easier for me to buy clothes if I had saved some money than it would be to sell the clothes when I needed money. He encouraged me to enroll in college.

Agnes introduced me to the Cottoys family, who were friends of hers, when I attended a function with her at their home. That was where I met Terry. Terry taught at the village school back home before he immigrated to America, two years before I did. He was as much surprised to see me as I was surprised to see him. We talked about home and what was going on with us in this country. Terry explained that he had resigned from his teaching position back home and immigrated to America because here he had educational opportunities he would not have had back in St. Vincent. He told me that he was attending school full time while working full time at Burger Tower, a chain of restaurants throughout the Philadelphia area, and he encouraged me to apply for a job there. Terry said that he was able to pay his tuition with the extra money he made from tips, saying that most of the time a customer would tip you if you acted friendly. "Speak no more, Terry," I thought. "I will be applying for a job at the company where you work, because I need to save as much money as I can to pay my tuition when I am accepted in college." Two days later, I applied for a cashier/waitress job at Burger Tower and I was hired. I immediately quit my job at McDonald's.

I was scheduled to work the 11:00 p.m. to 7:00 a.m. shift with my co-worker Cindy, who taught me the tricks that Burger Tower's employees played. She taught me how to use one pack of coffee to make up two pots of coffee, mixing both pots together so they would both taste the same. We rang up one pot of coffee and kept the money from the other for ourselves. I was scared at first, because I considered what we were doing to be a form of stealing, but Cindy convinced me otherwise. She said that Burger Tower got their full return from the one package of coffee, so we weren't stealing. After I worked with some other employees I realized that everyone else was doing the same thing. My weekly salary was more than I had made working for McDonald's, and there were times when the money from the extra pots of coffee and our tips were more than our weekly salaries. Although the job fulfilled my financial needs, it had its drawbacks.

I hated working the night shift. Sometimes when I rode the bus home, I would fall asleep and miss my stop. When I tried to sleep at Agnes' house in the morning, I would be kept awake by the noise of the other occupants in the household, especially Miss Lizzie and Ann. Not considering that I worked at night and needed to sleep in the day, Miss Lizzie, Ann, and Agnes' children would say that I was lazy, because only lazy people slept during the day. Lacking sleep, I became very agitated. I knew that if I wanted to maintain my sanity, I had to find a place to sleep during the day. That was when I decided to become more involved with Simeon. We began an intimate relationship, and his apartment became my place for sleeping.

Agnes was always aware of my whereabouts. I even told her about Ethel, a Jamaican woman ten years my senior with whom I had exchanged telephone numbers after we had met on Germantown Avenue. Like Rita and Cynthia, Ethel had immigrated to England and lived there for many years before she came to America. Agnes seemed to dislike her because of the earring she wore in her pierced nose, but Ethel and I became friends nonetheless. It seemed to me that since most of Agnes' relatives were against me, for reasons unknown to me, I needed Ethel's friendship. Ethel would listen to my vented frustration when the others would curse at me for no apparent reason. Several time I was tempted to curse them back, but I was afraid one of them would report me to Immigration. Finally, the day came when I had had enough. After one of Agnes' relatives slapped me in the face, I decided to move out.

I remember calling Ethel, crying and telling her that Joe and I had had an argument over a pot I was using which he wanted to use. When I told him that he would get the pot when I was finished with it, he slapped me in the face. Ethel was furious and offered to have me move in with her. She lived in a three-room rented apartment in the Germantown section of Philadelphia. It wasn't long before I realized that her style of living was completely different from mine. Whereas I dated only Simeon, Ethel went to bars regularly, and most of the time brought different men home with her. She even tried to get me to go to bed with a man she brought home one night. Ethel brought the same man to her apartment several more times, trying to convince me that he would be a perfect boyfriend for me. When I refused to get involved with this man, Ethel got mad and told me that I couldn't live with her any longer. I was scared. I had not too long ago reached the milestone of my twentieth birthday, I had immigrated to America less than a year before, and I didn't know many people. I thought I was about to become homeless, because I didn't want to move back into Agnes' house, even if she were to invite me. I thought about asking Simeon to let me live with him, but I decided against it, not wanting to be in the same situation as my mother.

Although my mother and Mr. Phillips lived together for many years and she gave birth to his many children, he never married her. I never understood why she would live with him in the first place, not being married to him. It seemed to me to be morally wrong. I resolved that I would never make the mistake of living with a man out of wedlock. Simeon was all right, but I thought I would never marry him, or anyone else, for that matter. Marriage was the least of my concerns. But then I reflected. "Lola," I told myself, "all that you are thinking is all right, but you need somewhere to live. You need someone who can rescue you, and you know of no other but Simeon. Simeon is your only hope, so forget about your morals and stupid pride and ask him if you could stay with him until you find your own apartment." With these thoughts urging me on like an inner voice, I called Simeon and asked if I could stay with him for a week or so until I found an apartment of my own. When he answered yes, I quickly hung up, packed my belongings, and got out of Ethel's place.

Not wanting to inconvenience Simeon and his roommate, I began looking for an apartment from the very first day I moved in. Working through several real estate agents, I signed a lease for a three-room apartment in West Philadelphia by the end of the following week. The rent would be sixty dollars a month plus utilities. With my salary, plus the extra money from the coffee sales and tips, I was able to pay the expenses of the apartment, save some money, and continue the financial support of my mother and grandmother back home. Two weeks after I had first moved in with Simeon, I moved into my own new apartment.

The three-room apartment that I moved into was not the best, but it was not the worst, either. It was situated on the third floor of a triplex house, and I chose the third floor for safety reasons. It was a fresh start for me. When I moved into the apartment, I bought a used refrigerator and a used bedroom set with mattresses, a new kitchen set with a table and four chairs, a frying pan, two pots (one small and the other medium in size), two spoons, two forks and two knives. I also bought some cheap curtains for the windows, some food, a case of beer, and an old music box from someone I knew. I was grateful to Agnes for lending me a small black and white television set, since I wasn't planning to buy one at the time. Having made these preparations, I began living alone at twenty years old in a big country where very few people knew of my existence, being kept company at times by the roaches that invaded the apartment, even though the landlord claimed to have exterminated it before I moved in. There were many nights when I arrived from work, switched on the lights and saw roaches running all over the place. Sometimes I talked to the roaches like human beings, asking them if they thought they were the tenants and I the intruder. When I was having visitors, I would talk to the roaches like a mad woman, asking them please to go in hiding until my visitors left. No matter how often the exterminator came, the roaches never left. I took to washing my dishes and silverware with hot water before using them. I went to bed hoping that they wouldn't crawl into my ear or mouth while I slept. None of them ever invaded my bed, but they did crawl into some food of mine. Once when I went to warm up some leftover food from the refrigerator, I found two roaches in the container. I freaked out seeing those roaches, and from that day I scrutinized every piece of food before I ate it. Still, I was so happy to have a place of my own that I never looked for another apartment.

Living alone was quite an experience for me. I worked regularly, slept when I wanted to, and played music and drank beer when I felt lonely and depressed. America is a wonderful country to live in, but it can be depressing country for someone who has no relatives and very few friends nearby. I felt fortunate to have met Simeon, as he was my only companion when I needed company. Simeon was the only guy who knew that I lived alone. I also went out on dates with Kevin two or three times. On our first date we met three blocks from my apartment. I told him that I lived with an evil aunt who would not allow him to pick me up in front of the apartment, and that he could not call me at a certain time. I told him that he should hang up if my aunt answered. In support of that ruse, I assumed the identity of the invisible aunt, and I even faked my voice to sound like her when Kevin called and I didn't want to talk to him. Later I decided to date Simeon exclusively, and I stopped dating Kevin without his ever knowing the truth about my living alone. Simeon visited me on the two days a week that I was off from work.

While working alone one night I was robbed at gunpoint. The robber took out a gun from his belt, pointed it directly at me, and demanded that I open the cash register and give him the cash. He told me I wouldn't get hurt if I cooperated. Knowing that my life was worth far more than the money in the cash register, I gave him the money without hesitation. He took it and fled. Although there were customers in the restaurant at the time, they all ran out when the robber pulled out his gun. It was only after the robber had left the store that I became terribly afraid and began to cry. I telephoned the Burger Tower main office and informed them of the robbery, and then I telephoned the police. The police questioned me and took a statement about the incident. Shortly thereafter, one of my supervisors came to close the store for the night, and he sent me home. When I telephoned Simeon and told him about the incident, he sounded as shook up as I was. He urged me to quit the job and look for another. "You could get killed on that job, Lola. Quit it and look for another," Simeon pleaded with me.

Simeon was right, but I felt I couldn't quit before finding another job. The reality was that I was an illegal immigrant, and finding another job would be difficult. No one would hire me if they knew I was illegal. As close in friendship as Simeon and I were, he did not know my immigration status, because we had never discussed it. Even if we had, I doubt that I would have told him. As Aunt Millie had warned me, my immigration status was to be a secret I couldn't share with anyone, not even Simeon. Fearing that I wouldn't be able to find another job, I went back to work two days after I was held up.

The company was very considerate of me. I was sent to work in another restaurant in a different location, but I continued working alone at times. While I was working alone two weeks later, I was held up at gunpoint again. It happened about midnight, on a cold winter night in February. The employees who worked the 3:00 p.m. to 11:00 p.m. shift had left about forty-five minutes earlier. I was serving coffee to two customers about fifteen minutes before the supervisor, a white middle-aged man, came to pick up the cash receipts from the previous shift, which were locked away in the safe. I was cooking hamburgers for two customers. As soon as the supervisor opened the safe, one of the customers leaped over the counter and the other customer stood in the entrance to the restaurant. The man who leaped over the counter pulled out a shotgun and pointed it at the supervisor, saying, "Mother fucker, lay down and open the safe, and give me all the money in it, and you better not touch anything, because I will blow your mother fucking head off if you do." Then the robber turned to me and said, "Sister, keep on doing what you doing and everything will be all right. Just keep on frying them burgers. If you keep frying those burgers, you won't get hurt." I kept frying the hamburgers. Meanwhile, two police officers drove by in a police vehicle. They even stopped in front of the store momentarily, but I was unable to attract their attention. The poor supervisor was lying down on the cold concrete. It was freezing that night, and he lay there trembling as the robber held the gun to his head. After the robber took the money from the safe, the two of them fled.

I began to tremble and cry. I was so terrified that I urinated on myself. The poor supervisor was trembling too, and his hands were shaking vigorously as he dialed to telephone the police. After he had locked up the store for the night, two police officers came to take the supervisor and me to the police precinct, where they took statements from us. They showed us some photographs and asked us if any of the persons on the photographs resembled the man that held us up, but we were not able to identify any. I was still frightened when on the bus to my apartment. I was too afraid to be alone in my apartment that night, so I telephoned Simeon and asked him to come and spend the night with me.

When Simeon entered my apartment, I told him what had happened to me on the job that night. He was concerned for my safety and pleaded with me not to go back. Before he left the following morning, he wrote the names and addresses of some companies on a note pad and suggested that I go to these companies and apply for jobs. The following night, when Simeon telephoned to inquire whether I had gone to apply for a job, I told him that I had, knowing that otherwise I would have to give my reason for not going, and therefore reveal my immigration status to him. Since I didn't want to tell Simeon about my immigration status, I continued to pretend that I was applying for other jobs when I wasn't. I lied and told him that I was only going back to work at Burger Tower until I found another job. Because of my immigration status, I had no choice but to return to the Burger Tower job, despite my realization that my life was in danger. The job provided me with the necessary income to live, and I was also able to take care of my mother and grandmother, who needed my financial support. Upon returning to work after my second robbery, the company changed my working hours from the 11:00 p.m. to 7:00 a.m. shift to the 3:00 p.m. to 11:00 p.m. shift, and they sent me to work in another restaurant in yet another location.

I was working at this new location when I first noticed the marks and open sores on the hands of most of the male customers. These customers' hands seemed enlarged, with marks all over them, like needle marks. I wondered what caused these marks, but I was afraid to ask the customers. One day I asked one of my regular customers, a policeman and a very religious man. Officer John came into the restaurant at about 5:00 p.m. daily to order his dinner, which he ate at the restaurant. He was the one who told me that most of my customers were drug addicts. When I asked him what he meant by that, he explained to me that the men were using needles to inject themselves with heroin. It was the first time in my life that I had ever heard of heroin and the effect that this drug had on the human body. I became really frightened when Officer John told me that using this drug caused some of the addicts to commit crimes that they would not otherwise commit. I had reason to be scared. Four weeks later, I began working at the new location, and I saw the robber who had held a gun to the supervisor's head during a robbery at the restaurant at the other location.

I noticed a man standing on the sidewalk, staring at me through the glass windows as I stood working in the restaurant. I was terrified, but I felt lucky when Officer John walked into the restaurant, minutes after I had made eye contact with the robber, who continued to stare at me. That was when I pointed to the robber and told Officer John that he was the man who had robbed us at gunpoint at the other restaurant. When he asked whether I was positive about the identification of this man, I told Officer John that I was sure he was the one. Office John went outside and arrested the man. I went to the police precinct and identified him from a line-up of several men. On the night of the robbery, I had told the police officers in my statement that the robber was approximately six feet, one inch in height, and sure enough this man whom I identi-fied was the same height. I was glad to know that this man would be put behind bars, and hoped that I would never see him again, in this lifetime anyway. However, I failed to take into consideration that there are others like him who are still running free.

A week later, I was robbed again. I was less than an hour on the job, and I was standing at the cash register about to give one of the addicts his change, when he pulled out a handgun. I don't know where he pulled it from. He pointed the gun at me, telling me to give him all the money in the cash register. He said that if I didn't do as I was told, he would kill me. Always considering my life to be valued much more than any money, I opened the cash register as fast as I could and gave him all the money. He took the money and left.

As had happened in the other restaurant, other customers who were in the restaurant ran away when they saw this robber point his gun at me. I couldn't understand at the time why those cus-tomers did not come to my assistance, but later I realized that I would have done the same thing had I been in their position. I tele-phoned the Burger Tower main office and then called the police to notify them of the robbery. A supervisor from the company came and closed the restaurant, and then the police took me to the police precinct to give a statement. It was while I was riding the bus home that I decided that I couldn't and wouldn't go back to that job. My life meant more to me than a job and some money. Money was necessary for life, but life came before money, my life any-way. As soon as I got home, I examined my bank statement. I cal-culated that I had saved enough money to pay my expenses, including feeding myself, for at least two years. I telephoned Simeon that night, informing him of the robbery. Before he could beg me to quit the job, I told him that I had already quit. He encouraged me to go to Philadelphia Community College and complete an application to attend classes, and he also advised me to look for a new job. The following day, I went to Philadelphia Community College and got an application and a catalog. I calcu-lated the tuition I would need if I were to enroll in school part time and the amount of money that I had sent to my mother to save for me back in St. Vincent. I concluded that I had saved enough money to pay for two years of my school tuition and that my mother should have saved enough money for me at home to take care of my grandmother and herself for the next two years. I also planned to look for a part-time job so that I could send my grandmother and mother more money. Having reached these conclusions, I completed the application to attend Philadelphia Community College.

When I was accepted at the Philadelphia Community College, I was excited. I made plans to begin school the first summer session, due to begin in April 1976, six weeks after I quit the job at Burger Tower. Since I was no longer at Burger Tower, I saw no point for me to go to court as a witness against the robber whom I had identified. I ignored the subpoena, not knowing that it is against the law not to appear in court when you were served a subpoena to do so. When I failed three times to appear in court, the sheriffs showed up at my apartment, notifying me that they had come for me. They told me I was to appear in court in front of a judge, since I had disregarded the subpoena and failed to show up in court. I was frightened. I think I looked even more frightened when I appeared in front of a very understanding judge, who explained to me that it was the law that I was to appear in court when I was subpoenaed to do so. The judge realized from my accent that I wasn't an American. When he asked about it and I told him my country of origin, he explained to me that the laws in my country were different from those in America, and he lectured me about American laws. Then he called the court to order, and I identified the robber and testified against him. He was convicted and sentenced to jail. Two women followed me as I was leaving the courthouse. One of them identified herself as the mother of the man who had robbed me. Both of these women threatened me, telling me that I had lied in court and that they were going to get me. I was afraid, and I fled that courtyard in a hurry to catch the bus home.

I was so frightened that I telephoned Zilpha to tell her what had happened to me in court that day. Zilpha was one of the Cottoys' daughters, whom I had met when I visited their family home with Agnes. Even though I was no longer living with Agnes, I stayed in contact with Zilpha and her sister, Pauline. Their parents, Mr. and Mrs. Cottoy, came from a village not far from my village back home. They had immigrated as legal immigrants to America, with most of their twelve children. I was aware that Agnes had informed them that I was an illegal immigrant. The Cottoy family also knew Simeon, and he and I were invited to attend the wedding of one of the Cottoys' sons when he was married to one of Simeon's former high school teachers. Simeon didn't attend the wedding because he had to work, but I went.

I remember that it was on the night of that wedding that I felt a stinging on the lower right side of my abdomen after Simeon and I had had unprotected sex. I knew that the stinging I felt was something new to me, and, though I did not know it at the time, I told Simeon that he had just got me pregnant. Simeon began to laugh and asked what made me think that I was pregnant. I explained to him what I was experiencing. The doctor had prescribed birth control pills for me to help relieve the pain that I was experiencing during my monthly cycle. Although the pills eased the pain, they made me feel sick all of the time. Hearing my complaint, the doctor had me stop taking the pills when I went to him for my regular checkup on Thursday of that week. I stopped taking the pills two days prior to having unprotected sex with Simeon. I had understood that I could continue to have unprotected sex for up to six months after I stopped taking the pills without getting pregnant.

From the night that Simeon and I had had sex I began to feel sick. As the days and weeks went by, I became sicker and sicker. I threw up everything that I ate or drank, even water. I hated the smell of deodorants, lotions, the apartment, food, and even the air that I breathed. I began losing weight. My body told me that something was wrong with it. Even though I had an idea of what was wrong with my body, I was hoping that it wasn't what I thought. Finally, I couldn't bear my sickness any longer, so I decided to visit a doctor for a checkup, at what was at that time the Philadelphia General Hospital. It was my first visit to that hospital. I thought it looked more like a place for ghosts than for the sick. After I waited for what seemed to be eternity to see a doctor, a nurse called my name, and I followed her back to the examining room.

After the nurse took my blood pressure, she told me to get undressed, handing me an old and not so clean white gown to change into. She told me that the doctor would be with me shortly and left, leaving me alone in the dark, dingy-looking room. Approximately half an hour later, an ill-mannered doctor entered the room. While examining me, the doctor said that he would need a sample of my urine. After he left the room, a nurse entered with a paper cup, gave it to me, and told me to go to the bathroom and urinate in the cup. I went to the bathroom, did as I had been directed, and gave the cup with my urine sample to the nurse. Twenty minutes later, the ill-mannered doctor reentered and asked when I wanted to be scheduled for the abortion. "What abortion?" I asked him. That was when he told me that I was six weeks pregnant. I stared at him with astonishment, even though my intuition had led me to believe that I was pregnant before the doctor had told me so. I composed myself and told the doctor that I would call to make an appointment for an abortion. The doctor left the office, and I got dressed, went out, and caught the bus to the stop nearest to my apartment.

While I was riding on the bus home and later after I got home, I reflected on lots of things. I thought about how I had protected myself from getting pregnant while I was attending high school at home. Andrew did me wrong when he married Dawn, but he did protect me and never got me pregnant. Since I had come to America, I had never thought about getting pregnant, because making and having children was not on my agenda. I had already decided earlier in my life that I wouldn't have children of my own. Now, I was faced with what they call in America an unplanned pregnancy. It was not only an unplanned pregnancy, but an unwanted one, too. I had to make a decision about the pregnancy, but I didn't know what to decide. I did know that having an abortion was out of the question. I couldn't take a baby's life and go to hell. God would never forgive me for taking a child's life. That was my religious belief about abortion, which I was definitely opposed to. I thought about adoption as an option, but I questioned adoption, too. Would I ever have the opportunity to see this child again if I were to give it up for adoption? If she were a girl, would the adopted parents protect her from incest and rape? Then I thought about my mother and the possibility of sending the child home to her, but I questioned that possibility, too. I wondered whether my mother might abuse my child, as she had abused me when I was a child. I wondered whether she would protect my child from the mental and physical abuse of Mr. Phillips, should he try to abuse my child as he had abused me. I also had thoughts about keeping the child, but I doubted that I would be able to do it. I believed at the time that I couldn't possibly take care of the child, financially or otherwise. I knew then that my pregnancy was a mistake, and, since Simeon was a part of it, I began to focus my thoughts on him, too.

I was emotionally upset with him and with myself. Even when Simeon was not present, I couldn't help thinking unkindly about him. I began cursing at him. "That son of a bitch got me pregnant and I don't know whether I love him or not. Why did he do this to me? Why? Why?" I fussed alone. It took me a while before I came to my senses and realized that I shouldn't blame Simeon for my pregnancy, that I should blame myself instead. Then I began thinking about what I might have done to protect myself. The more I thought, the more I cried. That night I cried myself to sleep. When I heard the telephone ringing, I refused to answer it, assuming it was Simeon calling me. I didn't want to talk to him, not at that time anyway.

When I awoke the following day, I felt sicker than the day before. I vomited until I felt weak. I felt dizzy, and I must have fainted. I recovered about midday, lying on the bathroom floor of my apartment, not remembering how I got there. I stayed inside my apartment for the rest of the day, thinking about my pregnancy and what I was to do about the unborn child that I was carrying within my uterus. I procrastinated about telling Simeon until 7:00 o'clock that night, when I decided that I had to tell him. Simeon was attending classes that night, and I knew he wouldn't be home until 9:30 p.m. I telephoned him when I thought he would be home and would have completed his schoolwork assignments. Simeon noticed that I was upset. He asked me what was the matter with me, even before I could tell him my reason for asking him to come over. I cried as I told him that I was pregnant. "What? When did you find out?" he asked in astonishment. I told him that I found out the day before. "Why didn't you call me and let me know as soon as you found out?" he questioned me, but I did not answer. For the rest of that week, Simeon came to visit me every night after he returned home from school. He was concerned not only about our unborn child, but also about me. My health was deteriorating rapidly. I continued to vomit every day, and I was losing weight. I stayed indoors most of the time.

Exactly a week after my first visit, the doctor told me that I was six weeks pregnant. I was talking on the telephone with a friend when someone kept ringing the doorbell of my apartment. I thought it must Simeon, since he was the only person who knew that I was home. But then I realized that he was at work. Not knowing who could be ringing my doorbell, I wasn't about to answer it. The person continued to ring the doorbell, as if to say, "Answer the doorbell, because I know that you are in there." Annoyed by the continuous ringing of the doorbell, I went downstairs in a rage to answer it, ready to ask whoever it was what the hell does he or she wanted.

I pushed the key into the lock and turned it. Before I could pull the key out of the lock and open the door, the white man who had been ringing my bell pushed the door open. As the door flung open, the man entered the building and showed me his badge. He identified himself as an Immigration officer and asked me: "Are you Lola Parker?" I answered, "I am Lola Parker." The man said that he would like to have a talk with me in my apartment, so I closed the door and he followed me to my apartment.

I sat in a chair as the Immigration officer began to interrogate me. He said that someone had notified the Immigration Department that I was in America illegally, and he asked me: "Are you here illegally?" I stared at him and answered that I wasn't living in America illegally, I was an American citizen. "Where were you born?" he asked. I told him that I was born in New York, but my parents were born in St. Thomas. I told him that my parents had sent me back to my grandmother in St Thomas right after I was born and that I had lived with my grandmother until she passed away a year ago and had then returned to the United States. The Immigration officer asked whether I had my passport with me. I told him I had left my passport with my aunt in New York. "You wouldn't have a problem going to New York to get your passport, would you?" he asked, and I told him that I wouldn't. "Do you have a Social Security card?" he asked. I gave him the card, and he wrote down my Social Security number and gave it back to me. "When can you go to New York to get your passport?" he asked. I told him that I couldn't go that day because I wasn't feeling well. I informed him that I was pregnant and that the doctor had ordered me to get some bed rest. He asked for permission to use my telephone and called his office.

When he hung up the telephone, he asked me again when I would be able to go to New York to get my passport. I told him that I would be able to go to New York the following day. He asked when I could bring my passport to him, and I told him the next day after that. He stared at me and asked again: "Are you sure that you are legal in this country?" I looked at him directly in the face as I told him that this country was my country too, that I was sure I was legal because I was born in this country. I felt that in telling him this lie, I was adopting America as my own, even though America had not yet agreed to adopt me. My reply did not hinder the Immigration officer from asking me more questions.

"You wouldn't have a problem going back on the plane, because you could go and come when you wanted to, right?" he asked me. I told him that I wouldn't have a problem going back to St Thomas, but I had no reason to go there, since most of my relatives lived in New York. The Immigration officer then said that the only reason he wasn't taking me with him was because I was pregnant, and I should go to New York for my passport and bring it to him on Wednesday. He gave me a card that listed his name and the address where I was supposed to turn over my passport. As he was giving me the card, he warned me that I had better not run away. He warned me that if I was illegal and did run away, he would catch me. "I will be looking forward to seeing you on Wednesday," he said to me.

I peeped through the window and saw him enter a black unmarked car, where another white man was waiting for him. They quickly drove away. I became frightened and began to tremble. It was only then that I realized I had just escaped deportation. Realizing that I was in trouble with Immigration reminded me of what Aunt Millie had told me when I lived in New York with Edna, that Immigration never comes looking for you unless someone reports you to them as an illegal immigrant. She also said that your friends were the ones who would most likely report you to Immigration, because your enemies wouldn't know your business. I was horrified to think that someone who was most likely a friend of mine had reported me to Immigration. It was even more horrifying to me that I hadn't a clue who the person could be.

My thoughts were focused on the unborn child that I was carrying within me. I thought also of the devious people I had left behind in the village back home. I couldn't see myself going back there to live among them, especially now that I was pregnant. I would rather commit suicide. But I knew that I loved life too much to commit suicide. Then I began thinking of ways to avoid deportation. Had it not been for my unborn child, I could have left everything except my clothes in the apartment and disappeared. Where, I don't know, but I would have done just that. I perceived my unborn child to be a hindrance to me, since it was preventing me from doing the only thing I thought I could to avoid deportation. "Don't be so severe about this unborn child being a hindrance to you, Lola," I thought. "Be grateful for the child, because if it had not been for the child, the Immigration officer would have taken you with him immediately. You know that, because he told you so." Yes, the child did help me, but I needed some other person to help me, too. I must have had a guardian angel watching over me, because I couldn't otherwise imagine how I could have come up with all those answers to the Immigration officer's questions. They were all lies, but I didn't fumble when I was answering him. I believe those answers helped me avoid deportation. "Ma, are you the one who is watching over me? If you are Ma, please help me because I don't know what to do next," I said to my invisible great grandmother. I spent the rest of the day thinking about what I would do next. The more I thought about my situation, the more I became afraid of the possibility that I might be deported. I knew that I had to reach out for help from someone, and Simeon was the only one I could think of. He was at work when I telephoned him.

After I told him about my ordeal with the Immigration officer, Simeon decided to leave work early that day. Simeon came to my apartment and told me that he wished he could marry me and file the necessary papers to get my status changed to legal immigrant. But he couldn't, because he was an illegal immigrant himself. He and I had dated each other for over a year, and yet, until that day when Immigration came looking for me, we had kept the secret of our immigration status to ourselves. Simeon, too, was frightened about the situation. It was imperative that I move out of my apartment by that Wednesday, since I had no intention of bringing my passport to the Immigration office, and I thought he would come looking for me again. Simeon's roommate, Chris, was also an illegal immigrant, so I couldn't live with Simeon without risking the deportation of the two of them as well as myself. I needed help from people I thought I could trust. The only ones I thought of were Zilpha and Pauline, the two Cottoy sisters.

I telephoned them, and both of them offered to have me stay with them. Then I telephoned Joshua, Agnes' male friend at the time I lived at Agnes' home, where he and I used to discuss how unfairly Agnes' families were treating her. Joshua offered to move the furniture in my apartment and keep it in storage until I was ready for them. Then I called Aunt Millie to inform her that I would be visiting her on that Wednesday. I didn't call Agnes, because someone had implied that it must have been one of Agnes' relatives who reported me to Immigration authorities, suggesting that I cut off all ties with Agnes because of her family's dislike for me.

The following day, which was Tuesday, I returned the television that Agnes had loaned me without telling her of my troubles. Regretfully, I also didn't tell Agnes that I was cutting all ties with her. Still, I felt I had to, because I was surrounded by so many uncertainties. Deep within me, I felt bad when I left Agnes that day. I thought I had betrayed her trust by not telling her, but I did what I thought was in my own best interest under the circumstances. Simeon and Joshua came to my apartment that night and moved out all of my furniture. I moved out of the apartment that night and slept with Zilpha. The following day, Wednesday, I traveled to New York to visit Aunt Millie.

I became sicker than ever while I was riding the train to New York, and I spent most of the time in the bathroom vomiting. When I arrived at her home in Queens, Aunt Millie greeted me with open arms. It didn't take her long to notice my illness, as I began vomiting soon after I swallowed the tea she made for me. When she inquired about my illness, I told her the truth about my pregnancy and my troubles with Immigration. Aunt Millie seemed sad as she listened to my story. Then she began fussing at me. She repeated that it must have been one of my friends who had reported me to the Immigration authorities, and that she had warned me before about such people. Although Aunt Millie was upset with me, she offered me some assistance. I couldn't live with Aunt Millie, because Edna was still living nearby, and Edna wouldn't lose the opportunity to notify Immigration authorities of my whereabouts if she knew. Aunt Millie was about to call one of her friends living in another area in Queens, asking him to take me in until she found some place for me to live permanently, but I declined her offer gracefully and returned to Philadelphia to live with Zilpha.

In the Eye of the Storm

Zilpha treated me kindly during the two months I lived at her home. Overwhelmed with the uncertainties of my future, I was depressed. I wondered where I would find a job and what I would do if I were successful in my effort to avoid deportation. I didn't want to work as a housekeeper/nanny again. Since the Immigration officer had recorded my Social Security number when he came to my apartment, I couldn't use the Social Security number that I used in the past to find a better job. I was smart enough to know that Immigration authorities could track me down by that Social Security number if I were to use it again. I was facing so many uncertainties that the thought of them made me more depressed. Since I was alone at the time and there was no living person for me to talk with, I began talking to Ma, my invisible great grandmother. I spoke with her as though she were sitting across from me, even though she had died when I was six or seven years old. "Ma, I am in trouble, lots of trouble. I am pregnant, Ma, with this baby I do not want, and I don't know what to do with it when it's born. Immigration is after me, and you know that I can't go back home to that village to live among those people. Those people hate me, Ma, as much as I hate them. I won't be able to find a job if I stay in America, because Immigration has my Social Security number on record. Without a job, Ma, I don't know how I would live. Ma! Oh, Ma! I am scared," I spoke and cried loudly. Thank God, no one was around and no one walked into the house at the time. Had someone walked in or been around at the time, he or she would have thought that I had lost my mind and gone crazy. I cried loudly for so long that I cried myself to sleep without knowing it

Ma patted me on my shoulders and comforted me. She told me not to worry, because everything was going to be all right. "Listen to me and do as I say. Call up the Social Security office and tell them that you need two application forms to apply for Social Security numbers for your children, and ask them to send the forms to you. Use the name I will give you as an alias when you apply for one Social Security card. You must use the number of that card to apply for jobs until you get your green card. Then she gave me the alias that I should use. Use your real name when you apply for the second card. You will need that card in the future," she said to me. Ma instructed me, step by step, how to complete the Social Security applications. After Ma finished instructing me, she patted me on my shoulder again. She assured me that every thing would be all right and that she was leaving. "Ma, Ma, please don't leave me. Please don't go, because I am scared." I begged of her, but Ma said that she had to go. She left, even though I cried and begged her to stay. My crying awakened me, and I sat up in the bed, realizing that what I thought was real was in fact just a dream.

Even though it was a dream, it was so real to me that I went looking for a telephone book. I needed to find the number of the Social Security office, which I found. When I dialed the number, the person on the telephone from the Social Security office asked me the same questions that Ma had told me in my dream that they would ask. I answered the questions as Ma had instructed me in my dream. I also completed the applications for the Social Security cards, as Ma had instructed me, using the alias name on one application and my real name on the other. I received the Social Security cards while I was still living with Zilpha. Unfortunately, Zilpha and her husband were having marital problems and were planning to sell the house, so I moved in with Pauline.

Zilpha and Pauline lived on different streets in the same south-west Philadelphia neighborhood. While I was living with Pauline, Zilpha telephoned to say that Immigration had come to her house looking for me. Zilpha's house was not the only place where they went looking for me. One of the tenants who still lived in my pre-vious apartment, and with whom I remained in contact, also tele-phoned to tell me that Immigration had come back to the apart-ment building asking residents if they knew of my whereabouts. Hearing all of this, I telephoned Ethel, the Jamaican friend that I lived with after I left Agnes. She also told me that Immigration had been at her place looking for me. I could understand that Immigration would be looking for me at my former apartment, because they knew that I had lived there, but how did they know that I had lived with Ethel and Zilpha? The person who was report-ing me to them knew of my whereabouts. As Aunt Millie had said, the person who reported me to Immigration had to be someone who was close to me and knew about my business. I thought at the time that the people knew of my whereabouts were Simeon and the Cottoys family, and I thought neither of them would knowingly hurt me. I wondered whether one of them could have told some-one else of my whereabouts without realizing that they were talk-ing to a person who was trying to hurt me, or to someone who was allied with such a person. I was paranoid. I felt insecure living with Pauline. I knew that I had to move, and I had to do it rather quick-ly.

Simeon and I discussed the situation. He agreed to keep my clothes at his place, and I asked his permission to take my shower there and change into clean clothes when I needed to. He wanted to know what my plans were and where I would live. I couldn't tell him, because I had no plans. I had nowhere to live and no place to call my home. With nowhere to live and no place to call my home, the streets of Philadelphia and the trains that run the subway tracks became my home. I rode the subways, day and night, travelling on the El train from sixty-ninth street in Upper Darby to Broad Street, where I caught the Broad Street subway and rode it from one end to the other. Sometimes I got off the train at Broad and Hunting Park and walked to a steak-and-egg restaurant that was located there. While in the restaurant, I ordered a cup of coffee, drinking it slowly, until I left to catch the train again. I would spend the rest of the night on the train, getting on and off at stops, while I tried to take a nap in between stops. When morning came, I got off the train and walked the streets until I got close to Simeon's apartment. Before entering his apartment, I checked for marked or unmarked cars with Immigration officers, and would only enter his apartment to take a shower and change clothing. Sometimes I would take a quick nap before I entered the streets again. Because I was pregnant, I tried to eat when I could.

While I was on the train one night, I thought about Joshua, and I wondered whether he could help me find a place to live. I thought I had nothing to lose if I called him, so I did. I explained my situation to Joshua. I told him that I needed to rent a room from someone who was not a West Indian and who was also living far away from the areas where Simeon and the Cottoy family lived. Joshua couldn't think of anyone at the time, but he promised to help me find a room if he could. He suggested that I telephone him again in a few days. When I telephoned Joshua, he had contacted one of his friends living in the Logan section of Philadelphia, and she was willing to rent me a room in her house. The Logan section of Philadelphia, where Joshua's friend lived, was quite a distance from southwest Philadelphia, where Simeon and the Cottoy family lived. That was the main reason why I decided to rent the room. When I met Shirley, we agreed upon the thirty-five dollars a week rent that I was to pay her. When I took my clothing from Simeon's apartment and moved in with Shirley, I informed Zilpha and Pauline that I had found a place to live, but I never gave them the address or telephone number of Shirley's house. I felt that without knowing it they might have been connected to the person who was informing Immigration of my whereabouts. Simeon and Joshua were the only two people who knew of my whereabouts, besides Shirley.

Shirley lived in a row house with her two sons. Thank God that I had taken Agnes' advice and saved some of my money in America. From that money, I was able to pay my rent to Shirley and did not need to depend on the money that Simeon would give me. I also thanked God that I had overcome homelessness and had finally found a place where I could sleep in peace at nights. I feared Immigration less at this time, because Shirley was a stranger to me and she knew nothing about my problems with Immigration. Although Shirley seemed to be a good person, she kept her house very untidy. Her two sons, Dale and Ronnie, disrespected her by cursing foul language in her presence. This seemed to bother me more than it bothered her. To avoid getting involved

with the goings-on in the household, and as a form of entertainment, I watched the 1976 Summer Olympics taking place at the
time, and I fell in love with the gymnastics. With great admiration,
I enjoyed the performance of the gymnast, Nadia, and I promised
to name my baby after her if it was a girl. Although I tried to pretend that I had no problems, my problems with Immigration were
in my every thought. Even more was it so after I telephoned
Pauline one day and she told me that Immigration had been at her
house looking for me.

When Immigration had come looking for me the first time, I
thought of a few people who could have reported me to them, like
Tim, a man I knew in St. Vincent who wanted me to dance with
him at a party in New York. When I refused, he cursed at me. He
said that I was acting as if I were better than he was, but we were
in America, and America equalized all of us. In response, I cursed
back at him that I didn't want him when he lived in St. Vincent,
and I still did not want him now that he was in America. He told
me that he would get even with me one day. I knew that he could-
n't have reported me to Immigration this time, because he did not
know of my whereabouts nor I of his. Several people had implied
that Agnes must have done it, but that was one possibility that I
never seriously considered. Agnes was not that type of person.
Others implied that it had to be one of Agnes' relatives that reported me to the Immigration officials. I thought at the time that it
might have been one of them, but I had my doubts. I couldn't
imagine how Agnes' relatives could have found out that I was living with Zilpha and that I went to Pauline after I left Zilpha. I
guess I was naive at the time, because I found out later that Agnes'
relatives knew more about me and my whereabouts than I thought
that they did.

It was Simeon's remark that he had no doubt he was the father
of my unborn child that led me to believe that I had more enemies
than I thought. I became so perplexed with Simeon's remark that I
asked him whether he was ever doubtful that he was my baby's
father. Simeon answered that he never doubted that he was the
father of my child and that no one would ever change that which
he knew was true. Then he explained to me that Virginia, one of
Agnes' sisters, came to his job, trying to convince him that Joshua
was the father of my unborn child. Hearing this accusation, I was
first dumbfounded and then furious that Virginia would make such
an accusation, that Joshua, who was a close friend and confidant,

who never disrespected me nor I disrespected him, was the father of my unborn child. When Simeon told me that, I felt such anger towards Virginia that if I had not been hiding from Immigration and people like her, I would have telephoned her and cursed the hell out of her. Then I began to wonder whether she could have been the one who had reported me to Immigration. I would never know for sure. All I was sure about was that someone was determined to have me deported from America just as much as I was determined to remain here. At that period in my life, I decided that Shirley's place was the safest place for me to live, even though the living conditions there were less than desirable.

One of Shirley's sons stole my entire jar of fifty-cent coins that I was saving as a gift for my unborn child. When I confronted him, he swore to his mother and me that he did not do it. After I confronted Ronnie about the coins he had stolen, Shirley changed her attitude toward me. She hardly spoke to me when I spoke to her. Then I became aware that Shirley was an alcoholic. When she was drunk, she cried and talked about her dead husband, whom she had shot to death some years ago after enduring his mental and physical abuses for many years. She said it was his physical abuses of her that made her snap and kill him.

Shirley explained that her husband had abused her almost every day of their married life together, causing her to be hospitalized several times for the lacerations she suffered from his violent abuse. Shirley said that she was tired of his abuses and had left her husband several times, but returned to him each time. She explained that on the night the incident took place, her husband was kicking and punching her, and with each blow he also threatened to kill her. Afraid that her husband was about to kill her, and horrified with fear, Shirley said that she snapped. She picked up a loaded shotgun and shot him to death. Shirley cried, shaking vigorously as she described the incident to me, and I wondered if the trauma she suffered that night was causing her to drink as much as she did. I also wondered whether she felt guilty about killing her husband or was still suffering from the pain and suffering that she endured as a battered woman. As Shirley was explaining the abuse that she had suffered from the hands of her deceased husband, I thought about my own mother and the abuse she was enduring from the hands of Mr. Phillips. I wondered whether my mother, if she had had a shotgun in her possession, would have killed Mr. Phillips, as Shirley had killed her husband. I thought about how

Shirley's past life of abuse was so similar to the one that my mother lived and was still living.

Besides the bad memories of her past that had such a negative impact on her life, Shirley had other problems. Her children were very troublesome and were always getting themselves into trouble at school and at home. Having to deal with the problems of her children had led Shirley to drink even more, causing her to curse at the children and call them all kinds of names. Because of Shirley's unpredictable behavior, I began to feel uncomfortable living in her household, and I knew that it would be a matter of time before I would stop living with her. I informed Simeon about the situation at Shirley's home and told him that I was seriously thinking of leaving Shirley's place to live on the streets again. He begged me not to leave Shirley, but I was determined to. After Simeon realized that he couldn't persuade me to stay at Shirley's house, he told me that he would help me find a place. He made me promise that I would never leave Shirley's place until he found another place for me. A few days after Simeon and I had had that talk, he telephoned to say that he had found me a place, and I should pack my belongings together, because he was coming to get me the following day. I had no idea where Simeon was taking me until I got into the car with him. That was when he told me that he was taking me to live with Henrietta, who he claimed was one of his friends. He explained that Henrietta knew about my pregnancy, and he assured me that she knew nothing about my problems with Immigration. "It was good that you didn't tell her, Simeon, because I wasn't about to tell her. The fewer people who know about my problems with Immigration, the better off I will be and the greater my chances of staying in America." These were my thoughts, and I shared them with Simeon, who agreed with me. Neither of us told Henrietta about my problems with Immigration.

Henrietta was a native of Trinidad. She and her two children, Daniel and Paula, lived in a three-bedroom row house in West Philadelphia. I saw her for the first time when I walked into her house. Henrietta greeted me with a bright smile, as though she had known me for years. After Simeon introduced me to her, she showed me to a room where I was to take my things and sleep, and she told me to make myself comfortable. She also told me that I was welcome to whatever food was in the house. From the moment I set my eyes on Henrietta, my intuition told me that she was good for me, because she accepted me, a perfect stranger, into her home and treated me as though I were a sister to her. As Henrietta and I became more acquainted with one another, I asked what Simeon had told her about me that she so accepted me into her house without any reservation.

Simeon had told Henrietta that I had nowhere to live because the aunt with whom I lived had put me out of her house after I became pregnant by him. Hearing that I was pregnant and was a native of St. Vincent, Henrietta said she had become sympathetic towards me, even though she hadn't met me. That was when she told Simeon I could come and live with her. Henrietta explained that we were all West Indian people, whether I was a native of St. Vincent or any other island. She said that, as West Indian people, we must help one another and that she was willing to help me until I was able to find a place of my own. Then she said to me: "Lola, I am much older than you are, and I would have been scared to death if I were pregnant and had nowhere to live. When Simeon spoke to me about you, I put myself in your position, and I felt obligated to help you, even though we had never met." Henrietta's words reaffirmed my belief and faith in God, because I believed that God had something to do with Henrietta's accepting me, a perfect stranger, into her home. I needed someone like her to rescue me and to bring some sort of stability back into my unstable life.

Henrietta and I, along with Jack, a boarder she had living with her at the time, all got along well together. We were indeed one happy family. Henrietta was a professional seamstress, and she would stay up late at night sewing after she finished with her daytime job. She taught me how to hem clothes, and Jack and I would stay up with her at night, assisting her with the hemming. The Christmas holiday season of 1976 was approaching, and Henrietta had lots of sewing contracts to complete before Christmas Day. Henrietta, Jack and I sat together in her sewing room after dinner every night, joking and singing as Henrietta sewed the clothing and Jack and I hemmed and pressed the finished goods. We were together in Henrietta's sewing room two nights before Christmas, when I began feeling some stomach cramps. I said to them jokingly that I was about to give birth to my baby, who wasn't supposed to be born until January 4. We stayed up that night until the early morning of Christmas Eve. By then the cramps in my stomach had ceased. Henrietta and Jack took a short nap before they left for work. I got out of bed later and did what I could around the house in preparation for Christmas Day, until Henrietta returned from work that afternoon. It was about 3:00 p.m. when my stomach began cramping again, but this time the cramps were more painful than the night before, and they were not stopping. When I informed Henrietta that I was having serious cramping, she telephoned Simeon at work. Simeon left work immediately and came to Henrietta's house. At first, Henrietta suggested that Simeon take me to the hospital and Simeon agreed with her. But I told them that I didn't see the need for me to go to the hospital, because I wasn't having contractions, I was having stomach cramps. Henrietta would have none of it. She was looking at me from the corner of her eye and saw that I was holding on to my stomach. She insisted that Simeon take me to the hospital. She assured me the doctor would send me back home if there were nothing wrong with me and that it was in my best interest to go and get checked by the doctor. I saw that she was concerned about me and I could not say no to her any longer, so I agreed with her. I asked Simeon to take me to the hospital. I was hoping that the doctor wouldn't keep me waiting in the hospital long, because I wanted to be back at Henrietta's house at a certain time to assist her with the Christmas decorations.

We arrived at the hospital emergency room approximately 6:00 p.m. on December 24. A doctor examined me, told me that I was dilating, and admitted me to the hospital, even though I wasn't in any pain. I was angry, because I couldn't understand why I was dilating when I had been told that the anticipated birth of my child would be January 4. While I lay on what seemed to be a bed with wheels, they pushed the bed and me onto an elevator. We got off on a floor with a sign marked "Labor Floor." They moved me from the bed onto another bed in a room. Then a nurse came into the room with a bottle with a tube and a needle connected to it. She pushed the needle into my vein. Simeon was afraid of hospitals and doctors, but most of all he was afraid of needles, so he left the room abruptly when the nurse appeared with the needle. The cramping in my stomach continued, and a doctor examined me for about ten minutes, while a nurse stood at the bedside and looked on.

There was another patient in the room, and although I couldn't see her, I heard her screaming loudly, "My vagina is bursting, my vagina is bursting." Hearing the screams of this patient, I became afraid, and I wanted to pull the needle from my vein, get the hell out of the bed, and run as far away from that hospital as I could.

But, since I couldn't run away, I just lay there on the bed in the room with the screaming patient. The doctor came and examined me again. Then he told the nurse that I was ready. "Ready for what?" I thought to myself. But I did not ask either the doctor or the nurse. They moved me from that bed onto a bed in another room. More people in uniform, including the doctor, gathered around my bedside, and one of the nurses instructed me to push, which I did. The more I pushed, the more she asked me to push. I was fed up with pushing, and I wanted to stop, but I didn't. I pushed and pushed until I felt something coming through the walls of my birth canal. I felt it when it entered my vagina. Someone placed a mirror in a position that enabled me to look on. I looked into the mirror and I saw the head of my child as it came out of my vagina. The doctor was holding the head of my baby when the entire body came out. It was 8:51 p.m. on December 24, 1976, when I gave birth to my child, a bastard baby girl.

Like her grandmother, who was an unwed mother when she gave birth to me, I was now an unwed mother giving birth to my child. Both mother and child were bastard children when they were born. From the minute that I laid my very own two eyes on her, I knew that my baby, my bastard child, was mine to keep forever. I knew I could neither give her up for adoption nor send her to either of her grandmothers in St. Vincent. Simeon had requested that, if I were to send the child to St. Vincent, she would live with his mother. I would never have granted him that request, and I knew I was keeping my baby from the minute that I saw her for the first time. I knew it when the doctor announced that she was a girl and he showed her to me. I affirmed it when I took her into my hands and held her in my arms, hugging her to my warm body. I just knew it. My child and I bonded the very first minute that my eyes beheld her, and I resolved to do everything within my power to take care of her. I meant to do everything within my power to take care of the child I had birthed, three hours and nine minutes before Christmas Day, and five days before my twenty-second birthday.

They took my baby away, and I was taken to a semi-private room, where I roared from the excruciating pain that I felt in my lower back. I felt as though someone was tearing away my flesh from my bones. In intense pain, I telephoned Simeon, telling him that I had given birth to our baby girl. I asked him to notify Henrietta. I was tired, but I cried from pain until the nurse came and gave me some medication. I took the medication and must have fallen asleep without knowing, because I was crying for pain when I awoke an hour later. I was experiencing so much pain that the nurse gave me an injection. I must have fallen asleep again without knowing, because it was daylight when I became aware of my surroundings. It was Christmas Day.

When I said Merry Christmas to the other patient in the same room with me, I told her that I was feeling better. She informed me that I had cried in my sleep for pain most of the night, only falling asleep after the doctor examined me and asked the nurse to give me another injection. After my conversation with my roommate, I asked the nurse for my baby. I wanted to hold her in my arms again. I felt joy within me when I looked at the face of the precious little thing that I had helped to create.

As I was holding my baby in my arms, I whispered in her tiny ears that things were going to be all right, and I began to cry, speaking to her for the very first time. At that moment, I felt an assurance within me that things were going to be all right. I reminded myself of the words from a song that the great raggae artist Bob Marley wrote: "Don't worry about a thing because every little thing will be all right." So I wasn't worried then, because I felt that everything would be all right for my baby and me.

I named my precious little girl Nadia Hope Parker. She was named Nadia after the gymnast Nadia, whose athletic feats had entertained me through that very depressive summer. Hope I had made up myself, and I called her by that name. Although her father's name was included on her birth certificate, she was to carry my surname, because he and I were not married. Nadia Hope Parker became Belitha Elitha Parker's bundle of joy from the moment she entered this world, and I vowed that she would remain my bundle of joy until I exited from this world. I was proud of her, and I promised to love her and care for her in the same manner that my great grandmother and grandmother had taken care of me.

Because of her birth and the promises I made to be the best mother ever, my life would never be the same. Hope's presence in my life taught me how to love someone unconditionally. I loved her without stipulation. Hope was the result of an unwanted pregnancy in the worst of times, but she became the one that I needed most at that time. Looking at her gave me the power to do things that I thought I couldn't do, like enduring the hardship of raising a child alone. As a result, I became more courageous in my effort to avoid deportation.

I lived with Henrietta for seven months, two of them after Hope was born. During that time she never accepted a penny from me for rent or boarding, nor did she ever make me feel unwelcome or uncomfortable. In February, I moved into a small, three-room apartment in a large apartment building in another section of West Philadelphia, living on my own again, this time with a sole companion, Hope. I was not employed, but I had enough money saved that I could survive financially until I found a job, which I hoped would be in no more than two months. I hoped not to become penniless and unable to take care of my daughter and myself, even though Simeon assisted me. Unlike my father, who had been no more than a sperm donor toward my existence, because he never assisted my mother with my financial support or otherwise, Simeon was a real father to his daughter. He assisted with the care of our daughter and supported her financially. He was even kind enough to pay the advance deposit of three months' rent required by the landlord before I could move into the apartment. I was grateful to him, but I planned not to depend on his financial support. I was determined to make it on my own.

I contacted Pauline and Zilpha, informing them that I had moved into my new apartment. Zilpha brought Hope three dresses when she visited me, and I expressed my gratitude to her for the dresses. I had to keep a low profile, because I was still hiding from Immigration authorities. But I did contact my Barbadian friend, Rita, who was still living in New York. She was the one who informed me that one of her friends knew of a lawyer who could get me a green card. When I inquired about the legality of it, she assured me that it was legal, because her friend had convinced her that it was. I had to admit that I was in a desperate position, having no job and a child to support. A green card would establish my legal residency in America and give me the legal right to work, thus making it is easier for me to find a job. I guess one could do desperate things when one is in a desperate position like the one I was in. In desperation, I gave Rita's friend five hundred dollars of the thousand she said that the lawyer needed to start the processing of my green card. She promised that I would have a green card in six months. At that time, she would give me the green card and collect the remaining five hundred dollars as payment in full. I was excited about the prospect of having my green card in six months, after which I would no longer have to live in hiding. Rita expressed her happiness for me, and we looked forward with great anticipation to the day when I would begin living in America as a legal immigrant. Rita and I kept in touch with her friend. Then, two months prior to the time that I was supposed to get the green card, she changed her telephone number. Since neither of us could get in touch with her and the time when she promised to deliver the green card was approaching, Rita and I decided to go looking for her. We went to her apartment in New York, but she never answered the doorbell. That was when Rita and I realized that her friend had taken my money and misled us. We confirmed later that a number of legal West Indian immigrants were exploiting illegal immigrants. Rita's friend was one of those who exploited their victims by claiming they were connected to lawyers who could legally get a green card for a price. It could not be proved that lawyers were involved in these scams, but the legal residents involved took the money and the victims never get the green cards they were promised nor their money back. They scammed us out of our money, knowing that we would not report their crimes to the authorities because of our immigration status.

Life had become more difficult for me than I imagined it would be, but I continued to do my very best to assure the livelihood of my child and myself. At least once a week, Simeon would baby-sit Hope, while I went out job hunting, without finding one. Besides the hardship of my finding a job, I experienced a frightening situation. While I was in the bedroom of my apartment one day, playing with Hope, I heard a loud bang on what I thought to be the apartment door. I ignored the first bang, but then there was a second and louder bang. So I went into the living room to check the door to my apartment. That was when I realized that someone was trying to break into my apartment and had almost smashed the door to my apartment into pieces. I slept at Simeon's that night, fearing for my life and my baby's. The following day, when I returned to my apartment, I said to myself that I would have moved out of the apartment if I had had enough to pay three months advance rent for a new apartment. Since I didn't have the money to move into a new apartment, I had no choice but to stay there and pray that no one would kill my daughter and me before I found a job and saved enough money to move into another apartment. I remained unemployed, but I never stopped looking for a job.

Since my weight and the size of my feet had increased after giving birth, I had outgrown all of my clothes and shoes. I needed a new outfit and a pair of shoes to wear when I went out job hunting, but I had little money. I went to the shopping area at fifty-second street in West Philadelphia and bought a cheap outfit and a pair of shoes. Then I bought the bare necessities that Hope and I needed to survive that week. I had only twenty-five dollars left in my savings account at the bank—all the money I had left to my name after shopping that day. I knew it was crunch time, and I began to panic. I feared that I would become penniless, unable to provide for my daughter and myself. I was desperate. I needed to find a job, so I made arrangements with Zilpha to baby-sit Hope for me on her days off. That was the last Monday in June 1977.

I awoke early that Monday morning and prayed to God as I did all the other mornings, but I added a special prayer asking Him to provide me with a job. As I was praying, I found myself overwhelmed with such emotions that I was grasping for air. As a result I was unable pray to God coherently. Because of my religious background and my spiritual beliefs, I had no doubt that God knew of my needs even if I could not state them in my prayer. After Zilpha left with Hope that morning, I put on the cheap outfit and my cheap fake leather shoes. In my cheap outfit, I felt groomed well enough for a job interview. Pauline had told me that Foster and Foster, an employment agency located at Broad and Chestnut, finds jobs for people. Since I didn't have much money, I decided not to take the bus, but instead to walk from forty-ninth and Walnut Streets in West Philadelphia to Broad and Chestnut Streets in downtown Philadelphia. That was approximately thirty-five city blocks, with some blocks longer than the others. As I walked, my feet hurt from the cheap shoes, but I continued to walk until I reached my destination. I went into a building at Broad and Chestnut Streets and took the elevator to the floor where Foster and Foster was located.

When I entered the office, I told the receptionist that I was looking for a secretarial job. When she asked whether I had experience in secretarial work, I lied and said that I did. I was confident that I could do secretarial work if given the opportunity. After I was interviewed, the receptionist gave me a typing test to determine the speed and accuracy of my typing. Thank God for Randell and the money that he used to give me while I was back home. Some of that money had gone for typing lessons, and I benefited from those lessons by passing the typing test, typing fifty-five words per minute with only a few mistakes. I also passed the math test that she gave me.

The interviewer, a white Caucasian man named Ted Pool, informed me that I had an excellent score on both tests and that I was an excellent candidate for a billing secretary job at Dread Valley Hospital. He explained the responsibilities of the job to me, and I agreed that I was qualified to do the job, even though I had no experience in medical billing. Mr. Pool scheduled an appointment for me to meet with Mr. Slick, the business manager for a group of orthopedic doctors at Dread Valley Hospital, a very prestigious hospital in the Philadelphia area. I had never seen an insurance form before, let alone completing one, and completing insurance forms was one of the main responsibilities on the job description. "Lola, don't panic, you can do it if you put your mind to it. You are not illiterate and you have lots of common sense. Remember what Ma Letteen used to say, that common sense was made before books. She said that if one had common sense, one would be able to do any bookwork. Lola, completing insurance forms is bookwork and you can do bookwork," I rationalized with myself.

When Mr. Slick was interviewing me, I lied and said that I had done billing. I also lied to him when he questioned me about my accent, saying that I was born in America and grew up in St Thomas (one of U.S. Virgin islands), as though he would know the differences between the U.S. Virgin Islands and the British Virgin Islands. I had now lied about my nationality to both the Immigration officer and Mr. Slick. "Mr. Slick, I need the job to take care of my child and myself. I have no other way of taking care of us, and I have only twenty-five dollars left in my savings account at the bank, which is not enough to take care of us. Please stop asking me all these damn questions and offer me the job," were my thoughts as Mr. Slick was interviewing me. He must have had an idea of what I was thinking, because he offered me the job. I was to pay the agency for finding me the job, and I guess Mr. Slick was supposed to pay them for finding me to take the job. That must have been the reason he told me that I wouldn't have to pay the agency if I didn't tell them that he had offered me the job, and he encouraged me not to tell them. "No problem, Mr. Slick. I need the money more than the agency does, so I won't tell them anything about your offer," I said to Mr. Slick. I called the agency and, as Mr. Slick had suggested, I told them that Mr. Slick had some other people to interview and that he would get back to them as soon as he made a decision. As I had been told in my dream by Ma, I applied for this job under my alias name, and I used the Social Security number that was issued to me for that name.

Before I began working, I needed to find an inexpensive, reliable babysitter for my daughter. With the assistance of Zilpha and Pauline, I did. They recommended Miss Elva, a neighbor living on the same street as their parents. The street was very accessible to public transportation. I had no problem taking my baby there on my way to work and picking her up after work. After I met Miss Elva and she agreed to baby-sit my daughter, I was happy. I looked forward to the beginning of the following week when I would start my new job as a billing secretary at this very prestigious hospital.

I began working at Dread Valley Hospital on July 3. My duties included answering telephones, completing insurance forms for patients, and submitting the forms to insurance carriers. I was to act as a liaison for patients and insurance carriers and collect payments from patients and their insurance carriers for services rendered to patients. I also did the bookkeeping for patients' accounts. I felt that I did an excellent job, and I was paid a very good salary that provided enough for my daughter and myself. The only free handout that I received for Hope was milk, cereal and juice from a government-run WIC program. After I began working, I was unable to take her for the appointments and she was cut from the program. Simeon also continued with his financial support of his daughter. He and I continued our relationship, even though I had reason to believe that he was involved with other women, having been seen at social functions among people who knew us.

I continued to keep a low profile, hiding from Immigration. When I was not at work, I stayed in my apartment and devoted my time caring for my daughter. Although I had no social life, Simeon did. People would telephone me and tell me that they saw him here and there at parties with different girlfriends. He would always deny it when I confronted him. Ever since we had begun dating, I could never recall seeing Simeon with another woman, except once. This was on a Sunday, when Rita came from New York to visit me. I took her to Simeon's apartment, thinking that he would be there. His roommate let us into the apartment. There we met another woman and an eight-year-old child. Simeon's roommate did not introduce us, which we thought would have been the normal thing to do. When Simeon arrived, he looked astonished, and I don't know whether he was astonished to see Rita and me or the other woman. He hadn't been in the apartment for long when he offered to escort the other woman to her car. Naive as I was, I never thought anything of it. The following day, someone called me, saying that she heard that I had met Simeon's other woman at his apartment. I was dumfounded. Of course, when I confronted Simeon he denied that the woman was his girlfriend.

One Saturday night, Zilpha insisted that I get out of the house and attend a party with her. She must have known that I would say that I had no babysitter and I couldn't go. Anticipating my objection, Zilpha had already make arrangements with one of her sisters to baby-sit Hope, so I went to the party with her, but reluctantly. Simeon and I were living apart, and neither of us had told the other that we were attending this party. When I walked into the party, I was surprised to hear that he was there, and even more surprising to hear he had escorted another woman to the party. I was standing a short distance from the bar. Our eyes met when he was walking across the dance floor on his way to the bar. Simeon seemed shocked to see me, and I guess he felt that he had no choice but to speak with me. "What are you doing here?" Simeon asked. I could have asked him the same question, but I didn't. Instead of answering his question, I said to him, "I hear that you are here with another woman. If you are, you better get rid of her now, because you will be with me from now on, and you will be going home with me when I leave this place tonight." He stared at me in dismay. Then he told me that he would be right back. "He had better be back soon if he knows what's good for him," I thought. This irresponsible thought was coming from an immature young adult who believed she was in love with the man who was the father of her first child. Simeon did come back to me soon after, and I made sure he stayed with me throughout the party. We danced together until the party was over, and we left the party together that night. Although Simeon never admitted that he had brought another woman to the party that night, I believed that he done so. I knew that the feeling I had within me for him was changing. I knew that my love for him was dying and that I would have to end my relationship with him someday.

Although Simeon never admitted to affairs with other women when I confronted him, deep within me I believed that he was involved with other women. Like Andrew, Simeon was a womanizer. Unlike my relationship with Andrew, in which I would be unfaithful to him when I found out that he was unfaithful to me, with Simeon I remained faithful. I would curse him and call him names. I even got physical with him one or two times, but he would always walk away from me and return after I had calmed down. Simeon did not like arguing with me. I remember what happened one Saturday night when he and his brother Calwin were at my apartment. After they ate the dinner I had prepared, Simeon announced that he was leaving to attend a party. I was angry that he had had the nerve to eat my food and go, and I assumed that he was about to attend a party with another woman. I wanted him to stay with me that night, so I instigated a brawl with him. Calwin was so upset with me that he told Simeon that he should kick my ass and leave. Simeon did not do as his brother suggested, but simply told me to behave myself. Then he left. The words that Calwin said to him that night never left me. I would always remember him as the uncle of my child who told his brother to kick my ass. Although I had reason to believe that Simeon was being unfaithful to me, he never showed me any disrespect. Up to that time in our lives, I had never seen him with another woman. He continued to profess his love for me, especially when I was angry with him and would tell him that it was over between us. We continued to live apart in our own separate apartments.

With the assistance of Zilpha and Pauline, I moved into a new apartment in a triplex building owned by Ronald, whose wife and daughter lived in the building. Unlike others that were occupied by many tenants, this building had only three tenants—the owner's wife, another single mother and myself. The three of us were each raising a daughter. Although I was still in hiding from Immigration, I wasn't as afraid as I had been before, because I had a good job and was able take care of my financial needs. I also had an increase in pay six months after I was employed, and another after a year, and Mr. Slick gave me excellent ratings on my performance evaluation. With my salary increases and the decrease in rent when I moved to the new apartment, I was able to increase the financial assistance that I sent to my mother and grandmother and also to increase my own monthly saving allotment. I did the very best I could for my daughter, and Simeon helped with her care, financially and otherwise.

Although I wanted to go back to school, I was scared, because I didn't want to chance getting caught by Immigration. Simeon thought otherwise and encouraged me to enroll in school again. Unlike the first time, when I used the name Lola and the Social Security number for that name, I now used my real name and that Social Security number when completing my application. Again, I was accepted into Community College and made plans to begun school the beginning of the first session of 1978. Simeon and I agreed that on the nights I attended school, he would pick up Hope from the babysitter and keep her until I got out of school. School was about to begin when the unforeseeable occurred. Simeon's employer transferred him to Washington, D.C., and he was unable to baby-sit Hope on the nights that I attended school. Had Simeon been a legal resident, he could have refused the transfer, quit his job and looked for another. But he couldn't risk losing his job not knowing if he would find another as an illegal immigrant. Simeon suggested that I move to Washington with him, but I declined for the same reason that he decided to go. I couldn't risk losing my job, not knowing if I would be able to find another in Washington as an illegal immigrant. Besides that, I had vowed never to live with a man unless we were married. Also, my determination to achieve my educational goals was the greatest concern to me at the time, not marriage.

Gwen took the place of Simeon, babysitting Hope on the evenings that I went to school. Since Simeon could not baby-sit for me at night, I had searched and found another baby-sitter. One of the Cottoy girls had recommended Gwen to me, and she was happy to have the job, because she was unemployed at the time. She would pick up Hope from the daytime babysitter and keep her until I could pick her up around ten o'clock on the nights that I went to school. Everything worked out well for me, both at work and school, until Gwen notified me that she could no longer baby-sit Hope. She had found a full-time job whose hours conflicted with the babysitting. I was devastated by the news. It meant that I would have to find another babysitter or else quit school. I was unsuccessful in my search to find another babysitter, so I quit school without notifying my professors or the school. I did not know that if I had notified the school or my professors, I could have received a withdrawal or incomplete grades for my classes instead of failures. I had no doubt that I could have earned at least a B for each of the three classes I was taking. I was disappointed with my failing grades and I felt dejected. I became more deter-mined than ever to find a new babysitter, so I could return to school. In looking for another babysitter, I had thoughts that I would have never been in such position if Simeon hadn't been transferred to Washington. I began to miss him and wish that he were still living in Philadelphia.

Simeon and I continued with our relationship, even though he lived in Washington and I remained in Philadelphia. We saw each other two weekends every month, and we spent our holidays together. I had no other man in my life, even though some of my friends and co-workers suggested that I should. I was focused on the things that I wanted to achieve, and it so happened that having a man was not one of them. Hope filled the void of my loneliness, because, besides being my child, she became my companion and trusted friend. Even though she couldn't talk back to me, she was the one I would talk to when I had problems and when I felt over-whelmed by the hardship in my life. Whenever I talked to her, I would afterwards become inspired with courage and feel that I could overcome whatever obstacles I feared. Hope attracted a few good people to us, like Lanell and the youngest of the Cottoys' daughters, Colleen, who assisted me with the care of my daughter in so many ways.

Hope was about three months old when I first took her to the Laundromat with me. The people at the Laundromat were all strangers. Among them was a lady I thought was from Barbados, because, when she commented how beautiful my daughter's eyes were, she spoke with the accent of a Barbadian native. Lanell, instead, turned out to be an African American. Hope's bright eyes attracted her. She fell in love with Hope and became a friend of mine. Our friendship was like that of a close relative. She was like an aunt to Hope, buying her very first snowsuit for her. She baby-sat Hope many times, taking her to spend nights at her own apart-ment when she thought I needed to have some time alone. She became Hope's Godmother. I will never forget Lanell, because she was a source of support for my daughter and me when we went through the roughest of times. I would be forever grateful to Lanell.

There was also Colleen. If Colleen had not volunteered to baby-sit Hope, I could not have returned to night school when I did. I had been unable to find a babysitter, no matter how hard I tried. Like Lanell, Colleen acted so much like a blood relative to Hope that many of the residents living close to the Cottoy family thought that she was Hope's mother, because she seemed to care for Hope like a mother. Colleen was still attending high school when she began babysitting for me on the evenings when I attended school, but she would insist Hope spent some nights and weekends with her. There were times when I would be home with Hope and Colleen would appear out of nowhere, saying that she had come to get Hope. When school was closed for vacation and Colleen was home, she would call me at work to tell me that she had picked up Hope at her daytime babysitter's house. Sometimes she would keep her for days at a time, and at these times I would always visit and spend time with my daughter, in the mornings before I went to work, and on evenings after I finished work. Colleen came into my life and assisted me with Hope when I needed that assistance most. I would be forever grateful to her for the things that she did, taking loving care of my daughter and solving my babysitting problems. In remembering the good things that Colleen did for Hope, I also cannot forget her sister, Zilpha, and her kindness towards my daughter and me.

Zilpha had a daughter who was three years older than Hope, for whom she bought lots of expensive clothes. Zilpha bought so many clothes for her daughter, Rose, that Rose outgrew many of her clothes without ever wearing them. Zilpha would give me most of the clothes Rose outgrew. I accepted those clothes from Zilpha, until her sister, Pauline, made an insensitive remark to one of her sisters about a dress that Hope was wearing at the time. Hope was dressed in one of the outfits that Zilpha had given her, and Toni, the sister of both Pauline and Zilpha, commented about how gorgeous the outfit looked on Hope. When I thanked her for the kind comment, Pauline remarked to Toni that I hadn't bought the outfit for Hope, that it was one of Rose's hand-me-downs that Zilpha had given me. I felt so offended by Pauline's unwarranted remark that as of that day I have never accepted another piece of clothing from Zilpha. I also never again dressed Hope in any of the outfits that Zilpha had given her. Although I was grateful to Zilpha, and would always be grateful to her for all those outfits, I was offended and embarrassed by Pauline's unwarranted remark. My determination to take care of my child with pride also strengthened me, and I became powerful in my struggle to win battles I thought would affect my pride and determination. One such battle that I fought and won was with Mr. Slick, when he tried to terminate my employment.

For the two years I had worked under Mr. Slick's supervision, he had given me excellent ratings on my performance reviews. That changed when I brought to Mr. Slick's attention my concern about patients' accounts that had been written off as bad debts even though those patients had paid in cash for the services rendered to them. I thought that by bringing my concern to Mr. Slick's attention, he would resolve the problem and give me an even better evaluation for my performance. I was naive. I had never been exposed to a situation like this one before, and I was unaware of the sometimes unethical politics of corporate America. I was about to learn a lesson.

I witnessed a change in Mr. Slick's attitude toward me from that day. He acted as though it wasn't a big deal that these accounts were written off as bad debts. He told me that reviewing these accounts was his job, not mine. On my next performance evaluation, Mr. Slick gave me a less than satisfactory rating, even though my performance on the job at the time was even better than the past year. Then he began to criticize my work, even though his criticisms were not warranted. There were about sixteen staff members in the department who did clerical and secretarial work, I was one of two blacks among them. Many members of the staff noticed that Mr. Slick was devaluing my performance, and some of them remarked that he was treating me unfairly. I was aware that Mr. Slick was treating me unfairly, but I was not aware that I could do anything about it. Then Shelly befriended me and told me how I could.

Shelly was the only Jewish secretary in the department. She commented to me that Mr. Slick was a bigot. It was the first time that I ever heard the word bigot, and I had no idea what it meant. I could have easily looked up the meaning of the word in the dictionary, but I asked Shelly to explain the meaning to me, since she was the one who used the word. Shelly explained that a bigot is a person who hates all blacks and some whites, mostly Jewish people like her. She went on to explain to me that Mr. Slick was discriminating against me because I was black, and he would do the same to her because she was Jewish. I didn't fully understand Shelly's explanation of a bigot, how Mr. Slick could discriminate against me because I was black, let alone discriminate against her because she was white and Jewish. It seemed to me that her explanation of the word "discriminate" was somewhat similar to "better than." It seemed to me like some of the people back home, who, because they held better jobs and lived in nicer houses, thought that they were better than those who did not have similar status in the society. I thought that all white people were the same, in that they had similar jobs, and lived in similar houses. So I didn't understand why Mr. Slick would discriminate against Shelly, since I assumed that Shelly came from a background similar to his own. I also didn't understand why some white people in America were discriminating against black people, and why those white people thought, regardless of their economic status, that they were better than all black people. I was not aware of the concepts of discrimination and racism until Shelly befriended me and educated me about their prevalence in this country. I learned everything that Shelly taught me about those things and I learned them well.

Although I continued to work, Mr. Slick was reducing my job duties, and he continued to downgrade my performance. I began to feel uncomfortable on the job. Thoughts of quitting came to my mind, but I knew I couldn't, because I depended on the job for the very survival of my daughter and myself. Also, I was attending Community College full time, and I needed the salary to pay my tuition. Then one day Mr. Slick threatened to terminate my employment.

Fearing that I wouldn't be able to take care of my child and myself if I lost the job, I decided that I had no choice but to fight to keep it. By that time my Jewish friend, Shelly, had taught me that there were laws that prohibited racial discrimination and what I could do within the laws to protect myself from Mr. Slick's racial discrimination against me. No one at that hospital, not even Shelly, knew about my background, and I intended to keep my background a secret from everyone at my workplace. I told everyone that I was a U.S. citizen, and I recounted the story that I was born in America and raised in the Virgin Islands, that my father lived in New York, and whatever else sounded good and believable at the time. When Mr. Slick threatened to fire me, I went to one of the top executives of the hospital and pleaded my case to her, letting her know that I had all intentions of retaining an attorney if Mr. Slick terminated my employment. I told her about everything, including the accounts of the patients who had paid their bills but had their accounts written off as bad debts. The executive officer was astounded by my accusation, but I had documents to support my accusation. When she asked what she could do to prevent me from retaining an attorney and pressing a claim, I told her that all

I needed was a job and the assurance that my supervisor would not harass me. She offered me a temporary position working as a billing clerk in the Human Resources Department until I was able to find a permanent position within the hospital. That was acceptable to me, and I accepted the offer without any reservation.

I am grateful to Shelly for her support of me. It was only with her support and my firm determination to fight for justice that I was able to go to the administrator. I was proud of myself, because for the first time in my life I felt that I had won a battle that was worth fighting for. I thought, "You came to America because you thought that America was the land of opportunity. You thought you would have the opportunity to find a white-collar job that you felt qualified to do. That all sounded good and promising to you, because you thought that you would be paid well for such job. With that money, you thought that you would be able to support the folks back home who needed your financial support, and you would be able to achieve your educational goals as well. No one told you before you immigrated to America that things were not so for someone like you who immigrated to America on a visitor's visa. No one told you before you came that if you stayed longer than the time that Immigration allowed one to stay in the country, you would become an illegal immigrant. No one ever told you that you wouldn't be able to find a decent job in America as an illegal immigrant, and that the only job you would be able to find as an illegal immigrant was as a maid. You probably would have decided against immigrating to America if someone had explained these things to you before you decided to come.

"Since no one explained those things to you, you immigrated to America at such a young age, to live with Edna, a perfect stranger. Before you came, Edna promised to be good to you, but she exploited you once you got here. When you found out about all those things, you wanted to go back home, but you chose to stay, because you believed at the time that staying in America was better than returning home. Because of the choice you made, you accepted jobs that you would never have accepted if you could have done better. First you worked as a maid, and later as a waitress/cashier. While working as a waitress/cashier, you were held up at gunpoint, not once or twice, but three times. You could have been killed, but you survived. Immigration came to deport you, and they missed the opportunity to do so. They took your Social Security number that was in the name that Ma Letteen had demanded everyone call you at birth. You were smart enough to know that Immigration would be checking those numbers as a means of tracking you to your place of employment, an easy way for them to apprehend you and deport you. You prayed, and you talked to Ma Letteen. She appeared to you in a dream, telling you how to get new Social Security numbers. She also instructed you should work under the Social Security for the alias name. When you did find a job at Dread Valley hospital, you used the alien name. The job paid well, enabling you to take care of yourself and your child, mother, grandmother, and you haven't abandoned your educational goals. You refused to quit school in spite of having to accept failures for classes for which you would have earned As and Bs, if you had had a reliable babysitter and had not had to quit those classes before completing them. When you thought that your job was in jeopardy, threatening the survival of your child and yourself, you fought to keep it, and you got a better one that paid more money. Girl, as an illegal immigrant in America, you have some nerve. You have more guts than most of the other illegal immigrants in this country, and even some of the legal ones and some who were born in America. Girl, what next?"

When I started to work in the human resources department of Dread Valley Hospital, it didn't take me long to realize that I was an outcast to most of my co-workers. I suspected it from the manner in which they talked to me. They stared at me as though I were from another planet There were many times when I spoke to some of them and they would pretend not to hear me. They mimicked my accent, and it appeared that some of them thought that because I spoke with an accent my intelligence level was below theirs, making me less of a human being. I learned from Shelly that Mr. Slick was a bigot, because he hated black people and some white people, Jewish white people especially. I wondered what one calls black people who hate other black people. Some of the few black people who worked in the department acted as though they hated other black people, including me. I noticed that although some white people were displaying some subtle dislike for each other among themselves, the black people displayed their dislike for each other more overtly.

My supervisor, Eloise, was a black woman, seventeen years my senior. She also supervised another black woman, Adalyn. Adalyn was older than Eloise, but I don't know by how many years. Eloise and Adalyn spoke ill of each other and openly displayed their dislike for one another. Eloise claimed that Adalyn was incapable of doing the work that she assigned to her, and Adalyn resented the fact that Eloise was her supervisor. It seemed to me that Adalyn was not performing well, but I was not certain it was because of her inability to do the job or because she hated Eloise and wanted to undermine her. The tension between Eloise and Adalyn escalated, until Adalyn decided to take a leave of absence from her job, as she said, "before I kill that bitch."

After Adalyn took the leave of absence, Eloise assigned most of her duties to me. In addition to answering the telephone, filing, and helping employees resolve their benefits problems, which was the job that I was hired to do, I had also to audit the employees' benefits plans, prepare the monthly billing statements, and act as the insurance carrier/employees liaison. I gained much valuable experience in the area of employees benefits administration from these added responsibilities. When I took over these responsibilities, I had to agree with Eloise that Adalyn's performance had been below average, especially with the monthly billing statements to the insurance carriers. Because Adalyn did such a poor job with the billing, the hospital overpaid their insurance carriers thousands of dollars monthly for employees who were ineligible for coverage, as well as for former employees whose coverage should have been terminated when they left the job. I was able to save the hospital thousands of dollars on insurance premiums by deleting ineligible employees. I also recovered money from the overpayment of past bills. Eloise showed her appreciation for the work that I did. But I questioned her judgment in not firing Adalyn for such poor performance.

Besides Eloise, there was Dorothy, the only other black supervisor in the department. She supervised the employment section of Human Resources. She was supposed to be looking for a permanent position for me elsewhere in the hospital, but my intuition told me that she wasn't. There was something about Dorothy that seemed deceitful, but I had no clue what it was. Dorothy acted superior to the average black person who worked in the hospital, but she was not the only one who acted that way. It appeared to me that most of the few blacks who held good positions in the hospital acted as though they were on cloud nine and the other blacks were on cloud one. Unlike the whites in high positions, who assisted and encouraged other whites to apply for higher positions when they became available, the blacks in high positions did not do likewise for other blacks. Blacks continued to degrade each other openly, while whites spoke ill of each other only among themselves, although they would openly speak ill of blacks. That was how I heard the rumors about Dorothy.

Rebecca was one of my Caucasian co-workers. One day, she and I were the only two people in our section, when Dorothy visited the section. Dorothy asked Rebecca a question and then left. Rebecca seemed upset that Dorothy had questioned her about something to do with her job. After Dorothy left, Rebecca said to me, "How dare that bitch question me about my job, when she is in a job that she isn't qualified to do?" Rebecca said that Dorothy had been promoted to her position because she was having an affair with the director of personnel, a white man. She continued to talk about Dorothy and other co-workers, including Eloise. I did not utter a word, because I was not about to participate in departmental gossip. I felt that I was there to do a job, and that was what I did. Rebecca was not the only one who gossiped about co-workers. It seemed to be the norm for most of them to talk ill about each other. I could not understand how they could work together, eat lunches together, and seem to be friendly with each other, and yet talk so ill about each other. There were times when I would wonder what they were saying about me, since I was the stranger among them. Even so, I was more concerned about the security of my job, my status as an illegal immigrant and my educational goals.

I was still a temporary employee, but I was paid high enough wages to enable me to take more credits in school, in hopes of getting my degree as soon as possible. I felt I had to get it before Immigration could catch me. I lived inexpensively, saving as much of my money as possible. My goals were to get my degree and to save enough money to take back with me to the islands if I were to be deported. I wouldn't care if Immigration deported me after I accomplished those goals. I felt that with a degree and some money, I would be able to take care of my daughter and myself if I were to return to St. Vincent. I reasoned that I would be able to buy a house of my own and that my degree would enable me to find a good job. I also knew that with a good salary, I would be able to continue supporting my mother and grandmother financially. All of these things would be possible only if I could stay in this country undetected by Immigration authorities until I got my degree.

I continued to make the necessary sacrifices as I pursued my goals. I lived in run-down apartments because of the cheap rent. I couldn't afford to buy myself breakfast and lunches from the hospital cafeteria, as most of my co-workers did. Instead I ate rice and eggs for breakfast at home before I left for work. I could have bought a bowl of salad for my lunch for only twenty-five cents, and that was what I did on most days. When I got paid, I treated myself to a sandwich. I never deprived my child of nutritious food, and she was always fed a balanced diet, including milk, all natural juices, meat, fish, vegetables and lots of fruit. She was not permitted any candy or junk food. I did my very best as a mother for my child, but there were times when my very best was not good enough to protect her. For example, there was the time Colleen was not able to baby-sit her, and Stella, one of her nieces did so. Stella had done some babysitting for me before. She lived with Dolly, her mother, who was very fond of Hope. I was on my way to Washington that Friday to visit Simeon, when I went to Dolly's house to pick up Hope. My body went chill when I walked through the door and saw my daughter's face. Instantly, I knew that something terrible had happened. My baby's face was swollen with finger marks. I asked Stella what had happened. "Who slapped Hope on her face? Who did such terrible thing to my child?" I asked Stella. She looked at me but said nothing, never answering any of my questions nor giving me any explanation of the marks on my child's face. In pain and disbelief, I fetched my baby and cried. I cried all the way as I rode the trolley to Thirtieth and Market Streets, where I caught the train to Washington. As I rode the train, I cried every time I looked at my daughter's face. I felt the hurt when I thought about the pain that my child must have felt when she received that slap. I hurt even more not knowing who had done it. My poor baby couldn't talk, and Stella never told me who had slapped her. I would always remember how numb my body felt when I saw my daughter's face that Friday evening. The sight of her face, with the pain and hopelessness that I felt on that day, would remain with me forever.

Because of that incident, I considered quitting school so I could spend more time with my child. But I didn't. I decided that to continue school until I graduated was in the best interest of both my daughter and myself. I continued to work on the job as a temporary employee, and I had hopes that Dorothy would assist me in finding a permanent position. Then, sadly, news came that Adalyn had died, a few weeks before she was scheduled to return to work. Eloise was quite pleased with my job performance, and she offered me the permanent position which Adalyn had held before taking her leave of absence. I accepted without hesitation. With the change from temporary to permanent status came a salary increase. I also became eligible for the tuition reimbursement plan, but I couldn't take advantage of it, because I was working under my alias name and enrolled in school under my real name. But the increase in salary enabled me to pay for more courses, and I took enough courses to qualify as a full-time student.

I had to manage the time that I spent at work and at school effectively, but it was the time I spent with my daughter that was of the greatest concern to me. I had no social life. On weekends, I dedicated most of my time to Hope, because I felt guilty not spending enough time with her during the week, especially on the nights that I had to go to school. Although Colleen took very good care of Hope and was a reliable babysitter, my routine on days that I attended work and school was very hectic. I went to school at night Monday through Thursday. On weekday mornings, when I had to go to work and school, I awoke at approximately six a.m. to prepare Hope and myself for the day. I left the house at 7:15 to catch the bus. In one of my hands, I carried Hope's bag with her supplies, a bag with my schoolbooks and supplies, and also my pocket book. With my other hand, I pushed Hope in the stroller. I had to walk four blocks from my apartment to the bus stop, where I caught the bus to Hope's daytime babysitter. After taking her to the daytime babysitter, I would walk three blocks to another bus, which took me to work. I would arrive on the job each workday by 8:20 a.m. My scheduled workday was from 8:30 a.m. through 5:00 p.m. After work, I took a bus to school because my first class began at 6:00 p.m. and the last ended at 9:00 p.m. After classes, I took two different buses to the Cottoys' residence to get my daughter, not arriving there before 10:00 p.m. I wouldn't get home until 11:00 p.m. most school nights.

Those were difficult times for me, as I tried to balance being a single mother taking care of my daughter, working a full-time job, and attending school full time. There were winter months when I walked to the bus stop and saw Hope shivering in my hands, as I stood on the corner waiting for the bus to arrive. Hope hated snow and sleet, especially when it fell on her face and stung her. At those times, she would cry at the top of her lungs. Those were the days when I wished that I were in a better position and able to buy a car, so I wouldn't have to stand at the corner waiting for the bus in snow and sleet. But I was doing the best that I could at the time.

Although the cold was unbearable in the mornings, it was worse at nights. There were many nights when I thought Hope and I would freeze to death waiting for the bus. I remember some cold nights when our teeth would chatter from the cold, and I would hold Hope close to my body with frozen hands. After the bus arrived and I rode it to the stop near to my apartment, I would walk home and be unable to unlock the door because my hands were too numb to hold the keys. I would have to use an elbow to press the doorbell to the Darnels' apartment. When she answered and walked to the entrance of her apartment, I would tell her about my hands and ask her if she could please get my keys from my pocket book and unlock the door to my apartment. I was fortunate, because she never refused.

I also remember one extremely cold night, as I stood with Hope waiting the arrival of the bus. We stood on that street corner for hours, but it seemed an eternity. It was so cold that my teeth chattered, and I felt Hope's body tremble as I held her close. I felt so cold, and Hope was trembling so violently, that I thought at one time our bodies would turn into ice before the bus arrived. Suddenly, a man drove up in a new car and stopped next to the curb where I stood. "Oh baby, it's cold out there. Do you want me to take you and your baby home?" he asked. Without thinking, I accepted the man's offer, jumped into the car with this stranger, directing him to my apartment building. He stopped in front of the building, and I got out of the car. He drove away before I could ask him his name or thank him for the ride. Under normal circumstances, I would never have accepted a ride from a stranger. But that night seemed different. That night I accepted a ride from a complete stranger without thinking of what might have happened.

Standing outside in the cold waiting for the bus was one thing, but living in an apartment where at times there was no heat or hot water was quite another. Robert, my landlord, was not living in the building when I rented the apartment, but his wife, Doris, and their eight-year-old daughter were. Rumor had it that Doris had suffered a nervous breakdown after Robert left her to live with another woman. Some of the children living on the same street were afraid of Doris, and they would call her "Crazy Doris." I found her to be a very pleasant person, and I was never afraid of her, even though at times I thought she looked crazy. She was said to be on disability. Doris stayed at home most of the time. On Sunday she attended church and twice a month she visited the doctor. Darnel was the other tenant who lived on the second floor. Like myself, she was a single mother with a daughter, about three years older than Hope. We three women, each with a daughter, lived in a building lacking heat and hot water when we needed them most. Oil was used to heat the apartment, and there were times when the oil tank was empty and we had no heat even after complaining to Ronald.

There were nights when the temperature outside was below freezing, and inside our apartment even colder. It was so cold at times that I risked our lives by turning on the gas oven, the only source of heat for my daughter and me, and keeping it on throughout the night. I remember one cold night that I greeted the dawn with a breath of relief and dressed my baby and myself without washing. I fled the apartment in a hurry, going to the Cottoys' residence. There I bathed Hope before taking her to the babysitter and bathed myself before I went to work. Besides having no heat or hot water in my apartment, I also had to deal with a leaky roof, which Robert failed to fix.

My apartment was on the third and top floor of the building. There were times when the rain came into my apartment as though I were outside. I had to use buckets to catch the rainwater. I complained to Ronald about the leak, but he never repaired it. These were some of the things that Hope and I shared. She slept on my stomach until she was over a year old, because I was afraid that she would die from what they referred to as crib death if I placed her in the crib to sleep. I was a single, inexperienced mother at the time, trying to do everything I could to protect my baby. It was a baby from an unwanted pregnancy, but one who, once born, was loved by her mother. We survived those days together, Hope and I. She was important to my survival as much as I was important to hers.

It was her presence in my life that enabled me to maintain my sanity. There were times when I needed someone to tell my problems to, but I knew of no one who would listen as Hope did. Some nights I would enter the apartment, throw my books about, and swear that I wasn't going back to school. On those nights I would pour out my heart to her, telling her my problems before she went to bed. Then I would cry to Hope as I lay her in bed, telling her that I would quit school, because working full time, attending school full time, and taking care of her full time was too much for me to handle. I would keep talking to her, staring into her beautiful eyes until she closed them in asleep. After more crying, I would come back to the reality that I couldn't quit school. If I wanted to provide her with a life better than my own, I would have to continue school until I graduated. Then I would reassure myself that I could do it, that I really could work full time, take care of her and also attend school full time. With that reassurance, I would pick up the books that I had thrown about the apartment and prepare to continue with my education. Even though there were times when I had problems that were beyond my control, and as a result received some low grades, I never quit school.

The low grades that I got in school did not reflect a lack of ability to do the work. Rather, they were resulted from some of the most difficult times that I had ever experienced. There were times when I would have a final examination scheduled, but couldn't take the exam because I had no babysitter. There were other times when I had to rush to finish my exam, because I had to pick her up at a certain time from the babysitter. I also had other distractions that prevented me from concentrating fully on my schoolwork, like the times when I would be overcome with the fear of being deported before I could complete school. Sometimes I would hear that Immigration had raided a workplace, caught many illegal immigrants, and deported them. That kind of news was troubling to me, and I would become frightened that Immigration would raid my workplace as well. There were times when I felt so paranoid that I would suspect every white male I saw of being an Immigration officer, even some of the white males who worked at Dread Valley Hospital. I felt desperate to get a green card, and when one is in a desperate situation, one can do desperate things. That was when I fell victim to yet another green card scam.

Janice, one of my friends from St. Vincent, was living in New York as an illegal immigrant, too. She called me one night to tell me that her husband, Cyril, who had been an illegal immigrant, was now legal, and that she herself was about to change to a legal status as well. Janice said that Cyril had paid two thousand dollars to get a legitimate American birth certificate from a person who worked in the office where they issue them. She said that the birth certificate was in Cyril's real name, and I thanked God for that, because I wasn't about to take on yet another alias. One alias was enough for me to deal with. Janice asked whether I was interested in paying the money for a similar birth certificate. I was reluctant about the whole idea, since I had already paid money for a green card that was supposed to be legal, and I had gotten neither the green card nor my money back. Nevertheless, I needed and wanted some sort of paper that would give me the legal right to be in America and prevent Immigration from deporting me. I told Janice that before I paid out any money, I wanted to see Cyril's document, and she agreed to show it to me. That weekend, I visited Janice in New York, and, sure enough, Janice showed me the American birth certificate in Cyril's name. I was convinced that it was legitimate. Before I gave them the money, I told them that I would like to know the name of the person who would provide the birth certificate and to have a face-to-face meeting with that person. I was told that I could not do so, because neither Cyril nor Janice had ever met this person, but had worked through another contact. That was how it was at the time with these scams, and probably still is.

Although I had some reservations, I gave them a thousand dollars and the information that they needed to provide me with a birth certificate. Two days later, Janice called to say that she and I would be getting our birth certificates in about three weeks. She suggested that I send the money to her, or bring it to New York in person, a week before we were expecting the birth certificates. Janice said that the person who provided Cyril with his birth certificate told Cyril that he could use it to apply for an American passport. Cyril applied for his American passport before I paid the balance to Janice, and before Janice had paid her own balance. As a result, we each lost only a thousand dollars instead of the two which we would have lost otherwise.

A few days after Cyril had applied for his passport, after midnight, some Immigration officers showed up at their apartment. They handcuffed Cyril and arrested him. That was when we realized that the birth certificate was a fake. It seems that there were a group of people in New York who ran a scam, where they took money from illegal immigrants and provided them with phony birth certificates. Cyril could not identify the person who provided him with the birth certificate, because he did not give Cyril his real name. He met Cyril at one location and took him to another to carry out the transaction, a location that Cyril couldn't identify either. Immigration officials kept Cyril in an American jail for a week or two before they deported him. Janice, on the other hand, was lucky enough not to be deported, too.

Janice was about seven months pregnant when the Immigration officials raided her apartment and took Cyril away. They told her that the only reason why they weren't taking her with them, too, was because she was pregnant. When I heard the news about Cyril, I became more worried, and from that time forth, I became more or less paralyzed with the fear that I would be deported before I was able to accomplish my educational goals. Besides dealing with my immigration problems, I had problems finding a suitable babysitter for Hope. Colleen was no longer able to baby-sit for me on a regular basis, and my daytime babysitter had become unreliable. When Mr. Cottoy had a day off from his job, and I had no other babysitter, he would volunteer, and he treated Hope as he treated his grandchildren. I would always remember his kindness. Because of the many babysitting problems that I had at the time, I began to take off from work and school regularly. I got low grades because of my absences from school, and I was afraid that I would lose my job if I continued to take too many unscheduled days off. As a result, I began to think about helping my mother come to America so she could assist me with babysitting Hope. She could also assist herself financially by getting paid to baby-sit other children. Then I wouldn't have to support her financially, because she would be able to take care of herself and assist with the financial support of my siblings back home. With this logical reasoning, I asked a friend who was an American citizen for her assistance. She wrote a letter to my mother inviting her to America, and she even provided my mother with a bank statement to send to the American Embassy in Barbados. But the American Ambassador in Barbados denied her a visitor's visa, and my mother was unable to immigrate to America. Although I was disappointed, I thanked my friend for trying. My mother could apply again after a year, and she would do so when the time came. In the meantime, I had to think about a solution to my babysitting problems.

When my daughter was four, I enrolled her in a day care center that was owned and operated by a church. Because the church members were the caretakers for the children, I assumed that they would provide my child with quality care, but it turned out that I was wrong in my assumption. Whenever I picked up my daughter from day care, she smelled like dogs and had dog hair all over her body and clothing. I asked the workers whether they had dogs in the building, but they denied that they did. One day, I decided to leave work early and showed up at the day care center unannounced. I was shocked to see that the children were taking their naps on the floor, with several dogs lying among them. I began to scream at the workers, and I took my child away from that center. I vowed that she would never return, even though I had no one to baby-sit her the following day.

As soon as I got home that afternoon, I gave my daughter a bath. Then I began to pray. In my prayer, and I don't know whether you would call it a prayer, because I didn't ask for anything, I questioned God about his fairness. I believed that the troubles I was experiencing in my life were a punishment from God, and I had no idea what I had done to God to deserve such punishment. After all, I hadn't committed any great sin, except fornication, and I had made a child and given birth to her. I knew of people who had had abortions, and to take the life of a baby seemed to me a greater sin than fornication. Yet those people didn't seem to have the problems that I had. I thought about the rapes that the pedophiles and rapists had committed on me when I was a child, and about how God hadn't done anything to stop them. I also thought about my immigration problems and my troubles on the job. The more I thought about how rotten my life was at that time, the more I questioned God about his fairness, and the angrier I became with Him. I was so angry that I questioned His very existence. At the end of all the questions and torments, I begged God to forgive me, and I prayed to Him to have mercy on my sinful soul. I asked God to guide and direct me in my most troubling times, and I believe that He did.

I believe that God was guiding me every day on the job, providing me with answers to the many questions that my co-workers were asking me. My co-workers wanted to know more about me. They questioned why I wasn't taking advantage of the tuition reimbursement plan, and I told them that my father had allocated money for my education and was paying my tuition. They must have believed me, because I wasn't questioned about it again. I told them that my father was well off and willing to pay for my education, even though he was disappointed when I had my child, especially out of wedlock. That lie also changed the attitude of some of my co-workers towards me. Some of them seemed to resent me because of the things I did for the betterment of my child's life as well as my own.

Hope was old enough to attend elementary school, but I refused to enroll her in public school, because public education in the city had a reputation for low academic standards. I enrolled her in a private school instead. At the same time, I had a few promotions on the job and some increases in my salary. When public transportation went on strike and my daughter refused to walk the thirty plus city blocks to school, I was able to buy a car. Before that, Hope and I would leave the house hours early, because she and I had to walk thirty-two city blocks from my house to her school, then I had to walk another twenty-eight city blocks to my place of employment. On the third day of the strike, I was tired and I assumed that Hope was, too. We had not walked three blocks when Hope sat on the sidewalk and refused to move. "Hope, get up. Get up and let's go, or you will be late for school and I will be late for work," I said to her, but she sat there and did not move. "Hope, please don't give me a hard time. Please, get up and let's go. I would lift you up, but I am too tired, so please get up from the sidewalk and let's go," I pleaded with her. She said to me, "Mommy, I am not giving you a hard time, but I am tired, too. I am too tired to walk. Go buy us a car, so we don't have to walk." Then she began to cry, and I began crying too. Then, I lifted my baby and carried her on my shoulders back to the apartment. I called work and told them that I was ill. I took the rest of the week off and stayed home with my daughter. That very evening, I called a friend and asked her to take me shopping for a car. I had enough money saved for a down payment on a car. I was also making enough money to pay the car loan and still maintain my lifestyle.

That very night I bought a car, which was a needed convenience for my daughter and me. We would no longer have to stand in the cold morning and night, waiting for public transportation. I would no longer have to listen to her scream her lungs out when snow and sleet fell onto her face. I got home at night by 10:30 p.m., instead of 11:00 or 12:00, as happened before I bought the car. I was also happy that I was able to buy a car of my own, but was naive to think that everyone, including my co-workers and my few so-called friends would be happy for me. I learned otherwise.

When I told Pauline, one of my so-called friends, that I had bought the car and showed her the car, I was shocked by her negative remark. She commented that I probably didn't have enough money to buy food, and yet I had bought a car, and a new one at that. I thought, "Pauline, I wish I could tell you that I have enough money in the bank to buy food for my child and me for a very long time and that I probably have more than you have. I wish I could tell you that I don't need an enemy, if you ever were my friend. But I can't, because you might report me to Immigration if I did." Like Pauline, some of my other co-workers had a similar reaction. They gossiped that I could not afford to buy a car and send my daughter to a private school on my salary. They commented that I must have been selling drugs. I wished I could tell them what I really wanted to tell them.

I wanted to tell them that I could afford to buy a car because I was willing to sacrifice some things for the sake of other things. I did not spend money on designer clothes and gold jewelry. I refused to spend my money on an expensive apartment or on alcoholic beverages at happy hour. Because I had made those sacrifices, I had saved enough money and to buy the things that were truly necessary, and buying a car was one of those necessities. I wanted to tell them that I wasn't a drug pusher, either. Marijuana was the only drug that I knew of. I had smoked that stuff back home when I celebrated my nineteen birthday. I didn't like the after effects. I couldn't control my motion, and I felt as though the substance was controlling me. Because I was opposed to being controlled by any person, let alone a substance, I vowed then never to touch that stuff again, and I hadn't touched it since and had no intention to do so in the future. I had never seen any other drugs, and I had no interest in seeing them, let alone selling them. I also had no plans to go to jail for selling drugs. I love freedom too much, and I wasn't about to risk it for anything in the world, not even money. I wanted to tell them that I was hiding from Immigration, and that that was the reason I was so focused on my education, hoping to attain my degree before Immigration found me.

I continued my progress in school, and in June of 1981 I completed the required courses at Philadelphia Community College to graduate with an Associate degree in Applied Science. It wasn't easy, but I did it. Although that was a great accomplishment for me, I didn't attend the graduation ceremony. I had pledged that the only graduation ceremony I would attend would be for my Bachelor's degree. With that pledge in my mind, in the fall of 1981, I enrolled in St Joseph's University as a full-time college student, and I began to attend classes there. I was about to face even more difficulties, both at work and at school.

I had become more acquainted with the people at work and somewhat friendly with some of them, having lunches with them at times. Those lunch periods enabled me to get to know the personalities of some co-workers. They talked to me about their private lives, especially their sex lives, as though it were public information. One of my co-workers said that she had met her husband, Leroy, while he was a patient in the hospital where she was working as a nurse's assistant. Joyce said that she was helping Leroy with his bath when she noticed his penis, the biggest she had ever seen in her life. She was immediately attracted to Leroy. They exchanged telephone numbers before he was released from the hospital. Leroy was living with his wife and children in a neighboring state. While Leroy's wife and children were visiting his in-laws one Sunday, Leroy telephoned Joyce, picked her up, and took her home to his house, where they had sex in the same bed that he and his wife slept in. She said that the rest was history, because Leroy had divorced his wife a year after they had met and married her. Then there was Bernita's story.

Bernita was married and living with her husband and their three children. She described her first affair. Bernita explained that she had left home that morning at the normal time that she would leave to go to work, but she went to her lover's house instead. Bernita said that she spent the entire day having sex with her lover until, as she said, "my pussy hurts.". Bernita said that she had sex with her husband that night, and when they were finished, the husband told her that it had been the best pussy he ever got from her. Then Bernita turned to me and said, "Men can't miss what they can't measure." I asked her what she meant by that, since she was staring directly at me when she made the comment.

Bernita told me that I was stupid to be single and not dating a couple of men. When I told them that I did have a boyfriend and that he lived in Washington, they laughed at me. Then Bernita suggested that Simeon probably had other women in Washington, so it was only fair for me to have other men in Philadelphia without Simeon's knowledge. She said that Simeon would never know if I had sex with another man, because he wouldn't be able to measure my pussy. According to Bernita, he could never miss what he couldn't measure, and she encouraged me to get another man. Well, Bernita, I wasn't looking for another man, and men at the time were the least of my concerns. I was more concerned about the security of my job and my new supervisor, who seemed not to like me, for reasons unknown to me. I was hoping that she wouldn't find any reason to terminate my employment before I attained my Bachelor's degree.

While I worked in the human resources department of Dread Valley Hospital, I experienced the good as well as the bad. I got several promotions when Eloise was my supervisor, but then Eloise was demoted and Elizabeth was appointed the new supervisor, even though she had had no experience in benefits administration. At first, Elizabeth and I got along well. She relied on my support, because I had the most experience and knowledge in our section. She gave me an excellent performance appraisal when she evaluated my work performance the first year after she was appointed to the position as my supervisor. Her excellent evaluation of my performance changed to satisfactory in the second year, and to less than satisfactory in the third year, even though I worked harder than my co-workers, who depended on me for assistance, too, because of my knowledge of the work. It didn't matter how well I performed on the job; it wasn't good enough, in Elizabeth's opinion. She criticized almost everything that I did. I didn't change my work habits, and I did the job to the best of my ability. I couldn't understand what I was doing wrong to cause Elizabeth to have such a low opinion of my performance. Whenever I asked Elizabeth what I could do to improve my performance, she evaded my questions.

Natalie, my Jewish co-worker, was the one who told me the real reason why Elizabeth was degrading my performance. She said that it had nothing to do with my job performance, that it had to do with rumors going around in the hospital instead. What did a rumor in this hospital have to do with me, I questioned myself. I asked Natalie to explain. According to Natalie, the rumor was that Elizabeth was having an affair with Wesley, who was the director of the department at the time. Wesley was a handsome black man, very articulate, and he dressed well. Natalie explained that it was also rumored that I was having an affair with Wesley, and that was the reason Elizabeth was treating me so unfairly. I was dumfounded by Natalie's remarks, because I didn't have enough time in the day for work, school, my baby and myself, let alone to be having an affair with a married man. Natalie said that Elizabeth would do everything in her power to discredit me, because she didn't like me, for reasons unknown to Natalie. Natalie advised me to be careful and to keep a record of my work, documenting everything that Elizabeth did to me that I thought was unfair. She said that to do so might be beneficial to me in the future. I thanked Natalie for her advice. She was not the only one to advise me in that manner. Heather, another Jewish worker, insisted that I document and keep a record of Elizabeth's unfair treatment of me. Natalie and Heather were very friendly with Elizabeth, but they were my secret pals as well. They were the ones who kept me abreast of Elizabeth's plans against me.

Although I was now informed about why Elizabeth was against me and knew of some of her plots to discredit my performance, I couldn't confront her. I would have betrayed the trust of my secret pals if I confronted her, and confronting her would not be in the best interest of my secret pals nor of myself. Natalie and Heather, unknown to each other, kept me abreast of Elizabeth's plots against me. Because I knew that my job was in jeopardy, I took a full course load for each summer session that I attended school. I would sit in the back of the classroom on the first night of each of my classes, so I could view everyone who came into the classroom. It was my purpose to drop the course and sign up for another if anyone from my job was in the same class with me. By this strategy, I was able to prevent anyone from discovering that I was using one name for work and another for school.

My last two years in college seemed to be even more difficult for me than my first two and one half years at Community College. It seemed that I had to spend longer hours studying, especially for the summer sessions when I took full course loads. Besides concentrating on work and school, taking care of and protecting Hope was the highest priority for me. As she grew older, she protected me as much as I protected her. Hope would never wake me if she answered the phone when I was asleep. When Hope approached age six, about the age when I had been first raped as a child, I was so concerned that someone would rape her, that I would check her vagina every night when I gave her a bath, to assure myself that no one had done it to her. I tried to be the best mother that I could, by doing things that I thought would benefit my daughter,. But there were people like Sally, one of my co-workers, who thought otherwise. Sally commented that she didn't think that I was a good mother, because a good mother wouldn't neglect her child for the sake of an education. Others suggested that a full-time job, attending school full time, and taking care of my baby were too much for me to handle. They questioned how I would have time to spend with my daughter. They suggested that I should quit school until she was older, but I never quit. Those comments and suggestions, criticizing my love for my daughter, did not deter me from doing the things that I felt I had to do. They made me more determined to continue instead, and they almost caused me to suffer a nervous breakdown.

Every Friday, I would pick up Hope from the babysitter and head to my apartment. But this Friday was different. When I picked up Hope, I felt exhausted. My body shivered as I drove the car nervously on the streets that led to my apartment, trying to avoid an accident. When I got into my apartment, I felt so weak that I lay across my bed without changing into my nightgown, and I fell asleep before 6:00 p.m. When I awoke around 8:00 p.m., Hope was lying next to me, and I realized that I hadn't fed her her dinner. She was hungry. Still feeling weak and nervous, I managed to fix her some dinner, fed her, and prepared her for bed. Then I laid her in bed next to me and again fell asleep. I slept through the night and awoke 11:00 a.m. the following day, which was Saturday. I remember giving Hope something to eat when I got up, but I went back to bed shortly thereafter and slept until 7:00 p.m. When I got up, I fed Hope again and went back to bed less than two hours later and slept until 11:00 a.m. Sunday morning. I tried to stay awake on Sunday, because I had my schoolwork to complete, and I had to prepare our Sunday meals, but I couldn't do either. I felt too tired to do anything. My head hurt, and my body ached and trembled. I felt weaker than I had felt the days before, so I lay back in bed and fell asleep again.

I was able to get out of bed on Monday and managed to dress Hope for school. While I was driving her to school, I felt dizzy and thought that I would collapse before I got to the school, but I arrived at the school safely. After I escorted Hope to her classroom, as I normally did, I drove to the doctor's office, thanking God that I didn't have to make an appointment to see him. When the doctor saw me and I explained to him what had happened to me over the weekend, he told me that I had overexhausted my body and that it was in a state of shock. The doctor explained that I could have suffered a nervous breakdown. He said that I needed lots of rest. Then he prescribed some medication for me and advised me to take two weeks off from work and to rest my body those two weeks.

I was afraid of losing my job, so I took only one week off from work, but I never took any time off from school. I continued to go to school, but my brain couldn't retain anything the teachers taught in school that week. I knew that I needed help before I collapsed. Then I wondered what would happen to my baby if I should die. I had no relatives living in America, just my baby and me. I wanted to change the situation and have my mother immigrate to America, but I couldn't assist her because I was still an illegal immigrant. I went to my friend, asking her again to assist my mother with her immigration to America. That was in April of 1983, almost at the end of my school years. Soon I would graduate and attain my Bachelor's degree. I was scheduled to walk in the graduation ceremony in May, and I would complete my final classes in the first summer session in June, 1983. I was close to the end, and yet it seemed so far away. I struggled to make passing grades for the twelve credits that I carried that semester. I would be satisfied even with a C for each subject, because I was tired, and was mentally and physically drained. But I couldn't quit trying, not then, anyway. I was too close to the end of the storms, to achieving my educational goals. In a few months, everything would be over.

I thought about the events that could take place after I completed my last class and graduated from school, like Elizabeth terminating my job or Immigration finding and deporting me. If those things took place after I graduated, it wouldn't matter to me one way or the other, because I would have achieved my educational goals and I had enough money in the bank to take home with me. I felt a sense of confidence within me. Suddenly, I wasn't afraid of anything or anyone, anymore, and I had a feeling of endurance, because the storm was almost over.

The Aftermath of the Storm

The storm ended when I completed and passed all the courses for that semester. Although I had three credits to take in the first summer session, I was eligible to walk in the commencement ceremony with the graduating class of 1983. I was excited, but I thought about not taking part in the ceremony, until Simeon convinced me that I should. He reasoned that I had worked too hard to achieve my educational goals not to take part in the graduation ceremony. I agreed with him. I invited a few friends to the ceremony, like Mary who had assisted me with Hope, taking her to church almost every Sunday. I also invited Ben and Maureen, my two friends living in New York, and Juliet, who had befriended me after learning that both of us were Vincentian. Simeon and, of course, my heroine, my daughter, Hope, attended the ceremony, too.

Hope wore a green dress with broad white collars to my graduation ceremony that day. As I walked with my class, Hope sat among the crowd of onlookers with her father, and I recognized her voice when she shouted, "Mommy! Mommy! There goes my Mommy. There goes my Mommy." I looked in the direction where I heard her voice and I saw her pointing at me. I was overwhelmed with emotion. That moment was the happiest of my adult life, other than the day when I gave birth to her and saw her for the first time. I could not have asked for anything more that day. I felt satisfied with everything in the world. I knew that the years I had spent in school were all worth it.

After the graduation ceremony, I wanted to spend the rest of the day alone with my daughter, but that was impossible. Ben and Maureen were spending the weekend with me, and Simeon was also visiting us that weekend. Juliet had asked that I stop by her house to pick up a gift. Her gift turned out to be a surprise graduation party. I was indeed surprised, and I thanked her and all the guests who were there.

When my weekend guests left on Sunday night, I prayed and thanked God that he had brought me this far in life. It was just a matter of time until I would complete the three-credit theology course and receive my longed-for diploma. It was the first time that I had ever had just one class in any session, but I had more difficulty in that one class than I did when I took two classes in other summer sessions. I struggled throughout the six weeks of class. At the end, I received a passing grade, and my days at St. Joseph's University were over. I planned to let my days on the job be over, too. I planned to quit at the end of August, sell my car, get my money out of the bank, pack our clothing, and leave America for good. But my plans never came to fruition, because, just as I was about to get to hell out, my mother with the assistance of my friend, immigrated to America in July of that year.

I didn't recognize my mother when I went to pick her up. Simeon had seen my mother a year earlier, when he had visited St. Vincent, and he was the one who picked her out from the crowd. I had not seen my mother in nine years. I couldn't believe what those past nine years had done to her appearance. She looked a lot older than her forty-seven years. I cried in silence looking at her. I wondered if it was the mental and physical abuses that she endured from Mr. Phillips that caused her to look so old and somewhat feeble. Then I looked at her hands and feet, and I saw the many calluses on them. "She has to get rid of them," I said to myself. I felt sympathy for my mother, and I wondered whether my body would have deteriorated like my mother's if I had stayed in St. Vincent. I planned not to let my mother return to St. Vincent anytime soon, so I changed my plans to return so that I could accommodate her needs. Because my mother did not have much education, I planned to assist her in finding a housekeeping/nanny job. With that job, I hoped that she would earn enough money to support herself and the children that she left behind. Most of all, I hoped her employer would sponsor her, thus enabling her to get a green card and become a legal immigrant. My mother would then be able to sponsor my siblings to immigrate to America legally, and they would be able to go back to school and further their education without fearing Immigration. When an employer offered her a job as a housekeeper/nanny, I thought of the good that my mother could do for her children and herself, and I encouraged her to accept it. The employer had also promised to sponsor my mother and all of her children under twenty-one. That meant that she and all her children would be eligible to receive a green card at the same time, if she worked for the employer until she was granted legal immigrant status. Unfortunately, my mother quit the job before the employer began the process to sponsor her.

My mother complained about her first job from the very first week, claiming the work was too hard and the children were difficult to care for. She quit in her third week of employment. I didn't want to force her to work, but I also did not want her to depend on me financially when she had the opportunity to be independent. I found my mother another job, but she wasn't on that job long before she began complaining. I felt that housekeeping work had been hard work for me, but I failed to understand how it could be hard work for my mother. After all, my mother had taken care of her house at home and cared for her ten children. I saw the housekeeping job as a step upward, more rewarding than the fieldwork that she had done at home. My mother stayed with me on her days off, so I explained to her the benefits of staying on the job. She agreed to stay, but not without complaining. I came to realize that, because of my mother, I would have to stay in America longer than I had anticipated.

Simeon's father had sponsored him, and he had received his green card a year before I graduated. Now that Simeon had his green card, he could sponsor me to get my own, provided we would marry. But I was still unsure. Marriage was still not in my plans, even though Simeon and I were considered to be boyfriend and girlfriend. We continued with our visits at least twice a month and spent all our holidays together. He continued to support his daughter, financially and otherwise. Although many who knew us would tell me that I was a fool to be with him and accuse him of dating other women, I never saw him with another female, and he denied having one. Simeon proclaimed his love for me, and I guess that I loved him as much as he loved me. In spite of the love talk that went on between us, I was glad to be independent of Simeon and capable of taking care of my daughter and myself. Nevertheless, he was the only man in my life at the time, and he seemed to look forward to my visits as much as I looked forward to his.

It was on the fourth of July weekend in 1983 that Simeon was supposed to visit me. He had telephoned on Friday night to say that he would be at my place at around 10:00 p.m. Saturday night. He was always hungry when he arrived, so I prepared a meal for him, even though my cooking skills were less than good. He never refused my cooking, not even when I made macaroni and cheese, which I prepared from precooked macaroni and grated cheese, mixed together and baked until the cheese melted. I awaited Simeon's arrival that Saturday night, but he never showed, nor did he call to say that he wasn't coming. I hardly slept that night from fear that he might have had an accident. I was reassured when I called his number and got a busy signal. But, for once in our almost nine-year relationship, I felt betrayed. I assumed that Simeon had had no intention of spending the weekend with me and that he had deliberately called Friday night to say he was coming in order to make sure that I had no plans to visit him instead.

"Simeon," I thought, "I have been faithful to you throughout our relationship, even when people would tell me that you weren't faithful to me. I never saw you with another woman, and whenever I questioned you about other women, you proclaimed your love for me. You claimed that I was your only lover and that you would never do anything to hurt me. Simeon, here I am lying in my bed and unable to sleep, because I am assuming that right this minute you are in your apartment, lying in your bed, in the arms of another woman, when you should have been in my arms instead." Then I told myself that I shouldn't get carried away, because I couldn't be sure that he was really with another woman. "Maybe he has a valid excuse why he couldn't come to visit you tonight after he said that he would." I said to myself. "Valid excuse, right, but he could have called, and he didn't. There is no excuse for him not to call. I have no proof, but I have a gut feeling that he has another woman spending the weekend with him. Otherwise, why would he take his phone off the hook, and why hasn't he called me to tell me he wasn't coming?" I couldn't sleep. I was anxiously waiting the dawn of the following day, Sunday, when I planned to go to Washington and pay Simeon a surprise visit. I drove to Washington with my daughter on that July 4th weekend of 1983.

Simeon was living in a luxurious high rise apartment building that included free parking. First, I checked the parking lot to see if I could locate his car, but I couldn't. I had keys to his apartment, but the main lock to the building had been changed since the last time I had used the key. Since I couldn't get into the building, I waited an hour in the parking lot, but there was no Simeon in sight. I decided to visit some of the Vincentian friends that Simeon had introduced me to who lived in Washington. I knew that he visited them frequently.

Brian and Miss Layne, who lived close to one other, were Simeon's closest friends in Washington. I visited Brian's house first. He was surprised to see me, and he seemed suspicious when I asked him whether he had seen Simeon that day or knew where he was? Brain answered that he had seen Simeon earlier that day and that Simeon told him he was expecting me. "Lord!" he said, "I wonder where my buddy Simeon could be?" "You know damn well where he is and who he is with," I thought, "so don't try to cover up for Simeon, because, frankly, you are not doing a good job, Brian. Your body language alone tells me you are lying." I left Brian's place and went to visit Miss Layne. I asked her the same questions, and she answered that she hadn't seen Simeon. I stayed with her for a while. Then I decided to return to Simeon's apartment building, Miss Layne accompanying me.

Simeon was still not at home, so I parked my car in the parking lot, in full view of Simeon's apartment, awaiting his arrival. Miss Layne and I were talking when Hope shouted, "Look Mommy, there goes Simmy (as she called her father). There goes Simmy in his apartment, and he is wearing a hat." Sure enough, there was Simeon looking through the window of his apartment as though he were looking for someone in the parking lot and at the same time hiding from someone. His car was not in the parking lot at the front of the building, so he must have parked in the lot at the rear. I drove to the rear of the building and saw his car parked there with the engine still running. At that very moment, I felt an unexplainable feeling within me, not a good feeling. My intuition had urged me to travel to Washington that day, and all the way to Washington I had had the feeling that I was about to catch Simeon with another woman. The feeling had become stronger since I arrived, and even more so as I stood in the lot looking at Simeon's car with its engine still running.

Our eyes met when he opened the main door at the rear of the apartment building. He looked shocked. I saw him throw a bag to someone who seemed to be following him, signaling that person to stay in the hallway. He stood at the door and stared at me in disbelief. "Simeon, bring her out. Don't send her back inside. Just bring your woman out, because I want to see her. I want to see what she has to offer you that I can't." I said to him in a loud tone of voice. Somehow I happened to maintain a calm composure. Simeon walked out of the apartment building and said to me, "Lola, I am sorry. You caught me and I apologize. I love you. She doesn't mean anything to me. Forgive me. Here are the keys to my apartment." He tried to give me the keys, but I refused to take them. "Please take the keys and go upstairs to my apartment" he said. "Don't let anyone see that we are arguing. Please, Lola, I am begging you to please give me another chance. Let me take her to the train station. I love you and I want you to be my wife." Then he looked at Miss Layne and asked her to talk to me and she tried to get me to take the keys. In the meantime, Hope had entered the building and seen the other woman. She came back outside shouting, "Mommy, I saw Simmy's woman. She is in the laundry room crying. Mommy, Simmy 's woman has long hair. Mommy, come with me and you will see Simmy's woman. Come with me, Mommy, come."

I hugged Hope and I told her that I loved her. She hugged me while her father stood there asking me for my forgiveness, pleading with me to take the keys and go to his apartment. I loved Miss Layne and respected her very much. She convinced me to take the keys, and Miss Layne, Hope and I went to his apartment. I never saw the other woman. Simeon came back to the apartment a half hour later, and I sat listening, not uttering a word, while he and Miss Layne pleaded with me to forgive him. Then he took Miss Layne home while I stayed in the apartment pondering whether I should drive back to Philadelphia that night. Since it was rather late, I decided to spend the night at his place and leave the following day.

I didn't sleep in his bed that night, and I said very little to him. I guess that I was in a state of shock. Normally, I would cry over an incident like that. But this time I didn't cry and I didn't feel hurt. I felt empty instead. I had no emotion, absolutely none. He tried to talk to me, but I didn't respond. Before I went to bed that night, I told him that it was over between us. Before I left his apartment the following day, I told Simeon that what we had had together would never be the same again, and I no longer wanted him or to be with him. "The only good thing that resulted from our relationship was Hope. Thank you for her. Because of her, my life has changed for the better," I said to Simeon. I told him that he could arrange with me to see his daughter when he wished to. I assured him that I would never prevent him from seeing his daughter or his daughter from seeing him. I resisted when he tried to hug me. I walked away, leaving him standing in the doorway of his apartment. I was on my way back to Philadelphia. I was hurting, but I still couldn't cry.

I had no doubt that it was the right time to end our relationship. I had graduated from school, and I was comfortable with the idea of spending the rest of my life as a single mother, knowing that I would try to do the very best for my daughter. Since the relationship between her father and me was over, I wasn't about to have another man in my life. I had lived with my mother and a man who wasn't my father, who had abused me mentally and physically. I wasn't about to let the same thing happen to my daughter. I planned, as soon as my mother was stable in a job, to leave her in America and return home to St. Vincent. I was living alone at the age of twenty, so my mother, soon to be forty-eight, could manage on her own. So I reasoned to myself as I made plans for a future with my daughter. I was disappointed that Simeon had betrayed me, and my heart ached, but I knew that it would be only a matter of time before I would get over it. After all, I had felt heartaches like that before, and disappointments by the score, as when Andrew got married to Dawn. All those were in the past, and I had gotten over them. Soon Simeon would be in my past and I would get over him as well. I knew that my heartaches and pains would soon pass.

Simeon called that Sunday night and pleaded with me to forgive him, asking that I gave him another chance. I abruptly hung up on him. In the past, I used to feel so hurt, and even cry, when I heard about his alleged affairs with other women. He used to deny those affairs, especially when I threatened to break off our relationship. I was naive enough to believe him most of those times, but this time was different. From the moment that I saw him with that other woman, whatever love I felt for him seemed to disappear. There was nothing that he could have said to me that day that would have made me feel differently. He knew, as well as I did, that I meant it when I told him that day that it was over between us. I guess that was why he was so persistent in asking me for forgiveness and another chance. He continued to call at night. No matter how much I insulted him and hung up the telephone on him, he never stopped calling.

One night I told Simeon that his telephone calls to me would soon come to an end, because I planned to return to St. Vincent. That was when he began to cry. The things he said to me that night touched my heart in a way that had never happened before. He admitted to me that he had had relationships with other women, both in Washington and while he lived in Philadelphia. Simeon explained that he had had those relationships because I was so focused on work, school and Hope that I didn't have much time for him. That much was true. He also said that he loved me, that I was a good woman and he didn't want to lose me. Simeon said that he believed me when I said that I had never been unfaithful to him He talked a lot that night. At the end, I told him that I wouldn't be able to forgive him, so it was in my best interest not to have him in my life. After we hung up, he called me back again and pleaded with me to marry him.

"Marry him, he must be crazy in his mind. Why would I want to marry a cheater of a man like him." I thought. I asked Simeon the same question. "Well, Lola, I would do anything for you, because I love you. If you don't love me any more, please allow me to do something to help you." I asked him what the hell could he do to help me that I couldn't do for myself. That was when he suggested that I should marry him for my green card, even if I didn't want to marry him for love. "Why the hell would I want to marry him for a green card now?" I thought. "I came to America to help my mother financially and to get her away from her abusive situation at home, and I have accomplished that. I wanted to reach my educational goals, and I have achieved that as well. He didn't offer to get me a green card before, so why the hell would I want to marry his ass for a green card now, when I no longer need it?" I told him as much, and then hung up.

"Lola, here you go with your foolish pride again," I said to myself. "Girl, the man is offering you a green card. Take it. You might want to come back to America later on in life. With a green card, you could do so without hassle from Immigration. How about law school? Did you not say that you would like to attend law school? With a green card, you would be able to enter law school, because you would be a legal immigrant. Girl, the green card is to your advantage, so accept the offer from him. After nine years of giving him your body, free of charge, that's the least he can do for you." This was how I reasoned to myself after I hung up. Then, I decided to call him back. We talked about his marriage proposal, and I told him that if I agreed to marry him, it would be a business marriage. We decided to talk about it some more, and, somehow, I agreed to meet him for further discussion—in Washington, because I didn't want him at my place.

I arrived in Washington by 9.00 a.m. that morning and met Simeon at his apartment. We talked with each other, and we quarreled. He reiterated that I was the cause of his having those affairs, because I didn't spend enough time with him. He questioned my love for him, since I had refused to move with him to Washington when he had asked me to. He went on and on and on, as though he were the victim in the relationship, not I. On August 4, 1983, one month after I had caught Simeon with the other woman., he and I went to a five and dime store and bought a fake gold wedding band for less than five dollars. We were married by a justice of peace in the Upper Marlboro Courthouse in King George County, Maryland. When we left the courthouse, he took me to lunch. We pledged to each other to keep our marriage a secret.

A few weeks after we were married, Simeon filed the necessary immigration papers for the processing of my green card. I realized that I would have to stay married to him for at least a year, until I received my green card. We resumed visiting each other on a regular basis. He also promised to be faithful to me, but I didn't believe him. He had made that promise before and broken it. It didn't much matter to me, because my feelings for him at the time fell short of love. Even though we were married, we lived apart. He continued to live in Washington, and I in Philadelphia with my daughter. Hope was growing up, and she would express a wish for a sister or brother, especially when she visited the Fields's family living across the street from us. She often said to me, "No one ever asked me whether I would like a brother or sister. I want a brother or a sister to play with me." One day she came to me and asked, "Mommy do you love me?" When I answered that I did, she told me if I did love her, I must get her a brother or sister to play with.

"Would you please have another baby, Mommy? Please Mommy?" she pleaded with me. I told her that I would consider having another baby.

I never wanted children of my own, but I loved my child without limit. I wanted to do things that would assure her happiness. If I were to have another child, I knew that Simeon would have to be the father. Unlike my mother, whose children had different fathers, I wanted the same man to father all my children. Since I had no intention of staying with Simeon, I wanted to become pregnant before I ended our relationship, and I succeeded. By September of that year, I was pregnant with my second child. Unlike my first, this was a planned pregnancy, and I was sick from the day that I conceived her until the day that I gave birth to her.

In the second month of my pregnancy, I began experiencing difficulties. There would be times when I was so sick that I would have to stay home from work. After eight months of difficulties, I had a placenta previa. It happened on a Monday morning, when I was preparing Hope for school and myself for work. I had just entered the shower when I noticed that I was bleeding profusely. My mother was home with me at the time, but I didn't want to alarm her. I got dressed and drove myself to the hospital, not knowing that it was a dangerous thing for me to do. When I got to the hospital and told the doctor that I had driven myself there, she said that I was lucky to have made it to the hospital without collapsing. She also explained to me that I was losing too much blood, and to save the baby's life and my own, she would have to perform an emergency c-section on me. I called Simeon to inform him, just before the anesthesiologist came to my room and stuck a needle into my vein. I remember waking up dizzy, seeing the baby lying next to me in the bed. My baby, who was supposed to born on June 14, was born on April 30, instead. Then I noticed that Simeon, Hope, and my mother were in the room, too. I looked at Hope and smiled. Then I looked at my baby again. I felt the same love for her as I had felt for Hope when she was born. I named her Nicholette Nicole Layne. Unlike Hope and I, who were born bastard children, Nicholette was what the people in the island would call a legitimate picme. But not too many people would know that, only those around my bedside that day. There was also Juliet, my friend who had had the surprise graduation party for me. I had confided to her the secret of my marriage to Simeon, asking her not to tell anyone else. Later I found out that Juliet had shared my secret with others, when another woman told me that Juliet had told her that I was married.

Before I got pregnant, Simeon and I had talked about my moving to Washington, but I had no intention of doing so. I still looked at my marriage to him as a marriage of convenience, not of love. I was still unsure of my love for him since I had met him with this other woman. When his job was transferred back to Philadelphia, he came to stay with me for a short time until he could find himself an apartment. He was opposed to living with me without letting it be known that we were married, and I was against telling people that we were married. I wasn't sure that I would want to stay married to him after I got my green card. Simeon and I got along well together while he stayed with me. After a while we talked about buying a house together. He suggested that we have a church wedding to announce our marriage. I was beginning to agree with him about having a church wedding, but our buying a house together was not meant to be, at least not at that time.

Simeon's younger brother, Joe, immigrated from St. Vincent about the same time we were making our plans to buy a house together. Simeon decided that he would take full responsibility for his grown brother, even though they had another brother living in Philadelphia at the time. He moved out of my place and rented an apartment where he and his brother could live. "Good for your black ass, Simeon," I thought. "You know what, I don't need you or want you in my life. I can take care of my two children and myself without your assistance, and it doesn't matter if I live in America or St. Vincent." Simeon continued to care for our children, financially and otherwise. He was still planning for us to be together after his newly immigrated brother found himself a job and was able to make it on his own. I, on the other hand, was planning to live back in St. Vincent with my children. I was just waiting for the green card that would enable me to travel back and forth without problems with Immigration authorities.

I was granted six months' leave of absence from my job when I gave birth to Nicholette, but I returned to work before the six months had expired. While I was on leave, Heather kept me abreast of what was happening on the job. Two months before the end of my six months' leave, Heather telephoned to inform me that Elizabeth was interviewing prospective employees for my position. She also notified me when Elizabeth hired Pete for the position, and she suggested that I return to work before I was scheduled to return. I promised Heather that I would think about it. I really wanted to confide to Heather that I planned to quit the job soon after getting my green card, but I couldn't, because Heather was not aware of my Immigration status, and I wasn't about to let her be aware. It was my secret.

Six months after Simeon filed the papers for my green card, I received notification from the Immigration Department that I was scheduled for an an interview with an Immigration officer. I was afraid that they would deport me if I showed up, so I ignored the first notification. When I received the second notice, Simeon convinced me that it was in my best interest to go to the appointment. When I went, I met with a female Immigration officer, who interviewed me. Instead of deporting me, as I feared, she granted me a six-month extension to stay in America legally. She also advised me that I was eligible to receive another extension if I did not receive my green card within that time. This interview took place about the same time that Heather suggested that I return to work early. Having been granted the extension by the Immigration authorities, I decided that it would be best to return to the job, since I didn't know how long it would take to get my green card. It was the same week that the new employee was supposed to begin that I notified Elizabeth by certified mail that I was returning to work myself.

Elizabeth had assigned most of my responsibilities to the new employee, Pete, a few days after he began. Our positions were both on the same grade level, and both required a business degree. However, Elizabeth was paying Pete a higher salary than mine, even though I had more seniority on the job and my qualifications for the position exceeded his. Heather made copies of Pete's completed application and gave it to me. She told me to keep them in a secure place at home, because I might need them if I decided to file a complaint against Elizabeth accusing her of unfair labor practices.

Three weeks after I returned to work, I received notification from the American Embassy in Barbados that I was scheduled for an interview with one of the counselors at the embassy. That meant that I would have to travel to Barbados, where my interviewer would decide whether I was eligible for a green card. If the counselor should decide against me, thus making me ineligible as a permanent resident, I would not be allowed back into America. At this time, I cared little whether or not I would be allowed back in. The letter listed things I had to do prior to the interview and documents I would have to bring with me to the interview. I was to provide them with a medical certificate from one of their recommended doctors to prove I was in good health. I was happy to see that two such doctors were in St. Vincent, which meant that I could have my physical done there. I also could spend some time with my relatives in St. Vincent, travelling to Barbados two days before my scheduled interview. I planned to depart from Barbados on the day of my interview, if I were granted the green card and decided to return to America. I also kept in mind that I would need another leave to travel to St. Vincent and Barbados, but that Elizabeth might not grant me another leave, since I had just returned from one. If she refused, I could quit, but I would rather not, because I wouldn't want to be out of a job before I found another one. I had to come up with another excuse for my leave. That was when I thought about visiting Dr. Rose's office, asking him to write a letter stating that I was sick and needed at least four weeks of rest. I was willing to pay whatever he would charge. I thought that Dr. Rose would be the perfect person to ask, because he knew me well and was aware of my situation with Immigration.

Dr. Rose and his family had immigrated from St. Vincent as legal immigrants many years before I did. Although he wasn't my family physician, I thought that he would be willing to give me the letter, because I wasn't a stranger to him. He also knew Simeon and my daughter, Hope, because at one time we had the same babysitter for our children. When I visited him at his office and told him what I wanted, Dr. Rose bluntly refused to write the letter for me. I was disappointed. As the people back home would say, he was one of our own, and being one of our own, I thought that he would understand my need better than someone who wasn't our own. I was wrong. But then again, even Jesus' own disciples had refused Him, so who was I to expect better. I left Dr. Rose's office knowing that I had to find a doctor willing to write me that letter. That was when I thought of Dr. Koch, a Jewish doctor whom I visited years ago when I suffered from a stomach problem. His office was located in Southwest Philadelphia.

Since I didn't have to make an appointment to see Dr. Koch, I went to his office right after I left Dr. Rose's office. There were some patients waiting to be seen by him, so I sat and waited until it was my turn to go into one of the examining rooms. When Dr. Koch entered and asked what could he do for me, I explained to him that I had just gone back to work from maternity leave, but that I needed to take another leave of absence for personal reasons. I told him that it was most likely that my employer would not grant me the leave without a medical reason. Dr. Koch said that he would write a letter stating that I was suffering from postnatal depression, and that I needed to be away from the job for at least two months. He dictated the letter and had his secretary type it while I waited. Then he handed me the letter, telling me to have my employer call him should they have any questions. "Lola, is this a coincidence or what?" I thought. "Jewish people, more than black people, are the ones who have come to your assistance whenever you had problems with the job. Shelly assisted you when Mr. Slick tried to terminate your employment. Heather and Natalie are assisting you and keeping you abreast of Elizabeth's plots against you, and Dr. Koch came to your rescue and wrote that letter when one of your own refused. God bless Shelly, Natalie and Heather, and, God, thank you for Dr. Koch." Because of his letter, Elizabeth granted me the leave without hesitation.

Ten years and approximately five months after I had left the land of my birth and immigrated to America, all alone, I was now about to return with my two daughters, Hope and Nicholette. My mother encouraged me to stay with my siblings in their house, the same house I couldn't live in before my immigration to America, because Mr. Phillips had thrown me out. I was about to return to a house full of bad memories, and to a village full of people who had caused me such pain and anguish for most of the nineteen years that I lived among them. I felt a chill in my body and a burning in my chest when I remembered my experiences living in that house among the people of that village. Even though most of my memories were bad, I was willing to return there, because my siblings, grandmother and some of my closest relatives were still living there. They meant a lot to me. Had it not been for them, I might have gone to St. Vincent and never visited that village, let alone stayed with my daughters in the house that I had been put out of.

There were so many thoughts in my mind as the plane began to descend upon the land of my birth. There was no one waiting for me at the airport, because I had not informed anyone of my returning and no one expected me. After I checked in with the Immigration authorities and cleared my luggage from customs, I walked out of the small airport and hired Leroy, a taxi driver I knew, to drive me back to the village. Leroy and I chatted the entire time while he was driving me to the village. The views of St. Vincent appeared the same as I left them over ten years ago— narrow winding roads, lots of green pastures with fruit trees and vegetable crops. School children still wore uniforms to school, and there were some improvements in the buildings, but not many. I gathered from Leroy that, although there had been changes in government officials, their philosophy in governing the people was the same, and the rich got richer and the poor got poorer. There was lots of unemployment, especially among high school graduates, and the people who were out of work were the poorer people most needing the work. As Leroy was about to enter Amondid Village, the village where I had lived before my immigration, I felt numb. I began to panic, as if I were about to face some sort of danger. I directed Leroy to my mother's house, where my siblings were living. When I got out of the taxi, some of my siblings ran to me, while others stood and stared, because they had no memory of me, having been small children when I immigrated to America,. I recognized my grandmother and ran to her. I hugged her and began to cry. She had a bandage tied around one of her feet to protect her ulcer, and her head was tied with a wrap. My grandmother seemed not to have aged over the ten years that I had been gone. She had been special to me throughout my childhood, and she was even more special to me in my adult life. I wanted to express that to her and to thank her for all the things that she had done for me. But I wasn't able to do it, and I don't know why. I thanked God for sparing our lives so that we could see each other again. Even though I told my grandmother how much I loved her, I wondered if she really knew how much she meant to me. I stayed up most of that night chatting with my sisters.

By morning, the news of my return had spread across the village like wildfire. I had to visit the town that day to take care of some business. As I walked to the bus stop, I was surprised at the manner in which some of the devious villagers greeted me, as if I were one of their favorite daughters. But as far as I was concerned, I was not. I didn't respond to their greetings, because I remained haunted by memories of the past. Being unable to forgive and forget, I continued my journey to the bus stop, where I caught the bus to town.

After my arrival in the town, I made an appointment to see one of the recommended doctors for my medical examination. Then I visited Randell, giving him the gifts I had brought him. Like my grandmother, he seemed not to have aged since I last saw him ten years before. He was surprised to see me when his secretary escorted me to his office and I gave him a hug. Later, I met him for lunch in the same dining room where we had had our lunches in the past. When I told him the details of my life in America, he said that he knew I was a determined person, but he never could have imagined how determined I really was. Randell said that with my education I would be able to find a high salary position in St. Vincent. He encouraged me not to return to America, saying I had already suffered enough there.

With complete honesty, I informed Randell about my marriage to Simeon and about our children. He wanted to see the children. He advised me to do everything I could to take care of the welfare of my children. Then he lectured me in a fatherly way on how I was to behave as a mother. That was just like Randell. We made plans to spend a day together with the children, and I was to visit him again when I came back to town for my doctor's appointment. After I left Randall, I was walking around some familiar places in town when I met Jason, one of Andrew's friends.

When he inquired whether I had seen Andrew since my arrival, I told Jason that I wasn't interested in seeing him. He told me that Andrew was no longer employed as teacher. He had become a politician and held a position as one of the ministers of government. He was working a few buildings away from where we were standing in conversation. Jason urged me to visit Andrew right then, and he and I walked to his office together. Andrew greeted me as though we were the best of friends. He even used his position to get my lab work done without an appointment. After we left the lab, Andrew invited me to lunch, but I declined. I was still angry with Andrew, having not yet completely gotten over the pain he caused me by marrying Dawn.

The following day, Andrew visited me at my mother's house, informing me that he was leaving the country to attend a conference related to his work, to be held in New York. I don't know what prompted me to give him my telephone number in America, but that's what I did, I also gave him permission to call me if he wanted to. "I love you Lola, and I always will," were his last words to me from this married man, who used to be my lover, or something like that, before he left my mother's house that evening—a house where he had not been permitted to visit me when we were lovers. Oh, time! Time is the essence of everything, because so many changes occur with time.

On the day of my appointment, I took the results of my blood work to the doctor. When the doctor read the results, he said that I was sick with some sort of serious disease and that I would have to have a series of injections before he could give me a clean bill of health. "Disease, what type of disease do I have, and when did I contract this disease?" I wondered. "I had a checkup six weeks after I was released from the hospital with Nicholette, and I was fine then." The doctor did not disclose the nature of my disease, and I did not ask. The following day, I went back to his office to be injected by his nurse, the first of six injections that I was scheduled to receive over six days. My buttocks hurt where the nurse first injected me and stayed swollen for days. When I took Hope with me for my second injection, the doctor noticed her and seemed puzzled. When he asked about it, I told him that Hope was my daughter and I also had another daughter, five months old. I told him both my daughters were healthy at birth. With that, the doctor stopped the remaining injections. He telephoned the lab technician, telling him that the lab must have gotten my results mixed up with those of someone else. He fussed about the inadequacy of the lab before giving me my medical report in a sealed envelope to take to my appointment with the officials at the U.S. Embassy.

Two days prior to departing from St. Vincent, my daughters and I spent the day with Randell. Randell never changed in his attitude towards me, assuring me that I could depend on his assistance if I ever needed it. It was the same caring Randell that I knew before I left St. Vincent. He never stopped caring for me, even when he was aware that I was married and had two children by another man. Although we spent the day together, we did not become sexually involved in any way. I would always appreciate the kind things he had done to make my life better, and I would forever hold a special place in my heart for him.

Ever since I had been reunited with my siblings, I felt saddened that the older ones did not attend high school. I was also disappointed that three of my sisters had mothered children of their own. My sister Marge, my mother's second daughter, had one child; May, my second sister, had two children, fathered by different men; Rox, my mother's fifth daughter and sixth child, also had a child of her own. I hoped they might have done better with their lives, and wondered whether I could have influenced their lives more positively had I not immigrated to America. I felt guilty when May and Rox told me that they would have gone on to higher education if I had not left St. Vincent. I felt heartbroken when they said that there had been no one to motivate them academically. They had all dropped out before high school, the norm for most people in our village. I wish I could have changed the hands of time and undone my sisters' pregnancies, making sure that they all attended high school, but I could not. Even though I was disappointed with what they had done with their lives, I couldn't give up on my siblings. I promised to do whatever I could for them. I wanted to do things for them that would have a positive impact on their lives.

Although I felt uncomfortable staying in the village, I enjoyed the time I spent conversing with my grandmother, siblings and relatives. Then came the day for my departure, and I felt sad leaving them behind. I thought of staying, never to return to America. But I had some unfinished business to take care of in America. I cried when I said good-bye to all of them, especially my grandmother. A few of my siblings accompanied me to the airport, and I held them and cried before I boarded the plane for Barbados. It was a sunny day, with the skies above clear and blue, just like the day when I first left the island to immigrate to America. As the plane lifted off and ascended, and I watched the birds from my window. Soon the plane flew out of view of the island of my birth and departed for Barbados, the first island I had ever visited, where I had fallen in love with the most wonderful and caring people, whom I would never forget.

Barbados was like a second home to me, and my friends were awaiting my arrival when the plane landed. I planned to spend three days in Barbados. I spent the first day visiting friends and on the second day went to the American Embassy to be interviewed for my green card. My interviewer was one of the meanest black women I had ever dealt with. She asked me questions that seemed to me not related to my application for a green card. At one time during the interview, I wanted to tell her that I had already gotten what I had gone to America for and I didn't need to go back there, so she could just deny me a green card. But I restrained myself. After she finished her interrogation, she said that the doctor in St. Vincent had forgotten to sign the medical report, and she would have to mail it back to him for his signature before granting me a green card. She said the embassy would notify me when they received the signed report from the doctor. "How dare this damn American come to Barbados, one of our West Indian Islands, and treat me as though she has more right here than I do. She is so damn mean, this big-breasted snob." So was I thinking about this woman, wishing that I could have told her exactly what I thought of her. But I left her office without uttering a word.

Another interviewer, whose name I did not know, had overheard her conversation with me and called me to her own office. She informed me that instead of waiting for the doctor in St. Vincent to return the forms, I could have another medical exam by a doctor in Barbados. She gave me a new medical form, with information about a doctor recommended by the embassy, and told me that if I saw the doctor that day I could return the form the following. Then she wished me good luck. I thanked her and left the embassy, going directly to the doctor's office, where I had another medical exam. I picked up the results and the signed form the next day and took them to the embassy. I was granted the green card. All of a sudden, as much as I loved Barbados, I wanted to leave the island, because both my daughters were sick. I walked across the street to the Pan American airline office to confirm my departing flight back to America.

Nicholette had had diarrhea ever since she drank her first bottle of Similac on the first day we arrived in Barbados. She must have gotten sick from the water that I used to mix the milk. And Hope had sores all over her body from mosquito bites. I had left America with two healthy children, and I was about to return with two sick ones. When I heard the announcement that it was time to board the plane for my flight to America, I hugged and kissed my friends good-bye. Then I had a flashback to the first time I had boarded one of these planes to America. I remembered how excited I was then, but now I was not.

Nicholette began to cry as soon as the plane began to ascend, and she cried off and on through the entire flight. The two passengers next to us moved to other seats, I believe, because of Nicholette's crying. As the plane was approaching Kennedy airport, I saw the shining lights again. This time I knew that they were not the lights to the gate of heaven, but the lights of a land where I was once eager to live, ten years ago. At that moment, I no longer felt the eagerness, because the beauty of the lights did not reflect the reality of my experience in this land. Although I had

had some good experiences, and I had achieved some goals in America that I would have never achieved in St. Vincent, I also had had some bad experiences. The bad experiences gave me second thoughts about living in there, now that I had a green card. I knew that I had some decisions to make. Would I stay married to Simeon? Would I quit the job at the hospital and look for another? If I decided to remain in America and on the job, should I continue to work under my alias or should I change to my true identity? How about my mother? Should I get her established and then return home to assist my siblings? Or would my siblings be better off if I stayed in America and helped them to immigrate here too? If I decided to return to St. Vincent, would it be fair to my two American daughters, raising them in a country other than the one where they were born? If I stayed in America, how would I deal with the racism that I would encounter as a black person? How would I explain to my daughters that many white people think that they are better than blacks simply because their skin is white? Did I really want to raise my children in a country with such hatred and bigotry? With all those questions on my mind, I wondered whether it was necessary for me to get a green card at all. I still couldn't decide whether to continue living in America or return home with my two children. I kept wondering as the plane was landing. After I was cleared by Immigration and claimed my luggage from customs, I walked to the area of the airport where people were awaiting the arrival of their loved ones. There he was, standing among the crowd with my girlfriend. Simeon hugged me and welcomed me back to America.

Isabelle Lewis was born in St. Vincent, West Indies and has enjoyed writing stories since her high school years. Since coming to the U.S. she has attained a Bachelor of Science degree and has become a Microsoft Certified System Engineer. She is employed in the technical field with a New York City Agency. She now resides in New Jersey with her husband and two children and is currently working on her second novel, *Free from the Shackles*.

The Journey of a West Indian Soul Order Form

Use this convenient order form to order additional copies of:

The Journey of a West Indian Soul

Please Print:

Name _____

Address _____

City _____ State _____

Zip Code _____

Phone ( ) _____

_____ Copies of books @ $16.95 each $_____

Shipping and handling @ $4.50 per book $_____

NJ residents add 6% tax $_____

Total amount enclosed
$_____

Make checks payable to Lewis I & E Company
Mail order to Lewis I & E Company
P.O. Box 8251
Cherry Hill, NJ 08002

You can also order books by contacting Lewis I & E at (856)-779-7369

Or visit us on line at:
www.lewisjourney.com